EYE FOR EYE

F. Lynn Godfriaux

WolfSinger Publications ~ Security Colorado

But if injury ensues, you shall give life for life,
eye for eye, tooth for tooth, hand for hand, foot for foot,
burn for burn, wound for wound, stripe for stripe.

Exodus, 21:23-25

Acknowledgements

I would like to thank the following people for their invaluable assistance in the writing of this book:

Steve and Brenda, Shelly, Elizabeth, and Sam: Thank you for reading and re-reading rough drafts and once again finding a way to help me change what needed to be changed without undue damage to my fragile ego.

Tim and the other SO's, and participants of FRIDPA: Thank you for your guidance, patience, and invaluable instruction in firearms and safety rules. Hopefully one of these days I'll get over my borderline fear of guns and actually have *fun* during one of the (bleeping) matches.

To Mom and Dad: Thank you for reading the first (really) rough draft and for your honest reactions. You helped me to write a much better story. I love you both.

To WolfSinger Publications: Thank you for your encouragement and support. This book would not be a reality if not for your publishing expertise, suggestions, and guidance.

To Joe, Erin, Josh, and Tori: I would get absolutely no where without your support, your patience, your love, and your encouragement. On days when I really wanted to throw the stupid manuscript away, you always brought me down from the ceiling and got me back on track. I love you with all my heart.

Author's Notes

Please keep in mind that while I have used real locations, buildings, and cities, I have freely made up details when my factual knowledge ran out. This is a work of fiction after all.

Prologue

"Mattie, you might have asked me to retrieve a glass for you," Hawk admonished, his British accent sounding tense.

"I don't have the energy to tell you where to look." I stood on my left leg and clung to the kitchen counter as pain streaked up my broken right leg encased in Plaster of Paris.

"Where is your domestic help?"

I sighed. "I sent William and Anna home. They're both exhausted. I can manage on my own." Gritting my teeth and wishing my husband were present to help me, I hopped one-legged along the counter and opened expensive cherry cupboards until I found a glass.

Shaking his head, Hawk plucked the glass from my hand, crossed to the sink and filled it with water. His black long-sleeved turtleneck and dark gray trousers heightened the iridescence of his gray eyes. I drained the glass empty, set it on the counter. The outside floodlights suddenly blinked on and through the kitchen windows I spotted a large white moving van disappear down the long winding drive.

"Sit down." Hawk's curt order distracted me from the curious presence of the van, and I tried and failed to hide my wince as I lowered myself into the wheelchair. He lifted my cast onto the steel leg support. I stared at the wrinkled black cotton T-shirt funeral dress I still wore, reflected miserably over the sunny warm mid-June Monday morning that now dragged into a warm stormy Monday night.

The outside floodlights blinked off. Tears leaked from the corners of my eyes, and I opened my mouth to ask Hawk to retrieve my sister's urn from the music room.

Without warning the double kitchen doors burst open and five men in black assault gear spilled into the kitchen. With spine-chilling silence, they fanned into a semi-circle, their eyes glaring with outright hatred at me through their black balaclavas.

Behind me, Hawk leaned over and curled his hands around my wrists, his fingers like steel cuffs as they pinned mine against the arms of the chair.

"H-Hawk…?" My throat constricted, my heart pounded hard against my chest and my lungs shriveled until I couldn't breathe as I stared at the lethal end of five automatic rifles.

Chapter One

"You're not going to being very useful with an aim like that."

Joe Healing Water, seventy, Southern Ute Indian, lay flat on his stomach amid the prairie grass and peered through his spotting scope. His dark gray hair trailed in a tidy, thick braid down the back of his long-sleeved red plaid shirt. He wore cargo jeans and a pair of worn, dusty cowboy boots.

Jeremiah Black Bear Tyler lay flat on his stomach as well, his legs splayed out behind him for stability. He studied the targets through the scope of his three-oh-eight rifle mounted on a small bipod. His short thick black hair glinted with steel-blue highlights in the fading twilight. He wore borrowed clothes from the older Indian, which meant a long-sleeve red plaid shirt with sleeves too short, and a pair of above-the-ankle cargo jeans he belted with baling string to hold them up. Bugs crawled over his exposed ankles, exploring their way along his calves and making him acutely uncomfortable. He squirmed, trying to settle himself deeper into the surrounding prairie grass bending low before wild, gale-force winds. At least he wore his own shoes, an old pair of Merino hiking boots, although trekking through the rough terrain around Wolf Creek Pass had worn down the soles.

Jeremiah Black Bear Tyler, also a Southern Ute, had grown up on the same reservation as Joe Healing Water. The Southern Ute Reservation lay in the southwest corner of Colorado, tucked just south of the Sangre de Cristo Mountains around Wolf Creek Pass, and adjacent to its neighbor, the Ute Mountain Ute Reservation. Despite sharing a border, neither of the occupants had much to do with each other.

A little over two weeks ago Joe Healing Water snatched Jeremiah, just out of a long surgery for a gunshot wound to his chest, from the Alamosa County Hospital, and hid him in a clinic on the Southern Ute Rez. Restlessness and an acute sense of impending doom drove Jeremiah to insist on hitting the road this morning despite Joe's argument his wounds were not yet healed enough for travel. Monday morning turned into late afternoon before they reached the barren flatness of the Oklahoma Panhandle.

The unrelenting sense of urgency gnawed at Jeremiah and he wished the old man would cut short this impromptu target practice so they could get back on the road towards Shawnee, where Mattie had endured her sister's funeral without him at her side. He didn't like her being alone and the sooner he and Healing Water got to Shawnee the better he would feel.

Low, ragged gray clouds raced across the expansive western Oklahoma sky. The wind buffeted them, whipping their clothes and carrying anything not securely anchored away to God knew where. Thunder rumbled in unrelenting commentary.

"Maybe we should call it quits." Jeremiah raised his voice to be heard, even though he lay only a couple of feet from Joe. The latter's spotting scope teetered as the wind threatened to dislodge the bipod. The two men glanced across their shoulders at the approaching system. The wind shifted against Jeremiah's face, warning him the massive storm front was bringing more than just heavy rain and gales.

"We should pack up and head for the Jeep," he advised.

"Can't quit yet, not before you've figured out what's messing up your ability to aim straight," Joe yelled back.

"I will be okay." Jeremiah started to rise.

"Well, your aim hasn't gotten any better," Joe accused, peering again through the spotting scope. "You haven't hit a damned thing."

"I know that," Jeremiah snapped. He inhaled in an effort to settle his mood, winced against the sharp stabs of two broken ribs. "Bullet holes do not support accurate shooting."

"Making excuses?" Joe was not smiling.

Jeremiah reached a hand inside the front of his shirt to scratch at the hospital tape holding bandages in place. "I am not."

Joe persisted. "You're almost three weeks out from surgery. Your aim should be better than this."

Jeremiah sighed and returned his attention to the scope mounted on the sniper rifle. "I can still out-shoot you."

Joe Healing Water snorted. "Like hell. Move over, son, and let me show you how it's done."

Jeremiah suppressed an oath. Sometimes, the old Indian could be a pain in the ass. Joe nudged Jeremiah away with his boot, then belly crawled to the rifle.

"Spot me."

Grimacing as the rough ground mashed against his chest, Jeremiah wormed his way to the spotting scope and peered through. He made a few adjustments before he settled on the targets that stood a half-mile away against the side of a small, sharply raised knoll. Premature twilight bled color into so many shades of gray, dirt and debris swirled across his line of sight. Behind them, lightning flashed with increasing frequency.

But it was the nagging worry over Mattie's safety that blurred his vision. Jeremiah swore under his breath.

"Worthless as a spotter, too, I suppose," Joe complained. "I'll take the can of beans on the right." He wriggled his torso against the ground, adjusted his legs, then grew still for so long he might have turned to stone.

"You are taking too long," Jeremiah snapped.

Without warning the weapon exploded, gun smoke shredding as fast as it appeared, the muzzle spewing a flash of flame. The recoil jerked Joe's supine body.

Jeremiah peered through his scope at the obliterated can. "Hit."

"Of course. Soup can on the left." Joe became still again.

Show off, Jeremiah thought, his mood deteriorating. He himself had failed to hit any of the large, stand-up profile targets, now whipped and bent as wind gusts threatened to pick them up and blow them into the next state. In the meantime, Joe was demolishing the smallest targets, the ones buried into the hill.

Joe remained motionless for longer this time, and Jeremiah scowled. Then came another violent explosion and recoil. Jeremiah squinted through the spotter scope. "Another hit."

Joe got to his knees, brushed dirt from the front of his plaid shirt. "Ready to practice for real this time?"

They exchanged places, and Jeremiah tried to ignore the pain in his chest and the acute urgency in his gut. Under normal conditions his accuracy matched Joe Healing Water's.

But not now. The bullet wound impaired his ability to fire accurately, the pain messed with his ability to slow his breathing and his pulse, and his compelling need to reach Mattie messed with his concentration. He shifted, tucked the stock of the rifle into his right shoulder, sighted through the scope, then grew still.

Joe lay motionless beside him.

"Beer can on the right," Jeremiah muttered, succumbing to the unspoken challenge. He slid the bolt action and chambered a round, then wiggled some more, trying to get comfortable.

"You're too restless. Settle down," Joe told him.

"Shut up." Jeremiah waited, trying to relax the muscles in his chest and slow his breathing and pulse, felt a minimal change in the latter. The wind gusted, and Jeremiah's forecaster instincts warned the approaching system was moving in fast. His window of opportunity shrank with every minute he prolonged his shot.

Patiently, he brought his wandering thoughts back to the view through the scope, the Foster's beer can blended so perfectly into the prairie grass as to be invisible. He waited, mentally seeking oneness with the weapon, the merging of the spirit of the bullet with the beer can, then reached his own spirit out to touch them. His right forefinger twitched, then squeezed. The explosion buffeted his ears through his protective headgear, the recoil jolted his body.

"Miss." Joe's eyes, black as flint, scowled at him. "We have a problem, if you can't do any better than that."

Jeremiah stared through the scope at the beer can. He sat up and crossed his legs, looked at Joe's shadowed face.

"I should not have missed. I cannot maintain my concentration." Jeremiah spoke formerly, without contractions, a conscious trait he acquired when he left the Reservation, a trait he used to maintain his native identity in the middle of the white man's society. He opened his mouth to tell the old Indian about his restlessness concerning Mattie.

"No shit." Joe straightened to his knees, then swung around to survey the blackening horizon behind them. "Damned weather. Looks like we're in trouble."

Thunder banged, lightning flashed long spidery electrical currents, striking the flat earth in an uninterrupted, unpredictable dance.

"*Damn.*" Jeremiah's oath got lost in the wind. He packed the bipod, rifle, and both scopes, zipped up the heavy duffel, then hoisted it across his shoulders. His wound did not like the added weight and pain streaked through his chest.

"We're not going to out-run this one," Joe yelled. The massive black monster gained momentum over the flat terrain as a classic wall-cloud formation sank like a slow-motion theater curtain until it dragged along the ground. Jeremiah spun around, assessing their surroundings.

No ditches, no bluffs, absolutely nothing to offer cover.

"Time to dig ourselves in," he hollered over the gale, as Joe turned and ran towards the little knoll they'd used as a backdrop for their practice session. Jeremiah followed, struggling against the screaming wind, the added weight on his back making the wound in his chest hurt until he couldn't breathe.

They reached the small hill and Joe dropped to his knees on the lee side to dig into the soft earth with his hands. Jeremiah pulled the rifle from the duffle. Using the stock as a makeshift shovel, he deepened the trench, grunting against the pain in his chest. The two men did not exchange a word. Both knew the tornado would be upon them in a matter of minutes.

The wind shifted direction and dropped to an angry growl. Jeremiah dug faster.

"Get in!" He waved for Joe to roll into the cleft. Flying debris and dirt dropped visibility to zero. Jeremiah felt the wind playing with him, threatening to sweep him off his feet. He pushed the older Indian into the tiny cleft, then wedged himself in, squeezing Joe into the deepest part of the hole. The twister swept loose earth into an ever-expanding debris field. Their only hope of survival lay in the outside possibility the small knoll might be just big enough to cause the funnel to hop over them or change direction. If the rope was any size at all, it would plow right through the small hill and their poor excuse for a storm shelter.

Dime-sized hail began raining down, and Jeremiah breathed a whisper of hope. Maybe, just maybe, the eye of the system was veering away from them.

The thunder morphed from flat explosions to electrical sizzles, lightning danced around the knoll.

Great, he thought. The knoll offered the only hope of cover, but it also represented the highest object in the area. He tried to squeeze further into the hopelessly shallow, laughably inept shelter. He really did not want to be struck by lightning. He would rather be swept away than fried to a crisp.

Mattie would be furious with him if she found out that once

again he'd waited too long, waited until the situation became dangerous and desperate. He had a history of pulling this sort of thing when she went on storm chasing escapades with him.

Hell exploded from the earth with the brutal savagery only Mother Nature could produce. Hail slanted into horizontal sheets, debris swirled into dust devils that gyrated around the parent funnel. Jeremiah felt invisible fingers grasping, pulling, tearing at him. Joe's hands wrapped around his waist, wedging him tightly against the damp earth. Time slowed. Jeremiah closed his eyes and held his breath.

Then, suddenly, it was over. Torrential rain pounded them, turning their ditch into a muddy, water-filled trough. Tailwinds knocked him to his knees when he crawled out of the ditch and tried to stand up. He turned and helped Joe.

"Lost your stuff?" Joe hollered.

Jeremiah looked around for the now missing duffel bag. Miraculously the rifle, covered with red, muddy Oklahoma clay, lay nearby.

"Looks like it. Maybe we will come across it on our way to the Jeep." Jeremiah squinted through the darkness and torrential rain. "Providing the Jeep is where we left it."

Another storm approached fast in the wake of the one now northeast of them, impossible to determine the severity, although Jeremiah's forecaster instincts noticed a subtle change in the barometric pressure around them. Maybe the first storm had expended the energy pent up between the warm air and cool air cells that invariably clashed around this time of year.

The two men worked their way across the soaked, muddy earth, around tree limbs and other debris on their mile trek to the Jeep.

"Have you run down any leads on how Carrot Eater got hooked up with the Charlie Network?" Jeremiah asked, using Gary Tacque's nickname from his days on the Rez. The heavy rifle rested across his shoulders and he had to shout to be heard. When Joe didn't answer, he figured the old man hadn't heard the question.

Joe proved the smart one, refraining from conversation until they reached the Jeep, parked off an exit of the eastbound lane of Interstate-Forty. The vehicle was upright, dinged with tiny hail pockmarks, and sporting a smashed windshield. The red paint job mixed well with the red clay covering it bumper to bumper.

"At least it's still here," Joe yelled.

The two men knocked away the remains of the windshield, then cleared shattered safety glass from the front seats and floor. Jeremiah lay the rifle behind the front seats and they climbed in. He retrieved a pair of sunglasses from the glove compartment. Joe would have to squint for the next several miles. He cranked the engine, then swung onto the ramp. The absence of the windshield made for a very windy ride, but they escaped the storm clouds as they neared Elk City. He took the exit, spotted a small gas station, and swung into an empty space in front of an auto repair shop next door. He cut the engine and climbed out.

"We might get arrested, looking the way we do," he grinned as he saw Joe in the pale glow of the overhead station lights. Both of them had red mud from head to toe. He half-heartedly wiped his face, felt the mud move around his eyebrows and through his hair, decided it wasn't worth the effort. He scratched at the surgical tape beneath his shirt, felt grittiness there, too.

"Ah hell, we're just a couple of redskins," Joe grinned, his white teeth brilliant against the red clay plastered over his face.

The middle-aged station attendant, as wide as he was tall with a bald scalp and round spectacles that magnified his blue eyes, burst out laughing when they appeared in the doorway.

"Looks like you boys got caught in the middle of a mud-slinging match." He wore grease-stained overalls and a gray uniform shirt that had been white when it was new. He was average height, his round cherub face was red with the classic spider veins of too much beer and not enough exercise.

From the doorway, Jeremiah glanced at a wall clock hanging behind the counter. Nine pm. He wondered whether Mattie might still be awake. She wasn't one to take sleep aids, and she didn't drink. He patted his pockets, then realized his cell phone was in the Jeep.

"Do you have a shower anywhere?" Joe asked from where they stood. "My friend and I got caught in some weather a few miles west of here."

Laughter shook the attendant. "No kiddin'." He leaned over and retrieved a key on a long wooden peg, then walked outside.

He angled his head towards the side of the building as he offered the key. "Sorry, fellas. No shower." He gave them a once over, then began laughing again. "I'd let you use the bathroom at the house, but the missus won't let you through the door looking like that." He paused and looked westward, where a light show danced along the distant horizon. "What size rope was it? Did you get a gander at it?"

Joe grinned. "No idea. We were too busy trying not to get blown to Kansas. Busted the windshield out of our Jeep. When does your neighbor open?"

The attendant shook his bald, shiny head. "He closed down a while back. Not enough business. You'll have to head east to find a repair shop and a place to stay for the night."

Jeremiah and Joe thanked the attendant, then took turns in the men's room and cleaned their faces off as best they could before climbing back into the Jeep.

"Ready to eat whatever happens to fly by?" Joe muttered as he settled into the passenger's side.

Jeremiah shrugged. "Consider it protein. We missed dinner." He adjusted his sunglasses, started the engine, cranked the heater, then retrieved his cell phone from the glove compartment.

"Calling Mattie?" Joe asked, watching him.

Jeremiah nodded, squinting in the pale, overhead station lights, and tapped the screen. He held the phone to his ear for several long moments.

"You talked to her since I dragged you out of the hospital?"

Jeremiah shook his head. He frowned. "No answer."

"Weather has probably knocked out some of the towers," Joe pointed out. Jeremiah dropped his phone into a cup holder, then pointed the Jeep onto the interstate. They had at least an hour before they reached a large travel complex. Without a windshield, that meant they would be eating a lot of bugs.

~ * ~

Jeremiah finished his shower at the Travel America station, then slid into the new jeans and sweatshirt he bought in the store. Reluctantly he coaxed his feet into his soaked hiking boots. He could have bought a pair of the mass-produced fake leather moccasins the store had for sale. He grimaced. He'd go barefoot before being caught wearing a pair of those. He was wadding up his ruined clothes to throw away when his cell phone chimed with several email and text notifications. He strode from the Men's Shower area and took a seat in an empty booth in the fast food section. He checked missed calls first, but none appeared from Mattie, which bothered him until he remembered she didn't know where he was or what had happened to him after he left the Alamosa hospital. In fact, no one knew where he was at the moment, which presented somewhat of a problem because technically that meant he was AWOL. He really needed to contact his handler, but put that thought aside and instead scrolled through messages. Several work-related emails and weather warnings concerning the F-4 that crossed Interstate-Forty on the western side of Oklahoma. His phone buzzed again with more weather warnings in their area, otherwise known notoriously as Tornado Alley.

Joe slid onto the bench opposite him. He wore blue cargo jeans and the same type of Oklahoma Sooner sweatshirt Jeremiah had on.

"Careful. People might think we're related," Joe grinned. His wet hair trailed down his back. "Want something to eat?"

Jeremiah nodded. "Anything will do."

Joe stood and headed to the counter as Jeremiah stared at an email. The subject had been typed in bold capital letters:

JEREMIAH BLACK BEAR TYLER.

That was all. Jeremiah frowned. Could be Spam, but he did not usually get junk mail through his phone. His thumb hovered over the delete icon. Taking the risk, he opened the email, felt his heart thump hard as his stomach did a long, slow nose-dive to somewhere around the soles of his feet.

> *Loved ones you will lose.*
> *We owe you that much, at least.*
> *Eye for eye, tooth for tooth.*
> *Beast for beast.*
>
> *---Charlie.*

"Jeremiah, what is it?"

Joe's voice filtered through the massive clog in Jeremiah's

brain. He looked up, met the old man's black eyes. A bag of burgers and fries sat on the table between them.

Jeremiah stared at him, trying to pull his thoughts together. "Have you talked to Hawk today?"

Joe shook his head, took a long drink from a large soda. "No, didn't see any reason to. Figured he'd call us with an update when events warranted." He pointed at the burger and fries. "Eat that. I paid for it."

Jeremiah ignored him. "Mattie is in danger." He turned his phone so Joe could see the message. "And if I am interpreting this message correctly, so is Mud Rain."

David Mud Rain Tyler was Jeremiah's younger brother, fourteen, and suffered from Downs Syndrome. Gary Tacque, who had married Mattie's sister Angela then poisoned her, subsequently kidnapped the boy and almost killed him before Hawk, Jeremiah, and Mattie managed a rescue that ended with both Mattie and Jeremiah suffering gunshot wounds from Gary's rifle.

Joe read the email and frowned. "Have you tried Mattie again?"

Jeremiah nodded. "No answer at her house. Her cell phone is turned off." He laid his phone on the table. "Hawk assured us he knew what protocol the Charlie Network would follow, that he would be dealing with one of their killers, two at most."

Joe fell silent. "We should've heard from him by now," he acknowledged, looking steadily at Jeremiah.

Jeremiah tried to ignore the urgency that now screamed like a banshee in his head. "There is severe weather all over the state, which is probably jacking up communications. And Hawk knows the Charlie Network inside and out. That is why he is in Shawnee instead of us."

Joe shook his head. "Mattie is family. We should've gone to Shawnee, not him."

Jeremiah pushed the food away, ignored Joe's scowl. "We need to get back on the road. I do not like the implications of this silence from Hawk."

"I wish the hell you were shooting better, that's for damn sure." Joe reached over, picked up Jeremiah's burger, unwrapped it, and took a generous bite. His eyes met the younger man as he chewed, and he shrugged irritably.

"Well, if you're not going to eat it, I will. I'm hungry, I paid for the damned thing, and I'm not letting it go to waste." What he didn't add was that eating helped disguise the fact he was as rattled by the email as Jeremiah.

He tried another tact. "Look. Hawk's about as good with regular communication as you are, and you suck at it. Just ask Mattie." He waved what was left of the burger. "He may be trying to contact us and can't get through because of the weather."

Jeremiah stared out the large plate glass windows of the fast food joint. "I should have taken Mattie with me when you got me out of the hospital." He winced and rubbed the bandages beneath his sweatshirt.

"Nothing to do about it now." Joe wadded up the empty wrapper. "Plans are already in place."

Jeremiah frowned. Trouble was, his instincts were screaming that leaving Mattie behind at the Alamosa hospital had been a bad, bad mistake.

Chapter Two

"Stand down." Hawk's words seemed alarmingly calm in the face of what had to be a surprise attack.

The five rifles lifted, but five sets of eyes remained fixed upon me.

Hawk's next words sent ice-cold chills straight down my spine.

"Freeman, what is the meaning of this?" He demanded. "You brought the entire team?"

The man in the center stepped forward. "Yes, sir. Marks is outside."

Insight came fast. Hawk *knew* these men. Not only that, they seemed to be referring to him as their *leader*.

"Permission to speak," said the man furthest to my left in a low voice tight with anger.

"What is it, Carson?" Hawk snapped.

In the meantime, thoughts flew through my head, rendering their conversation into slow motion.

These men were not here to attack Hawk, which meant they were here to attack me. Five soldiers. With assault rifles. And a whole lot of anger. I began to tremble. Hawk's hands became unbearably tight against my cold skin. My fingers tingled as numbness oozed through my hands, then spread over the rest of me.

"Why not kill her now? Why all the elaborate shit? Excusing the language, sir."

Hawk released a long, measured breath that ruffled the top of my short black, curly hair. "Because that is not what Charlie wishes."

The figure Hawk had called Freeman shouldered his rifle and stepped to the sink. Hawk maneuvered the chair until my elevated leg bumped against the mercenary. The man reached into his flak jacket and pulled out some slender rubber tubing, fastened it to the faucet, then withdrew a tiny circular saw, which he attached to the free end of the tubing. I jerked when he bent down and drew the hem of my dress to mid-thigh, exposing the entire cast.

"Don't!" My voice cracked, the word came out as a choked

whisper.

"Keep still," Hawk ordered, as Freeman grasped the heel of my cast with his free hand.

"B-but what is he doing?" My voice shook. Freeman flicked a switch and the cast cutter whined.

"This is a waste of time. Cut it off when we have her in the trailer," Carson spat venomously.

Hawk stepped between the men and me. "Cut the chatter, Carson. I've my reasons. I need not explain them to you. Any more insubordination, and you'll be scrubbing the loo for a week."

I couldn't take my eyes off the cast cutter. "D-don't…don't do that." Hysteria ballooned in my chest. I reached out with both hands. "It hurts. I can't…." I broke off when Freeman's eyes met mine. Their murderous ferocity stopped me in mid-sentence.

"Gag her and get it over with. *Sir.*" Carson again, obviously not worried about cleaning toilets.

Hawk drew himself to his full height, which reached about six feet. "Carson, assist Marks with keeping an eye out for unwanted visitors. *Now.*"

With exaggerated movements, Carson snapped to attention. "Yes, *sir.*" He shouldered his rifle, whirled around, and stalked through the kitchen doors.

A fine wet spray dampened the edge of the cast and misted onto my black dress as metal teeth bit into the hardened Plaster of Paris. I clamped my teeth, gripped the cold metal arms of the chair, and fought down burgeoning terror. Freeman guided the cast cutter upwards. I felt the heat through the padding, struggled against fear, disgust, and embarrassment as he worked his way up my leg while his comrades watched with cold, horrible detachment. Despite my efforts to block them, thoughts began whispering what might happen after the cast was off, and I shook so violently the cast rattled against the metal leg support. I wished frantically William and Anna were still in the house, then realized if they were, they would be in danger, too, these men would kill them to keep them quiet.

Freeman maneuvered the cast cutter to my knee. The heat from the saw radiated along my thigh, pain from the pins and screws holding my lower leg together ground until my leg felt about to burst into flames. I slapped a hand over my mouth to muffle a sob I couldn't control.

Hawk, who had been looking on, took a step forward. "Freeman."

The man looked up.

"Give it a rest to allow the saw to cool." He swung his attention to the remaining three men and jerked his head towards the kitchen doors. "Give me two minutes with her."

I noticed irritation flicker across Freeman's eyes, but he obeyed, switched the tool off, and laid it on the counter, then followed his comrades.

The heavy wooden kitchen doors swung slowly shut, and Hawk and I were alone. Hawk reached up to his right ear and appeared to remove some sort of communication device, which he wrapped tightly into his fist. I stared at the stapled incision along his jaw line, thought about the trust I had placed in him in the middle of the Colorado Rocky Mountains when we were chasing down my brother-in-law, and couldn't control the tears that tumbled down my cheeks. My fingers clamped the arms of the wheelchair with such force I couldn't work them loose.

Hawk squatted until our eyes met. "Mattie, listen to me." His voice sounded low, urgent. "I asked you once to trust me. I'm asking you again to do the same."

I looked away. "They're here to kill me. And…and you're… you're one of them."

His expression closed down as he raised his hand to his ear again. "Charlie wants vengeance for the death of their team leader, your brother-in-law, Gary Tacque. They know you killed him, and now they are here to kill you. But not without a spot of emotional revenge first. Killing you outright is a bit too quaint for this lot."

Hawk straightened, stepped behind the chair. His hands pinned my wrists again. His mouth brushed my ear as he whispered, "It will go better for you if you find the courage you possessed on that mountain."

The doors swung open and the men filed in, each one of them capable of violence I could not imagine. Where had they come from? How had they managed to gain access to my parents' house without being seen?

Why oh why weren't the police and S.W.A.T. storming the

house and rescuing me?

Where was Jeremiah?

Charlie wants vengeance for the death of Gary Tacque.

My brother-in-law. The man responsible for killing my sister and nearly killing my husband, his younger brother, and myself, all in order to inherit my vast family fortune.

Charlie. Was that Hawk's real name?

Despite his insistence, I couldn't trust him. My sister and my parents had trusted Gary Tacque, and now all of them were dead.

Were Hawk and my brother-in-law in this whole thing together?

I had killed Gary on the side of the mountain along Wolf Creek Pass because he was about to kill my husband. Hawk disappeared from the mountain only to materialize tonight and bring his mercenary comrades.

Terror morphed into a sudden jolt of raw anger. These men and their warped sense of loyalty, the utter vileness these monsters exhibited in thinking they were above the law. When Freeman picked up the cast cutter and knelt in front of the wheelchair, I braced my wrists against Hawk's fingers, ready to kick the madman in the face with my good leg.

Hawk's cold voice hissed. "You will keep utterly still and quiet, do you understand? I can promise a good deal of pain beyond your wildest imagination, should you say or do anything to provoke these gentlemen."

I squeezed my eyes shut and clamped my teeth until my jaw hurt, then snapped my eyes open and glared at the man cutting the cast.

A gloved hand caught me across my right cheek with such force my head snapped and sent a streak of pain through my shoulders and down my back. The entire right side of my face felt lit on fire. Hawk remained silent, his fingers biting into my skin. The other three men lifted their weapons, ready to aim lethal barrels.

I turned my head slowly, avoiding eye contact, and watched Freeman from the corner of my eyes. When he saw me properly cowered, he lowered his raised hand and turned his attention once again to the cast. I closed my eyes and felt the cutter eat through the remainder of the Plaster of Paris. When he finished, Freeman shut the tool off, his fingers lingering at the padded top that wrapped around my thigh.

"That will be quite enough, Freeman." Hawk released my wrists, then stepped in front of the wheelchair. Freeman retrieved the rubber tubing and tucked everything into his vest.

"Williams, Allison, over here," Hawk ordered.

Two of the men stepped close. I tried to notice distinguishing features, but all of them had identical builds, and the balaclavas hid their features, rendering it impossible to tell one from another.

"Grip the edges just so," Hawk instructed, and together they removed the cast from my leg. I gasped and gripped the chair arms again, as the cast gave way to expose the rust-colored stain of Betadine and dried blood all over the skin of my broken leg.

"The brace and bandages are with the rest of the equipment?" Hawk's voice penetrated the sudden ringing in my ears and a bout of dizziness that brought me perilously close to passing out.

"Yes, sir." Freeman's voice. I recognized the deep timbre.

Hawk must have nodded. "Right then. Move out. Quickly."

Two of the men wrapped thick arms around my waist and legs, creating a chair, and carried me through the kitchen doors, the large dining room, then into the front room to the hallway. Two team members waited by the front door.

"All clear," one of them said. The other one opened the front door, and I was carried swiftly down the staircase into the darkness beyond the front entryway floodlights. Headlights appeared along the drive, and the large shadow of an enormous fifth-wheel hauled by a triple axle diesel truck lumbered to a stop beside us. Thunder rumbled a continuous monologue as lightning flickered and flashed, creating a strobe effect as a storm system approached. Wind swirled and tugged at us.

"Set her down." Hawk motioned towards the back of the camper. The two men settled me onto the rear bumper. I gripped the metal support and focused on not crying out. My leg felt like it had been amputated. Hawk opened a rear entrance, climbed inside, reappeared moments later with a heavy black leg brace and rolls of bandages. He knelt down and I hitched up my dress enough for him to wrap my leg before applying the brace. The wet pavement of the sweeping driveway felt warm against my bare feet. The strengthening wind blew against my face.

"Why did you cut off the cast?" I choked out when he straightened.

He motioned towards the brace. "More portable. Less identifiable. And, if necessary, effectively immobilizing if taken off."

The men took turns storing their weapons and outer gear in the camper. Two of them retrieved large metal cases.

"Near the furnaces should be sufficient," Hawk instructed as they turned towards the house. I watched them sprint up the stairs and disappear through the front doors. Too soon they reappeared empty-handed. Apprehension began whirling around my insides. With a start I realized the men had removed their flak jackets and headgear. I stared at them, but they were dressed in black T-shirts and black cargo pants, their haircuts and clean-shaven faces identical. I was a photojournalist for crying out loud. Why couldn't I distinguish simple facial features?

Hawk turned to me, the wind pressing his long-sleeved turtleneck against his chest. "This is the house you and your sister grew up in?" He had to raise his voice to be heard over the wind.

"That's none of your business, *Mr. Charlie,*" I snapped.

"Fond memories, I expect," he said, ignoring my remark.

I gritted my teeth. "Not so fond since I've buried my family."

I didn't want him to know the truth, that the house represented my refuge among the death that surrounded me. The music room held Dad's two seven-foot grand pianos. The pianos my sister and I slept under when we were kids, the ones we played beneath as we giggled and carried on while our parents rehearsed for upcoming performances. Photo albums, furniture, family knick-knacks, all represented irretrievable loss if anything were destroyed.

Angela's urn still sat on the lid of one of the grands.

"Fond memories you'd rather not admit then," Hawk countered, seeing straight through my lie. I've never been a good liar anyway.

"Regardless," he continued, his tone coldly detached. "A significant part of your life. Your identity. Your family. Irreplaceable if lost." He hesitated a fraction, then added, "Or destroyed." He jerked his head towards the two men who had carried the cases into the house. One of them walked over to me and with a sneer held up what looked like a cell phone. Then as one, the men turned towards the house.

I closed my eyes, felt the urge to beg Hawk not to go through with what he was about to do.

Killing you is a bit too quaint for this lot. His earlier words rang through my head.

The shock wave of the explosion hit us before sight or sound. A solid wall of air hit me, knocked me onto my elbows. With a muffled *W-U-U-U-U-M-P-H*, the entire structure lifted, then collapsed into itself. Smoke, dirt, and debris mushroomed into a thick black impenetrable cloud followed by orange fingers that engulfed my parents' home. The place that held all of my childhood and most of my adulthood memories disintegrated into a pile of rubble.

Chapter Three

Thick smoke enveloped me, and I inhaled a lung full and couldn't control a fit of choking, or maybe I was sobbing. Blackness engulfed me, and I thought I just might topple onto the wet pavement.

"Get her inside." Hawk's voice seemed far away. Mentally I dug deep, gripped consciousness in a metaphorical chokehold, refused to allow the inner darkness to win. Forcing my eyes open when strong hands gripped my arms, I glared at the face on either side of me despite the fact my eyes either wouldn't or couldn't sharpen their blurred features.

The inside of the camper resembled a miniature office rather than a vacation home. My vision cleared, and things shifted into focus. Stark white mini-blinds provided privacy from outside prying eyes; dark leather armchairs surrounded an oval Formica wood table. Muted colors looked like they belonged in a utility building. A compact kitchenette occupied the center of the trailer, narrowing the passage to the other half, which held a cage containing four dirt bikes and more seating space that obviously could be folded into sleeping quarters. A small mirrored door stood opposite the cooking area, and I assumed that to be the bathroom. The pristine interior and clean, tidy décor did not match my impression of what these thugs would use for housing. One thing was for sure. They traveled in style.

Hawk moved to one side and the two men carried me through the kitchenette to the spacious seating area. As they lowered me to one of the couches, I caught movement from the corner of my eye and watched Hawk quietly open a small kitchen drawer, then slip something into his trouser pocket as he slid the drawer closed before bringing a finger to his ear.

"We're aboard," he murmured. He turned as the two men retreated to the opposite end of the camper where the other men grouped. Hawk reached into one of the overhead cabinets, retrieved a couple of pillows, and eased them behind my back, then shifted my leg until it rested solidly along the cushion. The fifth-wheel jarred and shuddered forward. I felt the slight decline of the driveway, then we turned right.

Hawk stood over me. "Comfortable?"

"No." I resisted the urge to look away and met his gray eyes with an angry glare, which I'm sure wasn't at all intimidating because my leg hurt so badly I couldn't sit still. Tears of pain leaked out despite my rapid blinking.

Okay, my restlessness wasn't just due to pain. I was terrified, the same uncontrolled panic I felt the night Hawk kidnapped me, threw me against the concrete wall in the bowels of a deserted parking garage, and demanded information I knew nothing about.

My parents' house had been blown to smithereens, just like my car when Hawk abducted me. Only this time I had not lost my camera equipment. No, this time he had just destroyed everything from my past and present, everything that would help keep my dead parents and my dead sister close in spirit. All reduced to ashes and rubble. I didn't know how to process the loss.

And on top of everything, my husband was totally out of contact. Again. It had been over two weeks since he and I had been taken to the Alamosa County Hospital, where he disappeared without a word or even a hint why. Friends took me to our apartment in Colorado Springs, then to my parents' home in Shawnee. Yet again I had no clue where he was, and I really needed him to come and get me. And beat the crap out of these guys while he was at it.

Kidnapped. Again. By a British agent who sure as hell appeared to be hooked up with the assassination mob he claimed to be hunting down.

"Hungry?" Hawk asked. I had a sudden urge to punch him hard where it would hurt the worst, give him some of the pain he seemed so willing to put me through.

But I remembered Freeman's hard slap against my face and swallowed the impulse. I sat with my back to the mercenaries but could not wipe the memory of their rifles pointed at me...nor their cold, murderous expressions.

All of them wanted me dead. My heart thumped so hard in my chest I thought it might just burst out and flop around on the floor.

"Mattie." Hawk's voice brought my attention back to his question. I shook my head.

"N-no. I'm n-not hungry." I pressed my lips together when I heard how badly my voice shook.

Hawk towered over me like some sort of dark horror movie specter. "You've not eaten all day."

I jerked my head up. "How would you know…?" I broke off and looked away. Of course he would have had me under surveillance, probably since I'd left the Alamosa hospital.

Hawk moved to a small stovetop where a camping pot puffed intermittent whiffs of steam. I hadn't registered the smell before now, but when Hawk lifted the lid and spooned something into a plastic bowl, the aroma of chili hit my nostrils. The rumbling movement of the trailer created a sour, nauseated feeling in the back of my throat. Hawk retrieved a plastic spoon from a drawer, then stood over me again and held the bowl out. Not wanting to give any of them more reason to hurt me, I accepted it without arguing.

I watched as he dished out servings to the men, who lined up in obvious routine and handed dinner along to the last man first. I wondered whether one of them did all the cooking, or whether Hawk would do it because he was in charge.

That didn't make any sense, I thought. He would delegate cooking to one of his minions, right?

I stared at the line of men, unfocused, and almost missed the motion Hawk made when he slipped his hand into his trouser pocket, then dropped something into the bowl of chili he held. I noticed the man standing beside him had his head turned as he handed a serving to the man behind him.

The pain in my leg ached and throbbed. Setting the chili onto the couch cushion, I held my braced leg with both hands and eased it until my heel rested on the floor. I didn't look at any of the men at the opposite end of the camper, but I could follow their movements from the corner of my eye. I picked up the bowl of chili and stirred it with the plastic spoon, the aroma and the nearby company twisting my gut into tight, painful knots. I watched and tried to discern features such as eyebrows and cheekbones, noses and head shapes.

The men lounged around the back, taking turns sitting in the expensive leather armchairs around the oval table. Conversation minimal as they ate, two of them came back for seconds, which

Hawk obliged. I wondered why he didn't join them, why he leaned against the kitchen counter and seemed to create a barrier between the men and myself. None of them glanced my way. I also noticed none of them made an effort to hide their faces from me, which I thought with a shiver represented a bad omen regarding my immediate future. I frowned. I could not tell one from another, could not give more than a basic description that would fit most males in the country. Even their skin color exhibited the same dark outdoorsman tan. And they all mulled around with a calm satisfaction that sent my nerves into hysterical override. They were too calm, too satisfied. They emitted absolute confidence of their success in avenging their leader's death.

Except for one. One of them had begun to fidget, his hands shaking violently as he tried to eat. I glanced at Hawk, who leaned against the small stovetop and worked on his own meal.

The man jumped to his feet, his small brown eyes staring at me with such hatred I shrank against the pillows even though the length of the trailer separated us. Hawk snapped his head up.

"What is it, Carson?" He barked.

"I…Sir, I'm having a hard time being around that woman without strangling the bitch. Sir." Carson's voice shook with strain. With stiff, jerky movements, he shoved past Hawk. Veins stood out along his thick, corded neck. His teeth clenched so tightly that his jaw muscles bulged. I watched him, careful not to make direct eye contact for fear he would start hitting me. I flashed back to my earlier impression that Hawk stood between the men and me as a barrier.

Well, I thought, if he was trying to protect me, he was doing a damned poor job of it.

"You…you have no right to eat, to drink, to *breathe*. If it was up to me…." The man's hand jerked, and the bowl he held flew at my face. His actions were so abrupt, so unexpected, I had time only to squeeze my eyes shut. Slimy chili hit me full in the face, trickled down my throat, seeped beneath the high neck of my black funeral dress. I sat rigidly still, expecting him to haul me to my feet and use me as a punching bag.

"Bloody fucking hell, Carson. What are you on about?" Hawk's voice, low and furious, punctuated the tense silence.

"Sorry, Sir." Carson sounded anything but contrite. "I'll get something to clean her up." As I opened my eyes, the meanness in his conveyed all too clearly the last thing he intended was cleaning up the mess, that he would leave a lot of bruises instead. His trembling hands brushed my face and I shrank back, sure I would not survive a beating from the monster. Instinctively I raised my hands, one of them still holding my uneaten chili. Carson slapped the bowl, sending the contents flying all over my chest and into my lap along with the mess already spilled on me.

"You will do nothing of the sort." Hawk sounded pissed as hell. "Go to the back. *Now.*" He did not move from his spot in front of the stove, but the venom in his words stopped Carson before his fists made physical contact with my face. He turned his head, his hands clenching and unclenching.

"Why are you protecting this bitch?" he challenged. Raw fury radiated through the cramped confines of the camper, creating a trap from which I had no means of escape. I could not tear my eyes away from Carson's large, powerful, shaking fists.

Hawk's answer split the silence like an axe splitting wood. "I am following bloody fucking orders. I suggest you do likewise."

"Fucking Brit," Carson seethed, "You don't belong here. You weren't part of Tacque's team." But he dropped his hands and stepped back.

Hawk kept his eyes on Carson. "Williams, Allison, get some sweat pants and a sweatshirt. And bring some wet towels."

Carson stumbled past Hawk and paced the cramped interior, his back ramrod straight, every muscle in his body twitching. I watched him from the corner of my eye and felt pressure building in my chest at the thought he might not stay there very long. He looked ready to spring at the two men who now approached my end of the trailer.

My heart pounded. I did not want to be undressed in front of these slimy assholes. I was having enough problems stifling surges of terror without the added threat of being stripped naked.

I crossed my arms over my ruined dress and nodded towards the clothes one of the men held.

"I-I'll t-t-take c-care of it." My voice shook abominably. I un-curled one of my arms and reached for the clothes.

"Mattie, you will follow directions." Hawk's curt order came from behind the two men. Chili was all over me, a great puddle of it sat in my lap. I could feel a wad of the disgusting stuff soaked into the neck of my dress and all over my chest. One of the men had brown eyes, the other had light blue eyes. I decided Allison was the one with blue eyes. I turned my head away.

Williams and Allison bent over and began working my dress out from underneath me, pulling it over my head and leaving a slimy trail of chili all over my cheeks and hair. My face flamed hot as red coals, and I clamped my lips against a shout of protest and mentally searched for something to take me away, to fill up my thoughts and give me courage when every fiber threatened to disintegrate. When one of the men began to wipe off my face and exposed chest with a wet hand towel, I almost lost it. Frantically I thought about my childhood, when Angela and I would listen to Mom and Dad rehearse for an upcoming duo piano recital.

Think of the music, I silently begged as I tried to recall names of pieces, or names of composers. I thought about Dad at his piano, and the vivid mental image gave me the feeling he was close, his strength supporting my flailing courage.

One of them used a thick terrycloth towel to dry me off, then guided my arms into the sleeves of a soft sweatshirt. A pair of hands grasped under my arms and lifted, and someone slipped a pair of sweats over my uninjured leg. The right leg of the sweatpants had been cut off to expose the brace. Closing my eyes, I shivered despite the thickness of the sweats. When someone dropped a blanket on me, I opened my eyes and watched the two figures cleaning up the floor and the couch. When they straightened and returned to the opposite end of the trailer, I closed my eyes again and huddled beneath the blanket. A vague musical strain drifted through my memory, and I listened with all of my heart and soul, wishing I could feel the vibrations as vividly now as when Angela and I lay on the floor beneath Dad's grand piano.

"Mattie, eat this."

Hawk's voice sounded way too close. I jerked my eyes open to find him squatting in front of me. I looked at the bowl of chili he held, then briefly met his steel gray eyes.

"I'm not hungry." My words came out in a hoarse, shaky croak.

"It's not a request." Hawk's voice had a cold edge that matched the coldness in his eyes.

"I'll feed it to her," Carson chided from the opposite end of the trailer.

"Shut up, Carson. You've caused enough problems already," one of the others snapped.

Hawk turned his head towards the back of the trailer. "Carson, pull out the rifles. All of them. I want them cleaned. Now."

I heard a beat of dead, rebellious silence before Carson answered. "Yes, sir."

Hawk turned his head to me again and opened his mouth, then shut it abruptly and brought a hand to an ear with what I realized now must hold some sort of communication device.

"Say again." He stood, the disgusting bowl of chili still in one hand. He turned and opened a set of cabinet doors to reveal a large flat screen, then picked up a remote, turned on the set, and surfed channels until he came to the weather station. The map behind the forecaster showed an outline of the entire state of Oklahoma. Red and orange rotating cells covered most of the state.

Hawk turned his head towards me. "Mattie, look at this and tell me whether we're headed into trouble."

I tried to match his cold expression, felt pretty sure I wasn't succeeding at all. "Tell me where we are and I can tell you whether we're headed for any of it," I retorted. What I carefully omitted was the fact, based on the location of the reddest part of the system, we were already directly in the path of the gigantic cell.

In the meantime, pain streaked down my leg. The Velcro brace didn't provide enough support. I balled up my fists, bent my left leg to my chest, wrapped both arms tightly around my knee and squeezed as hard as I could. Hawk couldn't help but notice my actions.

"You're in pain." He moved the short distance to the small kitchenette, set the bowl on the tiny counter. I kept my eyes averted as I heard sounds of opening and closing cabinets, but glanced around in time to watch him retrieve a small plastic bottle of water from an under-the-counter refrigerator. He closed the short distance between us and held out a large, oblong white tablet.

"Take this." Hawk placed the tablet in my hand, then held out the water bottle.

I really wanted to tell him no, to prove to him and his gang of imbeciles that I was tough and unafraid. But pain screeched through every nerve.

"Why make her comfortable?" Carson again, his voice floating from the back of the trailer.

Hawk spun an about-face. "Carson, control your mouth!" His words rattled the thin metal walls of the fifth-wheel.

Dead silence followed.

"CARSON!" Hawk bellowed.

The trailer rattled again, attracting my attention. The shuddering wasn't from the volume of Hawk's voice. I jerked my eyes to the television screen just in time to read the location of an approaching funnel cloud.

A tornado. On the ground. In our vicinity.

"Yes, sir." Carson's voice sounded belligerent.

Pre-occupied with his insubordinate team member, Hawk had yet to notice the telltale behavior of the trailer.

Apparently, he wasn't done reprimanding his assault team. "All of you will leave the woman alone until I order otherwise! Do I make myself quite clear!"

Sudden commotion and stamping feet, and I guessed six men suddenly jumped up.

"YES, SIR!" Came a loud, ear-ringing male chorus.

Hawk turned to me. "Take that," he repeated brusquely.

I decided it would not be wise to argue with him, opened the water bottle, and swallowed the medication.

He retrieved the bowl of chili, thrust it close to my face. "Eat."

Since I wasn't about to bring the dangerous weather situation to his attention, I obeyed and choked down a few bites of what had to be the spiciest concoction on the face of the planet. My forehead broke out in beads of sweat with the first bite, my mouth felt like I could breathe fire after the second. I chugged some water and managed to swallow another bite.

"Now, about the weather status." Hawk turned his attention to the flat screen and began muttering under his breath. One of his hands lifted to his ear, then he turned to me. "We're traveling west on Interstate Forty."

I looked at the red splotches surrounded by large orange rings that far outnumbered the amount of yellow and green bearing down on Shawnee.

"None of it looks good," I ventured. I heard footsteps and one of the men joined us to stare at the screen. I prayed they would be too preoccupied with the swirling colors to read the trailer. Hawk had muted the sound, and the forecaster's lips silently wagged on about location and severity of the cell.

"Any sign of a tornado?" the man asked.

His question told me a lot. Anyone from the southwest knew these kinds of cell combinations meant tornadic activity. Add the tornado warning ticker tape, and he should have known the situation without needing to ask. The jolting shudders coming from the trailer told me the driver was experiencing horrendous crosswinds. As if acknowledging my silent assessment, the trailer perceptibly slowed.

"The driver's requesting permission to park beneath an overpass." Hawk looked at me, waiting for an answer.

I really wish I were a good liar. If I could convince them to keep going, we would find ourselves in a highly dangerous vehicle in a highly dangerous tornado that might wipe out the whole rig, and with luck, few of the men in it.

But I was not a good liar. And Hawk knew it.

"An overpass won't give us much protection, if a rope of any decent size comes our way," I shrugged with as much nonchalance as I could muster.

"Rope?" The guy standing beside Hawk glanced down, his brown eyes familiar. I wondered whether he might be Williams. Or Allison. I couldn't remember which eye color I'd decided belonged to which man.

"Funnel cloud. Tornado," I explained.

"Any guess what size?" Hawk's voice sounded calm, and I realized with a shiver he might be unfamiliar with tornadoes, that he did not comprehend the heart-stopping violence we faced.

I glanced at the news feed in time to read that a large funnel cloud was on the ground and heading for Interstate Forty just west of Shawnee.

The trailer lurched and swayed again. Hawk put a finger to his ear. "He's pulling off. Says the wind is too bad to continue."

The huge camper veered onto an exit. The driver slowed, then made a laborious turn, the vehicle rolling several yards before shuddering to a halt. Wind gusts buffeted the sides with such force I couldn't hear anything above the noise. The high-pitched, whining wind gathered momentum, the brittle machine gun sound of debris pounded the outside of the fifth-wheel.

"How long do you think this will last?" Hawk yelled over the noise.

I glanced again at the weather screen and the tremendous cell bearing down towards the little dot marked Shawnee. The swirling epicenter was almost upon us. Abruptly, the screaming pitch of the wind dropped, and the buffeting seemed to ease.

Hawk glanced at me. "Is it over?"

Yeah, I thought, *for about thirty seconds.*

I nodded. "The wind is dying down." And it indeed sounded less forceful, typical just before the epicenter arrived. So I was telling the truth. I just wasn't acknowledging which part of the truth I was telling him.

"You're quite sure?" Hawk's eyebrows lifted doubtfully.

"Yes." I sounded strong, convincing.

Nodding, Hawk brought his hand up to his ear. "Move out. We need to keep going."

His ear-piece squawked so loudly that he winced. Evidently the driver was not happy about the order.

"I have information on good authority, and we're watching the weather system on the telly. Move out," he barked.

More squawking, louder this time.

"Never you mind what your radio chaps are telling you," Hawk snapped.

The fifth-wheel shuddered, began to move forward. I prayed the driver would be forced to make a large U-turn. Either direction, it didn't matter.

Hawk's attention was on the guy standing at his side, so I stole a quick glance at the television screen. The massive swirling red cell loomed close to the ribbon that indicated Interstate Forty.

A U-turn would expose the side of the trailer to the front of the tornado, the most destructive edge of the monster. With any luck, the tornado would rip the camper to shreds.

The low pitch of the wind suddenly broke into a shrieking roar, the trailer whipped around as though caught on a carnival Tilt-A-Whirl, and metal ripped with an ear-splitting screech. I grabbed for the cushions and glanced over my shoulder. The men stood in a group, their legs splayed in a useless effort to maintain balance, their eyes wide with shock.

"DOWN! NOW!!" Hawk yelled as he hit the floor. The men toppled and tumbled over each other, their arms waving wildly as they hit first one side of the trailer, then the other. Hawk's hand snaked up and pulled me onto the floor with him, my braced leg banging with a blinding, nauseating jolt when I fell off the couch.

I prayed hard the outside monster would blow through the trailer, killing the monsters who cowered inside.

I prayed the tornado would kill me, too.

Because if any of us survived this, Hawk would know I had purposely misled him, and he would throttle the life right out of me.

Chapter Four

The camper lurched wickedly, throwing us around like rag dolls, the metal frame screaming in cacophonic shrieks with the deep-throated roaring wind. Hawk gripped me hard, wedged me against the floor, as the frail metal frame twisted and tore, the storm sounding like dozens of thundering freight trains and high-pitched banshees. The tornado dragged us in circles, lifted the enormous camper like a feather, then slammed it onto its side. The wreckage slid heavily down an incline, thick, red, wet clay peeling the side right off and threatening to bury every one of us trapped inside. With a long convulsion, the mangled heap shuddered to a halt. The wind screamed around us, buffeting the wreck, teasing us as it threatened to scoop up the camper again, then seemed to grow bored with the game and suddenly dropped in intensity. The remains of the camper became silent as the wind moaned and wailed with less and less volume.

"Bloody fucking hell," Hawk breathed, his chest and arms trembling against me.

He wasn't the only one. My body shook, my teeth chattered until I thought I would bite my tongue. Pain ripped through me, spots danced before my eyes.

"Freeman!" Hawk's voice cracked. He cleared his throat twice before trying again. "Freeman! Williams!"

One by one the men answered.

Freeman's voice squeaked out an octave higher than normal. "No serious injuries, sir. Just shaken up."

Hawk shifted and I caught his profile from the corner of my eye as he pressed his hand to the earpiece. "Masters!" He waited a couple of beats. "Masters! Check in!" He stood, stumbling and swaying until he found solid footing in what was left of the fifth-wheel. Ripped metal edges created bizarre angles among the wreckage.

"Bloody fucking *hell*." Hawk's voice sounded stronger. And furious. "Freeman, go to the cab and check Masters. Williams, get these motorbikes undone and outside. Allison, bring me a spare pair of your black fatigues. The rest of you get the weapons and ammo out of here and find a place to hide them until we're clear. Williams, help them when you're done with the bikes."

Sounds of scrambling feet reached my ears, and I shifted enough to prop my head against a hard metal object. I looked at the wreckage around us, everything covered with chili, which for some wild reason gave me immense satisfaction. I wrapped my arms hard around my chest and rubbed up and down, trying to generate some warmth.

"Freeman, is the back door clear?" Hawk called over the activity.

"Yes, sir. Going to check on Masters now."

"Check the fuel tanks. Make sure we're not leaking diesel."

Hawk bent to some drawers. I heard the crisp rattle of plastic packaging before he picked his way through the debris to me. Behind him, Allison held some blurred objects that I assumed were clothes. I blinked my eyes. I couldn't talk, could hardly breathe, and my whole body seemed about to seize into one monstrous cramp from the conflicting sensations of brutally freezing air and the white fire that consumed my leg.

"Quite clever of you, Mattie, throwing us into the middle of that," Hawk growled between clenched teeth. He leaned over me, unceremoniously pulled the sweats and my underwear to expose my right hip, then sank what felt like an incredibly long needle into my skin.

"Allison, put those down and get me some towels, bandages, and duct tape," he snapped. "Looks like strawberry jam back here."

"Sir." Freeman's voice. He sounded hoarse and incredibly close. Like inside my head close. I marveled how acute my hearing seemed.

But I couldn't see a damned thing. The freezing sensation began melting into a general sense of numbness.

"What is it?" Hawk's fingers reached through the brace and applied heavy pressure against the back of my right knee.

"Masters is shaken up. Fuel tanks are intact, no leaks. The gooseneck tore clean through the truck bed, snapped both axles. The camper and the truck are ruined."

Hawk shifted, released my knee. "Allison, take over here."

Vaguely, I felt the metal sides vibrate as the men exchanged places. Steel fingers pressed against the artery located behind my knee. Hawk's voice came from far away.

"Clean things up and get the bleeding under control."

I closed my eyes and felt myself slip away into darkness.

~ * ~

Allison squatted beside Mattie, lifted her eyelid, then checked her pulse.

"She's out cold, sir. Pulse is rapid but strong." He pointed to the black brace that supported her right leg. "I'll have to get that off, and I can't do that unless I've got some help."

Hawk nodded. "I'll fetch someone." He stepped over the mess, rain and wind buffeting the remains of the camper. He reached the rear entrance and dropped onto the grass outside. The heavy rain drenched him within seconds.

"Marks!" Hawk hollered into the communicator, swiping at his face in a useless effort to brush away the water. A lot of crackling followed, then Marks answered.

"Sir!"

"Help Allison with the woman."

A split second of hesitation, then, Marks replied. "Sir, Cumbers and I are in the middle of digging a cache for the weapons. Neither of us is in the vicinity."

Hawk muttered and oath. "Where's Carson?"

"He should be at the wreckage, sir. He was helping Freeman with Masters."

Hawk tapped the earpiece. "Carson!"

Having overheard the entire conversation, Carson answered immediately. "I'll help Allison."

Hawk's jaw clenched. He didn't want Carson anywhere near Mattie, but at the moment he wanted Freeman at his side, so he had no other choice. "No injuries, understand?"

"Yes, sir."

Freeman, carrying a powerful flashlight, waited beside the camper. The bright halogen beam cut through the thick darkness, illuminated sheets of rain. Carson passed through the light on his way to the back of the wreckage.

"We've a problem." Hawk muttered to Freeman. "No way to avoid the bloody coppers."

"I was thinking the same, sir." Freeman agreed as they clambered into a ditch and stopped next to a dark figure leaning against the open door of the diesel truck. Freeman angled the light so the three men could see each other without being blinded.

"Okay there, Masters?" Hawk asked, squinting at the driver through the rain.

"I tried to tell you not to go nowhere," the driver wheezed. In his sixties, he wore a button down gray uniform shirt and pants, all soaked through. "I been driving this route all my life. We were damn lucky the thing veered when it did, or we'd be in Kansas now." His hand shook when he rubbed his gray, shaggy, dripping beard. "Sweet Jesus, that was close."

Freeman interrupted, his voice tight. "With all due respect, sir, why did you ask the woman for advice about the damned weather when Masters told you not to go anywhere?"

"What would you suggest?" Hawk pressed, directing his question to Masters and ignoring Freeman's challenge.

"Well, we ain't goin' nowheres til we get a tow truck here." His dark brown eyes peered from beneath thick bushy gray eyebrows. His wet gray hair blew wildly in the wind, looking more like a Halloween specter than a man. "Probably forty-eight hours, anyway, based on the number of wrecks around us."

"Bloody hell," Hawk muttered, squinting through the downpour at various shadows and blinking red lights littering the highway around them. Williams, evidently finished with unloading the bikes, joined them.

Masters frowned at the three men, understood their unspoken demand to find a quick solution. "I'll get on the horn and call in some help. I got a friend nearby who runs his own moving business. Might lend us one of his smaller vans." Shaking his head until water flew from him like a shaggy dog, Masters climbed into the truck.

"Fortunately, we've got some time before anyone shows up," Freeman ventured. "Masters will report no injuries, so we'll be a ways down on the response list."

Hawk nodded, his expression cold as his eyes swiveled between Freeman and Williams. "Williams, check on Cumbers and Marks. We've weapons and several hundred pounds of ammo to hide." He squinted through the heavy downpour and watched two men appear through the rain.

"You boys okay over here?" One of them asked. Darkness and soaked clothes hid most of their features, and Hawk realized the strangers would see much the same with him. He kept silent to hide his accent and let Freeman do the talking.

The latter nodded, water streaming through his military cut. "We're fine. Just in need of a tow truck."

One of the men grinned, his teeth white against his wet skin. "Don't we all." He and his companion waved, then trotted back to their own problems.

~*~

Carson hauled himself into the wreck, spotted Allison kneeling close to the unconscious woman. He picked his way through the debris and growing puddles.

"Whatcha got?" he asked Allison.

The latter shook his head. "Don't know. I haven't been able to take a look yet."

Together, the men worked off the brace and padding on Mattie's right leg, revealing a long, jagged gash that stretched from her mid-calf to her knee and across the recent surgical incision. Though bleeding, there did not appear to be any sign of arterial involvement.

"I've got this," Carson murmured as he assessed the wound. "Go help the others."

"But Hawk told me to..." Allison started to object. Carson waved an impatient hand. "I'm senior here, and I'm telling you I don't need your help."

Allison stood slowly. "You know he wants her alive," he warned after a long hesitation.

Carson grunted. "They need you more out there. Steer clear of Hawk for now and go help the others with the weapons and ammo." He watched Allison crawl over the wreckage and disappear through the door before turning his attention to Mattie. His lips curled into a malicious grin. "I'll take care of you," he cooed.

A good while later, his expression smug, Carson jumped down from the camper and hurried over to where Hawk stood in conference with Masters beside the truck. The downpour had eased to a steady light rain, which everyone ignored since they were soaked to the bone anyway.

"Sir, I've changed her clothes, put her in a pair of fatigues. She had a deep cut along her leg, which I got sewn up and bandaged. She's still out of it. I've got her wrapped up in a couple of blankets and comfortable. I told Allison to help with the weapons."

Hawk squinted at Carson, then turned to Freeman. "The two of you transport her to the house in Norman." He stopped, stood for several minutes in silence. The wind swirled in gentle, almost playful gusts around them. He turned a slow circle, scanning the dark horizon. "Bloody weather. I'd give odds to know what's headed our way."

"Give me a few minutes." Masters disappeared into the cab again, and after a bit leaned out and shook his head. "Hell, looks like we're in for a night of it. Another system on its way. Probably hit us within the hour. I radioed a friend over yonder, near Weatherford. It'll take him a while. Traffic's backed up for miles."

Hawk tramped through the darkness with Freeman and Carson. They climbed into the back of the camper and Hawk paused to stare at the surrounding mess, then quirked his thick, dark eyebrows at Carson.

"I thought a little re-arranging back here would help throw the cops off the scent," Carson offered.

"Bloody brilliant," Hawk admitted.

Motorcycle magazines, newspapers, laundry, and the remains of the chili littered the inside of the camper. The motorcycle cage, held up by a twisted section, was now empty. Mattie lay on a camping pad in a dry spot near the door.

Hawk stepped around the debris and bent down beside her. Covered in blankets she appeared very pale, but her breathing seemed quiet and even. Straightening, he picked up one of the motorcycle magazines, thumbed it, then threw it back into the mess.

Freeman and Carson picked their way around the wreckage and began checking storage areas for any stray weapons or forgotten boxes of ammunition.

"With respect, sir, anyway you look at it, your accent's going to stick out like a sore thumb," Freeman commented.

Hawk frowned. "Quite right." He tapped his communicator.

"Allison. Report in."

The communicator squawked. "Allison here."

"How are things?"

Allison's voice came across tinny and garbled. "No issues."

"Meet me at the back. Tell the others to stay on watch for coppers."

Freeman made his way to the door and dropped onto the ground. Carson joined him, and the two men turned their attention to the dirt bikes propped against the outside. Allison took a while before he joined them.

Hawk exited the wreckage. "I'm exchanging places with Cumbers and Marks until the response units clear out. You understand what to do?"

"Yes, sir." Freeman nodded. Hawk crossed the grass to the truck cab. The distant flash of emergency lights dotted the interstate. Strobes from more rescue vehicles could be seen approaching from the west.

Freeman watched Hawk walk away, then turned to Carson. "She's still out of it. I think the boss gave her something more than Morphine," he muttered. "You ready to load things up?"

Carson nodded.

"Let me get my gear." Freeman disappeared into the camper, then came out with a black motorcycle helmet, heavy leather jacket, and gloves. After he had everything on, the two men located a helmet for Mattie. Carson produced a long black raincoat, which they carefully slipped over her.

"Not much we can do to camouflage that brace," Carson observed as they carried the unconscious woman through the door and over to one of the bikes.

"Better than have blazing white Plaster of Paris," grunted Freeman. While Carson supported the limp woman, Freeman straddled the bike, then Carson settled her behind him. Freeman hunched forward until he felt her weight solidly against his back. Using duct tape, Carson strapped her wrists together beneath the raincoat.

"Will that hold?" he asked Freeman.

"Ought to. Help me adjust the coat." They worked the belt of the coat around Freeman's waist, strapping it until Mattie's hips were snug against Freeman's. Carson used plastic tie restraints to loosely bind Mattie's feet alongside Freeman's ankles.

"How does it look?" Freeman asked.

"On the freeway and with this weather, we should be good," he nodded. "I'll ride on the inside, so passing cars can't get a close look." Carson strode to another bike. With a crank, both engines roared noisily to life.

Hawk walked from the truck where he and Masters had been listening to radio chatter. He checked the restraints holding Mattie against Freeman and nodded his approval.

"Remember, keep it legal and don't attract attention. If the motorway looks backed up, take back roads. Don't use GPS unless absolutely necessary," he advised.

Carson waved a salute and the two dirt bikes made their way slowly to the pavement, then disappeared into the darkness. Hawk listened until he could no longer hear the engines.

He turned and addressed the next problem. Allison stood beside him.

"Change into jeans and whatever T-shirts you can find, cooperate with the police no matter what they say, and just maybe we'll eke out of this without attracting undue attention."

Allison nodded, and Hawk radioed Cumbers for directions to the weapons cache before darting into the trailer for a change of clothes. He located Cumbers and Marks, updated them on the state of things, then sent them to the wreckage.

Hours of laying on a fresh mound of dirt that buried the weapons gave Hawk precious time to assess the situation. He was fully covered in black and held thermal vision optics as he surveyed the activity around the wreckage several hundred yards away. Blue light bars of three Oklahoma State Patrol cars flashed brilliantly in the darkness, the units angled around the wrecked fifth-wheel. Another storm had come and gone, fortunately without any more of those damned twisters. The rain continued, creating misty conditions that hid him from wandering motorists and authorities.

Powerful spotlights bathed the site in foggy white light. Hawk watched several miniature specks moving about the truck and camper. A mobile repair unit worked on separating the damaged vehicles, while a large tow truck parked beside the diesel truck.

The mist swirled and eddied around him, growing thicker as

the wind lessened. Hawk watched the slow progress of separating the fifth-wheel from the truck. They needed to get back on the highway and out of the area. Hawk did not want to rely on the fickle temperament of Lady Luck.

~ * ~

"You sure you don't want your camper towed in?" Luke James, known to his friends as EllJay, asked as he guided the controls of the tow truck ramp. He opted to wedge the ramp beneath the raised back of the truck, then maneuvered the rig until the wreckage slowly inched onto the flatbed. "There's just no tellin' who might drive by and decide to loot the thing while we're gone."

Masters knew the tow truck operator from way back. "I'll take my chances, EllJay. Right now, I really need a ride to Vance's place."

"Vance Miller? The moving guy?" EllJay nursed a golf ball-sized wad of tobacco in his right cheek. Short and wiry, he normally wore a cowboy hat and boots, except in conditions like tonight. He valued his Stetson too much to ruin it in this kind of weather. He turned and spat, wiped his mouth with the back of his hand. "What you want to go all the way out there for?"

Before Masters could explain, one of the state troopers walked over. Water streamed from the rain cover protecting his hat. Dampness soaked through his uniform despite his raincoat. "I gotta say, I didn't think you folks would be in very good shape, not with the way things looked when I drove up."

Masters turned to him. "I done more sliding than rollin'. The camper took the brunt of it."

The state trooper flicked his eyes towards a nearby overpass. "You should've parked over yonder. Would've saved you a lot of trouble."

Masters grunted. He should have ignored the Brit's instructions and stayed put. He shrugged. No sense crying over spilt milk.

"So let me get this straight. You were driving the truck, but the rest of you were in the fifth-wheel while you were on the road?" The officer was fishing, and Masters felt uncomfortable having to lie. He had a good reputation with the state troopers and didn't want to screw that up. Out of habit he lifted a hand to massage his beard, felt the soggy hair matted against his clothes. Fortunately, one of the men standing beside him stepped forward.

"Yes, sir," Cumbers replied.

"Looks like someone was cooking back there," the officer commented.

Cumbers looked embarrassed. "Yes, sir, that was me. Masters here had pulled over and I was cooking us up some chili. I told him to get started again while I cleaned up."

"I'll need to see some identification and registration for the truck and camper."

Allison joined Cumbers, and the other team members drifted over. A second state trooper joined the first as they gathered IDs."

"You're aware it's illegal to be in any sort of towed recreational vehicle while moving?" The first officer asked when his partner took the IDs to their cruiser. "I'm going to have to cite you for illegal use of the camper."

Cumbers nodded. "I understand, sir." There followed a lot of standing around as the light rain misted around them.

"Ever been caught in a twister before?" the officer asked.

Cumbers shook his head. "No, sir, and I hope I never am close enough to witness another one."

"They can create quite a mess," the state trooper nodded towards the wrecks littering the highway. His partner returned with the ID's.

"They're clean," he said as he handed them to Cumbers, who distributed them among the rest of the team.

The trooper's mouth cracked into a wry smile. "Well, seeing how you're working with Jim Masters, I'll let you guys off with a warning. But take some advice and follow the rules from now on."

"Yes, sir. Will do," Cumbers nodded as he replaced his ID in his wallet. "Thank you."

Masters hitched a ride with EllJay when he towed off the ruined diesel truck. The wee hours of the morning saw him return in a small moving van. While scattered emergency crews concentrated on cleaning up the massive debris, Cumbers and Williams emptied the damaged camper of as much as they could, then stacked clothes, personal gear, canned goods, and kitchenware into the back of the van. Last to go in were the remaining dirt bikes. With Cumbers' directions Masters located Hawk and the weapons. Quickly and unobtrusively the men loaded the duffel bags and backpacks.

"You think we might get pulled over for a surprise inspection?" Cumbers asked as the van shuddered forward. He and the rest of the team sat on the hard metal flooring.

"Not likely," Williams interjected. "Not with everything that's going on. They're too busy to bother with routine inspections."

"I suggest we get off the interstate anyway," Allison ventured. "No sense pushing our luck."

Hawk nodded. He relayed the conversation to Masters via his earpiece, and soon they felt the van slow and veer onto an exit. The cumbersome vehicle bumped and swayed across narrow rural roads. Masters checked in when they reached the outskirts of Norman. He found a secluded place to park, and the men unloaded the van with silent efficiency.

"Thank you." Hawk handed him a thick wad of bills. "If anyone comes around asking questions, don't hesitate to tell them what you know."

Once Masters and the van disappeared, Hawk and his men transferred the weapons to the dirt bikes. Cumbers and Williams set off, returned in due time to collect more gear. It took two more trips before they had everything cleaned up.

After the bikes left with the last of their equipment, Hawk and Allison set off on foot. He allowed his thoughts to wander as they trekked through the quite dark town. Despite a few scary hours, he still seemed solidly in charge of things. The entire team assumed they were still on task for their next target.

Hawk hoped Tyler and Healing Water were on their way. According to their original plan he was to meet them in Shawnee with Mattie safe and sound and things well under control. He allowed himself a string of mental curses. Their original plans had been blown to hell and back, and any delay in Tyler and Healing Water's arrival would muck up their ability to assist him in taking out the Charlie Network before they did anymore damage.

And he had no way of alerting them to the damage already done.

Chapter Five

Jeremiah frowned as he drove east along Interstate Forty. He could not calm the frantic urge Mattie was in acute danger. He tried to rationalize, blaming the compelling feeling on the weather, his reaction to their close call, the severe storm cells engulfing most of the state. He and Healing Water were still at least an hour west of Oklahoma City. He dug his cell phone from the front pocket of his jeans.

"Joe, check the news. See what areas were hit, especially around Shawnee."

Joe Healing Water grunted and took Jeremiah's cell.

"What does it say?"

Joe brought the cell phone to his ear. "It's not saying a damned thing."

Jeremiah scowled. "Very funny." He pulled the Jeep to the shoulder, then plucked the phone from Joe's hands and swiped the screen, found the weather site, and scrolled through the report.

"Several tornadoes have touched down across the state," he read. "Looks like none of them hit populated areas. Kansas is getting it now. Hold on." He went silent.

Joe watched him. "Expecting me to read your mind?" he prompted.

Jeremiah glanced at him. "Shawnee and eastern Oklahoma City got lucky. An F-4 blew through between the two. Reports of damage along the interstate, but it missed both cities. We will be sitting on the highway for a while before we get to the Lamont home."

Jeremiah tossed the phone into one of the drink holders and tried to control an irrational surge of anger over the thought of a long traffic delay. He accelerated the Jeep back onto the interstate. Their only luck so far tonight was finding a mobile windshield repair truck at the Travel America station.

"Looks like the twister ripped a damage path between the western edge of Shawnee and the eastern border of Oklahoma City." Jeremiah ran through a mental map of the area. Too close, he thought, focusing on the white strips passing beneath them. Mattie was at risk. Doppler radar was good, but not pin-point accurate. Her home could have been hit. He wouldn't know until they reached Shawnee. He glanced at the speedometer, wanting to go faster, hating the crosswinds that buffeted the Jeep around like a child's toy.

"I'd suggest calling Mattie, but that would blow our position," Joe commented.

"Land lines and cell service will be spotty at best right now, and signals need to be kept clear for emergency communications," Jeremiah muttered.

They reached Oklahoma City and Jeremiah's frown deepened.

"Damn. Look at that." He slowed as a long line of red taillights appeared over a rise. Bodies of twisted cars, several flipped onto their backs like mechanical turtles, littered the highway just east of Oklahoma City. Debris and wreckage lay strewn about as far as the eye could see. Tree trunks had been stripped of their bark. Others lay uprooted, their tangled anchors exposed where the monster literally ripped them from the earth. Piles of tree branches lined the sides of the highway as clean-up crews worked to clear the area for traffic. They crested another small hill and saw the traffic being diverted onto an exit because both east and westbound lanes ended abruptly, large gaps of raw red earth carving deep tracts where the freeway used to be.

"Look over there," Joe pointed towards the wide median where the wrecked body of a large fifth-wheel camper lay. "That one got picked up and slung around a ways before the wind let go."

The Jeep crept along in bumper-to-bumper traffic, passing several eighteen wheelers slung onto their sides.

"Naw, not much damage. It was only an F-4." Joe stared out the passenger window. Jeremiah ignored his sarcasm and focused on getting to Shawnee.

It was well after sunup when they reached the exit that took them to the Lamont estate. The panicked feeling in Jeremiah's gut spiked as he turned onto the long winding drive. Noting the absence of tree damage, he tried to calm his nerves.

"Shit." Joe's expletive echoed Jeremiah's as they reached the break in the trees to the grounds around the house.

Or, more accurately, where the house should have been.

Jeremiah hit the brakes in front of the remains of the broad staircase that now led to a mound of rubble. He leapt from the driver's side, turned a full circle at the sight. Dirt and debris littered the flowerbeds near the destruction, but the fragile, multi-colored blooms appeared otherwise unharmed. The long paved driveway lay pristine, trees around the property intact.

"This was not weather damage." He spoke barely above a whisper.

"Agreed." Joe's voice matched Jeremiah's.

Jeremiah sprinted to the Jeep, grabbed his cell from the drink holder, and called 911.

"We'll get someone out there as soon as possible," the dispatcher said. "Units from other counties are coming to help."

"Damn." Jeremiah cut the call and jogged to where Joe had already started searching the ruins. The pressure in his chest threatened to explode into uncontrolled panic.

"No one, not even K-9 units, are going to be here for a while." He stood on top of the staircase and pressed both hands to his head.

"Mattie!" The shout was out before he realized he had yelled her name. "Mattie!"

Joe straightened and turned. "Jeremiah, you're losing it. If she's alive, she won't be able to answer." His black eyes drilled through Jeremiah's. "Remember your training."

Jeremiah stared at the man, then inhaled deeply. He tried to think through the panic, and moved carefully through the massive wreckage, tossing bricks one at a time onto the grass. He couldn't control the shake in his voice as he continued to call out Mattie's name. Each time he stopped and crouched into the rubble, hoping to hear a faint reply.

"Does this place have a storm cellar?" Joe asked as he worked. Sweat dampened his shirt and jeans. The mid-morning sun brought heat, compounding already humid conditions.

Jeremiah paused and straightened. He tossed the brick he held onto the growing pile.

"Yes it does." He scanned the wreckage, trying to imagine the door to the storm cellar. He released a frustrated sigh. "But I cannot tell in this mess exactly where the cellar door would be."

Both men turned as a fire truck, ambulance, and three Shawnee police cruisers, their light bars flashing, crawled slowly along the driveway. Fire fighters, ambulance medics, and cops spilled from the vehicles and ran towards them.

"Any evidence of gas leaks? One of the firefighters asked Jeremiah.

Jeremiah shook his head. "No."

"I'll call into the utility company and have everything turned off." He reached into one of the deep pockets of his heavy fire jacket and pulled out a two-way radio.

"Do you know the address?" Jeremiah asked, then paused. Of course they did. They had to have the address in order to show up.

"Give it to me again," the firefighter told him, then relayed the information to the dispatcher.

Uniforms, faces, and arms were soon covered in fine red dust. Jeremiah's hands became scraped and bloody from digging through the debris. Mid-morning stretched into mid-afternoon when the sound of tires on pavement made Jeremiah look up.

A K-9 SUV pulled to a stop, Jeremiah saw the cage in the cargo area. An officer appeared from the driver's side, strode to the back and raised the hatch. A German Shepherd leaped to the ground, pulling at the heavy leash, and the officer led the dog towards the wreckage.

Hours later Jeremiah began to breathe a little easier. The dog had not picked up the scent of either live or dead bodies. Rescue personnel found the storm cellar, but it was empty.

Jeremiah scowled. As relieved as he was Mattie had not been in the house, her absence did not make sense. She *should* have been in the house. Or at least she ought to be here now, in the aftermath of the destruction, asking what happened. She should have called friends, at least William and Anna. Either way he looked at it, Mattie and a crowd of concerned neighbors ought to be present.

So where the hell was she?

Brick dust covered himself and Joe as they worked systematically alongside the emergency crews, throwing bricks into the growing pile, inching their way through the rubble.

Jeremiah straightened abruptly with sudden insight that something was missing. He turned his head to yell at Joe when one of the cops waved at him. He tossed the brick he held into the now enormous pile on the grass, brushed off his hands, and met the cop on what was left of the staircase.

"Officer Miller," the cop introduced himself. He stood about Jeremiah's height, which topped out at six feet. He wore a vest beneath his Shawnee Police Department uniform, his short-sleeved shirt exposed thick biceps and forearms. His brown hair-cut in a close military crew, his brown eyes looked like they didn't miss much.

This is odd," Miller commented, surveying the grounds. "Never seen tornado damage quite like this." He turned to Jeremiah. "Then again, I'm still new to this part of the country. Been hearing stories all day how these things hop around." He paused, giving Jeremiah time to comment.

Jeremiah glanced at the pristine grounds and kept his thoughts to himself.

Miller continued. "The fire chief thinks there isn't enough surrounding damage to be a tornado strike. Too much burn evidence."

Jeremiah met the officer's eyes. "Rogue funnels are common with systems as big as the one last night."

The officer nodded, then retrieved a small notebook from one of his front shirt pockets. "You know the people who live here?"

"Yes. George and Ginnie Lamont." Jeremiah hesitated, following his natural instinct not to offer more information than necessary. But Mattie was missing, and despite assurances from the K-9 officers no one lay trapped beneath the rubble, Jeremiah could not rid himself of the image of Mattie lying dead under a pile of bricks. Shuddering, he drew a breath and added, "They died several months ago in a car accident."

"Any children?" Miller asked as he jotted some notes.

"Two," Jeremiah replied. "Angela, who died recently, and Mattie, my wife."

Officer Miller raised his head and stared at Jeremiah like a bug under a microscope. "Sounds like a lot of death in a short amount of time."

"Jeremiah hesitated before answering. "Yes, sir. It is."

"Mind following me over to the car?"

Jeremiah and the officer descended the stairs and walked to the police cruiser. "Know where the second daughter is?" Miller asked, glancing at his notes. "Mattie, right? She's your wife?"

"I thought she was here." Jeremiah stopped.

"And?" the officer prompted.

Jeremiah shook his head. "No, sir. I do not know where she is at the moment."

Miller did a slow three-sixty. "Looks like someone's been maintaining the property. What about live-in staff?"

Jeremiah hesitated again. "Their names are William and Anna. I do not know whether they were here last night."

"So you were not at the house last night but your wife was?" Officer Miller asked, jotting some more his notebook.

Jeremiah chose his words with care. "As I said, my wife's sister just passed away. The funeral was yesterday morning. Mattie would have been here at the house. I left after the funeral to do some storm chasing. Mattie and I live in Colorado Springs." He was weaving lies around the truth now, and the feeling made him acutely uncomfortable. Under the present circumstances he wasn't convinced he could fake it well enough to fool the cop.

"I think I remember reading about that in the paper. What a run of bad luck." Officer Miller glanced up. "Didn't mean for that to come out sounding callous."

Jeremiah inclined his head towards Joe. "I spent the afternoon with Joe over there. We were watching cells develop on the western side of the state."

Officer Miller paused. "So you're a storm chaser?"

Jeremiah acknowledged with a slight nod. "When I am not working at the Boulder Forecast Center in Colorado."

Officer Miller scanned his notes. "You and your wife came down for her sister's funeral?"

"Yes." Jeremiah affirmed.

Miller's astute brown eyes snapped up. "And yet you left to do some storm chasing?"

Jeremiah worked hard to maintain a neutral expression. "Yes."

"What time did you leave?" Officer Miller asked.

"After the funeral. I left while the house was still full of people here for the reception, so she would not be alone while I was gone." *What a pack of lies,* Jeremiah thought.

"I'll need a driver's license or some form of ID," Miller held out a hand. Jeremiah retrieved his driver license.

"Please wait over there," Officer Miller motioned towards one of the many large flowerbeds in full bloom. Jeremiah ambled over.

~ * ~

Miller put his mouth near the radio clipped to the right shoulder of his uniform. "Dispatch, get on the horn to the Sheriff. I need him to contact one of the detectives on duty."

He turned and studied the scene. Something hinky was going on. He hadn't been on the local force long enough to be familiar with all the citizens of Shawnee, but the name Lamont rang a bell. Several bells, in fact. He ran Jeremiah's ID through the system while he waited for a call back. His cell buzzed, and he answered.

"Detective Harrison Gates here," said the voice on the other end. "Dispatch gave me your number. Watcha got?"

Miller spent the next several minutes explaining the situation and his observations.

"Lamont. Lamont," Gates muttered. Miller could hear the guy tapping his computer keyboard. "Says here George and Virginia Lamont were killed in a traffic collision in Kansas back in January. He had a brother who died a couple of years ago. Another TC."

Miller jotted notes as he waited.

"Whoa." Gates released a low whistle. "Impressive family fortune. And Marigold has a sister who just died. The brother-in-law died a little over two weeks ago." He fell silent for several minutes. "So this Jeremiah Tyler. Did you run him through the system?"

"Yeah," Miller acknowledged. "Nada."

Gates paused. "Says here he went AWOL from the Alamosa County Hospital. How's he seem to you?"

"Too damn calm to not know where his wife is at the moment," Miller replied.

"What's he doing?" the detective asked.

Miller winced, then admitted, "He and a friend were going through the rubble when I arrived."

"Get him out of the scene and tape the area off. Get any other civilians outta there, too. My partner and I will get there in a bit." Gates hung up.

~ * ~

Jeremiah turned his attention to the officer when he walked over.

"I need for you and your friend to wait here," he instructed, handing Jeremiah his license. Jeremiah waved at Joe to join him, and the old Indian brushed his hands on his jeans and picked his way through the destruction. Miller retrieved a roll of yellow police tape and some stakes from the trunk of his cruiser. Soon fluttering yellow tape roped off the entire scene.

The cop didn't seem interested in continuing their conversation. Thirty minutes passed in silence when a Pottawatomie County Sheriff cruiser and a black sedan pulled to a stop nearby. A Deputy Sheriff angled from the cruiser and joined Miller.

Two men appeared from the sedan. The driver, a short man, dressed in a brown summer suit and tie. The passenger was tall and rail thin, his white short-sleeved Polo and dark blue dress slacks hanging on his bony frame. Officer Miller and the Deputy Sheriff walked over, and the four men conducted a long conversation. Jeremiah and Joe watched. The four men finally turned and strode over to where they waited.

"Detective Harrison Gates, Pottawatomie County Sheriff's department." Detective Gates appeared to be in his forties, had an ample bald spot before his light brown hair started, and was outgrowing the suit he wore. His light brown eyes scanned Jeremiah and Joe with uncomfortable intensity. He motioned to the man beside him. "And this is my partner, Detective Jason Reeves."

In his twenties, Reeves looked like Ichabod Crane, right down to the Adam's Apple bobbing up and down in his throat. His thin brown hair seemed permanently plastered to his head, and for all appearances he looked like a classic, painfully introverted computer geek.

"Mind if I ask a few questions?" Gates studied Jeremiah, then Joe.

Jeremiah tucked his hands into the front pockets of his dirty jeans and frowned. The appearance of two detectives did not bode well.

Reeves crossed his arms as he gently rocked back and forth on the balls of his feet. Even though he and Jeremiah were the same height, Reeves tilted his head back and stared at the two of them down the very long bridge of his aquiline nose.

"Full name, I believe, is Jeremiah Black Bear Tyler? And Joe Healing Water?" Reeves cut in before Gates could continue, his lips pressing into a smile that did not reach his eyes. An uncomfortable premonition crept up Jeremiah's spine. Joe stood nearby and did not offer any comment.

"And your wife is Marigold Annabelle Tessence Lamont Tyler?" Reeves continued, ignoring the warning look from his partner, who still smarted from being saddled with the young detective because of convenient family political connections.

Jeremiah sighed. "Mattie, for short. Yes."

"Thanks, Jason. I'll handle things from here." Gates pulled out a small notebook and pencil, then glanced at Jeremiah. "We can go over to the Sheriff's office if you want."

Jeremiah shook his head. "No, here will be fine."

"Will you take me through the events of the last twenty-four hours? Just to catch me up on what's going on." The older detective sounded civil enough.

"We came down for Mattie's sister's funeral in Shawnee..." Jeremiah started.

"Angela Marie Lamont Tacque?" Gates interjected.

"Yes," Jeremiah confirmed.

"She was twenty-four." The detective checked his notebook.

"Twenty-four is too young to suddenly die like that," Reeves cut in, demonstrating his lack of social etiquette that grated everyone's nerves in the department.

Jeremiah ignored the younger man's rude interruption. "Yes," he responded to the older detective's statement.

Gates stared at him like a bug under the same damned microscope Miller had been doing. "Awfully young. Terrible tragedy. I imagine it hit your wife pretty hard."

"Yes, it did." Jeremiah agreed.

Gates' eyes narrowed. "Didn't hit you as hard, though, did it?

I mean, you admitted to Officer Miller here that you didn't even stick around for the reception."

"There were reports of severe weather." Jeremiah winced. The guy was rapidly backing him into an uncomfortable corner.

"So, naturally, since you're a weather forecaster, the approaching storms would take priority over your wife's loss." Gates studied him.

Jeremiah stared silently at the detective. There was nothing he could say that wouldn't sound like back-pedaling. He carefully avoided looking at Joe.

Gates flipped through his notes. "Angela was recently married, isn't that right?"

"Yes. To Gary Tacque. They eloped a few months ago." Jeremiah felt his spirits sink. Great. The guy had done his homework.

Reeves continued to rock on his feet, uncrossing his arms and slipping his hands into his pockets, listening but not taking any notes. His Adam's Apple bobbed whenever he swallowed. "But he died recently as well?" he broke in.

"Yes." Though Jeremiah kept his expression neutral and his body relaxed, inside he felt as though his entire world was falling apart. Their questions felt like an interrogation rather than a simple interview. If the tone of the two detectives kept up like this, he and Joe might end up cuffed and stuffed in the back of one of the cruisers.

"An awful lot of death in your family." Reeves peered down his nose.

Jeremiah released a careful sigh. "Yes."

"And your sister-in-law passed away in a Denver hospital, even though she and her husband reside a few miles from here, in Norman, I believe?" Gates interjected.

Jeremiah nodded. "That is correct." He wondered whether Joe was going to jump in at some point and help him out of this mess, but figured the old Indian would keep quiet and let him drown. Damned stubborn old fool. Smart old fool, he amended, since he would be equally silent if Joe were being drilled like this.

"Gary Tacque died of gunshot wounds." Detective Gates jotted more notes. The wind blew his suit against his legs.

Although monosyllabic answers would be his best defense, Jeremiah needed to clarify the facts surrounding his brother-in-law's death. "Yes. My wife shot him with my nineteen-eleven handgun. It was self-defense."

Gates looked up from his notes. "According to statements in the police report, he shot you, and your wife shot him?"

Jeremiah nodded. "Yes." The wind buffeted them with increasing force, and he glanced at the southwest horizon where a thin black line indicated an approaching system. It appeared that this evening would bring a repeat of severe weather.

"Yet, ballistics on the bullet retrieved from your chest wound did not match the rifle found on Gary Tacque."

Jeremiah stared at the detective. Of course ballistics would find the discrepancy. He and Hawk argued over that problem when Hawk described his plans to take out Gary.

"What?" He asked, realizing too late his response sounded wooden and entirely too calm.

The detective studied him. "You didn't know that?" His brown eyes drilled through Jeremiah's black ones as though trying to see into his head. He paused briefly before adding, "Then again, you disappeared from the Alamosa hospital shortly after you came out of surgery."

"I do not recall that leaving a hospital is illegal," Jeremiah stated flatly.

"It's not good form to just disappear. You should've at least signed out AMA," the detective shot back.

Reeves interrupted. "And now your wife seems to be missing and her house has been destroyed."

Jeremiah's eyes narrowed. He did not like the young detective. "Yes, and several severe weather cells tracked across this area last night."

Gates shook his head. "This destruction was not due to weather, Mr. Tyler. You're a meteorologist. You of all people should recognize the signs."

Jeremiah barely resisted the urge to step back and cross his arms.

Detective Gates put away his notebook. "I find it interesting that all of your wife's relatives have died within a short period of time, and now your wife is missing. You're not going to tell me you're unaware of her extensive family fortune?"

Jeremiah felt his jaw clench. Out of the corner of his eye he saw Joe straighten.

Reeves stopped rocking. "And if your wife is found dead, Mr. Tyler, you do realize you will become a very rich widower?"

Chapter Six

I woke up slowly, reluctant to leave the warm cocoon of protective darkness. Sharp, hot stabs radiated down my right leg, and I tried unsuccessfully to suppress a moan.

"Mattie, wake up. There's news you ought to see." Hawk's voice spiked my anxiety level, and it took all my courage to open my eyes.

I lay on a couch. Gray concrete walls with a generous growth of mildew running up the corners and a general sense of dampness gave the impression of a basement. I suspected we were still in Oklahoma and this might be some sort of storm cellar. With slow movements I rolled to my left side and folded my arm under my head. Pain engulfed me, and I squeezed my eyes shut against the discomfort. The throbbing felt different, more intense, searing with heat that had not been present after surgery. My stomach felt slightly nauseated and closing my eyes made things worse rather than better. I opened my eyes and watched Hawk take a seat in a low, sagging brown armchair that looked like a Goodwill reject. No one else was in the room.

"You need to see this." He nodded towards the small flat screen television on a table across the room. Using the remote, he turned up the volume as a commercial about toilet paper ended and the news came on. I recognized the news team as one from Oklahoma City, the one on which Gary England served as meteorologist during my childhood years.

Which meant we were somewhere near Oklahoma City and it was early evening. The weather forecast finished. I wondered what day it was, but didn't want to ask.

The background scene showed a picture of my parents' property and the demolished house. The news anchor, a man in his thirties with a smile that revealed gleaming white teeth, wore an impeccable dark suit and matching tie, his dark blonde hair sprayed into perfection. His brown eyes looked at me through the camera, inviting me to believe every word he said.

"...of the famous Lamont estate was reported earlier today. The Pottawatomie County Sheriff's department initially reported they thought the house was destroyed by the storms last night. However, we have now learned Jeremiah Tyler, the husband of one of the Lamont daughters, may be involved and is considered a person of interest in the developing investigation. The Sheriff's department is not saying what may have happened, but it seems apparent they are no longer thinking the house was destroyed by storms." Mr. Blond turned to his female co-anchor. "Sue?"

"Thanks, Steve." Sue smiled, her shoulder-length light blonde hair styled to add softness to her prominent cheekbones and anorexic thinness. She wore a sleeveless cherry red dress, heavy make-up that accented her blue eyes and red lips, disguising her too big head and her way too skinny body.

I winced. My photojournalist eye again. I could never seem to turn the damned thing off, especially when it came to the news broadcasters and anchors, who reveled in the attention they got from the news coming in from the rest of us risking our lives to get important information to the notoriously uninformed public.

The television camera zoomed in. "Well, in the past few hours, some very interesting events have developed." Sue smiled at me, her brilliant teeth blinding. "The police are searching for Mattie Lamont Tyler, whom they consider to be missing and in danger. So far there has been no word of her whereabouts."

Steve turned towards his co-anchor. "Does the Sheriff's office have an idea what happened at the Lamont estate, if it wasn't the weather?"

Sue swiveled her impeccable face to her impeccably dressed news partner. "No, Steve. So far, they're not releasing any information."

Steve picked up on her unspoken train of thought. "So, its possible investigators might suspect Tyler of trying to inherit the extensive Lamont fortune."

I rolled my eyes. Great. Those two intellectually challenged bozos were using their camera time to speculate. Nothing was less useless than planting wrong conclusions into the heads of their audience. Get the majority thinking Jeremiah was behind this, and in a town as small and protective as Shawnee someone might try whipping up a lynch mob.

"Damn," I muttered at the television screen.

"There is evidence that indicates his involvement, Steve." Sue turned back to the camera. Her blue eyes gleamed. "Our own news team has uncovered several very interesting facts."

I missed Sue's report on the interesting facts. "Wait." Like a slow motion replay, the news report sank in.

"Jeremiah is *here*?" I breathed. I swiveled my head to face Hawk, then thought of the assault team and swallowed the string of possibilities that suddenly popped into my mind.

Whoever took Jeremiah from the Alamosa County Hospital had known he was still in danger. And while Hawk implied to me he was on our side, I suspected he was bluffing to maintain my trust. A frightening conclusion dawned, curling my insides.

Hawk wasn't protecting me, he was setting me up to be killed and building enough circumstantial evidence to get Jeremiah framed for my murder. It wouldn't take a genius to put together a case accusing Jeremiah of going after the Lamont fortune, especially now that I represented the only surviving family member.

Jeremiah had no idea what happened to the house or to me. And the Sheriff's department would no doubt grill him for answers he honestly did not know.

Jeremiah would immediately realize something other than a tornado destroyed the house. And he would hide that knowledge, which would make him appear suspicious to authorities. The cops didn't know my husband from Adam, didn't know he would not volunteer information even if they took him in for questioning. He was an expert at uninformative answers.

I should know. I'd been married to the man for the last seven years.

Sue continued, her face filling the television screen. "Gary Tacque's body was found around the Wolf Creek area in Colorado, which is very close to the Southern Ute Indian Reservation. Jeremiah Tyler grew up on that Reservation, and we have exclusive information that it was his handgun that killed his brother-in-law."

"Well, yeah, that's because it was the gun I used when I shot him," I argued at the screen, ignoring Hawk's irritated expression.

"That's pretty incriminating evidence," Steve nodded, his mouth grim while his eyes sparkled over the news.

"Gary almost killed Jeremiah, you idiots," I barked at the screen. "I shot Gary in self-defense. And I told the police all of that! Get your flipping facts straight!"

"There's more." Sue paused and glanced at her notes, which I thought nastily she didn't need. She already had everything committed to memory.

"What a couple of imbeciles," I ranted, waving a frustrated hand at the television. They don't care if they screw up the story just so long as they have something to tell the almighty camera!"

Hawk held up his hand. "Quiet, or you'll end up gagged and trussed."

"Oh, go to hell," I spat. "Jeremiah laid the damned thing down right beside me before he went to the edge to wave at the rescue helicopter. Gary shot him while he was waving, would have shot him again if I hadn't killed him!" I glared at Hawk.

"Why are they jumping to conclusions like this? Why aren't they waiting until they know the truth?" My voice cracked. "They haven't even mentioned Gary shot Jeremiah in the chest! They're reporting half the facts, as usual!"

Hawk's long legs stretched out in front of him. "Ballistics on the bullet they removed from your husband's chest wouldn't match Gary's rifle." His voice barely rose above a whisper.

I shook my head. "But I was *there*. I saw Gary come up to the cave. I saw him point his rifle at Jeremiah. He was going to shoot him again!"

Hawk quirked an eyebrow at me. "You never wondered why Gary's first shot didn't kill him? Why would he have hit your husband in the chest? He was a sniper. He would have shot him through the head."

I stared blankly at Hawk. "But there was no one else around who could have shot Jeremiah...." I trailed off. The answer oozed through my brain slowly, reluctantly. "You were the only other person on that mountain." My words came out haltingly. I didn't want to believe what my revelation told me.

"Yes." Hawk's eyes locked on mine. My chest constricted, and suddenly I couldn't breathe.

"But you said Gary disabled your rifle. That's how you got that cut along your jaw," I choked out, barely able to get my mouth to move.

Hawk's predatory eyes bore through me. "Gary disabled my rifle after I hit your husband in the chest."

I pushed myself into a sitting position. Pain streaked up my leg. *"You…you…you shot Jeremiah."* I whispered through clenched teeth, unable to break eye contact.

Hawk looked away. "Yes."

His admission shocked me. I stared at him, then dragged my eyes back to the television screen. "You tried to kill him. And now you're setting him up. You're framing him."

Hawk opened his mouth, but I cut him off. "It's not going to work, you know. Jeremiah will tell them. He signed legal papers. He can't inherit anything."

Emphatically, Hawk shook his head. He leaned forward, his voice low. "Mattie, listen to me. A proper solicitor will find loopholes. Authorities know that."

My world threatened to collapse into a black hole of raw emotion. I would soon be dead, and Jeremiah would be accused of my murder. I shook all over with the knowledge of my helplessness, to save myself, to help clear Jeremiah of being convicted and sentenced. "This is your fault," I choked out.

Hawk pressed his fingers against my lips, then turned his attention to the news report. I jerked from the contact, and he dropped his hand.

The scene behind the newscasters switched to a picture of Gary and my sister, both smiling, their arms entwined. I wondered whether the picture came from Las Vegas, where they eloped a few months ago.

Only a few months. They had married in February. It was now the middle of June. My parents were killed in January, Angela and Gary eloped shortly after the funeral, and now both Angela and Gary were dead. All because of greed over the enormous Lamont family fortune.

Sue's voice continued. "The police may suspect Tyler lured the couple to Colorado, then found a way to get rid of them without raising the suspicion of local authorities."

I swiped at tears. "That's ridiculous. Don't they even know how ridiculous they sound?"

"You need to understand the situation…." Hawk urged, his voice barely above a whisper.

I cut him off. "I already more than understand the situation. You and Gary have been in this whole thing together. Did you decide you didn't want to share all that money and figured out a way to get rid of Gary?"

Hawk opened his mouth, but I jerked my attention back to the television screen when Gary and Angela's faces faded and a picture of my husband appeared on the screen. The photograph looked awfully close to a mug shot.

The camera focused again on Sue and Steve. "Of course, everything is conjecture at this point, but the Pottawatomie County Sheriff's department has opened an investigation. This was taken by one of our news staff at the scene of the Lamont Estate," Steve reported. "There is quite a lot of evidence, albeit circumstantial at this point. The destruction of the Lamont estate, the deaths of Gary and Angela Tacque, and now the apparent disappearance of his wife, Mattie Tyler."

The camera swung to Sue, and she looked directly at me through the camera lens. "If you have any information concerning these events or the whereabouts of Mattie Lamont Tyler, please contact the Pottawatomie County Sheriff's Department."

A shot of my face filled the screen, with phone numbers listed underneath. I looked away and stared at the grimy cinderblock walls around me.

What drove Hawk's actions? If he was after my family fortune, why hadn't he killed all of us on that mountain? Setting me up to kill Gary meant one less person to split the money, but if both of them were after the family fortune, then it would have made sense for Hawk to team up with Gary and kill Jeremiah, Mud Rain, and myself in Wolf Creek Pass. Hawk could have killed Gary later, after we were dead.

The answer swept in. Hawk needed me alive in order to access the money. That explained his pretense of protecting me from the rest of the Charlie team. Would he kill them, too, once he forced me to sign over the Lamont fortune?

Either way I looked at it, Hawk's current trap appeared impeccable. Jeremiah's disappearance from the Alamosa County Hospital had thrown a wrench into his plans, so he now used me as bait to draw my husband from hiding, simultaneously leaving behind enough circumstantial evidence to get Jeremiah locked up.

Oh my god. I swallowed. I knew from personal experience how ruthless Hawk could be. I also knew I would sign anything to protect Jeremiah. I had to get away from Hawk and his team and help get the police on the right track. They were totally screwing things up right now by focusing on my husband. They needed to be looking for Hawk, dragging his lying British butt in for questioning, then throwing him in a cell for the rest of his worthless life.

Heavy footsteps clomped down the steep wooden staircase at the opposite end of the room. Six men, all dressed in identical military camouflage pants and green T-shirts, spread into the small, dank basement. I tried again and failed to see individual features among the flattop haircuts, clean-shaven faces, hard jawlines, and heavily muscled bodies.

My vision swam, and the scene blurred into a single grotesque creature with multiple arms and legs. I barely suppressed a scream as the monster crawled towards me, reaching, clawing....

Trembling and feeling cold as death, I shrank against the couch and threw my arms over my face. When nothing happened, I peeked open an eye. The bizarre image was gone; they were men again. Icy cold waves washed over me even though my right leg seared with hot, flaming pain.

"There's rather nasty weather predicted for this evening. We'll have to postpone our plans to the morrow," Hawk said as the men moved about the room. Two of them dragged metal folding chairs beside Hawk and took a seat. The other four leaned against one of the walls. I thought I recognized Carson because his eyes were the smallest of the group. I remembered how they looked like beetle eyes when he stood over me in the camper.

"I see you've something to eat," Hawk commented from his slouched position in the ratty armchair.

"Sir, would you like some?" The man sitting beside him asked.

Hawk shook his head. "In a bit. Thank you, Freeman."

"Getting damned tired of chili," Carson spat out, holding a plastic bowl in one hand, a plastic spoon in the other.

"Cut the belly aching, Carson," one of the others snapped.

The bowl Carson held shook badly. I watched his face and saw a wild look creep into his small brown eyes as he stared at me. I wondered whether he would walk over and throw his dinner in my face again.

"Why can't we go with things as planned?" Carson's voice

trembled with anger. His face turned red, his neck muscles strained with tension. He shoved food down as though he hadn't eaten in weeks.

Hawk regarded the man. "Because it increases the odds of failure. We won't be afforded a second chance."

"What about her in the meantime?" Carson jabbed his plastic spoon at me.

"What about her?" Hawk's cold voice echoed in the room. A muscle twitched around his eyelids, and I wondered whether Carson's agitated behavior might be getting under his skin.

"I'm tired of treating the bitch like a goddamn guest." Carson threw the plastic bowl and spoon against the wall, then stalked over to the couch.

"How's your leg feeling, bitch?" He sneered, a look of cruel triumph in his eyes.

"Carson, what is with you?" Freeman stood and braced his legs, his arms at his sides. The other men straightened.

Carson started pacing, his movements jerky, his entire body trembling. Perspiration beaded his forehead, trickled down his face. "I thought this mission was to avenge our fallen, not act like fucking escorts."

"Enough, Carson." Hawk stood; his voice cutting through the tension in the room.

Carson ignored him, his lips curling into a nasty grin as he glared at me. "I fixed your leg after you almost got us killed in that fucking storm. I told Allison I'd take care of you." The muscles along his jaw clenched. "But it'll take a fucking week before your leg rots off, and I don't want to wait that long."

I heard Hawk inhale sharply. "Carson, what in bloody hell are you on about? You're barking mad!"

Carson jerked his attention to Hawk, his small eyes narrowed into tiny slits. "With all due respect, Sir, I think it's time we cut her throat."

Pain levels slid into the background as my eyes locked on the enormous, wicked-looking knife in Carson's hand. I jerked into a sitting position and tried to wiggle away from the man.

"I told you not to do anything stupid!" One of the men strode from the wall, his blue eyes blazing with anger. "Don't go and tell me you fucked things up!"

"Carson, Allison, stand down." Hawk demanded.

"Why are you protecting this bitch?" Carson brandished the knife.

"Hey, man, watch where you wave that thing!" Allison warned, leaping back. The rest of the men circled Carson, their bodies tense, ready for a fight if Carson lost control.

"It's none of your sodding business how I treat her," Hawk snapped.

I tried to swallow. My life depended on Hawk's control of his team. The men out-numbered Hawk, and palpable hatred emanated from all of them.

But if Hawk was after the Lamont fortune, he needed me alive. I knew without a doubt none of the men realized the real purpose behind his actions. He was playing with their revenge mission, using them like pawns in a chess game. He was the mastermind behind it all, and I had no doubt he would kill both Jeremiah and me once he had his hands on my family fortune.

But he needed me alive to sign the necessary documents.

"Carson, stand down," Hawk repeated, moving between the agitated man and myself.

"You're protecting her. You're not here to avenge Tacque. You're here for something else." Carson glared at Hawk. "Don't think the rest of us haven't seen the way you're treating the bitch."

"Carson, get a grip. You've already screwed things up." Allison stepped in close.

Carson swept the group surrounding him with the knife. "Back off. Unlike the rest of you pussies, I'm not standing by and letting Tacque's killer be treated like a fucking guest."

I noticed the other men slip behind Carson and realized Allison was providing a distraction. Two of them suddenly grabbed Carson, and I thought out-numbered six to one, he had no chance.

I was wrong. Carson spun with insane speed, breaking away, the black blade of the knife a blur as he swung his arm in a low lethal arc.

Allison screamed as blood gushed with pulsing velocity onto the concrete floor. I screamed, then clamped a hand hard over my mouth. The bloody knife appeared briefly among fighting arms and legs, then disappeared as it drove forward again, searching for another target.

With swift, silent movements, Hawk whipped a forearm around Carson's neck, then viciously jerked his head with his free hand. A sickening crack punctured the chaos, followed by abrupt, utter silence.

Carson slipped from Hawk's hold and crumpled into an unnatural heap. Hawk knelt over Allison's writhing, bleeding body. The dying man's gasping screams weakened to whispers. No sound broke the silence as Hawk gripped the soldier's face in both hands and looked him straight in the eyes. Blood flowed in horrible, gigantic quantities across the concrete floor. Hawk remained motionless, holding the dying man's head until his body relaxed, then stilled.

The awful metallic stench overpowered my control, and my stomach violently retched. A strong hand gripped my hair; another hand caught me under my chin, steadying my head until the terrible vomiting stopped. I lay weak and shaking on the couch, tears running down my face, choking sobs racking my body.

Hawk stood slowly. "Williams, Freeman, work on cleaning this up. Marks, Cumbers, and I will take care of the bodies." He kept his voice flat, void of any emotion.

Horrible, deathly silence fell over the room as the men worked. Two men disappeared up the stairs, returned a few minutes later with several heavy-duty large black trash bags. I thought I would scream and not be able to stop if they started chopping up body parts. One of them produced a roll of duct tape, and the two of them and Hawk fashioned rough body bags. In the meantime, Williams and Freeman, both with blue gloves on, mopped and scrubbed with plastic brushes, pouring the pungent contents of a bottle of bleach onto the floor.

Time slid by. I watched with terrified fascination as Hawk stripped both bodies of clothes and all personal items, then used duct tape to seal up the bags. The room reeked of bleach and death.

"What now, sir?" Freeman asked. His question sounded academic rather than panicked.

"We bury them. The weather and the late hour should keep prying eyes to a minimum." Hawk stood over the two bags, his expression closed.

"How soon do you want them found?" Freeman asked.

"Sunrise should suffice." Hawk's eyes met mine.

I wondered why Hawk would want the bodies found, then realized law enforcement would have no idea where the bodies came from. Even if identified there would be no leads connecting them to Hawk's team.

And if Hawk's orders included hiding the two bodies anywhere near my parents' house the police would intensify their investigation on Jeremiah.

Chapter Seven

Late Tuesday afternoon the two detectives escorted Tyler from the Lamont grounds to the Pottawatomie County Sheriff's Office in downtown Shawnee, though if left up to him, Reeves would've cuffed the dirt bag and transported him in one of the police cruisers. Gates wanted to put him in the conference room, Reeves argued they stick him in the interrogation room. Gates reluctantly agreed, and Reeves pressed to be allowed to ask the questions.

"Go easy, Jason. Make him feel like we're on his side. We'll get more out of him that way," Gates advised. Reeves nodded and didn't say a word. He spun on his heel and headed to the interrogation room. With a shake of his head, Harrison Gates left. He had a lot of interviewing to do.

"You saw your wife at her parents' house?" Reeves stood across the table from where Tyler sat. Thunder rumbled outside the courthouse building that held the Sheriff's Department, and the detective secretly hoped the humid, stuffy conditions in the room would wear down Tyler's resistance. The fool should be feeling hungry, trapped, isolated, and stressed.

Reeves meant to break this guy before Gates returned. The Sheriff assigned him to help Gates on this case, and he intended to prove he was not the inexperienced rookie everyone seemed to think. What he had on Tyler so far amounted only to circumstantial evidence, but Reeves felt the investigation would soon turn up something concrete enough to arrest the guy. He knew in his gut Tyler was their man. He and Gates only needed to wear him down until he confessed.

"Answer the question. You saw your wife at her parents' house?" he repeated.

"Yes." Jeremiah replied. He wasn't lying. He had seen his wife many times at her parents' house. The last time was January, when he and Mattie attended her parents' funeral. If the young detective wanted to ask stupid questions, that was his problem.

Reeves peered down his nose and quirked his eyebrows. "No one remembers seeing you either at the service or at the house afterwards."

Jeremiah shrugged. "I was there." *In January, that is,* he thought.

"Including Reverend Kelley, who presided over the service." Reeves studied Tyler, then leaned forward, pressing his knuckles against the table. "Surely you must see the uselessness of lying to us."

Jeremiah stared back.

~ * ~

Gates swung his battered sedan into the courthouse parking lot, got out and locked the car, then strode as fast as his stocky legs would take him. A phone call from one of the deputies advised him to get back to the station and leave the collecting of witness statements to the Shawnee Police.

The courthouse was listed on the National Register of Historic Places. Built in 1935, the three-story building was constructed of faced stone blocks, presented ornate windows with metal trimming with three large medallions on the front windows depicting the head of an Indian, the scales of justice, and the head of a pioneer. Three sets of heavy wooden double doors led inside, a broad ornate staircase led to the second and third levels. The Pottawatomie County Sheriff's Department took up the third floor, and a ratty partial attic that had been the jail was used now for holding suspects and criminals waiting transfer to the new county jail. The broad flight of granite stairs leading to the building had him puffing hard, and he debated whether to take the newly installed elevator to the third floor. A glance at his gut convinced him to haul his butt up the three flights of stairs.

He stood outside the observation room door for several minutes, panting and heaving, then entered, quietly closed the door, and walked to the observation glass. Five minutes told him Reeves had ignored his instructions.

Damned politics. Anyone listening to Reeves' crappy line of questioning would immediately know he hadn't yet learned the finer points of conducting an interrogation. A glance at Tyler's expression told him the man knew more than he was admitting. He didn't doubt for a minute Tyler was hiding something, but they needed to get Tyler on their side.

And then there was Tyler's chest wound and subsequent disappearance from the Alamosa County Hospital. Initial police reports indicated Tyler had been wearing a vest. His attempt to pawn Tacque's shooting off on his wife soured Gates' opinion of the man, especially since his wife wasn't present to defend herself. Reeves should be asking him about that, instead of asking vague unhelpful questions about funerals.

Why had Tyler been wearing a vest?

Gates corralled his wandering thoughts and turned his attention from the observation window to the door as a middle-aged woman in a black business suit entered.

"Hey, can I talk to you for a sec, Detective?"

Gates nodded, and the woman closed the door. She was about his height, slender, wore her gray hair short. Reeves' voice through the intercom caught his attention, and he looked up in time to see the detective stand.

"You are aware we can hold you for forty-eight hours before we have to let you go?" The young detective challenged.

"I am," Jeremiah said.

Reeves glared at him. "I'll be right back. Think about your position here, Mr. Tyler."

Gates watched Reeves leave the interrogation room and with a sinking feeling turned his eyes to the observation door. The young detective strode into the room, shut the door behind him.

"Well? What do you think?" Reeves demanded, puffing out his chest and ignoring the woman standing beside Gates.

The older detective shook his head. "Jason, all we have is circumstantial evidence right now. Any lawyer will chew us out for holding him, especially with the way you've been badgering the man."

"Any luck yet locating the weapon that killed Tacque?" Reeves asked, changing subjects.

Gates shook his head. "No. Searches at Tyler's Colorado Springs apartment haven't turned up a thing."

Reeves slid his hands into his pockets, tilted his head until he stared at Gates down the bridge of his nose. "The son-of-a-bitch probably got rid of it long time ago."

"We also haven't located the weapon that matches the bullet found in Tyler," Gates continued patiently. "You keep forgetting the Alamosa report stated Tacque was shot in self defense by Tyler's wife, since Tyler was unconscious and bleeding out at the time."

Reeves shrugged irritably. "She covered for him." He jerked his head towards the observation window. "And the dirt bag isn't talking now because he knows we have to let him go."

Gates barely avoided rolling his eyes. Reeves' stubbornness would give Bob Stoops and the Oklahoma Sooners a run for their money. He turned to the woman beside him. "What did you want to tell me, Ellen?"

"Sir, I've been following up on Angela Lamont Tacque's funeral, and I've got the statements officers gathered from friends who attended the funeral and the reception. One of the officers ran down the two staff members, William Burns, their butler, and his wife Anna, who does the cooking. They're the ones who've been keeping up the place." Ellen held up several sheets of printed computer paper and adjusted her glasses.

"Well?" Reeves prompted.

Gates leaned against the wall and folded his arms, the material of his suit coat tight around his back and chest. He needed to get on a gym schedule, start taking off some of the weight he'd put on over the last several months since he'd quit smoking.

"No one saw Jeremiah Tyler either at the funeral or at the reception."

Reeves looked annoyed. "We already know that."

Gates raised a hand to silence his partner. "We're aware of that, Ellen," he echoed gently.

"He wasn't even in town." Ellen glanced at him, then went back to her notes.

Reeves rolled his eyes, reminding Gates of a Halloween mask, the way the whites shone completely around his irises. "I suppose you're going to tell us next Tyler used military C-4 to blow up the place. We already know that, too." He was skinny enough to be a marathon runner, but to Gates' knowledge the kid never exercised. He must have a wild metabolic rate. That and his youth, and the kid didn't need to worry about how much he ate.

Gates frowned. "You've got him tried and convicted, Reeves. You're not going to get very far with that kind of thinking."

Ellen's next statement got both men's attention. "When I did a background check on Tyler, I ran into a whole slew of firewalls. It took me a while, but I found out that Tyler started as a Marine, then went over as an operative with CIA. It looks like he was still on their active list as of six months ago."

"Really?" Gates straightened from the wall and reached for Ellen's notes. "You sure about this?" He scanned the information.

Ellen nodded.

Gates looked at Reeves. "That would explain his reluctance to talk to us."

Reeves' confident grin turned haughty. "That's bullshit, Harrison, and you know it."

Ellen coughed gently. "I've got something else. His wife wasn't alone in the house. The officer who interviewed the domestic help reported that both of them saw a gentleman with Tyler's wife before they left the premises."

"Any details on the guy?" Gates asked her.

Ellen nodded. "He had a British accent. The butler remembers seeing him when he stuck his head in to check on Tyler's wife."

Reeves started rocking on the balls of his feet. "Which means Tyler has an accomplice. I'm thinking he planned to blow her up with the house and thought authorities would be dumb enough to think it was a tornado hit."

Gates rubbed his forehead. "We didn't find her body under the rubble."

Reeves nodded his head so vigorously Gates thought it might just wobble off his skinny neck and roll around the room. Ellen stood in silence and listened.

"Exactly."

Gates stared at his partner. "Okay, Reeves, quit acting like Stephen Hawking and please tell me what you're thinking." He slid his hands into his pockets. He used to carry a pack of cigarettes in his right pants pocket so he'd always have them available. Too many times he'd forgotten his jacket in the car or in his office. His wife badgered him into quitting last December as his Christmas present to her.

Damn it. He needed one now. Instead of smoking his way through problems, he had started eating his way through them. And now his pants were too tight, too. Yeah, definitely time to start hitting the gym.

Reeves stopped rocking. "His accomplice didn't follow the plan. He may be holding Tyler's wife as hostage to get more money."

Gates studied his partner. "I didn't hear any of that in your line of questioning."

Reeves grinned. "Because I didn't want him to know that we're onto him. If we let him go, he'll start looking for his wife. Or find a way to contact his accomplice and find out what the hell happened. Either way, he'll lead us right to her." Reeves crossed his arms and started rocking on his feet again, which made Gates feel slightly motion sick.

Gates fell silent. Rescue crews had found a wheelchair underneath the rubble. And the cars were in the garage. The accomplice angle made sense. It would explain why she hadn't been in the house when it blew. Gates squirmed uncomfortably in his suit. Maybe he should break down and buy a larger size.

"If we let Tyler go, we can tie this up before the Feds get involved." Reeves grinned at Gates. "Might even get me promoted."

"Yeah. He might also rabbit on us," the seasoned detective observed. If Reeves was right about all of this, he was conducting a brilliant interrogation. But he wasn't acting like a partner and sharing his thoughts, and that got under Gates' skin. He rubbed his thumb and forefingers together, imagining the feel of a cigarette.

Reeves shook his head and assumed that irritatingly superior expression again. "No, he won't. He'll stay close to try to locate his wife."

"Maybe." Gates shook his head. Something about Reeves' deduction bothered him.

Reeves bulldozed ahead. "Maybe the accomplice has killed his wife already. We won't know until the guy contacts Tyler, and he can't do that until we cut Tyler loose."

Harrison Gates studied the kid for several long moments. "So why the hell did you insist on bringing him in?"

Reeves stopped rocking, slid his hands into his pockets, and puffed out his chest. "To give me time to line up surveillance."

"You should've told me what you were thinking," Gates scowled. "I could've been working on getting things ready."

"I've already got it covered," Reeves asserted.

Gates couldn't help the irritation that slipped into his voice. "You're supposed to keep me in the loop." He shook his head. "One of these days, Reeves, your cockiness is going to bite you in the ass."

~ * ~

Jeremiah looked up when the door opened and the young detective appeared, shut the door carefully behind him, then leaned against the wall and crossed his arms.

"Well, it looks like for the moment at least, you're clear. My partner has turned up some evidence that is taking this in another direction."

Jeremiah kept his expression carefully neutral. Years of field experience told him the detective was lying. Just so long as they let him go, that was all that mattered.

"Am I free to leave?" He asked.

"Yes."

With a noisy scraping of chair legs against the tiled floor, Jeremiah stood.

"Stay in town and give us your contact information should we need to bring you in for some more questioning," Reeves warned.

Jeremiah's expression remained bland. "Of course."

The detective opened the door and followed Jeremiah down the hall to the booking room where the desk clerk handed over his wallet and cell phone. Jeremiah recited his cell number and the name of a nearby motel.

"Remember, don't try leaving Shawnee, or I'll run you down and put you in the county jail." Reeves watched Jeremiah leave through one of the broad double front doors of the courthouse.

~ * ~

Jeremiah called Joe as soon as he walked a couple of blocks and gave him a brief summary of the interrogation. The prairie wind brought the sweet scent of rain. Storm clouds created a premature twilight.

"This has turned into a real SNAFU." Joe did not sound happy.

"Rapidly deteriorating into FUBAR," Jeremiah agreed. "As

long as they focus on me, they will look in all the wrong places for Mattie."

"Your face is all over the news," Joe muttered. "Maybe the Charlie team will let their guard down, now that the police are after you?"

"Not these guys," Jeremiah grunted. "Charlie has not left a trace. If they had, I would not be a suspect." He stopped in the shadow of one of the downtown stores and watched a Shawnee police cruiser, headlights off, a couple of blocks away.

"I would give an eye to know what screwed things up," Jeremiah murmured as the cruiser pulled to the curb. The two young cops assigned to watch him were novices, no doubt about that.

Joe swallowed a curse. "Hawk needs to find a way to let us know where he is and what the hell happened, even if he has to resort to smoke signals."

"Very funny." Jeremiah started walking again. The cruiser pulled out and followed. He sighed and tried to ignore them.

"The cops are betting I will lead them to Mattie. Which means I have an escort."

Joe coughed. "Well, that'll be easy, since you stick out like a sore thumb."

Tyler watched the cruiser's reflection in a store window as he thought. "Meet me at Mattie's favorite restaurant this evening. Around eight."

"Which one would that be?" Joe asked.

Jeremiah chose his next words carefully. "Her childhood restaurant. The one she and Angela always loved. Remember the story?"

"Gotcha. You be careful, Jeremiah," Joe warned. "You're not going to be any help at all if you end up back in cuffs."

Jeremiah checked his watch. Six p.m. He had a few hours, no leads, and no idea where to start looking for Hawk and Mattie. Joe was right. Hawk needed to send some type of signal, the sooner the better. He prayed Mattie was alive and Hawk would protect her. But time was running short. Charlie had out-maneuvered all three of them, blown their plans to hell and back.

He glanced at the glass front of a restaurant. Even though he had nothing to go on, at least he could make something up; give those two cops activity to report for their effort before he lost them. He pushed through the restaurant door, asked a waitress for directions to the public library, then strode purposefully on his way.

~ * ~

Rain pelted Jeremiah; stormy prairie wind gusted and wailed as yet another system hit the Shawnee area. He trotted along the side of the two-lane highway, sure in the fact the weather conditions hid his movements, dropping into a drainage ditch whenever traffic approached. He had lost the Shawnee police, who no doubt fell for the misdirection and would stakeout the eateries in downtown Shawnee. He slowed when he reached a thick wooded section bordering the Lamont property, then crouched among the damp vegetation and waited. He was early, but he could use the time to confirm he had not been followed.

The slightest rustle nearby and Joe slipped beside him from the surrounding shadows.

"You make too much noise," Jeremiah whispered.

"You might as well be wearing cow bells. I've been here for hours, heard you a mile away. A buffalo stampede makes less racket." Joe countered. "C'mon."

"Not yet," Jeremiah shook his head. "We wait. I want to make absolutely sure no one has followed us."

Joe grunted, the two men crouched, their backs against a large oak tree, and settled in for a long surveillance. The storm passed, leaving the air warm and humid. Dripping water created soft rhythmic music as yellow police tape circling the ruins fluttered with faint phosphorescence in the darkness. A police cruiser came up the drive, its headlights exposing the destruction. It sat idling for a while, then slowly rolled back to the main road.

Jeremiah nodded. "Now we can move."

The pair slipped through the trees until they reached the tiny wooden bridge Mattie and her sister spent their summers having picnic lunches on throughout their childhood.

"There's a gardening shed behind the house, down the hill a ways," Jeremiah murmured.

Joe shook his head. "Is that your idea of a safe house?"

Jeremiah quirked an eyebrow. "Can you think of something better?

Joe grunted. "I reckon they wouldn't think us stupid enough to hide out at the crime scene."

They slipped onto the open grounds behind the house, and Jeremiah led the way to a small sturdy building at the back of the Lamont property built from the same brick as the main house. Joe helped him open the heavy wooden door, revealing a spacious interior filled with an impressive large riding mower, various gardening tools hanging from the wall, and shelves of supplies. A small BMW motorcycle stood in one corner.

Pale yellow light flickered as Jeremiah lit an oil lantern.

"You might want to keep that from the windows, unless you want us found." Joe advised. He looked around. "You know the police will eventually search this."

"I imagine they already have. Which makes it a perfect place to hide." Jeremiah moved to the furthest wall, lined floor to ceiling with shelves of various gardening and maintenance items. While Joe watched, Jeremiah slid the shelves out, then disappeared behind them.

"This way." Jeremiah's voice sounded distant, and Joe's brows furrowed. He stepped around the shelves and discovered a low trap door in the base of the wall.

"Grab the bottom of the shelf and pull it behind you before you shut the door," came Jeremiah's voice from the pale round pool of light emanating from the opening. Joe followed his instructions, then crawled on his hands and knees along a large corrugated drainpipe, the light flickering weakly off mildew and mold. The old Indian's features spread into a broad grin, the creases in his face emphasized in the lamplight.

"You've decided to bury us early?" his voice barely reached beyond his lips. He wondered whether Jeremiah heard him. He bumped into Jeremiah and looked up.

A concrete wall blocked their way.

"It may take both of us to get this open," Jeremiah said. "It has been a while since anyone was down here."

"How in the hell did you know about this?" Joe panted. Jeremiah thought the older man looked a little blue and suspected the air quality in the tunnel lacked enough oxygen for two men and a lamp.

"It ought to be here," Jeremiah muttered, his fingers searching along the bottom of the wall. "Ah." He jerked on something, then turned to Joe. "We need to push together." He gripped the top right hand corner of the slab, and Joe wriggled in as close as he could and shoved his fingers beneath the lower corner. Gritting their teeth, the two men pressed their shoulders against the cold concrete and shoved.

It took several tries, but finally the slab of concrete shifted, then reluctantly swung inward. Jeremiah took the lamp and disappeared into the darkness. "Hurry up, before you pass out from hypoxia."

Joe followed him through the hole, then felt the edge the concrete slab and pushed it closed. He stood up and looked around.

The room he found himself in appeared to be a large underground basement. Bunk beds, tables, a desk, and some scattered armchairs made up the furniture. A picnic table held two small electric stovetop units attached to a small red gasoline generator. Jeremiah lit two hurricane lanterns, then began opening cupboards and closets that lined the walls. He retrieved green T-shirts and military camouflage cargo pants.

"Here. Change into these. Then find us something to eat. It is close to midnight, and I have not eaten since this morning." He began stripping off his soaked clothes. Joe did likewise.

"What is this place?" Joe asked, laying his wet clothes on one of the tables to dry.

"Underground bunker beneath the Lamont estate, left over from the Cold War years in the fifties when everyone feared a nuclear strike." Jeremiah laid his wet clothes over a couple of chairs.

Joe turned in a slow circle, confused. "But isn't this the storm cellar the police checked out?"

Jeremiah shook his head. "That storm cellar is located beneath the other side of the house."

Joe whistled in appreciation as Jeremiah began taking inventory of their supplies. Cases of ammunition for handguns, hunting rifles and pump-action shotguns. Other cupboards contained stacks of canned goods, bottled water, MRE's.

"Did Mattie's father build this?" Joe asked.

Jeremiah crossed to a computer desk, leaned down, and released a satisfied sigh. "Batteries are good. George must have replaced them before his accident." He straightened and faced Joe. "As for your question, the answer is no. According to George, the previous owner showed him the bunker when he bought the estate. Said it was not on any of the blueprints." Jeremiah removed the weapons and laid them out where he could see them. The room had circulation; he could feel a slight breeze. The weapons appeared to be cleaned and oiled.

"You must've updated some of the supplies," Joe commented as he perused the canned goods and picked out a few which he carried to one of the small metal stovetops.

"George and I did over the years. Neither of us wanted to open something from the fifties." Jeremiah reached to a shelf above the computer desk and pulled opened several cabinet doors, revealing an array of small closed-circuit security monitors. He flipped switches and the screens popped into life, showing various black-and-white images of the Lamont property. His red Jeep sat to one side of the broad staircase, and he wondered whether the young detective had ordered a tracking device planted on the vehicle.

"I also installed a surveillance system. We have our own command center, right under the noses of law enforcement. We can keep an eye on police activity at the crime scene." He watched as the dark shape of a large van with its lights off rolled slowly up the driveway. Two figures appeared from the van and moved to the rear panel doors, reached in, then pulled out two oblong objects that looked suspiciously like bodies and dumped them onto the ground.

"And anyone else who might decide to show up," he added after a minute.

Chapter Eight

The stench of the bleach mixed with the lingering stench of blood, and I had trouble controlling the urge to gag. I thought if I had to spend much more time down here I would be adding the stench of puke, too.

Time dragged. I hurt all over and closing my eyes didn't lessen either the pain or the memory of the man bleeding out all over the floor, so I stared at the flat screen television. Even down in the basement I could hear thunder crashing as another system moved through the area. I wondered whether Hawk's team would try to carry out their plans under the current conditions. While the inclement weather would hide their activity, a tornado might just blow them and their cases full of bombs to hell.

Which would be just fine with me.

I thought about all the evening television dramas the networks ran. The good guys always saved the innocent people from getting blown up or shot. Then the inevitable super-smart, model-perfect, manicured and trimmed crime detection team managed to solve the murder in just under fifty minutes because during the commercials they came to all the right deductions, made all the right phone calls, brought in all the right people for questioning. They never followed wrong leads like the local yokels seemed bent on doing. The Pottawatomie County detectives were too busy chasing after Jeremiah when they should be scouring the crime scene for clues to Hawk and company.

Freeman came downstairs and crossed the room to where Hawk sat in the armchair. I finally could recognize him because he stood slightly taller than the rest of the team.

"The van is ready," he said, taking a seat in a metal folding chair.

Hawk ignored him and kept his eyes on the weather channel, which showed a large splotch of red approaching Cleveland County. "That doesn't look inviting," he muttered after several beats of silence.

Freeman turned his head and stared at the screen. "After what we went through last night, I agree." His head swiveled back to Hawk. "But I think it would be foolish to wait. If we don't blow the place tonight, we'll have to sit here another twenty-four hours. Too much danger of discovery if we stay that long in one location."

Hawk pressed his lips against his fingers. "I'd rather like to avoid another round with response crews if bad weather wrecks the van."

"Williams, Marks, and Cumbers will be down in a minute." As Freeman spoke, the three men descended the stairs. Two of them hoisted one of the bagged bodies onto their shoulders and carefully disappeared up the stairs again. A few minutes later, they returned for the second body and carried it upstairs, too.

"Where to? The town dump?" One of them asked when they returned.

Hawk shook his head. "The Lamont property. The place we blew up last night."

Freeman snapped his head to Hawk, his brown eyes narrowed in a frown. "But that's going to take a couple of hours, especially in this weather. The town dump is closer, more convenient."

"The dump no doubt will have security cameras," Hawk countered, his eyes on the television. "We've managed to stay off grid. I want to keep it that way."

Freeman's expression turned thoughtful. "Upping the heat on her husband?"

Hawk nodded. "Quite."

Freeman's lips curled. "The cops should find the bodies easily enough when they spot freshly dug earth."

Hawk remained motionless, his expression closed. "One would hope, but sometimes even the obvious proves obtuse." He nodded towards the three men, and they disappeared up the stairs again. A door slammed, then silence fell over the room.

Hawk switched to a news station and I watched the world news come and go, then a repeat of evening local news and wished I could somehow find a way to escape these horrible men.

"We went through Carson's things. Didn't find anything that might have caused him to break like that," Freeman murmured.

Hawk said nothing.

Freeman persisted. "He was hyper since the mission started. I put it down to his hatred of her. Do you think he might've been popping something?"

Hawk remained silent and motionless. He might have been carved from granite.

Freeman shook his head. "I can't figure out what happened to him. He's been with the team for a couple of years. Smart, quick, the most consistent aim out of the entire team."

"In retrospect, I would guess Meth, by his symptoms." Hawk ventured.

Freeman leaned forward and rubbed his forehead. "It doesn't make sense. Where'd he get it? Why would he even try the stuff? He would've known what drugs would do to him."

"Any history of PTSD?" Hawk asked.

"Naw," Freeman shook his head. "He was too mentally strong for that shit." He sat in silence, shaking his head, obviously mulling over the events. "Had to be something else, and the only idea I can come up with is some sort of drug-induced mania. But if it was drugs, how did he do it? We would've seen him shooting up."

"I'd guess oral ingestion," Hawk murmured.

Freeman closed his eyes and ran his hand over his short dark hair. "How he managed to dope up without anyone's knowledge is nothing short of miraculous." He sounded distressed and more than a little doubtful. "Someone would've seen him using it." He fell silent. Tension created lines around the corners of his down-turned mouth.

"Out with it." Hawk told him after a long silence.

Freeman leaned forward, resting his elbows on his knees. The muscles of his forearms and biceps stood out in the stark overhead lighting. "Carson was the youngest of the team. There was nothing in his prior history that even hinted at drug use."

"As you've clearly pointed out." Hawk sounded impatient. "What about before he joined the team? Did you run his background check?"

"I sure as hell did." Freeman's eyes cut to Hawk. "It's your background I'm not so damned sure about."

Hawk rested his arms on the chair. "My actions speak for themselves."

Freeman's lips thinned. "Your actions might be covering ulterior motives."

Abruptly, my head split into a massive wave of pain and the room began to spin. I closed my eyes, felt my stomach lurch, the odors of bleach and blood assaulting my nostrils. I jerked my eyes open, and watched in silent horror as millions of black bugs converged over the walls. I bit back a cry, gripped the cushions of the couch, snapped my eyes shut, and tried to reason through what I'd just seen. When I risked another peek, the walls appeared normal again. I began trembling as icy cold waves rocked through me.

Freeman stood and walked the length of the room, ran a hand over his bristly hair, returned to his chair and sat down again. "Our team has been rock solid until this mission." He hesitated, then added, "You're the new addition."

Hawk turned cold eyes to the man. "I am following Charlie's orders. I suspect my treatment of the woman tipped Carson over the edge."

Freeman met Hawk's stare. "Tacque was Carson's mentor. Carson's admiration of the guy bordered on hero worship." He paused. "All of us did. Tacque was a hell of a leader."

"If you're interpreting my actions towards the woman as protection, then you've yet to understand the finer points of revenge." Hawk's words barely reached above a whisper.

Freeman stared at him. "Your methods are different than Tacque's."

"Precisely why I am still alive and he is not." Hawk broke eye contact and settled further into the chair. "I am aware that all of you would rather like to slit her throat." His statement came out academic, as though they were talking about some sports event.

"Especially after what happened to Carson and Allison. It's her fault," Freeman snarled.

Hawk sighed. "Quite."

I clamped down hard on the panic that surged.

"The time is close. But not yet," Hawk muttered. "No, not quite yet," he repeated in a barely audible whisper.

"Back to my point about waiting," Freeman told him, changing the subject.

Hawk released a slow sigh. "Her husband's younger brother. David Mud Rain Tyler, I believe. Tacque had him at one point, but the lad survived. He's with temporary guardians here in Norman." His eyes cut to Freeman. "I don't want to risk complications."

My first impulse when I heard Hawk's words was to beg both of them to leave Mud Rain alone. Jeremiah's world revolved around his younger brother, and he had almost died trying to save Mud Rain from Gary. I almost died trying to save my husband.

I could not believe these monstrous men could have a bond so strong they would go to such lengths to avenge one of their own. The entertainment world never portrayed them that way. There was unrest and infighting, which always helped the good guys win in the end.

But there was no unrest pulling this team apart except for Carson, and he was dead. If anything, the remaining team members seemed to have unified under Freeman.

A lot of time slid by in silence after that. I must've drifted because I jolted awake when I heard the opening and shutting of an upstairs door.

Hawk heard the return of the team members and nodded to Freeman. "Tell the others to join us."

Freeman got to his feet, stretched, and ascended the stairs. Hawk rose and walked to the table. I thought he was going to turn off the television, but instead he retrieved several sheets of white computer paper and returned to his chair. Uncomfortable silence fell between us, broken by a clomping of feet as Freeman and the others descended into the room.

I focused my attention on the television screen, not wanting to hear details of how they were going to kill Bill and Becky Parsons, close friends of my family since I had been a child. I couldn't bear to hear Mud Rain was yet again at risk.

And in the meantime Jeremiah had dropped off the map. Did he suspect Mud Rain was in danger? Would he find a way to warn the Parsons? Would he risk calling the police? Was there any way on earth he could find out my location, arrive in the nick of time like they always did on the television shows, and beat these guys to a pulp?

He was the lead suspect in the destruction of my parents' home. He faced arrest and possible incarceration from the trap Hawk wove. Worse, he faced death from Hawk and his team. My mind kept coming back to the question of who had snatched Jeremiah from the hospital and tucked him into hiding. I racked my brain, trying to get my jumbled, restless thoughts to make sense. I thought about Jeremiah, and I wondered whether he had disappeared on his own after surgery.

Had Jeremiah realized Hawk shot him? Had he suspected he was still in danger and left the hospital on his own? Whom would he have contacted?

Joe Healing Water.

I had no idea why Joe's name popped into my mind, but it more than fit, I thought. Joe had been in the area. He had called Hawk with the location of Jeremiah's Jeep when we set out after him.

"That would be a very nice hit." Freeman's words interrupted my train of thought, and reluctantly I tuned in to their discussion.

"The advantages outweigh the risks," commented one of the men.

"Not tonight." Hawk sounded annoyed. He studied the sheets of paper he held. "The weather creates too much of a problem. We stay here. Tomorrow evening looks better, according to weather reports."

I closed my eyes and wished someone knew where we were and could stop these men. Their planning was flawless. And the weather would once again hide their activity. It seemed as though even Mother Nature was on their side.

Hawk glanced up from the papers in his hands, threw me a strange look, then turned his attention to the men. "We'll take her with us, then decide how best to dispose of things."

If he was using some form of psychological torture, he was very good at it. I tried and failed to keep the horror of his words from affecting me.

"I...," I swallowed, clamped down on the terror, and tried again. "I...need to use the facilities." I watched Hawk, praying for some miracle that would distract these men long enough for me to climb through the bathroom window. It was a ridiculous, stupid plan, but it was the only one I could think of.

Hawk's eyes snapped to mine, and I hoped my expression did not give away my thoughts.

"There's one behind you." He looked like he was about to add something, but then shut his mouth.

I stood, almost cried out as I put weight on my braced leg. Hawk rose and grasped my arm. I tried to wave him off.

"No. Don't touch me." The words ran out of my mouth before I could stop them. The panic in my voice bounced off the concrete walls.

Hawk ignored me and assisted me around the couch to the bathroom. I grabbed the edge of the sink.

"I've got it from here."

He shrugged and released me. I closed the door. When I looked around my heart fell down around my toes.

No window. Not even one of those little vent windows. How in the hell did this house get built without a frickin' window in the bathroom? I used the facilities, but I didn't flush when I was done. Instead, I took up precious minutes trying to figure out a way out of the house, away from Hawk and his men.

I thought about the two dead men and the fact the team was now two members down, raising the possibility they might actually have to leave me briefly unattended. That would be my only chance to get away, and I could not allow some stupid pain to get in the way.

I flushed the toilet, took my time washing my hands. I opened the medicine cabinet, a plain white metal box with a generous amount of rust eating away at the edges. Nothing but a disposable razor and a can of shaving cream occupied the inside. I closed the medicine cabinet and opened the door.

I started to limp back to the couch, put weight on my broken leg, released a soft, involuntary cry of pain, and gripped the door jam with both hands. I closed my eyes, tried to stop the spinning in my head.

Vice-like fingers gripped my upper arm. My eyes snapped open to find Hawk beside me. Without a word he helped me back to the couch, and I slumped down. Tears trickled down my face, partially from the pain in my leg, partially from the fear of being so close to a killer, partially from the physical contact that drove home the point of how absolutely helpless I was to defend myself.

I watched the backs of the team members as they worked on two more metal cases identical to the ones they used to blow up my parents' house. I did not see the contents, did not want to. I kept my eyes on the television screen, but I didn't register any of what I watched. My mind was too busy arguing with myself on the impossibility of any type of escape from these monsters.

I was also racking up a good deal of animosity towards Jeremiah. He had escaped Hawk's radar and disappeared from the Alamosa County Hospital, but he had left me behind.

Why? Why hadn't he taken me with him? If he suspected Hawk, he would know I faced danger as long as I was within Hawk's reach.

As though someone in the news media had read my thoughts, the television screen suddenly showed a picture of my husband, and the number for Crime Stoppers underneath. I prayed none of the men would notice the report, but of course Hawk chose that moment to look up.

"Quiet," he ordered, and silence fell over the room.

"…has disappeared," the news anchor reported. His voice rang out clear and strong. "We will interrupt normal programming to give updates on this breaking news. If you see this man, do not approach him. Please contact local police immediately."

The four men glanced at the picture of my husband before the screen changed back to an off-hour infomercial.

Hawk swung his attention to me. "I suspect Tyler is aware of the situation by now."

"He doesn't know our location. But he may try to get to his brother. We need to blow the house tonight," Freeman declared.

Hawk shook his head. "The weather will limit his movements. He's too busy evading the coppers. He won't suspect his brother is in danger."

"But he'll know what took down the first house. I'd feel better if he were behind bars. As things stand, I think we should go tonight." Freeman argued. He turned to stare at me, but my thoughts turned inward and I missed the dangerous glint in the man's eyes.

Jeremiah somehow managed to dodge the Shawnee Police and Pottawatomie County Sheriff's Department, but I could see no way for him to uncover my location to rescue me from Hawk. I could only hope he would intuit the danger facing the Parsons and Mud Rain.

How much more death and destruction would Hawk and his team of miscreants carry out? Would they aim for the National

Weather Station located on the south college campus? Would keeping me with them force Jeremiah into the open? Would Hawk kill my husband before my eyes?

My attention jerked back to Freeman when he walked over to the couch. The corners of his mouth quirked as he bent down. I pressed against the cushions in an effort to open some space between us.

"We're avoiding anything with GPS, so we need directions to the Parsons house," he said, staring at me. Hawk made a movement, but then he stilled. I looked back at Freeman.

"Give me directions." His voice sounded too calm, and shivers trembled through me.

Before I realized what he intended, he pulled up the right leg of my sweats, exposing the brace.

"Let's see what this looks like." With quick movements he undid the Velcro straps and opened the brace, then unwrapped the padding. My entire lower leg was bloated and purple.

Hawk practically leaped across the room. "What in bloody hell did Carson do to her leg!"

Ignoring Hawk, Freeman studied my face. "It looks as though Carson forgot to remove the tourniquet he used."

I stared at the grotesque appearance of my leg and clamped a hand over my mouth. Without warning, he wrenched my knee sideways.

Blinding white streaked across my head. Someone screamed, hoarse and agonized. I was pretty sure it was me, but my head was so full of pain I couldn't think. I fell onto my side, shaking, trembling, unable to do anything to ease the pain.

Freeman's voice, mellow and terrifyingly calm, floated across me. "Give me directions."

All those stupid television shows, all those ridiculous movies in which the hero withstands all forms of torture and pain, proving his or her mental, physical, emotional strength. All those heroes.

All those stupid, sissy actors who pretend to withstand the impossible, ignoring reality and the limits of human tolerance.

White-hot flashes streaked through my body. I felt Freeman's hand on my knee and reached out in a frantic effort to stop him from wrenching my leg again. I think I shook my head. Consciousness waned.

"Do not faint." Freeman's voice sounded so close as to be coming from inside my skull. I think I moved my head. I'd forgotten his question. I would answer in a heartbeat if only he would repeat his demand.

He seemed to read my mind. "Directions to the Parsons' residence," he repeated, his voice soft, frighteningly intimate.

Clinging with mental fingers to consciousness, I stammered as I replied. "On t-the other s-side of t-the f-freeway. W-west of campus." I felt the warmth of his hand against my skin and wished desperately that I could melt into the couch and disappear. I heard men's voices arguing, some rapid shuffling.

"Mattie." Hawk's voice sounded close. I opened my eyes and stared straight into his light gray eyes, inches from my own.

"What type of neighborhood?" His voice held urgency. Terror seized every muscle in my body. I wanted him dead, dead, dead. And I wanted Freeman and all the others dead, too. And I wanted someone to take me away to somewhere safe, without pain.

I desperately wished I could lie well enough to convince them the Parsons lived in a gated residential community guarded by twenty-four-hour security. That it would be impossible to get in and blow up their house without the entire Norman police department descending upon them.

Hawk bent his head close; his breath brushed the side of my face. "Do not lie to me."

I had no idea what the other team members were doing. They could have been shooting each other and I would not have noticed. My whole attention rested on Hawk, his cunning brilliance that was responsible for so much immeasurable, intolerable, unbearable pain and loss.

My mouth was dry. I couldn't swallow. I barely managed a tiny shake of my head.

"What type of neighborhood?" Hawk repeated, Freeman standing directly behind him. His words sounded like canon booms in the room despite the fact that he hardly spoke above a whisper.

"Woods. T-trees. L-l-like m-my p-p-parents." I choked the words out.

I would lose my leg if one of them didn't undo what Carson had done. I felt fingers tighten around my knee and barely controlled the impulse to beg for mercy.

I can promise a good deal of pain beyond your wildest imagination.

Hawk's words, whispered in my ear at my parents' house.

Why oh why hadn't Jeremiah taken me with him when he disappeared from the hospital in Alamosa?

"Gated?" Hawk searched my face for deceit.

I nodded. Tears streamed down my face. I brought up a hand and covered my mouth to keep from begging. I couldn't break eye contact.

His eyes bore through me. "The code?"

I closed my eyes and tried to think. Was there a code that automatically called the police?

If there was, Becky never told me. All I knew was the code to let myself through the gate when we went to visit.

I felt fingers tighten and shook my head. "D-don't." I bit into the side of my hand in an effort to control the overwhelming hysteria. "I'm t-trying to think."

"Think quickly." Hawk's voice again, low, insistent.

It seemed to take forever, but I finally visualized the gate controls and imagined punching in the code. I told him the sequence.

"I'll handle this." Hawk picked up the brace. He fumbled around the back of my knee, and I thought that maybe he removed the tourniquet, but I couldn't be sure. He re-wrapped my leg then closed the brace. I felt him adjusting the Velcro straps, his hands lingering on the device. I lay on the couch and closed my eyes, refusing to look at him, refusing to face the fact that I was going to die soon. Probably tonight. I had no strength left, no ability to move if an opportunity arose to escape. I understood fully the need to cooperate at any cost, to cross to the side of the enemy in order to avoid more pain.

Somewhere in the recess of my mind the words "Stockholm Syndrome" formed. I didn't care. I was too scared.

Chapter Nine

Joe walked over and studied the sophisticated surveillance screens. "Looks like we've got company. Doesn't look like cops," he frowned. His wet gray hair straggled down his back, slow to dry in the humid, damp conditions.

Jeremiah stepped close to the monitors, trying to pick out features of the two figures. "Neither of them looks like Hawk," he pointed out after a long silence. "Nor Mattie."

"Can't see the make of the van," Joe muttered, squinting at the screens.

They watched the dark, motionless vehicle, headlights off, thin wisps of exhaust drifting from the tailpipe and faintly visible in the heavy downpour.

Jeremiah glanced at Joe. "Two figures. Both exited from the passenger side. No movement from the driver."

"Which means there are three of them." Joe paused. His black eyes studied the monitors for several silent moments. "Think this is the signal we've been waiting for?"

"From Hawk?" Jeremiah's eyebrows furrowed. "What are the chances this is a random dump?"

"Too large to be coincidence. Which means these bozos are connected with the destruction of Mattie's house and her disappearance." Joe glanced at the younger Ute, reading his mind. "Could've done without the damned body bags."

Both men turned their heads and studied the scene on the security screens. Uncomfortable silence fell thick and heavy between them.

"Let's review what we've learned so far," Joe stated, carefully keeping emotion from his voice. "We now know Hawk miscalculated the number of men who would show up at Mattie's house. Obviously he couldn't figure out how to warn us."

"Obviously." Jeremiah's jaw clenched.

"Okay, so more than two showed up last night to take out Mattie. They blew up her house instead." Joe watched the images kneel and hoist a body bag onto their shoulders. The men carried their load up the remains of the broad staircase.

"Obviously." Jeremiah repeated.

He spun and strode to the long picnic table in the middle of the underground room. Hunting rifles, pump-action shotguns, and several handguns lay on the wooden surface.

"We need to know who occupies those body bags." He loaded one of the handguns, screwed on a suppresser, and set the gun down again. Joe watched him.

"I agree." Joe picked his next words with care. "And if your wife is in one of those bags, we need those three clowns alive to lead us to the rest of them." His statement hung in the silence between them, both of them fearing the truth, neither knowing what to say to lessen the tension.

"Hawk might be in one of the bags," Jeremiah walked back to scan the monitors.

"Yeah, well if that's the case he proves my point," Joe declared flatly.

Jeremiah looked at him. "Which is?"

"Entaffs." Joe squinted at the monitors again.

Jeremiah's eyes narrowed. "You are making that up. SNAFU and FUBAR are standard military references. There is no such thing as an *entaffs*."

Joe grunted, his hands tucked loosely in the pockets of the borrowed cargo pants. "Well, there should be."

Jeremiah waited. "And your definition...?" he prompted when Joe wasn't forthcoming.

"Never Trust A Foreign Spook."

"You need to find something useful to offer besides making up unhelpful acronyms." Jeremiah scowled as the two images dropped their load onto the soggy ground.

Joe snorted. "If some soldier can make up shit like 'Situation Normal: All Fucked UP' and 'Fucked Up Beyond All Repair', then I can damn well make up my own as the situation warrants. This is definitely in the SNAFU category. NTAFS certainly fits."

Jeremiah crossed to a wall of cabinets, opened one and extracted a small box from which he took a tracking device. He returned to the table and picked up a collapsible sniper rifle.

"I must admit Hawk is really good when it comes to smokescreens." Joe watched as the two men descended the stairs, hoisted the second body bag onto their shoulders.

Jeremiah's words came out low, angry. "The Lamont estate has been destroyed, Mattie has disappeared, and now we have two bodies."

Joe spun around, his black eyes flashing. "You're not going to help Mattie by killing those clowns."

Jeremiah collected his gear. Ammunition, thermal optics, small two-way radio were some of the things he loaded into a military backpack.

Joe watched the two men drop the second body bag beside the first. One of them tramped to the van and retrieved a shovel. "That's odd. Looks like they're taking time to bury whoever they killed."

"Whomever." Jeremiah corrected.

"Whatever. Not my language." Joe looked at him. "Use the tracking device, not any of your weapons. Understand?"

Jeremiah reached into a floor-to-ceiling closet and retrieved a pair of thin gloves and a balaclava. He slid the handgun with the silencer into a thigh holster, then tucked the small tracking device into a pocket. He slipped into a pair of thin rubber-soled shoes, then went to the desk. He opened a drawer, removed a cell phone and an earpiece and small transmitter.

"Can't use mine," he told Joe.

Joe nodded towards the phone. "Got any juice?"

Jeremiah changed the battery from his phone to the new one. "Does now. Keep me posted on their movements, especially the driver," he instructed as he tucked the communication device into his ear.

"Mattie and Hawk might be in the van. Maybe that's why the driver hasn't appeared," Joe ventured.

Jeremiah looked at the monitors and shook his head. "Unlikely. If Hawk were on the premises, he would have made an appearance by now."

Joe's aged fingers gripped Jeremiah's arm with surprising strength. "Remember, son. We need someone to track back to where they're holding Mattie. You kill them, and you'll alert the rest of the team."

Jeremiah dug the small round object from his pocket and held it up. "Hence the reason for the tracking device."

"Just don't want you going postal on me, that's all." Joe

dropped his hand and turned his attention to the monitors.

It took Jeremiah longer than he wanted to spend crawling through the pitch-black tunnel to the equally dark gardening shed. He dropped his backpack beside the motorcycle, then opened the heavy wooden door of the building. Darkness hid his movements as he eased through the door, then took a moment for his eyes to adjust to his surroundings. Lightning flashed to the southwest, which meant Norman was getting hit by weather that would soon reach them.

Jeremiah did not retrieve the night vision goggles from his backpack, did not want the added distortion and limited depth perception issues. Keeping the van in sight, he slipped among the trees towards the drive. The two men stood at the top of the stairs, apparently taking turns with the shovel. Jeremiah quelled the strong urge to quietly take out both men, then the driver when he exited the van to investigate. He paused in the thick foliage and watched the two figures for several minutes. They worked with methodical efficiency as they took turns with the shovel, their progress rapid despite the muddy conditions. Dread coursed through him and he fought down panic, forced himself to focus. He needed to confirm whether Mattie occupied one of those bags.

"You're doing good so far. Don't spoil it by doing something stupid." Joe's voice whispered through the earwig.

"You are not anticipating finding your wife in a body bag," Jeremiah snapped, then clamped his lips shut. Breaking silence within earshot of the enemy would do him no good. Sounds carried easily. He waited for Joe's reprimand, but the earpiece remained silent. Exhaling slowly several times, he felt his heart rate slow and the pressure inside his chest lessen. Several minutes passed before the familiar feeling of professional calm settled into his chest. His stomach refused to untwist.

"Good boy. Stay on task," Joe whispered.

Jeremiah tapped the earpiece.

The two men straightened, one dropped the shovel, and they dragged the first bag into the shallow grave. Satisfied they were unaware of his presence; Jeremiah crept from the trees and crouched, shut out thoughts of his wife lying in a muddy grave amid the rubble of her parents' house. Instead, he envisioned the mercenaries keeping her alive, using her to flush him out.

Aware the driver was no doubt watching rear and side mirrors, Jeremiah dropped to his belly and crawled towards the van. Rain began falling as he paused at the edge of the tarmac, then slithered beneath the vehicle. Retrieving the tracking device from his pocket, he fastened the tiny transmitter securely to the underbody of the van, then drew his weapon and waited.

"They're done." Joe whispered. Jeremiah touched the earpiece.

In character with highly trained professionals, the two men did not utter a word as they returned to the vehicle. Jeremiah watched their legs and boots, both covered in thick muddy, red clay, as one of them walked to the rear, opened a door, and replaced the shovel. The passenger door opened and both pairs of legs disappeared into the cab. The driver shifted gears and the van rolled down the driveway. When the vehicle cleared Jeremiah's body, he eased into the grass and lay motionless, listening for any indication his presence had been detected.

"Tracking device engaged," Joe whispered. "Good work. Stay there until my signal."

Thunder cracked hard as lightning connected earth with sky in one long, thick electrical bolt.

"Okay, they're on their way. You're clear. Go after them." Joe's voice sounded relieved.

Jeremiah tapped his earpiece and stood. But instead of following Joe's orders he jogged through the increasing downpour to the mounds of freshly dug earth. He had placed an uncomfortable amount of trust in Hawk to protect Mattie.

"Get back on task!" Joe's voice snapped in his ear. "We don't want to lose those bozos. I'll check the bags after you've left."

Ignoring him, Jeremiah collapsed to his knees and yanked off his balaclava. The graves were no more that a couple of feet deep. Rain turned the red clay into thick, slick mud that he clawed with increasing frenzy, not caring that his green camouflage turned brick red as he pushed the mud away to access the bags. His heart pounded in his chest, his hands shook, and he shuddered violently when his fingers hit the first bag. Rain pelted the muddy plastic. Thunder crashed again as lightning threw his shadow across the ground with garish distortion.

He felt a pair of feet, moved to the other end of the grave, dug again. His heart stopped in his chest when he felt a face. With shaking hands he ripped the thin trash bag and leaned close, squinting as another lightning bolt revealed features.

"Well?" came Joe's irritated voice in his ear.

"Not Mattie." Jeremiah blew out a shaky breath.

"Hawk?"

Jeremiah shook his head, aware that Joe could see his movement on the security screens. "Not him, either," he added unnecessarily.

He moved to the second grave and began to dig again. He located the face, felt increasing anxiety when his hands told him this body was smaller. He ripped the second bag open.

"Another male. Not Hawk," he breathed as a wave of relief washed through him. "Looks like Hawk has been busy."

"Satisfied? Think it might be a good idea to follow that van now?" Joe whispered in his ear. Jeremiah's fingers shook when he reached up to tap the ear piece.

"Don't bother burying them again. Hurry up. Looks like the van is heading south. My bet is they're headed to Norman." Though Joe sounded aggravated, Jeremiah picked up an undertone of relief. He'd been as worried as Jeremiah about whose bodies those bags contained.

Jeremiah tapped the communication device, stood and allowed the heavy downfall to sluice some of the mud from his clothes.

Pressure filled his chest again as another thought occurred. Mud Rain lived with the Parsons in Norman.

He needed to catch the van and locate the team's hiding place. The weather might slow down their actions, force them to postpone another possible hit, but he could not afford to take the risk. If the assault team were located in Norman, then the Parsons and his younger brother were in imminent danger. If the team planned a mission, the early hours and the current weather conditions would provide ample cover.

"Want your sniper rifle?" Joe whispered in his ear. Jeremiah paused, confused.

"The one in the Jeep," Joe clarified. "You're more familiar with that one."

Jeremiah hurried to the Jeep still parked at the edge of the long drive, but his rifle had disappeared from behind the front seats.

"Police must have found it," he muttered. He sprinted to the shed.

The small motorcycle Jeremiah used was fast, versatile, and about as low profile as he could ask for. He kept to back roads as he raced to Norman. A small GPS tracking screen was clipped on the handlebars, and the faint blip did not alter course. The large storm cell continued to bring heavy rain and an impressive lightning show.

An hour later the blip on the GPS screen stopped along the west side of the Oklahoma University campus. Jeremiah rode through town and parked behind one of the carefully landscaped hedges on campus, across the street from the house where the van parked.

Mid-June, several hours into Wednesday morning, and stormy conditions kept campus students indoors, traffic minimal. Jeremiah had no trouble remaining out of sight as he reconnoitered the house.

It was clear now Hawk had woefully underestimated the Charlie Network. Hawk's original plan, to lure Tacque's former teammates to Shawnee, capture and interrogate them, was a total disaster.

Jeremiah's jaw clenched and he frowned as he forced away thoughts about the argument he, Hawk, and Joe had concerning Mattie. Hawk swore no harm would come to her. She seemed the perfect target to lure members of Tacque's team, and Hawk claimed he had connections through his knowledge and investigation into the Network.

A cold chill crept along Jeremiah's spine. At the time, he reluctantly took Hawk's word on the chain of events and agreed not to contact Mattie until this was over. Hawk insisted he represented the best choice to lure and intercept the team Charlie would no doubt send after Mattie; assured both himself and Joe the network would not risk sending more than a pair of assassins to take out their target.

Exactly what were Hawk's connections with this assassination network? His presence at the same baseball game in the same section as Mattie on that fateful Sunday afternoon seemed incredibly coincidental.

Gary Tacque had been a killer. Hawk was a killer. Gary had gone after Mattie's sister, Angela. He married her, then poisoned her in a way that made her death appear self-induced if not natural, then tried to kill Jeremiah's younger brother. Tacque had been after the Lamont fortune.

What if Gary hired Hawk to take out Mattie? What if in reality, Hawk was part of the Charlie Network, too?

Jeremiah pushed away nagging doubts and concentrated on the fact two dead bodies in the ground at the Lamont estate, two grave diggers, and one driver meant the Charlie Network had sent a team of at least five to the Lamont estate. Hawk had been caught off-guard, had not been able to slip a warning message to himself or to Joe Healing Water. One of two possibilities existed. First, Hawk's position was now compromised because he had risked ordering the remaining team members to bury those two bodies all the way in Shawnee instead of somewhere close in Norman. He had used the bodies as a signal, hoping Joe and himself would realize the situation and follow the van back to his location.

The other possibility was Hawk had buried two bodies on the Lamont Estate as a lure into a trap.

Jeremiah released a measured sigh. His first and only priority involved rescuing Mattie and getting her to safety. The van parked in front of the house meant at least three team members occupied the residence. If he notified police about a home invasion at their current location, he might get a street full of squad cars before the killers had a chance to leave. He pulled out his cell to call emergency when the eerie, ear-piercing wail of the tornado sirens wound up. He released a string of curses. He tried 911, got a busy signal. He called Joe.

"Contact Bill and Becky Parsons," he ordered, trying to keep his voice low but still audible over the cacophonic wailing. "Tell them to get themselves and Mud Rain out of their house immediately. I cannot get through to emergency. The tornado sirens are going off and emergency phone numbers will be jammed with callers. Then find some transportation and get down here." Joe's voice came over flat, emotionless. "First of all, I need to be here when the cops find those bodies. Second, since the local cops no doubt stuck a tracking device on your Jeep, I'm out of luck in the transportation department, unless you're expecting me to hotwire some rattle trap piece of junk."

Jeremiah muttered an oath. Two dead bodies at the Lamont estate also meant the police would soon be doubling their efforts to find him. He didn't doubt for a minute the young detective would assume Jeremiah baited him by burying those two bodies on the Lamont property. Reeves would be gunning for him, would label him armed and extremely dangerous. That alone increased the chance of him being shot on sight, even though technically law enforcement wasn't supposed to do that sort of thing.

In the meantime, the sirens wailed away. How could he warn the Parsons their lives were in danger from something far more dangerous than an approaching funnel? Jeremiah debated the risk of leaving his surveillance post and ride to the Parsons' house.

"You still there?" Joe's voice asked through the cell.

Jeremiah shifted, glanced to the hedge concealing the motorcycle. "I am sure their next target will be the Parsons and Mud Rain."

Joe grunted. "They may also be heading to the OU weather center. They know your connections; they will know Mattie worked there, too."

"Damn it, Joe." Jeremiah glanced around for an emergency campus phone. Nothing. "I need to get a message to the Parsons!"

"You need to stay on task," Joe snapped. "Stick with them. Mattie's with them. If they head for the Weather Center, that'll give you enough time to run over to the Parsons and get them to safety. From the sounds of those sirens, they may already be in their storm cellar."

Jeremiah didn't waste breath arguing with the old Ute, but he knew the Parsons would be anywhere but their storm cellar. Hell, half the town would be in their yards trying to spot the damned tornado.

The front door of the house opened, and Jeremiah cut off Joe and jammed the phone into his pocket. Wind lashed him, rain pounded, lightning flashed with psychotic frenzy. He watched four shadows run out, tried to squint through the storm to recognize any of them. Another man appeared half-dragging a slender, limping figure.

Mattie.

The figures crawled into the van and the vehicle pulled from the curb and disappeared into the storm. Jeremiah jumped on the motorcycle and followed.

Sirens wailed, wind threatened to blow him off the small motorcycle; lightning danced and gyrated around him. He prayed the van would head to the Weather Center. He needed only a small window to get the Parsons and his brother to safety. He tried to dig his cell from his pocket to attempt to reach emergency again, almost lost control of the bike and dropped the phone. His heart sank when the van headed across town towards the gated residential community where the Parsons lived.

The van jerked to a stop at the gate, the driver punched in the code Mattie had no doubt been forced to provide, then swung into the residential area. Jeremiah slipped the motorcycle beside the gate and vaulted the wall. Sprinting through a thick grove of pecan trees, he slowed when the Parsons' house came into view and darted to a massive oak tree on the edge of their large property. The tree groaned and thrashed in the wind, rain pounded him, and he hoped the Parsons were in their storm cellar this time. Low, black clouds scuttled across the sky, signaling the approaching wall cloud. He slipped the backpack from his shoulders, unzipped it, and reached for the sniper rifle.

The rear panel doors swung open and four figures leapt out, one of them pulling a figure with his hands bound behind his back. Whipping out the semi-automatic handgun, Jeremiah aimed but could not focus on a clear target through the rain. If he took time to assemble the rifle, the killers would be in the house and the Parsons would be dead. He bolted upright and set off at a dead run towards the house. Even then he didn't move fast enough to prevent what happened next.

The last figure jerked his head in Jeremiah's direction and aimed what had to be a handgun, but the wailing sirens, pounding rain, and the screaming wind buried the flash and the report. Jeremiah dived for cover behind a low hedge, peered around in time to see the assault team burst through the front door. He leaped up and ran for the breached entrance.

The violence of the storm did not cover the sudden blast of a shotgun.

Time slowed to a standstill. His feet refused to run any faster, he couldn't get to the front door no matter how hard he tried.

He reached the steps when someone slammed heavily against him, throwing him away from the house and crashing onto the lawn. A heavy concussion boomed and a fireball lit the night like a bonfire, sizzling and spitting in the heavy downpour. Pain exploded through his chest, his head bounced against the soggy wet earth, sending more pain streaking through his skull. His ears rang as wind howled and sirens echoed around his head. He twisted and struggled beneath heavy, oppressive weight pinning him to the ground. Then the earth shuddered and another explosion engulfed him.

Chapter Ten

The clock in the corner of the television screen read two-thirty Wednesday morning. I was more than just awake. I was terrified.

Hawk stood in front of the screen.

"This storm system will provide the perfect cover." Freeman argued, his voice tense.

Hawk looked at me, then turned back to the man beside him.

"I agree we mustn't wait, but I want to check the conditions from upstairs. This rat-trap cellar muffles things, and I'm not overly fond of being tossed about like a bloody rag doll again."

Hawk disappeared up the stairs. Freeman watched, then turned to the other men.

"This weather creates the perfect conditions." His words came out in a tight, low voice.

"Agreed." The remaining three men nodded.

"People will see you," I blurted. "The security firm always makes rounds about now."

Freeman and the others whipped their heads towards me.

"And how would you know that?" Freeman challenged.

"B-Becky told me," I stammered, wishing I sounded more convincing.

"You're lying." Freeman waved a dismissive hand and turned his attention to the others.

"Leave them alone," I pleaded, unable to stop the words. "They don't know anything about what's happened. They don't know about Gary, they don't know where Jeremiah is, they're not…" The rest of my plea turned into so much mumbling when Freeman crossed the room and gripped my mouth with cruel strength.

"I don't care what Hawk's plans are, the rest of us have had enough of you," he snarled under his breath. I listened for Hawk's step on the stairs, but dead silence came from overhead. I wondered what in the world he was doing.

"We're running out of time. I don't want to get caught out in daylight. Too much chance of someone seeing us," One of the men pointed out.

Freeman glanced at his watch, then at me. His brown eyes looked like they belonged to a stone gargoyle rather than a human being.

"We need to move now." He inclined his head towards the cases lying on the table. "Marks, put a timer on those."

The man closest to the wall nodded, turned and pulled out the bottom drawer of a set of filing cabinets.

"Toss me that roll of duct tape," Freeman ordered, his hand still gripping my mouth. I shrank against the back of the couch. I raised a hand in a feeble gesture, which he swatted away. He released me and ripped a piece off the roll.

"Okay, okay," I blurted, but he slapped the strip across my mouth.

"I told you to shut up." He unwound more and reached for my hands.

"Leave them free," one of the men behind him advised quietly. "She'll be easier to transport with use of her arms, with her leg and all."

Freeman glared at the man who had spoken.

"Just saying," the man muttered apologetically, raising his hands.

"I'll be upstairs," Freeman's eyes cut to the ceiling. "I don't know what our fearless leader is up to, but it's time we made amends." He took the roll of duct tape and ascended the stairs.

The tape clung to my face like cement, mashing my lips against my teeth. I watched Marks retrieve two objects from the drawer and open each case. The other two men looked on as he worked. I couldn't figure out why Freeman wanted timers with these, since the ones they used to blow up my parents' house had been detonated with a remote control.

A solid thud shook the ceiling, and I assumed Freeman and Hawk were moving ammunition and weapons. My mind envisioned men with rifles raised storming into the Parsons' house. I looked at the three standing at the table. All of them wore black gear, though none of them had a rifle. Each of them checked the handgun strapped to their thigh.

Marks walked to the bottom of the stairs.

"Timers are in place." His voice, though not loud, echoed up the staircase.

"Set them for two minutes," came Freeman's voice from above. He sounded out of breath.

"Got it." Marks returned to the cases, made some adjustments, then snapped the lids closed.

"Rifles?" One of the men asked.

Marks tilted his head. "Upstairs." His eyes swept the basement. "Check everything, make sure we don't leave anything behind."

The other two nodded, though I couldn't figure what there was to check, since the room was bare except for the few pieces of ratty furniture. The two men pulled on Latex gloves, retrieved rags from one of the filing cabinet drawers, and began wiping down every surface. They checked cushions, beneath furniture, and the bathroom even though I didn't remember any of them using it. When finished, they tucked their cloths into a pocket, then grasped my arms and pulled me to my feet. With powerful hands they half-carried me across the basement and up the stairs.

At that moment the unique, ghostly wail of the tornado sirens wound up.

We reached the upper level and the two men dragged me into the empty living room. Freeman stood at the front door, frozen as he listened to the wailing sirens. He whipped around to me.

"What are those?" he demanded, fear in his voice.

Of course I couldn't answer him. I had duct tape all over my mouth.

"Does that mean there's a tornado on the way?" He sounded furious.

I nodded.

"*Shit.*" He yanked the front door open. "Hold her in the kitchen while we load the van," he snarled.

I tried but couldn't locate Hawk as the men dragged me into another room. Panicked commotion came from the front room.

"Bring her now!" Freeman yelled over the blaring sirens. The two obeyed, half-dragging me with them. My right leg felt like a ton of lead. Pain shrieked through me, my cheeks puffed out behind the tape as I panted and groaned. My nose ran, my eyes streamed, and I thought with so much moisture the tape would surely soften and lose its grip. But it didn't, and I mentally cursed every one of these dirt bags for denying me a last chance of being saved by screaming my lungs out when I got through the front door.

Of course, no one would hear a damned thing because of the blasted sirens, so Freeman wouldn't have needed the stupid duct tape after all.

One of the men ran ahead to help Freeman with equipment as the other dragged me through the front door. The van sat at the curb amidst lightning flashing everywhere, wind and rain blowing through the trees, sirens adding a surreal wail. The man dragged me along in a death grip, forcing me to put weight on my leg to avoid falling. We were the last out of the house, the last to crawl into the back of the van. Through the rear panel door window I caught a glimpse of part of the Oklahoma University campus before a hand gripped my hair and yanked my face towards the wall of the van and shoved me hard onto the metal floor. There were no seats except those up front for driver and passenger. I sagged against the inside, my leg grinding with agony. I watched as three of the men donned black close-fitting gloves and black ski masks. I recognized Freeman's face when he slid behind the wheel.

Five men. Hawk must be in the van with the rest of the team. I spotted his face in the darkness and wondered why his was the only one uncovered. Freeman started the engine and the van shuddered along the narrow college town streets, turning corners, ignoring lights. Despite not being able to see where we were going, I knew we were heading towards the Parsons' neighborhood, and soon their house would crumble into a heap of rubble, too. I prayed the engine would quit, I prayed for a flat tire, I prayed for a cop to stop us because of a gut instinct something was wrong. I even prayed for the tornado to drop on top of us and destroy the van and everyone in it.

None of my prayers got answered. Evidently, God was on break tonight.

The movement of the van jostled my leg and sitting on the hard metal floor emphasized the pain of grating bones until I wished I could faint. Too soon we rolled to a stop in front of the gate that led into the prestigious residential community where the Parsons lived. In my mind I pictured the grand homes that sat on multi-acre, heavily forested grounds, all of them sprawling ranch-style miniature mansions. I thought of the security company that made rounds and hoped one of their cars would be on site, but the boulevard proved deserted due to the dangerous weather conditions.

I whipped my head around in time to catch a glimpse of the Parsons' house through the windshield before the van passed and rolled to a stop.

Their house was lit up like a Christmas tree. I prayed Bill, Becky, and Mud Rain had retreated to the storm cellar, but I knew they would be upstairs keeping watch through windows and monitoring the weather station for as long as the power remained on.

"I'll watch the woman," Freeman yelled over the cacophony, twisting around to face the rest of the team. "Marks, take the cases. Cumbers, assist our leader. Williams, watch their back." He and Marks exchanged a brief nod, and Marks quickly opened the cases, slipped a hand inside no doubt to start the timers, then snapped them closed again.

Two minutes. That's all the life Parsons and Mud Rain had left. I squeezed my eyes shut against the mental picture of the imminent explosion.

I opened them again when, without a word, the men drew handguns from their thigh holsters and pushed past me. I turned my head away, not wanting to see the evil in their eyes, their cold commitment. I also did not want to make eye contact with Hawk. He had been behind all of this, and now he was about to lead the others on another killing spree. Tears streamed down my face as the duct tape muffled uncontrollable sobs.

The back of the van emptied as the men jumped into the raging storm. Freeman watched their progress, and with a start I realized no one was watching me. Frantically, I looked around for something I could use as a weapon.

The end of a tire iron lay in one of the grooves of the floor. Keeping my eyes on Freeman, I groped with my left hand until my fingers felt cold metal. Praying it wasn't strapped down; I carefully wrapped my hand around the end, then lifted.

It left the floor with nary a sound. Taking a deep, steadying breath, I laid it along my left leg. I needed to get to my feet, but that much movement would attract Freeman's attention.

I could do this, I thought. I had to. It was the slim opportunity I had prayed for. Maybe God was listening after all. I forgot about pain and immobility, closed my eyes, and imagined how Freeman would move. He was a big man, and the cramped space of the van would create a disadvantage. All I needed was one swing. But I would have to be on my feet if I had any hope of an attack. The van shuddered and swayed in the storm, making standing difficult enough without a broken leg.

I opened my eyes and flicked my attention to Freeman's back, being careful not to stare. If he turned around, my window of opportunity would close and never open again.

Slowly, I bent my left knee to my chest, the ribbed metal flooring cold beneath my bare foot. With my right hand, I groped for something along the wall to use as leverage to haul myself upright. I tightened my grip on the tire iron, counted silently to three, then threw all my strength into my left leg and my right arm.

"What the fuck...?" Freeman shouted as something through the windshield caught his attention. My movement jostled the van, and he jerked around.

"Sit down bitch!" he roared, the volume of his voice within the confines of the van making my ears ring.

Come here and make me! I glared at him, my retort muffled by the duct tape. I braced my left leg and hunched awkwardly. I was off-balance, on one leg, trying to maintain my footing in the shaking van. I gripped the tire iron in my left hand and held it out of Freeman's line of sight. Pain consumed my right leg and I gritted my teeth behind the duct tape and refused to allow tears to flow.

As Freeman lunged to his feet faint popping noises erupted outside, barely audible through the sirens and the storm.

"Fucking bitch, I'll kill you!" Freeman bent forward, his large body cramped in the tight confines of the van. He reached a hand out to grab me. I planted my right foot, bit my tongue against the pain that scorched up my leg, grabbed the tire iron with both hands, and swung the makeshift weapon in an upwards arc with every ounce of strength I could muster.

The end of the tire iron caught Freeman on the side of his face. He went down with a surprised grunt of pain, and I swung the iron sideways and brought it down as hard as I could against the back of his head.

Freeman crumpled onto the floor of the van. I did not waste time checking to see whether he was still conscious. Using the tire iron as a makeshift cane, I hobbled to the rear doors, turned the handle, pushed them open. Rain-drenched air tasted like freedom and I struggled to control the adrenaline as I eased onto the street. Cold wet pavement met my bare foot. I couldn't feel a thing under my right foot, even though I knew I should because it was as bare as my left one. Hail mixed with rain stung like a swarm of bees. The sirens continued to wail, forlorn and ominous.

The sickening, familiar sound of an explosion buffeted me as I collapsed against the back of van. A soft orange-red glow penetrated through the storm, and I choked back a sob.

Bill and Becky, and Mud Rain were dead. My head whirled with the emotional impact, and I collapsed onto my left side. Water ran along the black pavement forming miniature lakes that raindrops pummeled into tiny waves, while runoff created rivulets that pulled and sucked at my arms and legs.

Any minute the killers would return to the van, find Freeman unconscious, find me in a heap on the pavement. They would probably shoot me. I didn't care. At least I would be together with my dead family and friends.

Shoot me, I thought, waiting to hear footsteps. *Get it over with.*

A deep, primal urge coaxed my eyes open. I lifted my head. None of the killers appeared, and I thought vaguely that maybe they miscalculated and got caught by the blast. After all, they used timers instead of a remote to detonate the explosion.

No, I could not be so lucky. These mercenaries were too professional to get caught in their own blast.

Move! Move now! the inner voice insisted. I reached up, yanked the duct tape from my mouth. My cheeks burned as skin peeled away with the tape, the pain sharpening my dulled thoughts. I grasped the bumper of the van and hauled myself upright. Using the tire iron, I hobbled across the street into the neighbor's yard.

I should pound on their door for help.

No guarantee anyone would hear me over the sirens. Besides, they might be among the more intelligent who headed for their storm cellar when the noise started. In addition, Hawk and his team would not hesitate to kill anyone who tried to help me. So I limped around the corner of the house and stumbled into a small grove of pecan trees before collapsing against one of the slender trunks. Rain fell in a torrential downpour, thunder shook the earth, the sirens felt like they came from inside my head, and I thought that in all probability no one heard the man-made explosion.

I dragged my right leg and struggled to another tree trunk and admitted the truth.

I was not going to put nearly enough distance between the van and myself before those horrible men returned and realized I was missing.

I kept waiting for the sound of surprised shouts, pounding feet on wet pavement as the killers spread out to look for me. Desperately I hoped they would consider flight a higher priority. I did not waste energy looking back. I closed my thoughts against the death of my friends, of Mud Rain. There was no doubt in my mind their house had disintegrated with the same deadly force that destroyed my parents' home. No one could survive that kind of destruction. Tears ran down my cheeks. I had absolutely no idea what to do. I couldn't make it to the main boulevard beyond the gate. I thought about waiting for emergency crews to arrive. Ambulance crews, police, firefighters, all of them offered safety and protection.

But could they keep me out of the reach of the Charlie Network? Hawk's team descended on my home without warning, blew up two houses, killed multiple people. Yet they had left no trace. They were like ghosts. Everywhere at once, invisible, sweeping down to attack me without anyone's knowledge.

And if I went to the police, told them about Hawk, the Charlie Network, would that clear Jeremiah? Or would they think I was a fool trying to protect my husband? The circumstantial evidence certainly condemned him well enough. And if they refused to believe me about Jeremiah, would they believe me if I told them I needed to stay hidden, avoid the inevitable media circus? Would they believe me about the whole Charlie Network, or would they chalk up my efforts as the rantings of a half-crazed victim suffering emotional loss and injury-induced delusions?

I needed to disappear. Otherwise, Hawk and his Charlie Network would find me and kill me.

I reached the gate, punched in the code, hobbled with painful slowness as the gate swung open, wondered why the van hadn't appeared yet. The sirens suddenly wound down, and the ensuing silence seemed profound despite the continued noise of the storm.

I made it outside the gated neighborhood and was ready to collapse when I saw an object so totally out of place it could only be a hallucination. I stared for what must have been at least a full minute.

A motorcycle leaned against one of the trees a little ways in from the street. I dropped the tire iron and limped over. Unable to control the sobs of pain, I stared at the object, then reached out and touched it.

It was real. I leaned down and noticed a small GPS screen attached to the handlebars. I frowned at the tiny blip, then swung my eyes towards the Parsons' property. The blip was not moving. The blip was near the Parsons' address.

The van was parked near the Parsons' address.

Thoughts slowed. I heard the rain around me, the thunder crash again as lightning met earth. I stared at the motorcycle, the one from the garden shed behind my parents' house. As surreal as it seemed, I realized it was true. Thoughts clicked and with sudden clarity I saw the picture.

Jeremiah knew about the shed, the motorcycle, and the bunker. He must have been nearby when Hawk's men took the bodies to Shawnee.

Had he been near the house where I had been held? Had he left to warn the Parsons, to get them away from danger?

Regardless of his actions, he was in the vicinity now. He had to be. I turned back towards the Parsons' house.

How could I contact Jeremiah and evade Hawk and his team? Or had Hawk and his team of killers intercepted Jeremiah? Was he dead now, too? Had he been inside with the Parsons and Mud Rain when Hawk and his men blew the house?

I put a hand to my head. Leaning against the security wall, soaking wet, in pain, I couldn't seem to unravel what it all meant, what I was supposed to do.

I glanced at the gate. Still no van. That didn't make sense. Even if I knocked out Freeman, Hawk and his team would have returned to the vehicle by now. I felt hot despite the cold rain and wind, and I couldn't get my eyes to focus. I tried to take a step forward and fell flat onto my face. My cheek banged against something cold, hard, and slender, and I curled my fingers around the tire iron. Slowly, painfully, I staggered upright, then reached the pavement and stumbled along the broad boulevard. I needed to put distance between myself and that stupid van, but I could hardly put one foot in front of the other. Using the tire iron to hold me up, I didn't have enough energy to stumble fast enough to get away from the main road.

Rain turned to a cold mist. Faces swirled around me, shifting in and out of focus, their features pale, their eyes hollow. I threw my arm over my face to protect myself, and toppled into the grass along the side of the pavement. I curled against the faces, afraid they belonged to the killers.

I must have blacked out, because when I became aware of my surroundings again, gray, early morning light filtered through heavy clouds. Lying on the grass on the side of the road meant that I would be difficult to find, but I needed help. I uncurled my arms and shivered.

I managed to regain my feet and kept moving, turning randomly right or left whenever I reached an intersection. I lost all sense of direction.

Vague realization made me stop and look down, and it took me a long time before I recognized I was no longer on street pavement, but seemed to be on some sort of broad, redbrick paving stone. I stared at the path. It looked familiar, like an old friend.

Why did the redbrick path look so familiar?

My vision cleared abruptly and I found myself staring at a mailbox. I squinted, focused on the address. Shock rolled slowly down my spine when I recognized the name and street.

I knew the person who lived here. He had been a close, close friend of my father and mother. I had no idea how I had managed to end up on his front walk, but I didn't waste the miracle. Dragging my right leg, I limped along the redbrick, reached the front door, rang the bell. When the door finally opened, I cried tears of relief.

"Oh my God. Mattie Tyler." Strong, familiar, gentle hands scooped me up, held me close, carried me inside. I thought irrationally how much water I was dripping all over the highly polished hardwood floors.

"I've been watching the news nonstop since I heard about your disappearance." The soft, familiar voice shook with anxiety. "The police and rescue are all over the Parsons' place. Explosion. The reports just came on with an update saying Jeremiah was found in front of the wreckage. The police are looking all over for you."

His words drifted through my mind, but I heard only jumbled noise that didn't make any sense. Gentle hands laid me onto a soft bed, covered me up with warm fuzzy blankets.

"I need to call an ambulance and get you to the hospital."

Images of police cars flashed before my eyes. I couldn't focus, could only see a blur of white hair and kind features. I shook my head violently in an effort to convince him not to call any rescue, no law enforcement. Clutching his arm, I began rambling, my thoughts jumbled up, sobbing as I tried to tell him what had happened, the danger Jeremiah and I were in, and if the police found out where I was, then the Charlie Network would find out, too.

Chapter Eleven

Dazed, weak, and disoriented, Hawk shook his head and tried to clear the pain and ringing in his ears. He rolled off whomever he had just knocked flat. Chunks of wood and brick jabbed his back and legs, pain throbbed through his head, the surroundings spun wickedly until he thought he might throw up. He shook his head again, unable to hear a damned thing except a god-awful ringing. He squinted down at the motionless figure beside him.

"Bloody hell, Tyler, you were to wait with Mattie in the van." Hawk felt his vocal chords utter the words but could not hear his voice. He tried to sit up, fell over into the debris. Duct tape still bound his hands, though in the chaos when Bill Parsons fired his shotgun, he managed to squeeze his legs through his arms to get his hands in front of him. Miraculously he still gripped the handgun he'd wrestled from Marks. But he felt like a trussed up Christmas bird waiting for the spit. Rain and wind pelted him, lightning danced and flashed with strobe-like frequency. He felt rather than heard constant, ground-shaking thunder.

All in all, it seemed rather like he'd been blown to Jupiter. Laying the gun on the soaked lawn, he raised his hands to one ear, felt something warm and sticky, brought his bound hands before his eyes.

Blood. A lot of it.

Memory oozed back. That ruddy Freeman caught him by surprise at the house, dazed him, bound his hands with the intent of leaving him in the Parsons' place when it blew. But instead of confronting three frightened civilians when they stormed the residence, Williams, Marks, and Cumbers ran into a hornet's nest. Bill Parsons, warned by Cumbers when he burst through the front door, had his military pump-action shot gun up and ready when they reached the living room. Parsons yelled for them to stop, saw Cumbers raise his weapon, and shot him. The slug smashed clean through Cumbers' chest and took out Williams standing right behind him. In the split-second Marks stood open-mouthed, Hawk dropped to the floor, swiped the man's legs from underneath him, then wriggled his feet through his bound hands. The cases sprawled across the hardwood floor to bang against the far wall, and Marks reached for his gun. Hawk kicked him in the head, then kicked the gun from his hands. Parsons yelled at him to stop, he yelled back there were more outside and to get Becky and the boy to the storm cellar. Scooping up Marks' gun and hoping Parsons wouldn't mis-read his actions and put a shotgun slug though his chest, Hawk straddled each of the downed killers and ended any possibility of further trouble from them by firing a bullet into the back of each of their skulls. Worried the sudden motion of the cases might have jarred the detonators, he crossed the room as Parsons' wife and the boy scrambled for the storm cellar, knelt down and opened one of the cases; saw with shocked disbelief a timer counting down final seconds. He screamed at Bill to run, then took off for the front door.

The first bomb detonated, smashing him through the wrecked front entrance and into Tyler. The second one blew moments later.

He pushed himself shakily to his hands and knees. Tyler had not stirred. Hawk leaned over, rain streaming down his face, and noticed the Ute's ears a bloody mess, too. He lay so still Hawk thought he might be dead, until he pressed his fingers beneath his jaw and felt a pulse.

Why in bloody hell did Tyler run for the house? Had he seen Hawk with his hands tied and assumed he needed help? He should've realized he needed to deal with Freeman in the van and rescue Mattie.

It was quite obvious Tyler and Healing Water correctly interpreted his message, and Tyler subsequently followed the van to Norman. Hawk squinted through the storm as a long-overdue thought wandered into his brain.

Why wasn't the bloody van moving?

He frowned. Freeman would've witnessed everything from the driver seat of the van and realized Hawk doubled-crossed the team. By all rights Hawk should have a bullet in his skull by now.

Was Healing Water in the van with Mattie?

If Healing Water was now in the driver's seat, he would've witnessed Tyler and himself getting blown to the ground and should be moving the van closer to offer assistance.

In either case, the bloody van ought to have *moved by now*.

Hawk stared through the wind-driven rain at the blurred, reeling, immobile lump of the van. Maybe Jeremiah took out Freeman, left Mattie in the van. Mattie had an injured leg.

Well, she could still bloody well manage to roll the van closer.

Something was wrong. Something in addition to blowing his cover to hell and back, almost getting himself killed, and witnessing yet another house blown to bits. It went without saying Healing Water and Tyler would not be pleased over the destruction of two family homes. Add in Mattie's current condition and the bloody situation pretty much spelled the end of any reconciliation between himself and the two Utes.

He worked his feet beneath him, tried to stand. His head wasn't having any part of the idea and spun so badly he thought it might just launch off his shoulders. He fell heavily to the ground and lay there, nauseous and on the brink of passing out. He moved his head and looked at Tyler again. In his current condition, there was no way he could take the Indian with him. He needed help.

The sick feeling in his gut grew until it felt like an alien about to tear its way through his throat. He lay there and fought the blackness. Rain pounded harder. Lightning flashed continuous electrical bolts, thunder shook the ground beneath him.

Think!

No doubt he was concussed; his ears full of blood which made strawberry jam of his balance. Walking would be impossible. He could lay there and wait for emergency personnel to show up.

He really did not want to end up in jail, which is exactly where he'd be if he waited around for first responders.

Hawk tried again to focus on the wavering shadow of the motionless van. Cursing the storm, the Charlie Network, Healing Water, and Tyler, Hawk squinted through the storm as another long over-due thought occurred.

No lights had blinked on in any of the neighboring houses.

Were the neighbors deaf as posts? Or did they sleep like the dead?

As if in response to his thoughts a light blinked on in the house across the street, like a pale yellow eye snapping open to peer into the darkness.

Bloody hell. Hawk made it to his hands and knees, retrieved the handgun and worked it into the waistband of his cargo pants, then tried to crawl across what seemed a mile of lawn. He needed to get himself, Tyler, and that bloody van out of sight before neighbors realized what had happened.

Hawk made it to the curb, used the side of the van to brace himself as he staggered to his feet. Sagging against the side, he lurched to the rear doors. It took him longer than it should have to realize what he saw.

One of the panel doors hung open.

That wasn't right. The team shut both doors after they got out. And even if they had forgotten, Freeman would've shut them.

And to make matters worse, neither Healing Water nor Freeman appeared.

Grasping the butt of the gun with both hands, Hawk staggered against the panel door. Weakness broke over him like a giant tsunami wave. He squeezed his eyes shut, mentally pushed through the incapacitating frailty, forced thoughts off the wild merry-go-round in his head.

"Mattie!" His voice vibrated, a buzz of noise distorted into nonsense by the ringing in his ears. It went without saying; he'd never catch her reply. He struggled into the back of the van, out of the elements raging around him.

A dark form sprawled motionless on the floor. Hawk jammed the handgun into the waistband of his pants, then crawled to the body, squinting in an effort to focus, his hands rolling the figure onto his side before his fingers pressed beneath his jaw.

It was Freeman, and he was dead.

Serves the bloody fucking git right, Hawk thought. He blinked, but could not see Mattie. His brain chugged out an incredible and unforeseen complication.

Mattie had somehow escaped.

He edged to the passenger window. He couldn't be sure, but he thought he saw shadowy forms running through the darkness towards the destroyed house. Lightning still flashed but with less frequency. No one yet seemed to have noticed the van sitting a block away. But since he couldn't hear a damned thing he would have no warning if someone approached the vehicle.

With a last glance around the interior to make sure Mattie hadn't somehow hidden herself in a corner, Hawk struggled to the rear of the van, checked to see no one stood nearby, then dropped onto the pavement. He fell heavily against the side and collapsed to his hands and knees. He had to get across the boulevard and crawling wasn't going to cut it. Bracing his hands against the side of the van, he pushed himself to his feet. Feeling like he was on a careening amusement park ride, he staggered across the black pavement. Darkness spun in front of him, and he fell hard to his knees. If anyone spotted him reeling like a wayward drunk they would know something was wrong. This was a gated upper class residential community, not the slums in lower London.

A grove of trees loomed around him. Hawk collapsed among the concealing trunks, closed his eyes and leaned his forehead against the cool, smooth bark. Blackness and buzzing surrounded him.

That was no good. Hawk opened his eyes, squinted again; trying to decide whether there was increasing activity across the street or whether his eyes were playing tricks. Slumped deep within the trees in the darkness hid him from curious eyes. He tried to think, to make sense of things.

Where in the bloody hell had Mattie got to? How in the world had she managed to escape with a broken leg? Had Tyler and Healing Water shown up while he and Parsons were fighting those bloody killers in the house? Had they killed Freeman? Had Healing Water whisked Mattie away while Tyler tried to follow him into the house?

Hawk rubbed his bound hands against his forehead and tried to generate enough strength to move. He cursed softly, vilely. Slowly, relying on training so ingrained he did not think, Hawk pushed himself to his knees, then used the tree as support to struggle to his feet. He made his way carefully from trunk to trunk, missing often and collapsing to crawl until he felt the next sturdy trunk beneath his tied hands. It would be too easy to get turned around and go in circles, or worse, end up in plain sight in the middle of the boulevard. He tried to keep the street to his right. Wavering, blurred figures appeared to be crouching around Tyler, who had not moved.

Bloody fucking Indian, Hawk thought. It would serve him right if he had gone and got himself killed. He and Healing Water should have stuck around to offer assistance, waited for him before whisking Mattie to safety.

Strobes of flashing lights caught his attention. Fire trucks, police cars, and ambulances filed down the boulevard, the rain softening the emergency lights until they twinkled like Christmas decorations.

Hawk stumbled deeper into the orchard, winced at the thought that a two-year-old could follow his trail, paused when he reached a wide-open lawn with flowerbeds and shrubbery. His strength gave out and he fell on his face, pushing his feeble legs and scooting along on his belly across the miles of open space, trying to use the landscaping for concealment and failing miserably. After what seemed like years, he reached an average height perimeter wall fortunately constructed more for looks than security. He scrambled over and collapsed into a thorny hedge. He lay there, unable to coordinate any sort of movement. The pain in his head roared like rockets blasting their way to the moon, and he just managed to control the urge to throw up all over the soft earth. He felt consciousness slipping and lacked the strength to fight it.

~ * ~

Emergency lights pulsated through the rain and over the ruins of the house as one of several Norman police officers on the scene ran to Sergeant Hayes.

"Sir, it's Jeremiah Tyler," he panted. "The one the PCSD put an APB out on. He's out cold. The medics are taking him to Norman Regional Hospital."

Hayes grunted as an ambulance siren wound up. "Anyone contacted the PSCD yet?" He hollered over the noise.

The officer waited until the emergency vehicle disappeared from the neighborhood, the siren fading in the distance. "Pottawatomie County Sheriff's Department is sending detectives down as soon as the weather clears," he answered.

Hayes scanned the destruction, the neighbors milling around despite the stormy conditions. He frowned when his eyes paused on a van parked along the curb. Squinting through the rain, he glanced up and down the dark boulevard but no other vehicles were visible, not even in the broad driveways.

"That seems odd, parking a vehicle on the street in this

neighborhood," he mused. He turned his attention back to the officer. "Start asking around; find the owner of that van."

~ * ~

It was well into Wednesday afternoon, the sun hung above a large bank of black clouds crowding the southwest horizon, the air hot and humid with the promise of more rain sooner than later. Detective Harrison Gates climbed out of his sedan. He had long ago shed his suit coat and tie, his sleeves rolled up as far as they would go. Jason Reeves exited the passenger side, wearing his usual white Polo shirt and blue slacks. They paused for several minutes and surveyed the destruction, then walked over to the Sergeant, who stood near a cluster of police cruisers.

"Harrison Gates, Pottawatomie County Sheriff's Department," he said, extending his hand. "This is my partner, Jason Reeves."

"Sergeant Jeff Hayes." The Sergeant carried himself with military crispness, his gray hair cropped close to his head. He looked both men up and down, saw arrogance in the young detective's expression, and took an instant dislike to him.

Gates waved an arm at the scene, now roped off with yellow police tape. "What the hell happened here?"

"Bomb Squad just cleared the area. Said it was some kind of detonation." Sergeant Hayes turned, but instead of heading to the pile of rubble, he led them to an unmarked white van parked about a block down from the site. Crime scene tape surrounded the vehicle, too. The men ducked under the tape and the Sergeant led the detectives to the open rear panel doors.

"It gets worse." Hayes sounded pissed as hell.

Gates shot him a look, then glanced inside. A body bag in the back of the van, the stench turned his stomach sour.

Hayes explained. "Got his head bashed in. No weapon yet. County Coroner is here. We're waiting on transport. Everything is tied up from the storm last night."

"Got a picture circulating?" Reeves asked.

"Not yet," the Sergeant replied. "We'll get those out once we get the bodies to the morgue."

Gates stared at the destruction, avoided eye contact with Reeves.

"Remind you of anything? Like the Lamont estate?" Reeves looked at him.

The Sergeant nodded at them. "I heard what happened in Shawnee. That's what I'm thinking. Maybe a terrorist cell?"

Reeves shook his head. "Tyler's a son of a bitch, but I'll bet my reputation he's not involved with a terrorist cell. He's just a greedy bastard willing to do anything to get his hands on his wife's money."

Gates shot his partner an irritated look, then added. "They wouldn't bother to hit individual homes. They'd be after bigger targets." The three men turned to stare at the pile of rubble. "Whose house is this?"

"William and Rebecca Parsons. I've been too busy giving out orders to find out anything else yet." Hayes turned his head to a group of officers busy with more crime scene tape. "Hey, Winston!"

The nearest officer turned and strode across the lawn.

"This is Detectives Gates and Reeves, from PCSD," Hayes said as an introduction. Winston nodded towards the two detectives.

"Any more information about the owners of the house?" Hayes asked.

Winston pulled a small notepad from the left breast pocket of his uniform and flipped some pages. "William and Rebecca Parsons. Lived here twenty-five years. No children, though neighbors say they've been caring for a youth with special needs," he told them.

"Any relation to the Lamonts in Shawnee?" Gates asked, but he already knew the answer.

Officer Winston shook his head. "Not so far, Sir."

Reeves turned his attention to the pile of debris. "This looks like a repeat of the Lamont place. Same thing. Exact same thing." He turned to Hayes. "Your boys found Jeremiah Tyler here?"

Hayes nodded. "He was out cold. Looked like the explosion caught him."

Reeves grinned. "We've got Tyler on site this time."

"Hey, Sarge! Over here!" Another officer waved at them from across the wide front lawn surrounding the Parsons' residence. He stood beside a large oak tree fronting a grove of tall, magnificent hardwoods in full foliage. The Sergeant and the two detectives walked over.

"I opened it up and took a look inside," the officer motioned towards a military backpack lying against the backside of the tree.

Hayes' face went purple. *"You did what?"*

The officer swallowed.

Hayes didn't give him a chance to explain. "You opened an unidentified backpack? Do you have a goddamn death wish? You could've been blown to hell and back! How come no one found this and notified Bomb Squad?"

The young officer's face turned beet-red.

Gates knelt down and stared at the backpack and the items inside. "A broken down sniper rifle, looks like," he commented as he leaned forward for a closer look. "Ammunition, thermal optics." He glanced at Reeves, then at Hayes.

"Yeah, we'll take care of it," Hayes barked. He turned to the young officer. "Get on the horn to Bomb Squad and tell them to get their asses back out here." He ran a hand over his short gray hair. "My god, I can't believe we missed this." He gazed at the destruction. "We've been focused on the mess under all that rubble. canines have nosed out some body parts. We've found three heads so far. All males."

Gates threw him a puzzled frown. "No sign of the wife?"

Hayes shook his head. "Not so far."

"What?" Reeves stared at the Sergeant. "Are you sure?"

"Anything else?" Gates prompted when the Sergeant frowned.

Hayes studied the detective. "I know it's early, but the County Coroner's preliminary report stated all three heads have gunshot wounds. Back of the head. Execution style."

Reeves nodded. "Ah, now I'm starting to get the picture. Tyler, he was armed?"

Hayes tramped his way across the rain-soaked lawn. Reeves and Gates followed.

"Well?" Reeves prompted, annoyed.

"I know what you're thinking," he said as they walked. "Tyler made it to the scene and shot the intruders. I hate to break this to you, but what we're finding isn't fitting that line of thinking. The weapon on him hasn't been fired. And there's no residue on his clothes or hands."

Reeves stopped mid-stride and caught Hayes by the sleeve. "Are you sure? Did your boys follow procedure?"

Hayes looked annoyed. "Of course we did. Bagged his hands, bagged his clothes in the ER, tested everything. We got nothing."

Jason glanced at the surrounding puddles. "No matter. The rain obviously washed things away." They walked over to where three body bags lay on the ground. CSI team members and three officers with K-9s sifted through the debris. The County Coroner hovered nearby as the pile of body parts grew.

"What a mess," Gates commented.

"Looks like we've got Tyler on murder charges this time," Reeves declared, his expression smug.

Gates ignored his partner's statement. He eyed the destruction and wondered whether CSI could possibly get things cleaned up before the next storm system hit.

"Any word on whether he's awake yet?" he asked.

Hayes pulled out his cell phone. "I'll call the hospital, get an update."

Fire trucks left one by one, then ambulances arrived to carry away the body bags. The hospital reported Tyler remained unconscious. Hours later an Oklahoma State Trooper arrived on the scene. A uniformed officer climbed out and walked over as Gates unfolded his already soaked handkerchief and mopped his face. Reeves stood talking to a group of Norman cops.

"Harrison, long time no see," he said as he extended a hand.

Gates shook it, his face breaking in to a broad grin. "Shawn Evans. How's life treating you? Still on the church softball team?"

Shawn laughed. "Yeah. Good stress relief. You should try it."

Gates mopped his face again. "What brings you out here?"

The state trooper's expression sobered. "I read that you and Reeves are on the Lamont case. I saw the mug shots being circulated. I may have something in connection."

"Let's hear it." Gates stuffed his soaked handkerchief into a back pocket.

"Well, early Tuesday morning I was on site of a wreck caused by the tornado that blew over Interstate Forty west of Shawnee." Evans opened his mouth to continue when Gates' cell phone rang. Gates held up his hand.

"Hang on a sec. I probably should answer this." He un-clipped his cell. "Hello, Gates here." He frowned. "Who the hell is this?"

His face blanched, and he whirled frantically towards the pile of rubble. "Oh, my God…who is this…damn it, don't hang up!" He punched in some numbers. "Dispatch? Track the call that just came through my cell." He stuffed his phone into a pocket, then ran towards the cluster of officers talking with Reeves.

"Get everyone over here! NOW! I just received an anony-mous tip that there are three people trapped in the storm cellar beneath this mess!"

Chapter Twelve

Awareness crept back when two hands eased beneath his armpits, and Hawk opened his eyes, squinting against the brightness of full daylight. The sun glared down from high overhead. Instinct told him it was early afternoon and that he had been out for several hours.

"Got yourself hid back here pretty good." Joe Healing Water muttered, then noticed the dried blood clogging Hawk's ears. He shook his head, saw duct tape wrapped around his wrists, pulled out a pocketknife, and freed Hawk's hands.

"You look like shit. Guess things didn't go the way you planned?"

Hawk stared at him, vague recognition flickering across his face. He tried to move but could not lift his head.

"C'mon. Might as well get you out of here before the cops show up and drag your ass to jail." Joe pulled the injured man gently to his feet, steadied him when he swayed, helped him lurch towards the open passenger door of a dented, rusty, pick-up truck idling on a narrow alley behind the gated community and pecan orchard.

Joe eased Hawk into the passenger side, shut the door, then got in and shifted. The gears rasped and rattled as he guided the floor stick into first gear. He glanced over; saw Hawk unconscious against the side of the door, then pointed the rattletrap vehicle down the alley.

~ * ~

Mid-morning Thursday, Jeremiah sat on the concrete bench in the holding cell, his elbows on his knees, his head in his hands. The dizziness was better and the ringing in his ears had diminished. But he couldn't get his thoughts to clear, nor could he put together the events of the past twenty-four hours. The doctor who released him into police custody this morning explained he suffered from a concussion, his confusion of events was common, and his memory would return.

Unfortunately, none of the doctor's explanations told him

why he was in a jail cell staring at a row of iron bars.

Door locks buzzed and a short stout man in a brown business suit entered the holding cell area of the Norman Police station. A young deputy sheriff accompanying him unlocked Jeremiah's cell. The man looked to be in his mid-forties and studied him with wide-set, serious brown eyes.

"Detective Harrison Gates."

Jeremiah rose to his feet, tottered, and reached out a hand to the concrete wall to steady himself. The spinning accelerated, his stomach began to roll, and he figured it better to sit down than throw up all over the detective. With a hand still on the wall, he eased himself back onto the concrete slab that served as a bed.

"How's your head?" the detective asked.

Jeremiah rested his head in his hands. "I have felt better."

"Do you know where you are?" When Jeremiah gently shook his head, the detective continued. "You're in the Norman police station. Do you remember why?"

Jeremiah met the detective's direct brown eyes. "No," he answered. "I do not."

Harrison Gates studied the man. His non-verbals supported his statement, but he remained wary. He'd met more than his fair share of pathological liars.

"My partner and I are transporting you to Shawnee." He waited for Tyler to ask why, watched for a flicker of understanding, memory of the Lamont residence explosion, something that would give him a clue the prisoner knew more than he was admitting.

Tyler revealed nothing.

Gates nodded to the deputy sheriff, who produced a pair of handcuffs. "Hands behind your back."

Jeremiah made it to his feet and turned around, felt cold steel as the young deputy sheriff snapped on a pair of handcuffs. He looked too young to be a law enforcement officer.

"I've got it from here." Gates dismissed the youth, took Jeremiah by the arm and walked with him down the hallway and out the exit to the parking lot where a Pottawatomie County Sheriff's Department cruiser sat. Gates glanced at the empty driver's seat.

"Looks like my partner is still in the building." He opened the rear door, guided Jeremiah's head as he angled onto the hard plastic. He leaned in, buckled Jeremiah in, then rested his arm on the hood of the car.

"My partner and I aren't exactly seeing eye to eye on this investigation. He's sure you're responsible. I keep trying to tell him all we've got is a bunch of circumstantial evidence."

Jeremiah listened, his expression cool.

"You got anything that might help us get on the right track?" Gates pressed.

Jeremiah released a measured sigh and allowed his eyes to drift to the building behind the cop. That the detective thought he would be naïve enough to fall for a very badly disguised good-cop-bad-cop routine was almost laughable.

Gates drummed his fingers on the hood of the car.

Interesting, Jeremiah mused, as he casually watched the man's non-verbals. The detective appeared more than a little agitated.

A thin, angular man with a skinny head and neck walked to the cruiser. His light brown hair added a somewhat lopsided look to his young, bony features.

Jason Reeves threw up his hands when he reached them. "Why did you insist we transport this lowlife to Shawnee, Harrison?"

"Most of our evidence is up there," Gates replied, his voice low. He made a downward motion with his hand in an effort to signal Reeves to keep his objections to himself.

Reeves ignored the gesture. "Well, we'd be better off keeping him here in Norman. We've got enough evidence down here to proceed. Our own department is overwhelmed with storm clean-up."

Gates shrugged and opened the passenger door. "So is Norman, after last night. Trust me, I've got my reasons."

"Well, your reasons suck." Reeves flopped behind the wheel, slammed the door, twisted the key to start the car, then shoved the shifter into gear. The two cops fell into a tense silence as the cruiser rolled through town, then accelerated onto the Interstate.

The sun shone in a cloudless sky. The southwestern horizon appeared clear, indicating a break from recent severe weather cells. Jeremiah watched the scenery glide past as they made the hour trek to Shawnee.

"What day is this?" Jeremiah asked, breaking the silence.

Gates turned his head to look at him. "Thursday."

"Time?" Jeremiah inquired.

Gates glanced at his watch. "Thirteen ten."

Jeremiah kept his expression neutral. "Pardon?"

"One-ten," Gates' eyes narrowed. "And don't give me that. You were military."

Jeremiah shrugged. "Served a while ago." He'd hoped security firewalls would deny them access to his military history. That they had gained knowledge about that part of his background meant they knew all about his expertise on everything from weapons to explosives. He sighed. They might as well cart him off to the state pen now.

"That kind of lame excuse won't get you anywhere," Gates snapped before twisting around to glare through the windshield.

Reeves snorted, and opened his mouth.

"Shut up, Jason," Gates ordered curtly. "Save conversation for when we get to the station."

Flat terrain slipped by as they cut east on the south side of Oklahoma City and headed for Shawnee. They reached their destination and led Jeremiah to the interrogation room.

"Sit down," Reeves said, pulling out a metal chair. Jeremiah hesitated; watching for an indication the cop might remove the handcuffs. When Reeves just stared at him, Jeremiah shrugged and sat down. It wouldn't take long before the young detective realized small discomforts would do nothing to improve Jeremiah's cooperation.

Jeremiah sat motionless on the chair in the tiny room with a one-way mirror on the opposite wall. Harsh fluorescent lighting threw hard-lined shadows onto gray-tiled floor, gray walls, gray ceiling. *A psychological trick*, Jeremiah thought, to depress the suspect into thinking cooperation would be the best way to go. His shoulders ached from the muscle strain of having his hands cuffed behind him for so long. He knew the drill, was familiar with interrogation techniques, had been through a few that made this room look like a five-star hotel. They were not going to get any information from him that he did not want to give, but maybe their questions would trigger some memory, help him fill in the blanks clouding recent events.

"Cool character, isn't he?" Reeves muttered in the room on

the other side of the mirror when Gates joined him.

Gates frowned as he studied the prisoner through the one-way glass. "You didn't uncuff him," he accused.

"Of course I didn't." Jason sounded surprised.

Gates muttered an oath, spun on his heel, jerked open the observation room door. Pausing with his hand on the doorknob to the interrogation room, he blew out several heavy breaths to control his irritation. The two hours he had just spent arguing with the sheriff had not convinced the elected official to remove the young detective from this case. He opened the door.

"Sorry for the delay." He helped Tyler to his feet, then removed the restraints. "Have a seat."

Jeremiah rubbed his wrists, then sat down, and rested his clasped hands on the table.

Gates mused over the paleness beneath Jeremiah's dark complexion. He was weak, still recovering from almost being blown to smithereens. His condition ought to work in their favor, although if Reeves insisted on conducting the interrogation he didn't think they'd get very far. The doc who had overseen him at Norman Regional Hospital informed them about his amnesia.

"I'll be right back." In his irritation with Reeves, Gates forgot to bring the information folder with him. He left the room, strode back to the observation room.

"So, you think he really has amnesia? Or is he acting?" Reeves nodded towards the one-way glass when Gates entered.

"I'll find out which soon enough." Gates snapped, scooping up the yellow folder from a table.

"Let me at him. I'll get a written confession before dawn." Reeves brushed his hands over his blue slacks then rested his hands on his hips.

"The key here is to get him to cooperate. Going in there like a bull in a china shop won't help." Gates turned towards the door.

Reeves jabbed a finger at the window. "He possesses all the knowledge to have blown both those places. It's all there in his folder, all his training with CIA over the last seven years." He gestured towards the folder Gates held. "And now we've got four bodies. One in the van, three found shot dead in the wreckage. I'll bet his wife's buried on the Lamont property. We should get the dogs back out there." Reeves' eyes narrowed. "And you're treating him like a house guest."

Gates fought down his irritation. "Any sign of the camper Evans reported?"

"What camper? Who's Evans?" Reeves shot back.

"The state trooper I talked with down in Norman. Evans stuck around after we rescued the family trapped in the storm cellar. He gave a description and license number. As damaged as it was, the trailer ought to be easy enough to find." Gates raised an eyebrow. "Haven't you looked for it? I told you to search salvage yards and abandoned vehicles lists."

"Busy work," Reeves snorted. "And not connected with this case."

Gates stepped forward, jabbed the folder at Reeves. "This whole thing stinks of professional hits. If Tyler is involved, it's a sure thing he's using accomplices. We need to follow every lead."

Reeves stiffened. "Professional hits my ass. This is all about the Lamont fortune. And Tyler's the only lead we need."

"I'll be back." Gates opened the door.

"Leave Tyler alone. This is my interrogation. Don't go in there and screw it up," Reeves warned.

Gates turned slowly, a feeling of dread oozing along his spine. "Since when did this become your interrogation?"

"Since Sheriff Orlando gave it to me." Reeves crossed his arms and started rocking on the balls of his feet. Gates released a resigned sigh and held out the folder.

Over the next several hours Gates paced the observation room. Reeves was bent on using time and isolation to wear Tyler down. If a lawyer got wind of this, there'd be hell to pay. A deputy sheriff ducked in and offered both of them coffee. He thanked the guy and took a cup; Reeves declined the offer and instead worked his way through a bag brought in from McDonalds. Gates thumbed through Tyler's folder in an effort to ease his exasperation. He felt more than a little uneasy that they were missing something, and sorely wished he'd followed up on the camper himself. His gut nagged that the state trooper's report represented an important lead.

As evening hours crept closer to midnight, Gates watched Reeves frown and glance at his watch. Tyler had been in that room for hours. Long enough for someone with something to hide to start getting nervous. Long enough for him to request use of bathroom facilities, to ask for something to drink, to inquire what was taking so long, to get up and pace the room to get the circulation going in his backside.

Tyler had not moved or uttered a word since Gates left. He sat motionless, staring blankly through the one-way glass. Not one twitch from him since the time Reeves stuck him there.

"Damn." Reeves scowled.

"His behavior doesn't bode well for that confession you're trying to waggle," Gates muttered. "Whether you're willing to admit it or not, Reeves, Tyler is going to be a hard nut to crack."

~ * ~

Just before midnight Reeves brushed off the front of his shirt, tightened his belt a notch, then left the observation room and opened the door to the interrogation room. Tyler turned his head, met his eyes with an unreadable, penetrating stare.

"Want something to drink? Need to use the facilities?" Reeves asked, standing in the open doorway.

Tyler blinked. "No."

Reeves' expression poorly hid his opinions. "Changed your mind yet about a lawyer?"

Tyler blinked again. "No."

"Okay, then." Reeves shut the door; felt an odd sense of relief that Gates stood watching through the observation room. Tyler's utter cool sent a sliver of apprehension up his spine. He pulled out the chair on the opposite side of the table, the metal legs scraping loudly on the gray tile. He sat down, laid the folder in front of him, flipped the cover open and thumbed through the pile of reports and photographs. Then he closed the folder, leaned against the back of his chair, and let his hands drop to his lap.

"You've left quite a body count."

Tyler stared at him.

Reeves persisted. "Three bodies were recovered from the Parsons residence. All three of them had been shot. Care to shed some light?"

Tyler stared straight through him.

Reeves opened the file, lifted a couple of sheets. "David Mud Rain Tyler? He's your younger brother, correct?"

To Reeves' surprise, Tyler nodded. "Yes. That is correct."

"Three bodies were recovered from the wreckage," Reeves repeated. "The coroner confirmed all three skulls had execution style bullet holes in their heads." Reeves watched Tyler closely as he spoke and caught the miniscule flinch cross the Indian's features. An emotional response Tyler could not quite control.

Finally, a crack in the cement.

Memory didn't take days to return, as Jeremiah felt sudden, total recall jolt his system. He heard the shotgun explosion as clearly as though someone had just fired one in the room. He pictured the Parsons and his brother lying dead, the sound of the explosion as the detonation crumpled the Parsons' house, the weight that pinned him to the ground.

Reeves saw the pain clearly on Jeremiah's face as recall hit him. "So you knew them," he stated, retrieving a pen from his shirt pocket and making a check mark on one of the papers. "Things will go easier for you, if you help us ID the bodies. Why don't you start with the one in the van?"

Jeremiah stared at the detective. The image of his brother, Bill and his wife Becky, all lying dead twisted his stomach into knots. A body in the van could only mean Mattie had been found dead, too.

Reeves studied the notes he'd made among the sheets in the folder. "Four males. Your accomplices, I would guess? Give us some names."

Jeremiah jerked his eyes to stare at the detective's bent head. *Four males?* His mouth fell open, but he checked his impulse, and snapped his mouth closed before Reeves looked up.

Because he was looking down, Reeves missed Tyler's shocked reaction. But in the observation room, Detective Harrison Gates saw Tyler's momentary lapse and leaped to his feet.

Something was wrong.

"Did you see that?" He asked the young officer who had brought the coffee.

"See what?" The guy looked at him, a rookie, fresh from the academy. His uniform still had that brand new never-been-worn smell. He was almost as green as Reeves. Gates scowled. Where was the brass going for recruits? Day care facilities?

"Keep an eye on him." Gates ordered, then strode from the

observation room. He had years of experience reading body language that had honed his gut into a reliable instinct.

And right now his gut was screaming that Reeves had just majorly screwed up.

Gates rapped twice on the door of the interrogation room, opened the door, poked his head around the edge.

"Reeves, may I see you for a moment?"

Jason leaned back in his chair and glared at him. "What is it? Can't it wait?"

Gates shook his head. "It's important."

"It always is," Reeves grumbled. He stood, scooped up the file, and stalked through the door into the hallway. He closed the door behind him gently enough, but Tyler had already seen his annoyance, which wouldn't help him get the upper hand interrogating the man.

Reeves tapped his foot against the tile floor. "What is it?"

Gates got straight to the point. "Have you told him the Parsons and his brother are alive?"

"No." Reeves snapped.

"Why not?" Gates pressed.

"Because I don't want to, Harrison." Reeves turned his back on him and reached to open the door.

Gates leaned forward. "Well, he thinks the three bodies you're talking about are the Parsons and his brother."

Reeves froze, then turned. "That's bullshit. He knows who's dead. He shot them."

"I'm telling you, he thinks the Parsons and his brother were the ones who were shot." Gates jabbed a finger at the door. "And you're screwing up the interrogation by assuming otherwise. Not only that," his voice lowered to a hiss, "You're missing a key sign that could blow this whole thing wide open."

Reeves tilted his head back and sighed at the ceiling. "Harrison, I am trying to get him to admit he's behind all of this. Did it ever occur to you he hired a group of mercenaries to kill his brother and the Parsons so he'd be in the clear to inherit the Lamont estate, then decided to kill the men he hired? It happens all the time, the mastermind behind the operation cleaning up loose ends." He looked at Gates. "Only he misjudged the bombs and the Parsons made it to the storm cellar before the explosion.

There's been no news about his wife, and I'll bet he knows she's dead because he killed her."

Gates fought a losing battle with his annoyance. "Then please explain to me why ballistics isn't lining up with your theory Tyler shot the mercenaries he sent to kill the Parsons and his brother."

Reeves rolled his eyes. "Screw ballistics! They're wrong half the time anyway. So it wasn't the gun they found on Tyler. He got rid of the one he used, that's all."

Gates shook his head, but Reeves jumped in. "Tyler was *there*. He was *at the scene*. He has to be the one. We just haven't found the weapon yet."

Gates jabbed a finger towards the closed door of the interrogation room. "He thinks the three dead bodies are the Parsons and his brother!"

Reeves snorted. "Just where in the hell are you coming up with that nonsense?"

Gates inhaled deeply. "By the look on his face when you asked him to identify *four males*. Your statement confused the hell out of him."

Reeves shook his head. "Give it up, Bill."

"Reeves, you're an asshole. And you're turning this investigation into a witch hunt." Gates spun on his heel towards the observation room. He might as well go home and crawl into bed with his wife.

With his hand on the observation room door, Gates spun to face the young detective. "If Tyler was responsible for killing those four dirt bags, your statement would not generate a confused reaction."

"He's acting," Reeves snapped.

Gates wagged his head. "No, he wasn't. The only reason for his confusion is because he thinks the bodies you're talking about are the Parsons and his brother."

Gates gripped the doorknob as he swayed slightly. He was beyond exhausted.

"Look, I'm tired of you trying to tell me how to do my job," Reeves spat, poking his finger at Gates across the distance between them.

"Yeah, well, I'm tired of watching politics screw up my efforts to conduct a legit investigation." He closed his eyes, inhaled deeply. Then he opened his eyes and looked at the young detective. "You're wrong, Reeves."

"No I'm not!" Reeves hissed. "He knows those four dead men. He shot them! He was in the house just before it exploded. He executed the three we found in the remains, killed the one in the van."

Gates leaned his forehead against the door, then straightened and tried again to get Reeves to understand. "His reaction doesn't fit the circumstances you just described."

"What's it going to take?" Reeves exploded, stalking down the hall to where Gates stood. "Shall I march the Parsons and his brother into the room and confront him? Do you think that will get the correct fucking reaction?"

Gates' eyes narrowed. "No, Jason. Show him the faces of the four dead males." He stepped forward and thrust his face close to Reeves. "And when you show him the head shots, make sure you're looking at his goddamned face."

Reeves resisted the urge to push the older detective away. Instead, he watched Gates enter the observation room and slam the door shut. A sliver of doubt trickled through his brain. Gates' gut instincts were legendary in the department. Reeves scoffed at the idea but couldn't shake a nagging doubt Gates might be onto something. He stood in the hallway, rubbing the back of his neck and staring at the folder in his hand. He'd been glad for the promotion to detective, but he'd for sure request a different partner in future investigations. Harrison Gates was over the hill and he was screwing up Reeves' chance of getting this wrapped up before the Feds got involved. He walked slowly down the hall, opened the door and stepped into the interrogation room.

Tyler had not moved; the pallor of his face the only sign of his physical distress.

"Sorry about the interruption," Reeves said, closing the door and resuming his seat. He opened the folder and retrieved four photographs.

"Need you to ID these." He saw Tyler swallow and allowed himself a tiny smile. Gates was wrong. Tyler was nervous about having to stare at the photographs and pretend he didn't know them.

Without taking his eyes from Tyler's face, Reeves laid the

shots of the dead bodies, faces up, one by one onto the surface of the table, taking time to arrange them carefully in front of Tyler.

Unmistakable shock flash across Tyler's face. His eyes snapped to Reeves with such intensity, the young detective almost leaned away.

"These are from the Parsons' residence?" Tyler's question was low, his voice unbelieving. He touched one of the photos with the tips of fingers that visibly shook.

Reeves nodded, cleared his throat. "You should know them, since you shot them."

Tyler ignored his accusation. "You have not found other bodies?"

Reeves felt their positions suddenly flipped; felt he was the one being interrogated. He didn't like the feeling.

"Tell us where to find them, and we will," he snapped, tired of the charade. "And while you're at it, you can tell us what you've done with your wife, Mattie Tyler."

Tyler's coal black eyes bore through him, and Reeves shuddered. The guy was a hell of a liar.

Tyler relaxed against the back of his chair, rested his forearms on the table, laced his fingers over the middle photograph, and released a slow, measured sigh.

He did not utter another word the rest of the night.

Chapter Thirteen

It took until late Thursday afternoon before Hawk came around enough to make any sense. Joe Healing Water, dressed again in his dried out jeans and red plaid shirt, scowled as Hawk struggled to sit upright on one of the lower bunk beds in the underground bunker.

"You've been out of it for over twenty-four hours, and I need answers."

Hawk gave him a blank, confused stare. His ears still rang, his head spun like a carnival ride. He shook his head and brought his hands up to both ears, felt heavy bandages.

"How in bloody hell am I supposed to hear through all this?" He knew his mouth uttered the words, but his voice sounded like a buzzing beehive.

Irritably, Joe waved him over to the computer desk, didn't offer assistance when Hawk almost fell on his face trying to cross the room. Joe sat down and stabbed at the keyboard.

What the hell happened to our original plans?

Hawk collapsed in a metal folding chair beside Joe and squinted at the screen. He shook his head in resignation, glanced at the Indian's cold black eyes.

"Charlie sent Tacque's entire team. Something unforeseen but in retrospect, not unexpected."

Hawk shivered violently and thought about the damp, muddy clothes he still wore. "I need some dry clothes before we resume our conversation, or I'll end up with pneumonia and you'll be burying me alongside those other two chaps." He rose and staggered to some large metal storage cabinets.

What he wouldn't admit was that he didn't want to answer the questions he knew the old Indian would ask, mainly because he didn't have any explanations. He rummaged around the storage cabinets until he found some dry clothing. Pulling on a green T-shirt and a pair of camouflage cargo pants, he stumbled over to the bed he had slept in and dropped his wet clothes. He felt two sharp jabs in the middle of his back and turned around. Joe gestured towards the computer screen.

Hawk mused over the unpleasant flashback when Joe Healing Water had him dead to rights with a shotgun in the middle of the Comanche National Grasslands in the southeast corner of Colorado. That was an experience he did not want to repeat, and the Indian had more reason at the moment to get rid of him than he had at that bloody petrol station in the middle of nowhere.

So he stalled. "I'm trying to get some bloody circulation going."

Joe stalked over and sat down at the desk.

Grumbling, Hawk followed. Reluctantly, he leaned his hands on the back of the folding chair and read the questions on the screen.

Who the hell gave you permission to blow the Lamont place? Where is Jeremiah? And where the hell is Mattie?

Wishing he could put a couple of miles between himself and Healing Water, Hawk straightened, rounded the chair, and sank down. His head hurt, his ears buzzed, his body felt like it had been flogged. He barely had strength to stand, much less defend himself.

"I've been unconscious for the last bloody twenty-four hours. Tyler's probably in jail. He wasn't moving after he and I collided in front of the Parsons' place," he admitted.

Bloody Freeman. Why did he have to go and set timers on those sodding bombs? Did he contact Charlie and receive orders to get rid of the entire team?

That didn't make sense. The Charlie Network would not be so callous with their mercenaries.

He squinted when Joe scowled at him and jabbed a finger at the computer screen.

"As for Mattie," Hawk hesitated, then plowed on. "I left her with Freeman in the van. I've no idea where she's got to."

Joe turned and stabbed the keyboard again.

Well, according to the news, your Freeman was found dead in the van, and the police are searching for Mattie.

Hawk sighed. "A bit awkward, this."

So far as he could see, Mattie's disappearance and Freeman's death meant that somehow she managed to bash Freeman's head in then make an escape on an infected, severely compromised, and unsupported broken leg. Impossible, Hawk mused, shaking his head, unaware of Joe's eyes on him.

How in bloody hell had Mattie managed to kill Freeman and disappear from the back of the van? And where the bloody hell had she gone? And if she indeed managed to escape on her own, why did she not wait for the police and emergency personnel?

His eyes met Joe's, who studied him like a falcon eyeing a fat rat. He blew out a sigh. "As for blowing two houses to hell and back, I lacked reason enough to convince six bloody killers not to."

Joe turned his attention to the keyboard, his stone-faced expression sending a chill along Hawk's spine. Bloody inconvenient, he thought, that he couldn't make a miraculous recovery and stand a better chance of defending himself. He gave in to the urge, peered beneath, then around the edges of the desk. When he straightened, Joe's eyebrows quirked.

"Looking for a bloody sawed off shotgun."

Joe snorted, stabbed the keyboard. Hawk leaned forward.

Don't need one.

Hawk grunted. In his current condition, he would definitely come up on the losing end if things got physical. Joe's aged fingers danced across the keyboard, and Hawk's eyes narrowed.

"For an old man who runs a station in the middle of nowhere, you seem quite familiar modern technology."

Joe ignored him and continued typing.

According to news reports, Tyler's in jail over at the Pottawatomie County Sheriff's office.

Hawk's scowl deepened. "Well, if you already knew his location, why drill me?"

Joe typed again, his expression stony.

Checking your reliability.

Hawk pursed his lips, rubbed his head with a hand. He shrugged and slumped against the back of the folding chair. Sodding Indian. Nobody seemed willing to trust anybody at the moment. For good reason, he reflected sourly. The last time a mission went this bad he himself ended up in hospital with third degree burns all over his back and legs.

You know who Charlie is?

Hawk folded his hands in his lap. "I've an idea. You're not going to like it."

He squinted at the screen as Joe stabbed at the keys.

Tell me and I'll decide that for myself.

Hawk stood and weaved across the room before collapsing onto one of the bottom bunks.

"Bloody hell," he spat. "I should've cut out on that bloody fucking mountain after the chopper arrived." He saw Joe typing again, rose, ordered his feet to walk a straight line. He stumbled, fell twice, struggled to his feet, uttered several scathing oaths that he regretted not being able to hear bounce around the underground room. He reached the desk and squinted at the computer screen.

Where's Mattie?

Hawk straightened, mused over the uncomfortable truth.

"As I've said earlier, I've no idea where she's got to," he stated flatly. "Or how she managed her disappearing act. Or how she managed with a fucked up leg to kill one of Charlie's best men before she made her escape from that bloody van."

Joe's fingers danced.

You were supposed to tell her Jeremiah was coming to get her.

Hawk dropped his gaze to the floor, rubbed his forehead with his fingers. "I was rather compromised at the time and couldn't get a message to her. I hoped Tyler would sum up the situation and get to her before Freeman could do any more damage." He gave up the idea of trying to walk across the room again and sat down beside Joe.

Joe's fingers typed again.

She must've panicked. After watching you torch her parents' house, she would've guessed what you were about to do and thought she was going to watch her friends and Jeremiah's brother die in the explosion. And being Mattie, she found a way out and took out your driver while she was at it.

"And in doing so, threw another ruddy wrench into our already wrecked plans," Hawk grumbled. He needed a shower, a shave, and his hearing back. A sponge bath and a disposable razor would be acceptable solutions to his first two problems. But it would take days, possibly a couple of weeks, before the tinnitus subsided enough for him to hear again.

Joe stood and walked to a small under-counter storage cabinet, retrieved a bottle of water, unscrewed the top and took a drink. Hawk found himself admiring the underground bunker.

The walls and ceiling were clay earth supported by four-by-four studs every sixteen inches or so. Thick, heavy hardwood trunks formed beams across the ceiling. He did not have to bend over, but the ceiling was within easy reach.

"Does Mattie know this place?" he asked.

Joe nodded. He took another long pull from the water bottle, set it down on the desk beside the keyboard, then resumed his seat and began typing.

Her father had it renovated and expanded after an F-5 tornado hit the state several years ago. He created the exit at the back of the property in case the house was destroyed and the inside access got blocked.

"So we've two exits?"

Joe shook his head, stretched his fingers, typed again.

Thanks to you, debris now blocks the passage to the house. Why?

"Because we need a second exit besides the one at the back of the property. Just in case." Hawk sat motionless. "So, Mattie knows about this underground bunker. Might she try to get here?"

Joe scowled at him and went back to typing.

She has no transportation, no way to get from Norman all the way to here. Especially with a broken leg.

Hawk stared at the screen for a long uncomfortable silence. Well, probably silence for Joe. His silence was filled with incessant ringing.

"How in bloody hell did she manage a disappearing act?" He shook his head. "Rescue crews should've found her, packed her off to hospital. Her leg was in bad shape."

Joe thrust his nose into Hawk's face. His mouth moved, his black brows furrowed with anger. Hawk didn't attempt to lip-read. He imagined well enough what the old Indian shouted.

Joe clamped his lips into a thin line, whipped around, and began typing. Hawk leaned over, saw the language and grimaced. He skipped down to a line that held a question he could answer.

How bad was her leg, you bastard?

Another question Hawk did not want to answer. He cleared his throat. "We removed the cast to make her more mobile, less visible. In theory, not having a cast should also have aided her escape when Tyler came for her." He started to add that it got banged up a bit when the tornado threw them around the camper, then thought it would help his longevity if he kept that thought to himself.

He wasn't about to admit the devastating, inhumane mutilation Carson created, tying that bloody fucking tourniquet the way he had.

"Might she be in a hospital?" He mused aloud. "And if so, can you access local hospital inpatient lists to find out?"

Joe shook his head, typed again.

Already thought of that one. I can't get a list of patients because of security measures.

Hawk motioned for Joe to move. Joe stood and Hawk took his seat in front of the computer screen. "Let me work on this a bit, see if I can get some information."

Joe leaned over, elbowed Hawk's hands out of the way.

I tried typing her name into every hospital site in the area, including Oklahoma City. I've also looked under Jane Doe.

"Jane Doe. An alias? I imagine she'd be admitted under something besides her real name, particularly if the police are trying to keep news of her whereabouts out of the media." He concentrated on working through firewalls and lost track of time before he finally leaned back and shook his head. Joe stood nearby the entire time, staring at the screen. And probably muttering oaths Hawk didn't want to hear anyway.

He sighed. "I've located several Jane Does, including one in the Norman ICU." He risked a glance at the old Indian.

Joe leaned over, his fingers jabbing the keyboard.

Some of those Jane Does are dead.

Movement caught his eye, and Hawk turned his attention to the security screens monitoring the property above them as a Shawnee Police cruiser pulled to a stop along the drive. Hawk straightened in his chair. "Took them long enough. A bit thick, if you ask me, not checking the Lamont scene before now."

Both men watched two officers exit the cruiser and stride towards the fresh mounds of earth. When they caught sight of the bodies, one of them ran back to the cruiser, his mouth against the radio snapped to his shoulder. The other ran for the trunk and retrieved yellow crime scene tape. In less than fifteen minutes, officers, cruisers, and media trucks swarmed up the drive.

Joe waved impatiently at Hawk to move, then began typing.

Maybe we should ask them if they've seen Jeremiah or Mattie.

"Your sarcasm is duly noted," he muttered.

Joe's expression hardened.

You'd better hope and pray Mattie's not one of those dead Jane Does.

Hawk stared at the typed statement for a long time. "ICU. That rings true. I'll bet Queen's money she's there."

Joe typed again.

If she's in ICU, that means she's critical. He folded his arms across his chest, his onyx eyes black and cold as he stared at Hawk.

Hawk ran a hand over his disheveled, dirty hair, then across the bristles covering his face. "What a bloody mess. I honestly tried to protect Mattie. Things blew out of control when Tacque's entire ruddy team walked in. I had no way to contact either of you, and I couldn't risk showing sympathy towards Mattie or they've had killed me on the spot. I was protecting her and changing plans by the minute trying to gain control of the situation. I had a spot of luck when Carson took out Allison, and I thought myself a proper genius when I sent that van out here with the bodies. It was Jeremiah's bloody fault, not mine, that he popped up in front of the Parsons when the place blew."

More typing. Hawk wondered briefly whether Joe might continue this interrogation indefinitely. If he did, he'd be disappointed, since Hawk had no more useful information to offer.

What do we do about Charlie?

Hawk shook his head. "That's not a priority at the moment. I'm more interested in Jeremiah." He stood, gripped the cabinets as he swayed. He turned his attention to the monitors again when a CSI truck rolled into view. Law enforcement and coroner personnel bent over the two bodies. An assistant retrieved two body bags.

What he did not want to admit was not only was Charlie a priority, but both Jeremiah and Mattie were in imminent danger until he and Joe could get them safely squirreled away in the bunker.

"Have I mentioned the Lee twins?" he asked, turning to Joe.

Joe typed.

Who the hell are they?

Hawk rubbed a hand over his face. "Part of the Charlie Network. Fortunately, neither was around when I convinced Charlie to put me in charge of the op. The two of them alone make Gary

Tacque's entire team amateurs. No doubt they'll show up soon."

He noticed Joe typing again and reluctantly leaned down, gripping the cabinet when he experienced another wicked bout of dizziness.

Jeremiah and Mattie are sitting ducks so far as Charlie is concerned. I need to know what you know about their organization. You're useless at the moment. It's up to me to get Jeremiah out of reach.

Hawk glowered. He didn't like being called useless, but Joe was absolutely right, at least for the interim until his ears healed. Two weeks was too long to expect Charlie to hold off on retaliation. He crossed to the under-counter cabinet, peered inside. Bottled water crammed the shelves. He shut the door and looked at the shelf above the counter. Brown foil packages of MREs, or "Meals Ready to Eat". He reached up and picked one out, then retrieved a bottle of water.

"Want one?" he asked, turning to Joe and holding up the MRE. The latter shook his head. He seemed occupied with something on the computer, and Hawk had tired of answering questions, so he stumbled over to the metal bunk beds against the far wall. There was enough sleeping accommodation for four average-sized adults. Wool blankets, pillows, and white cotton sheets lay folded at the end of each of the bunks. He sat down on the bottom bunk he'd occupied until a few hours ago, tore open the MRE, and added some water. He felt for the capsule, broke it, and waited while the resulting chemical mixture heated, warming the contents. He realized he'd forgotten an eating utensil.

"Damn," he muttered, rising stiffly to his feet and weaving his way to the cabinets. He rummaged through several drawers before he found plastic utensils, retrieved a fork, returned to the bunk bed. As he ate he watched Joe, who had not turned his attention away from the computer since the end of their conversation.

If only Mattie had stayed in the van. They would have cleaned up the rest of Gary's team, gotten her to hospital, and could be on their way to dismantling the Charlie Network. As it was, the first team was dead, and Mattie and Jeremiah would become prime targets for retribution. They sent six men to avenge one man's death. How would they react to the decimation of an entire team?

No doubt Charlie knew of his double-cross by now. Their

snipers were the best in the world. They knew his and Joe's basic location. Hawk and Joe could remain in the bunker for a while, but not indefinitely. Charlie might very well send the Lee twins, both the best of the best in the Charlie Network. They would need only one shot. The Charlie Network would descend upon the area, force them into the open, and that would be that.

Hawk stared at the concrete floor as he ate, so absorbed in his thoughts he did not see Joe stand and wave him over. Nor did he notice when Joe strode across the large underground room. He did notice when Joe smacked the back of his head, sending a shot of pain slicing through his skull. Startled, he jerked his eyes up.

"What?"

Joe walked back to the computer and sat down. Leaving his meal on the bed, Hawk rose and followed. Joe closed an email account, then began typing.

So, got any plans for getting Jeremiah out of jail before someone from Charlie Network kills him?

Hawk sat in the metal chair. "Not particularly. I'm rather at a loss at the moment." He glanced up and watched the monitors as CSI personnel loaded one of the body bags onto a gurney, then maneuvered the gurney down the stairs and into a waiting ambulance. He returned his attention to the computer screen.

"What are our assets?"

Joe rolled his eyes and typed.

We ain't got none.

"That's bloody cold of you." But Hawk silently agreed with him. Their current position appeared worse than pitiful. However, that line of thinking would get them nowhere. "I agree we could be in a better position, but we have neutralized the team Charlie sent to take out Mattie," he countered.

Joe shook his head.

More like taken a bat and beat up the hornet's nest. Like the queen bee wasn't already out for blood.

Hawk stared at the words as bells began ringing in synchronous clash with the tinnitus. He turned his head slowly to stare at Joe. "You know who Charlie is, don't you?"

Joe's closed expression revealed nothing.

Hawk stood and limped over to where he had left his unfinished MRE. Picking up the remains, he stumbled to a large black trash bag near the entrance of the tunnel and threw the rest away, then turned and faced Joe from across the room. The two men remained motionless for several beats before Joe broke his stare and turned back to the computer screen.

Enlightenment came fast as Hawk stared at the old Indian. Joe Healing Water grew up on the Southern Ute Reservation. From his contacts and research, Hawk knew the Charlie Network worked either from the Southern Ute Reservation or out of the Ute Mountain Ute Reservation. He had learned more than he wanted to know about Reservation conditions when he contacted Charlie and offered his services. Gary Tacque had been a team leader, but he ultimately answered to someone higher. And while Hawk had an idea, he was unfamiliar enough with American Indian culture and the two Reservations to be able to reach a conclusive decision.

Joe Healing Water, a Southern Ute who spent his life on the Reservation. A Southern Ute old enough to have witnessed the birth of the Charlie Network. He knew the Ute identity of Gary Tacque.

And he had suddenly picked up and left the Southern Ute Reservation to set up shop in the middle of nowhere. Hawk mused over Mattie's surprised reaction when she recognized him in the tiny gas station in the middle of the Comanche National Grasslands. Evidently she and Jeremiah knew Joe Healing Water; yet she had been unaware of his relocation.

Joe Healing Water, who also had a sniper background.

Hawk drew a breath, forced his wobbling feet across the room again.

"Level with me, Joe." His voice sounded like so much buzzing to him, but he knew he spoke loud enough to be heard.

Joe Healing Water glanced up.

"Why did you suddenly relocate to the middle of nowhere? Was it because you knew too much about the Charlie Network? Were you on their radar?"

Joe stared at the computer for a long time. Hawk watched him, mentally urging him to give an answer.

Joe's fingers slid up to the keyboard, began typing.

Mary Eagle Feather approached me several years ago about an idea to help the Ute Mountain Ute People. She knew my background, wanted me to cross the border and help her and her son. I was in a position to give them names of sharp shooters who might be interested in joining them. I was blind and didn't see where they were going with their idea. Mary Eagle Feather started using the sharp shooters to carry out assassination contracts. I told her I didn't want to be any part of that. She put a contract out on me, and I figured I'd live longer if I disappeared. So I did.

"And who is Mary Eagle Feather's son?" Hawk asked, though he thought he knew the answer.

Joe's fingers moved.

Gary Tacque. Aka Jay Wild Horse Houser. Aka Carrot Eater.

Hawk rolled his eyes to the ceiling. "Aka, Mattie's brother-in-law and leader of the team who responded when she killed him on that bloody fucking mountain."

Chapter Fourteen

Mary Eagle Feather sat at her desk and stared through the window at the small, decrepit National Historic ghost town of Victor, Colorado. She was in her mid-fifties, tall, slender, with waist-length straight black hair generously streaked with gray. She wore a heavy taupe wool cardigan over an off-white cashmere turtleneck sweater, and an expensive deer hide floor-length skirt decorated with beadwork and turquoise. A turquoise pendant hung from a thick silver chain around her throat. Rabbit fur boots kept her feet warm. She wore no makeup, did not need any. Her natural beauty remained stunning, seemed to grow more pronounced as she aged.

Her black eyes stared beyond the grimy pane of the window. A narrow two-lane strip of pavement dipped steeply downhill on the north end, rose steeply uphill at the southern end, and served a handful of decrepit buildings in the middle. Mounds of dirty snow banked the town, crowded around dirty buildings, shone with blinding whiteness on surrounding hills in the high June sun. If she had her way, the strip mine between Victor and Cripple Creek would have long ago bulldozed this filthy town along with its National Historic sign. If she had her way, Cripple Creek, the larger tourist attraction a few miles away, would also be buried under a mountain of waste.

But she had to exert patience. Patience, like the White Man demonstrated patience as they slowly killed off her People. Mary Eagle Feather smiled a slow, grim, satisfied smile.

She had uncovered a way to decimate the precious National Historic towns. And just as the White Man's government had destroyed the Ute Mountain Ute Nation, broken treaty after treaty, so she would see to it she returned the favor and ruin two national treasures the White Man held dear. Their destruction would come through the means that had created them.

Gold and silver mining.

Her smile grew. The small town of Victor, Colorado, considered Mary Eagle Feather a major asset. Billboards on every street corner boasted their town had their very own, authentic American

Indian leader on their council. A large majority of the residents wanted her to run for Mayor.

The destruction of Victor would take several more years. She looked across the antique desk of her office room located in the nineteenth century building preserved by the National Historic District people. Chan and Wan Lee, identical Asian twins, sat in silence across from her. They waited for instructions, but she was not yet ready to tell them.

"This has gotten messy," she said instead.

Chan Lee, dressed in jeans and a blue Colorado sweatshirt, nodded. "Quite." His British accent conflicted violently with his Asian features. Mary Eagle Feather had known him for almost ten years, and she still had to control her tendency to jolt whenever he spoke.

"We should not have sent so many. Freeman and Carson would have been enough." Wan's accent matched Chan's, right down to the pitch and resonance. His haircut, clean-shaven face, and features all matched his brother, rendering it impossible to tell them apart. The only difference lay in the fact he wore black jeans and a gray non-descript sweatshirt.

Mary Eagle Feather scowled. "That's not the problem. We broke protocol and got in close to the target."

Chan nodded. "Close and personal revenge rather than using a shooter's nest. I agree. We miscalculated." He sat with quiet, professional assurance. His brother exuded the same demeanor, but shook his head at his brother's remark.

"Hawk was our mistake," Wan countered.

Chan's eyes darted sideways towards his twin, then back to the woman sitting across the desk. "Hawk was a necessary risk."

Wan leaned forward, turning to face his brother. "I told you not to hire him. You, of all of us, knew his operative background. You were his bloody superior officer." Wan gripped the arms of the chair, his eyes sparking with anger. "And because of your sodding stubbornness, he took out Freeman and his entire team." Seeing Chan's frown he leaned back, relaxed his hands, inhaled deeply, released a sigh before he met the woman's cool expression. "Hawk was a mistake. A big one."

Mary rested against her wooden desk chair and returned her attention to the scene beyond the window. "Six bodies and two destroyed homes between Norman and Shawnee, according to media reports. Hawk's face is not among the pictures being broadcast, so we must assume he's behind their deaths. My son's entire team, all of them excellent shooters, all of them highly experienced, longtime members of the Charlie Network." Neither her expression nor her tone revealed any emotion.

Chan's frown deepened. "The team ought to have managed Hawk well enough, taken him out if he posed a threat. When you informed me that he contacted you, I recommended him as an opportunity to keep him under surveillance." He paused.

Wan's voice came across low, tight. "He killed them, the bloody sod. He out-maneuvered us."

Mary considered both men for several moments, then inhaled and shook her head. "I thought perhaps his near death two years ago would work in our favor. He could very easily have fit in well with our group. Operative background, forced to go underground, excellent marksman." Mary's eyes teared up. Her only son, Jay Wild Horse Houser, her pride and joy, dead because of that Tyler woman and her husband, Jeremiah Black Bear Tyler. And now her son's team were dead. All of them.

Avoiding eye contact to hide her emotions, Mary stared out the ancient, filthy windowpane held down by lead weights in the frame. Spring this year brought weeks of heavy wet snow and frigid conditions. Victor lay just above timberline, and the weather was as unpredictable as the Coyote. Clouds brought another foot of snow just last week, and the unusually cold weather generated a string of tornadoes through the Plains states.

"Gary thought him an excellent choice when I mentioned his name a year ago," Chan ventured, sounding mildly defensive. He used Jay Wild Horse's alias out of respect. Neither he nor his twin had ever used Gary Tacque's native name.

"I told you he would never dirty his hands." Wan shook his head, his lips pressed into a thin line. "And threatening to expose his operative background would not phase him. Not in the least. He's too British. Too clean."

But Mary ignored them as she stared out the window. Chan noticed the moisture on her cheeks and with a small hand motion waved his brother silent.

The past folded around Mary Eagle Feather, enclosing her

with warm memories of her only child, her son, her pride and joy. His presence by her side gave her the strength and direction to carry out what otherwise would have remained frustrated dreams. Jay Wild Horse Houser, aka Gary Tacque, had been born off the Reservation. His father, a rich French businessman, had enjoyed Mary's youth and American Indian beauty only to desert her when she became pregnant with Wild Horse. Returning to the desperate, poverty-ridden conditions on the Ute Mountain Ute Reservation meant no opportunity for either her or her unborn child. So she traveled to Washington D.C., sought assistance from the Bureau of Indian Affairs, seduced the officer assigned to her, lied about her Ute Mountain Ute background, claimed she was the last surviving member of a deceased Southern Ute clan who wanted to return to her People. Charlie Underwood had been sympathetic, kind, supportive. A middle-aged bachelor with no family of his own, he asked her to marry him, vowing he would move to the Southern Ute Reservation with her and work with the natives to improve conditions.

Of course he broke his promise, just like every person connected with the White Man's government. Shortly after the birth of her son in a white man's hospital, Mary asked Charlie to transfer to Colorado and take her and her infant son to the Southern Ute Reservation. Charlie refused, claiming he needed to spend a few more years in Washington before he relocated. When he balked at her suggestion to allow her to leave without him, she poisoned him, called emergency help in a feigned state of panic, convinced first responders and ensuing investigators he became depressed over the fact he was not the father of her child. An unexpected inheritance from Charlie's estate introduced Mary Eagle Feather to the power of money. She invested her newfound wealth, then moved to the Southern Ute Reservation under the guise of a distant, extinct clan, and eased into the population. The introduction of casinos brought a degree of prosperity to the native population, Mary became a casino manager and made sure money went to the Rez rather than the Government, and Wild Horse grew up in the traditions of his People.

But being a half-breed on the Southern Ute Reservation proved difficult, and Wild Horse began running away from the insults and treatment as an outcast. He spent his youth roaming the large reservation, often disappearing for months. Mary Eagle Feather fretted over his safety, but dismissed her concerns when her son returned a different person, a man among his simpering, pathetic teenaged former classmates. The day he demonstrated his marksmanship stirred deep, formerly dormant spirits in Mary Eagle Feather's soul.

The idea germinated slowly in Mary Eagle Feather's subconscious. She quit her job at the Southern Ute Casino, returned to the Ute Mountain Ute Reservation, and found her adobe home a crumbled derelict. Wild Horse continued to live in the wilderness of the two Reservations, kept in touch with her after she moved. On his twentieth birthday he came for a visit, and she approached him with the idea of using his talents to save their People. Wild Horse resisted the idea at first. He hated the notion of returning from a wandering, free lifestyle to one of structure and timetables; argued against helping a culture that had outcast him, until Mary told him it was the White Man's blood they rejected, not his Native heritage. The idea of exacting revenge grew on Wild Horse, and together they formed clever ways to gain more wealth. Wild Horse's short stature and features made him appear much younger than his years, but infiltrating the foster system proved unprofitable and more trouble than the project deemed worthy. Mary married into wealth four times, but realized the increasing occurrence of "natural deaths" would come back to haunt her if she continued down that path. And anyway, the whole process just took too long.

Then Wild Horse came home with an idea so unique, so perfect, Mary felt her heart soar. She chose the name of their new endeavor in honor of the Bureau of Indian Affairs officer she murdered, and so their venture became known as the Charlie Network. Wild Horse branched out, personally selecting and grooming individuals into an extraordinary group of shooters, then developed such an impenetrable screen around their new group that discovery proved impossible. He avoided using natives, fearing they would stick out too much in alien cultures. Soon their reputation for clean, untraceable hits gained international attention. Money from their successes went into the ailing Ute Mountain Ute People. Clinics, housing, preservation of their history, there was so much to do and so little time left.

"Belaboring our mistakes will not fix the problem." Mary's voice broke the long silence. "The question now is how to get our hands on the Lamont fortune." She closed her eyes, inhaled, then fought down emotion.

"Apprehend Tyler. And his wife," Wan murmured into the silence.

Mary opened her eyes. "Do we know where the Tyler woman is?"

Chan shook his head. "The coppers haven't a clue. Tyler's in Pottawatomie County Jail. It's possible the woman went underground with Hawk and Healing Water."

Mary's eyes narrowed. "Healing Water. He's behind their success. I should have taken care of him a long time ago, before he fled the Rez."

"Wan and I shall address Healing Water and Hawk," Chan urged, his voice low as he leaned forward in his chair.

Mary shook her head. "There will be another time for that. We've acted rashly and have suffered heavily because of our impatience. Once we're sure none of the bodies can be traced back to the Charlie Network, we'll take care of those two." She stood, stepped from behind the desk and crossed her arms as she once again stared through the grimy window.

Over the last twenty years, the small mine between Victor and Cripple Creek had become a monstrosity, using their gigantic trucks and bulldozers to destroy the beautiful mountains Mother Earth created. Those same ugly gigantic trucks built their own ugly gigantic hills of strip mining waste.

She turned slowly to face the twins. "For now, we need to cement our claim to the Lamont fortune. Wild Horse was on track, he almost succeeded."

Mary stopped when the sound of heavy, stumbling footsteps on the stairs came from outside the closed office door. She leaned against the cold window and frowned. She knew those footsteps, knew what their stumbling meant, and hated the repulsion at the thought of what she was about to see.

The three of them turned their heads when the office door opened. In stumbled a man in his thirties, Ute Mountain Ute native, with the traditional short stockiness so characteristic of her People, his shoulder-length black hair plaited into two oily, dirty braids. He wore dirty jeans and an equally dirty black sweatshirt that stretched broadly across a pronounced paunch. Brown slush covered his cowboy boots.

"Gray Hare, what are you doing here?" Mary stood with her back to the window and scowled at her cousin, then couldn't control the way her nose wrinkled when she caught a whiff of his body odor.

Gray Hare's lips spread into a wide grin with brilliantly straight, white teeth. "Got my Government check yesterday." He glanced around the sparsely furnished office, obviously looking for a place to sit down. There was none, so he stumbled over to the side of the desk and wriggled his backside onto the highly polished surface.

"But you're supposed to be working the casino?" Mary frowned at her cousin, hoping he would pick up her hint to get off of her desk.

Gray Hare's glazed black eyes squinted at her expression and his grin broadened. He was either too drunk to focus on her expression, too simple minded to understand her non-verbal message, or was being his typical difficult self and refusing to acquiesce. He shrugged. "What for? They don't let me gamble on the job, and walking around in a security uniform don't pay enough." He waved his check. "Besides, the Government pays me for doing nothing. Why should I disappoint them?"

Mary lifted her chin. "So you're going to spend the weekend inside a bottle instead."

Over the years a strip of small gambling casinos had popped up along the northeast entrance of the Ute Mountain Ute Rez. The intent had been to lure tourists to lose their money gambling in Reservation casinos because they could avoid the heavy taxation of other locations. In reality, the natives fell victim to the flashing lights and fancy décor, losing most of their government checks on gambling and the rest on booze.

The money from the Lamont fortune would contribute towards a new clinic, as well as more counselors for the widespread alcoholism that plagued the Reservation. Mary envisioned new schools that resurrected their history and their pride, their fighting abilities, their native language, and their land management skills. New schools and clinics meant decent jobs, an alternative to the jobs in the casinos. Money also meant bribes for political favors.

The one thing she had not found a solution for was the apathy generated by free government checks. They were being paid to do nothing, so that's what they did. Alcoholism took most of them in their prime. Diabetes plagued the rest.

Meanwhile, Gray Hare and his filthy jeans threatened to leave scratches all over her antique desk. She stalked over and made swatting motions at him.

"Get your dirty behind off my desk."

"Then give me a chair to sit in," Gray Hare complained as he slid down.

"Go downstairs and get one from the front room." Mary opened the right bottom drawer, retrieved a can of furniture polish and a soft cloth.

"And lug it all the way up those stairs?" Gray Hare released a rumbling chuckle. "You care more about the furniture than you do your blood kin." He shuffled to the wall behind the door and slid down onto the rough floorboards.

Mary grimaced. "You're going to end up with splinters in your backside." There were disadvantages of occupying an original town building, like the rough plank flooring the National Historic people refused to replace. She slid her eyes in the direction of the twins, who remained seated and silent. Chan flicked his eyes in her direction, acknowledging she could not risk talking business in front of her cousin, no matter how drunk he might appear.

"Don't get comfortable, Cousin. If you're here for the weekend, I will put you to work." She finished polishing the surface of the desk, then carefully replaced the can of furniture polish and the cloth in the right bottom drawer and sat down.

"Like one of those big trucks? That would be fun," Gray Hare grinned again.

"Unlikely, since not only are you always drunk as a skunk, you don't own a heavy equipment license," Mary snapped, annoyed with Gray Hare's sudden appearance, annoyed she couldn't think fast enough to get him out of the office. She wasn't as sharp as she had been ten years ago. Mid-fifties were taking their toll, despite her efforts to fight off the effects of middle age. Over the last few years she had begun shifting decisions more and more to Wild Horse. He had been brilliant, quick with answers regarding potential clients, patient and thorough when a problem needed working through.

Mary Eagle Feather leaned against the back of her chair, her black brows knitted so closely they almost touched.

"We've a meeting…" Chan broke off abruptly when Mary cut angry eyes towards him. Her cousin might be drunk, but he would undoubtedly pick up on Chan's British accent. Gray Hare had been a Reservation cop, decent shot, and a hell of a tracker before alcohol ruined him.

Gray Hare's chin drooped towards his chest as his head nodded. Mary cast her eyes at the twins, noticed their attention currently on Gray Hare, and slid her cell phone from one of the deep pockets of her skirt.

Wild Horse had created a unique code system early on that allowed them to use unsecured communications without fear of detection. She used the code now to send a message including a description of the Tyler woman to sleeper members of the Network, then slipped her cell back into her pocket.

Gray Hare's breathing slowed then deepened, and soft snores implied he'd fallen into a drunken stupor. Mary stood and stepped to the front of the desk. Chan and Wan rose, the three of them forming a tight circle. Mary inclined her head.

"We need Jeremiah Tyler," Chan breathed in a whisper. "And we need his wife. There's still time to complete what your son started."

Mary's expression turned reflective. "Black Bear's an agent. On top of that, he's Southern Ute. Breaking him would give me great pleasure."

"Chan and I will do it," Wan whispered in a tone of revenge he couldn't quite disguise.

Mary's eyes sharpened on the twin. "You would never break him," she snapped. "Not Black Bear. This confrontation is between him and myself."

Chan maintained a neutral expression, kept emotion out of his voice. "What of his wife? She controls the money."

Wan nodded, working to exert the same calm his twin demonstrated. "She's the weak link."

Mary pursed her lips as she thought. "We don't know where she is."

Chan nodded. "I'll check with the Norman and Shawnee P.D.s. See what information they've gathered." He turned to his brother. "Wan, find Hawk and Healing Water and maintain surveillance."

"We've no idea their location," Wan objected.

"Tyler's in Shawnee. They'll be in the area," Chan pressed. "One of them will pop up."

"They'll be close to the Lamont place," Mary inserted softly. "It's possible that since we don't know where the Tyler woman is, they might not, either."

"What about Tyler?" Wan asked.

Mary Eagle Feather waved a dismissive hand. "He's in jail. If they release him, his movements will be easy enough to follow."

Chan glanced at the woman. Strong as she was, her memory had noticeably weakened over the last couple of years. He wondered whether she might be suffering early stages of dementia. Fast upon that thought came the unpleasant realization that grief over her son's death might hasten an undiagnosed disease process.

He chose his words carefully. "With respect, ma'am, Tyler disappeared the first time coppers released him. Remember, they hadn't a clue where he'd got to until he showed up unconscious at the second explosion."

Mary fell silent. Chan and Wan understood Hawk, knew better than any of the other members how to handle the British operative. Besides that, they were the next best shooters in her Network.

Correction. They *were* her best shooters, now that Wild Horse was dead.

But she needed a third person to tail Black Bear, should he be released. Stalling for time to think about the problem, she glanced over at the slumped, sleeping form of her cousin. Too bad he was such a mess. He might have proved useful if he could keep his head out of the bottle.

"It is possible Tyler doesn't know his wife's location, either, in which case he'll try to search her out, should he be released," Chan murmured into the silence between them.

Mary nodded. "Following him might lead us to the Tyler woman. But until he's released, I want you looking for her."

"When we apprehend Tyler and his wife, where should we

bring them?" Wan asked.

Mary Eagle Feather glanced towards her sleeping cousin. His snores were loud enough to fill the room. She could feel the vibration through the heavy soles of her winter boots.

"This location is too high profile," she murmured. "There are too many eyes here. Too much curiosity."

"What about the Reservation?" Chan suggested.

Mary Eagle Feather shook her head. "No, too much chance of interference there as well." She frowned, deep in thought. What would Wild Horse do?

She felt his spirit float through the walls of the building and melt slowly with hers. The idea came suddenly, brilliantly, as though he had spoken to her.

"We will use my son's cabin on Wolf Creek Pass," she murmured, sliding her eyes yet again towards her cousin. Gray Hare appeared to be sleeping, but he had been wily over the years he worked as a cop and could be faking it while trying to pick up their conversation. His snoring seemed less noisy when they were talking.

Chan shook his head. "Neither of us knows the location," he objected, motioning towards his twin.

"I've an idea," Wan spoke softly. "I don't relish the thought of depending on the fickleness of the police to release Tyler. They might hold him without bail, what with the number of bodies piled up. And we can't run down the woman without risk of exposure. What I have in mind would put Tyler in our hands *and* flush out Hawk and Healing Water."

"What are you thinking?" Mary Eagle Feather's eyes regarded the twin, trying to discern some small characteristic that would help her to distinguish one from the other.

"We nick Tyler."

"And how do we do that? He's in a cell." Mary Eagle Feather's undertone held obvious irritation.

In the true nature of identical twins, Chan realized Wan's idea. A smile curled the edges of his thin mouth. "We borrow a couple of uniforms and make it look as though Tyler masterminded his escape. The ruddy coppers won't realize he's been abducted. No doubt the building has closed circuit cameras. I'll assure our faces are seen. Once the news media gets our images on the telly, Hawk will realize the truth. He knows my identity, knows I've a twin. Abducting Tyler will force them out of hiding. From that point, we'll have opportunity to control their movements when they attempt a rescue." He paused. "I see one problem with this." He looked at Mary Eagle Feather. "How do we lure Hawk and Healing Water to the cabin?"

Mary Eagle Feather's lips curled into a slow, confident smile. "Healing Water knows the location of the cabin. He will know that is where I will hold Black Bear."

Chan studied her. "Are you quite sure?"

Mary Eagle Feather nodded. "Oh, yes. Healing Water will think like I think, will understand that Victor and the Rez are too risky. He will head for Wolf Creek Pass."

Chapter Fifteen

Total peace washed through me, dissolving the pain, healing my leg, making me whole again. I could run, laugh, enjoy the wonder of Life. I no longer suffered the angst of missing loved ones. They were here with me, all of them, smiling gentle reassuring smiles, letting me know without ever speaking a word that I was okay and that all was well. Wonderful, beautiful silence surrounded me, embraced me with warmth, comfort, safety.

~ * ~

"Detective Reeves. Detective Gates. Please, listen to me. The man who shot those three men had an accent. I don't care what you're trying to tell me about tunnel vision and whatnot in a life-threatening situation. I know what I heard. The man who shot those three men was *not* Jeremiah Tyler." Bill Parsons sat across the table from the two detectives. He was in his mid-fifties, completely bald, wore crimson OU sweats borrowed from a neighbor. A small stout businessman, Oklahoma born and raised, he had lived through more tornado warnings than he could count. Reaching his right arm out, he squeezed his wife's hand as she sat beside him.

Becky Parsons remained quiet despite her strongly adverse feelings towards the two detectives. Large, black circles of exhaustion ringed her vivid blue eyes. Friends and neighbors had loaned her and her husband clothes, a place to stay, food, and invaluable emotional support. She wore a flowered scarf to cover her short white hair and a pair of OU sweats, which made her already small frame appear even more frail.

Detective Harrison Gates noted Bill's exasperation and threw a quick glance at Reeves. The latter, his arms crossed, stood to the side of the long oval conference table, rocking on the balls of his feet as his narrow brown eyes studied the couple down the long, aquiline bridge of his nose. His expression held disdain and disbelief, his voice patronizing when he spoke.

"Mr. Parsons, will all due respect, you were in a state of panic, your life and the life of your loved ones were being threatened. It would be impossible for you to notice an intruder's features, much less an accent."

Gates barely controlled his temper. Reeves needed a crash course in effective communication and controlling his body language. He was treating the Parsons with the same abrasive attitude he'd used with Tyler. He thought back to last night when the young detective grilled Tyler until the wee hours of the morning instead of allowing the man a chance to tell his side of things. Reeves refused to accept the coroner's report filed earlier this morning on the six bodies found despite the fact two professionals had worked non-stop since the bodies reached the morgue. He even ignored the ballistics findings supplied by the lab and submitted a request for a third coroner to repeat the autopsies and a different lab to re-run ballistics tests. And because of his connections through an uncle's political pull, he got what he wanted.

Damned rookie. Gates' eyes slid to the broad plate glass window of the conference room. Friday morning and already dark clouds crowded the southwest horizon, promising another storm system sooner than later, which meant emergencies would yet again overtax their already insufficient staff. He glanced at the flag fluttering limply in the oppressively humid conditions.

Gates brought his attention back to the occupants sitting around the large oval table, with the exception of Reeves, who stood irritatingly to one side and kept peering over Gates' shoulder. He needed Reeves to get his head out of his ass and start asking different questions, to quit sending patrol cops on useless, time-wasting errands to look for the kinds of answers that would support his conclusions, rather than allowing the collected facts to tell their own story. In his own desperation to find a way around the chokehold Reeves currently had on things, Gates requested the Cleveland County Sheriff's Office to drive the Parsons from Norman to Shawnee. He wanted to watch Tyler's interaction with the couple Reeves was accusing him of trying to kill, though he doubted Reeves astute enough to notice a bulldozer in the room, much less the finer points of nonverbal clues.

~ * ~

Bill Parsons watched the two detectives, noticed the older one's thoughts wander when he gazed through the window. He quietly ticked off his own observations in his head. Gates obviously was not pleased with his rookie partner. He made a mental note to research Jason Reeves, find out how an officer so inexperienced had managed to land a detective position so soon in his career. Not that he could use any of it to help Jeremiah with his current problems, but he would file the knowledge anyway. No telling when tidbits of information might prove useful in his other line of work.

In the meantime, the tension between the two detectives meant key evidence and clues were being missed. He sighed, tried another tact, carefully maintaining his façade of the victimized homeowner.

"Look, detectives. Two days ago my wife and I lost our home. All of our family pictures, heirlooms, records, possessions, gone, *Poof!* In the blink of an eye. All because of these strangers...these *killers* who invaded our home in the middle of the night. We're peaceful folks. We live in a peaceful neighborhood. We attend church on Sundays. To have something like this happen to us is unbelievable. I wouldn't protect anyone who committed an act of violence like this, not even if they were family. If Jeremiah had been a part of the break-in, believe me, I would be telling you." He paused, hoping his words would sink in, then continued.

"But to think Jeremiah Tyler could be responsible for something so random, so irrational...so *hideous*." He threw up his hands. "It's ludicrous! Everyone in town knows the Lamonts, everyone knows about their wealth. Believe me; all of us who knew George and Ginnie and watched their two girls grow into wonderful young women put Jeremiah under a microscope when he started courting Mattie. In the seven years he's been with the family there has not been one *iota* of a hint he married Mattie for her family money." He stopped, wiped his eyes with the sleeve of his sweatshirt because he no longer owned a handkerchief. He inhaled deeply before continuing. "I cannot say the same about Gary Tacque, who married Angela less than six months ago. And now she's dead."

Gates nodded as he jotted notes on a legal pad. Bill glanced at Reeves again, noted the stubborn set of his jaw.

"But if you're dead set on trying to pin this whole thing on Jeremiah, there's not a thing I can say that will change your mind."

He sighed, leaned against the soft conference room armchair and pinched his nose with the thumb and forefinger of his right hand. Good Lord, maintaining his cover was tricky under normal conditions. The present situation made his efforts exhausting, lack of sleep complicated things even further.

Gates rubbed his face with his right hand, felt the bristle of a day's worth of beard, realized he had forgotten to shave this morning. He'd collapsed on the couch when he got home sometime during the early hours after Reeves finally ended Tyler's interrogation. He hadn't bothered to change clothes. He'd slept a couple of hours, wolfed down breakfast, pecked a distracted kiss on his wife's cheek, and headed out the door to call Norman PD to bring up the Parsons.

Reeves leaned against the conference room window. He badly wanted to order Gates out of the room and take over things on his own, but reluctantly admitted such behavior might not impress the couple. Bill Parsons seemed too calm, too in control, and it bothered the young detective. But Gates would throw a major conniption if he tried to grill the guy now, especially in front of the wife.

Parsons faced him calmly across the table, and Reeves straightened and began rocking on his feet again. The man's statements threatened his theory. Despite his efforts this interview was not going the way he wanted it to go.

Harrison Gates sighed. "In the space of less than a week, we've had two residences destroyed with identical types of explosive devices, and a body count that's kept two county coroners busy. The local news media is screaming for answers. We've even made national news."

Bill Parsons nodded. "I understand the amount of pressure both of you are feeling. I'm sure the constantly changing weather conditions have complicated your progress."

Reeves cleared his throat. "What my partner is trying to say is Tyler's the only connection between all events. And now you're trying to tell us he's not behind any of it, that someone with a foreign accent is responsible?"

With a calm Reeves thought too perfect for the situation, Bill Parsons leaned back and nodded. "That is correct."

Reeves crossed his arms and stopped rocking. "If you're so

sure Tyler wasn't involved, then describe this man and his accent," he challenged.

"Reeves, cool it," Gates warned.

Bill Parsons thought quickly, weighing what information he should share, and what the detectives would believe. "My ears were ringing from the shotgun blast, I was yelling at him to drop his weapon, he was yelling at me to get Becky and Mud Rain to safety, shouting there were more of them outside." He hedged on telling the complete truth. "So while I can't say for certain his exact accent, I can tell you with absolute confidence the man who shot those three men was *not* Jeremiah Tyler."

~ * ~

Gates eyed the folder in front of him, debated about leafing through the contents, decided not to because he already knew what it held. Shawnee, Oklahoma, was a small town, a friendly town. He hadn't seen this much violence in years, much less in the span of a week. He twirled a black *Ticonderoga* pencil between his fingers as he thought.

Reeves' inexperience was costing them valuable time, threatened the loss of critical evidence if they didn't correctly read the crimes scenes before the next storms hit. The corners of his mouth pulled down into a disgruntled, sour expression. He darted a look at Bill Parsons' shiny bald scalp, imagined himself looking exactly the same way sooner than later. His mood dropped to sub-basement level.

A sudden *snap* broke the silence in the room. Gates frowned at the splintered pencil between his thick fingers, threw the fragments into a trashcan located beneath the conference table.

Reeves inhaled noisily through his nose. "Personally, it would help me feel better about reconsidering Tyler's position as a suspect if he would tell me where his wife is," he told the couple.

Bill nodded. "I know it would. But Jeremiah hasn't done anything to his wife. I'm sure her disappearance is as much a mystery to him as it is to the rest of us." He rubbed the arms of the conference chair with the ends of his fingers. "Have you identified any of the three dead men? Or the one found in the van?"

"No," Gates shook his head. "Not yet."

Reeves straightened from the wall. "Wait a minute." He

crossed to the conference table, opened the folder lying in front of Gates. Thumbing through the pages, he pulled out some hand-written notes. "The Lamont's butler said there was a stranger with an English accent with Mattie Tyler on Monday night." He stud-ied Parsons from the top of the paper. "Would you say this man's accent was English?"

Bill winced internally, shrugged nonchalantly. "Possibly. Like I told you, my ears were ringing like crazy. My statement would never stand up in court."

Reeves glanced at Gates. "I wonder how good Tyler is mim-icking a foreigner."

"Oh, for heaven's sake, Detective," Bill interrupted. "You just said yourself the domestic help reported the man was a stranger."

Stung by Bill's reprimanding tone, Reeves swung his attention to the couple. "Why in the world would you load slugs into a shotgun for home defense?" He shot back, his voice tight. "You should know a slug will take out the target and anything behind it. Two of those bodies had quite an impressive hole through them."

"Why the accusatory tone, detective?" Bill retorted. He felt Becky squeeze his hand. He squeezed back, but refused to follow her non-verbal warning. "If I choose to load slugs into my shot-gun, that's my business, damn it. And it was a home invasion. I was well within my rights."

Becky Parsons straightened in her chair and met the young detective's brown eyes. "We went to the firing range last week. Bill was showing me the difference in recoil depending on what kind of ammunition is loaded in the shotgun."

Reeves rolled his eyes. "That's ridiculous. Any woman your size shouldn't be handling a shotgun in the first place. And you should've changed out the shells before you left the range."

"Detective!" Bill Parsons bristled.

"Back off, Reeves!" Gates snapped simultaneously.

Becky ducked her head in an attempt to hide a sudden rush of tears. She wasn't sensitive as a rule, but she was exhausted, dis-traught, and homeless. And she really didn't want to sit there and be reprimanded. She automatically reached for her purse, realized she didn't have one, and raised a hand to hide her eyes since she didn't have a tissue.

Gates saw her distress, got up and retrieved a box of Kleenex from a table near the door.

"My apologies, Mrs. Parsons," he murmured, setting the box near her elbow. Becky nodded and pulled several tissues. She pressed them to her eyes, then dabbed at her nose.

Bill Parsons glared at Reeves. "I've just about had enough of your behavior."

Gates regarded his partner stonily. "I understand that circumstantial evidence makes Tyler appear suspicious." He stopped, bit down on the urge to tongue-lash Reeves. "But we need to look for concrete evidence."

Reeves glared at Bill Parsons. "Give me answers that will supply real evidence. Do you really have no idea why four men broke into your house?" Reeves stepped forward, leaned over Gates' shoulder, slid the folder to one side, and drew an imaginary line with his thumbnail down the open pages. "Because I see definite ties that you seem bent on ignoring. You and your wife care for Tyler's younger brother. Tyler has strong motive to kill his wife's family as well as his wife. He has the knowledge to construct explosives, and his behavior has been less than exemplary. He's the common denominator in all of this, and I don't believe in coincidence."

Bill Parsons grew still. His bright round blue eyes drilled through the detective.

"Reeves," Gates growled, sensing Parsons about to blow.

But Reeves pressed his lips into a thin line. "According to the coroner's report, three of the men were shot execution style. Tyler has military background, is a CIA agent. He knows all about killing. The man with the accent, whoever he is, could very well be a paid assassin working with Tyler."

Bill Parsons leaned against the back of the chair and folded his arms across his chest. "So, according to you, Jeremiah Tyler hired four assassins to kill the three of us. No." He held his hand up. "That would be five assassins. I left out the body in the van. *Five assassins,*" he repeated, "show up at our house, and then Jeremiah kills the men he sent to kill us. Assuming the one with the accent is an accomplice, as you suggest, he stood by and watched while Jeremiah killed the other three." He leaned forward suddenly, his voice dropping to a low murmur. "But let's ignore for a moment just how ludicrous that theory sounds and look at the explosion. Why risk blowing up the house when he's on the premises? But no matter, according to you he blows our house up to kill the three of us, after he shoots the assassins he hired to kill us. Then he gets caught in the explosion and almost killed, and the accomplice with the accent meanwhile has disappeared."

Reeves stared at him. His Adam's apple bobbed when he swallowed. For the first time he seemed to realize how ridiculous the whole thing sounded.

Bill Parsons leaned back. "Good luck trying to get any prosecuting attorney to swallow a story like that," he snapped.

Uncomfortable silence filled the conference room. Gates watched Reeves try to stare down Bill Parsons; Parsons was not intimidated.

"When did you last see or talk with Jeremiah Tyler?" he asked after a while.

Bill Parsons broke eye contact with Reeves, turned his attention to Gates. "The last time I can think of was several months ago, at the Lamont funeral in January."

Becky Parsons nodded. "We've talked to Mattie since then, and Jeremiah calls to check up on Mud Rain, but we hadn't seen either of them since the funeral until we got a call about Mattie being in the hospital over in Alamosa." She paused. "Of course, both of us saw her last Monday at Angela's memorial service."

"Was Jeremiah Tyler present?" Gates asked.

The couple shook their heads.

"And that doesn't seem at all abnormal to either of you?" Reeves interjected, placing his knuckles on the table and leaning forward. "Because it sure seems abnormal to me. What kind of husband would be absent at a time like that, when his wife needed his support?"

Becky stared at him. "You have a point," she admitted. Her husband shook his head.

"Not necessarily, Becky." He looked at Gates. "Jeremiah and Mattie both were seriously injured and hospitalized. Jeremiah was in emergency surgery for a gunshot wound to the chest."

"And his wife suffered a gunshot that shattered her right leg. Yet she managed to make it to her sister's funeral, while her husband conveniently disappeared from the hospital after surgery."

Reeves' statement hung in the air.

"His absence doesn't implicate any involvement." Bill Parsons rubbed a hand over his bald scalp. Reeves noticed the gesture and thought it a sign of nervousness.

"Whether you want to believe it or not, you must admit the possibility exists," he pressed.

Bill Parsons leaned forward. "Whatever I tell you is not going to change what you want to believe. What I know is Jeremiah was not with those men who busted through the front door."

"And you have no idea why those men targeted you?" Reeves repeated.

Bill Parsons shook his head. "No idea whatsoever. And I take it from your questions Jeremiah isn't talking."

Reeves spoke before thinking. "No, he isn't. The most we've gotten out of him was his reaction when I showed him the pictures of the three dead men. Evidently, he thought the bodies we were talking about were you and your family."

Sharp gasps filled the room as Bill and Becky leaped to their feet.

"You mean you didn't tell him we're alive?" Bill's voice lifted an octave, his eyebrows threatened to reach all the way up to his bald scalp.

Reeves straightened, realizing too late his mistake. "Mr. and Mrs. Parsons, please. I've been conducting an investigation here. We've got six bodies, a missing wife, two destroyed homes, and the only connection between all of the above is Jeremiah Tyler."

"You...." Bill Parsons swallowed the rest. He stood rigidly still, his back ramrod straight. "I'd never make it in law enforcement, I can tell you that much. Wouldn't be able to stand having to work with idiots like yourself."

"Please, sit down," Gates waved for the couple to take a seat, his voice gentle in an effort to regain the confidence Reeves had just obliterated. "Maybe you can help us with locating Mattie Tyler. Can you think of where she might have gone? A friend of the family perhaps? She's injured, probably scared, probably not thinking clearly. Her fingerprints are all over the van that was parked in front of your house. It's possible she managed to get away and has run to someone whom she feels she can trust."

Becky Parsons shook her head. "There's any number of close

friends here in Shawnee. If you and your resources haven't located her by now, we certainly can't help you."

Bill inhaled deeply. "May Becky and I visit Jeremiah?"

"No." Reeves blurted.

Bill's jaw clenched. "Did it ever occur to you Jeremiah isn't talking because you already consider him guilty? He's not going to entrust knowledge about his wife's safety to anyone he doesn't trust, including law enforcement."

Reeves dug in. "He needs to trust me. I'm not letting him out of jail or allowing him visitors until he gives me information on where his wife is."

Bill shrugged. "Then you'd better be damn well be prepared for hell to freeze over."

"You seem very sure of yourself on this," Gates cut in before Reeves could reply.

Bill Parsons nodded and looked down at the detective. "I've known Jeremiah Tyler for a long time. You're not going to get a thing from him if he doesn't want you to know." He nodded towards his wife. "But Becky and I might."

~ * ~

Detective Harrison Gates leaned against his chair, ignored Reeves agitated motions, and stared flatly at Bill for several silent minutes. His gut told him Bill Parsons had a connection with Jeremiah Tyler beyond being a family friend. His knowledge of Tyler's personality and qualities seemed too thorough for casual acquaintance. Possibilities began whirling around his overworked brain.

He nodded. "Okay. I'll take you back."

Bill relaxed a little. "Thank you, Detective Gates. I understand the pressure the two of you are under. Maybe we can help you get to the bottom of this."

"Can I talk to you outside?" Reeves gestured angrily for Gates to follow and stalked from the room.

"Excuse me." Gates rose and followed Reeves out the door.

Bill covered his wife's cold hand with his warm one, he knew she was nervous and still reacting to the shock of recent events, and gave her fingers a tight, reassuring squeeze.

"How are you holding up?" He murmured gently.

"I'll be better when we can talk to Jeremiah," Becky whispered. "I don't like these detectives. They're looking for an easy solution, not trying to get to the truth." Her eyes drifted to the window. The wind had picked up, the flag now flapping wildly as the system approached. Clouds scuttled low overhead, promising rain before long. She should be at the OU campus Weather Center in Norman, not here in the Pottawatomie County Sheriff's office. Bill should be talking to their insurance adjuster, and Jeremiah should be with Mud Rain rather than sitting behind bars.

The door opened and Detective Gates gestured. "This way." He escorted the couple to a partial attic of the old building. He held the door for them, then led them to a short row of ancient cells that had been the county jail until being shut down by the Health Department several years ago.

"Tyler, you've got visitors," he announced.

Bill and Becky stared at their friend through the bars of the old cell. Jeremiah looked up, his expression lined and haggard, his eyes hollow and withdrawn. Scanty black bristles made his pale face look dirty and ill-tempered. Dried mud covered his clothes.

Jeremiah inhaled sharply and visibly forced down emotion. He stood slowly and walked the few paces to the bars. He glanced at Gates, who remained in near proximity.

Becky covered her mouth with her hand and squeezed her eyes shut for several seconds. She took a deep, steadying breath, opened her eyes, met Jeremiah's stare.

"How can we help?" she whispered.

Bill Parsons struggled to control his temper. "This man's barely two weeks post-op for a life-threatening gunshot wound," he seethed between clenched teeth.

"The Norman doctors said things were mending well," Gates replied, keeping his voice carefully neutral.

"Mud Rain?" Jeremiah's voice was hoarse, barely recognizable.

Becky nodded. "He's safe, Jeremiah. He's with Irma."

Jeremiah shook his head. "No, he is not safe, and now neither are the Greenbecks. We need to get him out of sight."

Bill stepped close to the floor-to-ceiling cell bars.

"Please step away from the cell," Gates advised.

Stifling an angry response, Bill obeyed. He felt Becky's fingers close around his clenched fist.

"Not safe?" He asked Jeremiah. "Have you said anything about this to the cops?" He immediately regretted his last question when he saw Jeremiah's expression turn cold.

Jeremiah shook his head. Becky saw the desperation he was trying to hide.

"Have either of you seen Mattie?" he asked.

The couple shook their heads. Behind them, Gates quietly retrieved a small black notepad from the inside pocket of his suit and began to scribble.

"What kind of danger is Mud Rain in?" Bill pressed.

Jeremiah shook his head, refrained from comment.

Bill nodded, understanding. "Detective Reeves has it in for you."

"We tried to tell him you're not involved in any of this, but he wouldn't listen," Becky added.

"I am involved," Jeremiah admitted quietly, flicking his eyes to Gates, who looked up. Their eyes locked, then Jeremiah shifted his attention back to his friends. "Just not in the way they assume. And they will not believe my explanation."

"I know how worried you are about Mud Rain and Mattie," Becky whispered. "We'll take care of Mud Rain. Please believe that."

Jeremiah whispered, "Thank you. Hide him. Quickly."

"And we'll start looking for Mattie," Bill offered. "We'll find her. You wait and see. We'll have the entire town of Shawnee out looking for her."

Jeremiah shook his head. "Take care of Mud Rain first. If the police do not know where Mattie is, she is currently safer than my brother."

"We'll find Mattie," Becky repeated in a shaky voice.

"I hope so." Jeremiah murmured. What he didn't add was he desperately hoped they would find her alive.

Chapter Sixteen

Dad sat beside me in the auditorium, his arm tight around my shoulders, his strength giving me safety, chasing away the terror, the pain, all of my worry. I did not have to be an adult while he was here with me. He would take care of me, keep me safe. Mom was onstage singing The Lord's Prayer *a cappella, and then she and Dad would finish their recital with a Schubert trio for clarinet, voice, and piano. I wondered why Dad was sitting in the audience with me when he really should be backstage. I asked him. "I wanted to be here with you during this song," he smiled gently. "Besides, I want to show you something." Mom's voice softened with incredible control, exquisite sensitivity on the last note, and as one the audience released a sigh of absolute, divine awe, then burst into applause. Instead of joining them, Dad ran to the stage, leapt up, and then grabbed one of the cords that controlled the backstage curtains and began swinging from curtain to curtain.*

I watched in confusion as other audience members copied his actions. Suddenly their professional recital became an acrobatic circus act, shattering my peace and sense of safety with their laughter and jeers.

~ * ~

Dr. Vance Trek, head of the medical staff at the University of Oklahoma Medical School, strode down the hall of St. Anthony's Hospital in Oklahoma City, well aware of the half-dozen medical students following with awed expressions. They should be in awe, he thought. His reputation as a trauma surgeon ranked among the best in the country, and the school board had lured him to become part of their teaching staff because of it.

He had been a medical student once, but that was before the profession grew soft, getting rid of thirty-six hour shifts, insisting on equal opportunity, decreasing the amount of assignments and research, softening the horrendously difficult exams. The entire profession now cowered before that most-feared, most arrogantly unfair term ever invented, the Malpractice Suit. He and his professional brothers saved lives. His knowledge and expertise made other professions look like kindergarten projects.

Years of standing in the trauma OR ruined his knees and hips. A bilateral knee replacement helped relieve some of the pain, but the artificial joints did not fix everything. He started exercising, lost weight, divorced his third wife to find a younger woman. He refused to color the gray that now generously streaked his thick, dark hair. Early sixties brought arthritis and fatigue that complicated the long hours he spent in the trauma OR suite. The invitation to become head of the prestigious OU Medical School seemed the perfect opportunity to pass along his vast knowledge and expertise.

That is, until he actually started working with the students.

His problem lay in the fact he did not like medical students. They were ignorant, stupid, and dangerous, their pathetic lack of knowledge and experience a threat to his own reputation. How was he supposed to impart his vast talents on such feeble-minded minions?

His cell buzzed, and he pulled out his phone to read the texted message. He stopped abruptly in the middle of the hallway, did not see the gaggle of students behind him collide into each other as they avoided bumping into him.

My God, he thought incredulously. *She's the one the Network is after.*

Dr. Trek tucked his cell phone away and strode into the Intensive Care Unit. Friday morning and the nursing staff would be trying to change shifts. He stopped at the desk and glared down at the clerk dressed in purple scrubs. If left up to him nurses and clerks would still be wearing white uniform dresses and caps. Whoever decided it was okay for the girls to wear pants ended the era of a physician's enjoyment looking at legs and peeking up hems.

"I need the night nurse for the patient in Room C." His rich baritone voice rang through the unit.

Sue, the desk clerk, glanced up and couldn't hide her grimace. Medical students grouped behind him.

"Sir, we've had a really busy night. Day shift is getting report now. Someone will be with you shortly." She tried and failed to hide an exhausted sigh. The patient in Room C, the patient Dr. Trek had performed long surgery on, was the reason for their crappy night. Dr. Trek swiveled his head around the unit and noticed the crash cart, cluttered with discarded plastic wrappings and drawers still ajar, parked outside the sliding doors of Room C.

"What happened?" he demanded.

Sue inhaled before answering. "She's our one-on-one patient at the moment, Dr. Trek. There's a nurse in the room while her night nurse is in the reporting room." She knew she was avoiding his question; knew the tirade he would create at the news no one had notified him when his patient coded. Officially he had not been on call, but he had a reputation of blowing up for no reason, and she was just too tired to fend off one of his temper tantrums.

Dr. Trek gave the desk clerk a cold stare. "I want to speak to the night nurse."

What a pompous asshole, Sue thought, creating a mental image that helped her feel better. "Yes, Sir. I'll go get her." She stood and headed to the room behind the nurses' station.

Meanwhile, Dr. Trek waved the med students into Room C. Each ICU room had a glass front that could open completely to allow x-ray equipment and a flock of personnel in an emergency. Tanned, patterned curtains gave a modicum of privacy from curious eyes. He pushed the curtains back when he entered, motioned impatiently for the students to fan out against the wall facing the patient's bed. A respirator cycled with rapid, hi-pitched sighs. EKG, blood pressure, and pulse-ox monitors beeped rapidly. He glanced at the green spikes marching across the screen in rapid tachycardia. No ectopy yet, he noticed. Soon, he suspected, the patient's straining heart would start to fail, and wayward beats would begin showing up. Only one of those premature ventricular contractions needed to hit the fragile QRS complex and it would be hello V-fib and good-bye patient. He thought about the nice bank deposit waiting for him when he reported her location to the Network. He swallowed uncomfortably as he recalled the terse instructions in the coded text.

She'll die soon. I won't actually need to do anything other than report her location, he mused. He forced his attention back to the patient in the hospital bed. Multiple intravenous tubes snaked from bags hanging from ceiling hooks. The linens looked freshly made, the patient bathed and made as comfortable as possible, fresh bandages on IV sites, fresh dressings around the recent tracheotomy he performed. Discarded dirty linens piled in a corner, and two large trashcans spilled over with remnants of chaotic intervention. A nurse in green scrubs sat in a chair with a bedside table pulled close, her computer and handwritten notes spread out in front of her. She stood as the group entered the room, more to avoid getting trampled underfoot than in deference.

Dr. Trek offered the female nurse a tight-lipped smile. She was tall, thin, her long blonde hair pulled back in a ponytail. She probably had great legs.

"What happened in here? Looks like a tornado hit the room," he demanded, not bothering to introduce himself or his medical students.

The nurse motioned towards her notes. "She coded again, just before shift change."

"Why wasn't I notified?" Dr. Trek puffed out his chest in indignation.

The ICU nurse stiffened. "That's not my problem. I'm just in here until day shift is done with their report. She wasn't my patient last night."

What she didn't bother to admit was she and the rest of the staff spent most of the shift in the room trying to stabilize the patient. They'd been short-staffed already, and this patient required two nurses for most of the night. The other six patients fortunately had been stable, but the entire unit ended up behind in giving medications and carrying out procedures.

With a derisive snort, Dr. Trek turned his attention to the group of medical students. "This next patient is a classic case of Adult Respiratory Syndrome, or A.R.D.S.," he began. "I performed a tracheotomy on her after her A-K surgery."

He went over and pulled the covers away from the patient to show the amputated right lower extremity. The patient's hospital gown came to mid-thigh. He brushed that back as well to expose the patient's abdomen and chest, fresh dressings covering the bilateral chest tubes protruding from both sides of her ribcage. He saw the nurse frown and thought he would enjoy grilling her later; demonstrate by example how to treat the nursemaids of the medical profession.

"Can anyone tell me why this patient has developed A.R.D.S.?"

A tentative hand raised behind the front row of students.

"Yes?" he nodded. Perhaps this group represented an improvement over the imbecilic idiots he interrogated last week.

"What does 'A-K' stand for?" A male voice faltered from the back of the group.

And to think he had one of the best reputations in the country. What Vance Trek wouldn't give to be ten years younger and heading for the surgery suites right now. With an exaggerated sigh, he answered.

"Above the Knee. Please keep stupid questions to the classroom." His eyes swept the group. "Who has done their research and knows this patient's history?"

Dr. Trek, nicknamed "Spock" by the medical students not only for his last name but also for his appearance, was a spitting image of the famous character. His black eyebrows angled sharply towards the bridge of his nose, and he had the uncomfortable habit of cocking his right eyebrow when interrogating unfortunate medical students who arrived to the classroom or clinical unprepared.

A female voice popped up from the depths of the stethoscopes and white lab coats. "This patient is a twenty-eight-year-old female admitted early Wednesday morning for high fever. She was unresponsive when she arrived to the ER by ambulance. Blood work came back showing she was septic. A recent gunshot injury to her right tibia-fibula was infected and circulation to the extremity had been badly impaired, possibly by something constrictive, maybe a tourniquet, which might have been used to control bleeding from a recent laceration. ER staff started her immediately on large doses of multi-spectrum IV antibiotics. She went to surgery for debridement of the wound, but the limb was too far gone, and you were called in to perform a right B-K amputation. B-K meaning 'Below the Knee'." The female voice clarified.

"Who's talking? Come up front where I can see you," Dr. Trek demanded. A female medical student. Not that females belonged in medical school, but if he stroked her ego a little, maybe he'd get to stroke other parts of her later.

The students parted and a tiny, chubby, middle-aged woman stepped forward. She didn't reach five feet, had the thin fragile, post-chemotherapy hair so common among patients who endured repeated heavy doses.

"Abigail Higgenbottom," she said, her voice firm.

Vance Trek cursed vilely beneath his breath. "Continue."

Abigail Higgenbottom cleared her throat. "By yesterday morning she was showing symptoms of Adult Respiratory Distress Syndrome. You took her back to surgery and took her knee and most of her thigh. The joint had been severely infected all along, and I don't understand why you didn't do an A-K amputation the first time. The pulmonologist on call decided to leave her intubated, against your recommendation according to his notes, forcing you to return a third time to do her tracheotomy. He put her on respiratory support with high PEEP settings to try to improve the gas exchange in her lungs and reverse her acidosis. So far she's been non-responsive to treatment and blood work is showing beginnings of kidney and liver failure. She coded twice last night." The tiny woman paused, stared at Dr. Trek with clear, intelligent brown eyes. "You charted after her tracheotomy that she won't last forty-eight hours. But Dr. Winehopp thinks if we can support her pulmonary function a little longer, she may stabilize and pull through. He's seen other cases worse than hers survive and make a full recovery."

Dr. Trek acknowledged the information with a small smile. "Okay, so you remember what you read in her chart. What caused her A.R.D.S.?"

Abigail inhaled and straightened to the top of her four-foot eleven-inch height. She had to tilt her head back at a significant angle to maintain eye contact with the surgeon.

"Adult Respiratory Distress Syndrome can occur with any major injury, most often from septicemia. In this case gangrene had set in, which complicated the infection. Exact epidemiology is unknown, but when it occurs the lungs become wooden and unable perform gas exchange, carbon dioxide builds up in the body causing acute acidosis and the onset of kidney and other organ failure. Treatment is high-pressure respirator, antibiotics for infection, morphine for pain if the patient is conscious."

"And the prognosis?" Dr. Trek asked.

"Not good, that's for sure," came a tentative voice from the back.

"I want numbers, not opinions," Dr. Trek snapped. Uncomfortable silence fell among the group. The rapid wheezing of the respirator and electronic beeps sounded extraordinarily loud.

Abigail cleared her throat again. "Well, if the high PEEP settings don't pop a lung, prognosis is about fifty-fifty."

A half-dozen pairs of eyes dropped automatically to the chest tubes protruding from the patient's chest to the gently bubbling containers collecting bloody drainage.

Abigail continued, carefully keeping emotion out of her voice. "In this case, the patient's bilateral lung collapse complicates things."

Dr. Trek turned to the nurse standing in the corner. "Any signs of cardiac stress over the last twelve hours?" he asked.

The nurse watched him with a steady, unintimidated expression. "You mean besides her tachycardia, hypoxia, poor capillary refill, and the fact she coded twice last night?"

Dr. Trek's eyes narrowed when Abigail smiled. He opened his mouth to retort when another nurse entered the room. He swung his angry eyes to her. "Are you night shift?"

The female nurse nodded. She was older, about his age, her gray hair cut short. "What can I help with?" she asked.

Dr. Trek was quick to reply. "You didn't page me when this patient coded."

The nurse moved to the computer and paperwork on the bedside table. She rifled through several pages. "No, Sir. We didn't. You weren't on the on-call list. Your med student was here all night. So was Dr. Winehopp, her pulmonologist. I didn't see the need to disturb you."

Dr. Trek whipped around to the medical students. "Which one of you spent the night here?"

Abigail looked over at the patient, then back to Dr. Trek. "I did. And I'll stay in the building; see how Winehopp handles her acidosis. He worked all night to keep her alive. He doesn't believe in giving up on a patient's chances, no matter how critical. Ever." Her words echoed in the ensuing silence. Dr. Trek stiffened.

"That kind of insubordinate attitude demonstrates one thing." He waited a beat before continuing. "You belong in a nursing program, not medical school." He walked over to the bedside and ripped bandages off the IV sites and chest tubes, and the gauze from around the fresh tracheotomy. "This inflammation is unacceptable," he growled to the two nurses standing on either side of the bed. He turned and waved the medical students out of the room, and the flock of white lab coats disappeared through the ICU double doors.

~*~

"Excuse me." Dr. Trek broke into the line at the coffee shop on the first floor of the teaching hospital. He ordered a latte, then found a corner table and pulled out his phone. He used the code to send his information, then stared at the reply. He'd joined the Network several years ago as an auxiliary, a pair of eyes to spot targets.

He'd never received an order to actually kill someone before.

~ * ~

"What an asshole," Sherry Mills muttered as she began re-placing dressings.

Karen Dempsy pulled the patient's gown to cover her and tucked the blankets around her again. "Go home, Sherry. You've been up all night. I can take care of this." She was twenty years younger than Sherry. She stroked the young patient's limp black hair, her brown eyes wet, her expression distressed. "Do you think he's right about her not making it?"

Sherry stopped what she was doing and met Karen's worried expression. "Keep the faith, Karen. Call the latest ABGs in to Winehopp. He's in the building somewhere, probably trying to catch a couple of hours sleep. We're not giving up on her." As she spoke, her eyes drifted up to the EKG monitor. A wide, distorted, disorganized blip interrupted the uniformity of the cardiac spikes.

Another premature ventricular contraction, aka PVC. An ugly one. She reached over and hit a button on the monitor to record the event.

~ * ~

At Reeves insistence he and Detectives Gates made yet an-other trip to the Lamont place Friday evening. Several storms had blown through, emergency calls once again jammed the system, and they were ridiculously short-staffed. Gates argued ineffectively that they needed to stay in town to help.

"What do you expect to find out here?" Gates asked irritably as he pulled his Ford to a stop in front of the staircase that led to the pile of rubble.

Reeves slid from the passenger seat. "I still think Tyler's wife is here somewhere."

Gates stood and surveyed the wreckage. Yellow police tape fluttered in the stiff wind. "You planning on using a bulldozer to move this crap?"

"I might," Reeves shot back.

Gates rested his hands on the hood of his car and sighed. "Look, Reeves. You've got a lot of potential as a detective, you just need to back off the one-track thinking and take a look at what the physical evidence is telling you, not what you want it to tell you. Circumstantial evidence is almost always misleading, and it's a mistake to prioritize that over the physical evidence we've obtained so far." He was about to add more when Reeves's cell phone rang. Reeves held up a hand.

"Hold that thought. Reeves here," he answered. Shock froze his face and the color drained away until Gates thought he might fall over in a dead faint.

"What do you mean, he's not there!" He shouted into his cell phone.

Gates groped for his cell and called Dispatch. "What's going on?" he demanded. He stood beside his car not believing his ears.

"Oh my God." He cut the call, wriggled his chunky frame behind the wheel.

"Get in, Reeves!" he yelled, trying to get the man's attention. Reeves paced back and forth waving his free hand, yelling at the person on the other end of the call.

Like yelling and pacing would do a damned bit of good. Cleveland County Jail was on the receiving end of Reeves' conniption.

Reeves ignored Gates and continued to shout. "Our desk told me a couple of your guys came and got him to take back to your place for questions concerning the Parsons' house! Are you telling me that your boys managed to lose him on the way down?"

Gates got out, stalked over to the other side of the car. "Get in, damn it!"

Reeves kicked at the debris around his feet. "You'll be handing out parking tickets for this, Hayes!" Angrily he cut the call and hit the speed dial to the Pottawatomie County Sheriff's Office. He jumped into the passenger's seat, slammed the door as Gates hurried around, slid behind the wheel, started the car, then swung a U-turn with a squeal of rubber on pavement.

"I need to speak to the dickhead who released Tyler to the two imposters posing as Cleveland County Deputies!" Reeves shouted into the phone.

A young male officer's voice came on the line.

"Deputy Phillips here."

Reeves glared at the road in front of him. Friday evening. What a way to start the weekend. "What kind of paperwork did they show you?" he demanded.

"Um, they didn't have any with them."

Reeves shook his fist at the windshield. "Are you telling me you released a murder suspect on no authority except a couple of uniforms?" Heads were going to roll over this screw-up.

Phillips' voice, though soft, came across rock steady. "Yes, Sir, that's what I'm saying. The two deputies behaved like they knew what they were doing. No one besides me was in the building at the time."

"Did security cameras pick them up?" Reeves demanded.

"Yes, Sir. Their pictures are already out."

"I'll have your badge for this!" Reeves cut the call. Gates opened his mouth.

Reeves shook his head. "Don't start in on me. I don't want to hear it," he growled as he glared out the passenger window.

"Call them back. Make sure they've put an APB out for Tyler as well," Gates advised. "I'm not going to say a damned thing. We're on this case together. I'm in as much shit as you are over this screw up."

Reeves put the call through. "Please tell me someone has put an APB out for Tyler," he tried to calm down.

"Yes, Sir," the desk sergeant replied. "It's out all over the state. So are the security pictures of the two imposters."

Reeves ran a hand over his thin brown hair. "What did they look like?"

Gates rubbed his forehead as he drove. God, what a mess. "Put it on speaker so I can listen in, too," he told Reeves, who jabbed a finger at his phone. Gates debated using his siren, then rejected the idea. No amount of speed would bring Tyler back now.

The desk sergeant's voice came over the speaker. "According to Phillips, they were the same height and features, dark skin tone, collar-length black hair, although they both wore sunglasses and hats that hid their features. Around five seven or so, same build. He said they looked American Indian."

"Seal off the entire building and get CSI in there to start dusting for prints." Reeves swore again.

"Harrison Gates here," Gates spoke up. "Find out whether Phillips got a look at the vehicle they were driving. If they arrived in a Cleveland County police cruiser, that'll narrow the vehicle search."

"Ah...." The desk sergeant's voice trailed off.

Reeves groaned. "Don't tell me. They came in an unmarked vehicle."

"Yep."

"Didn't Phillips get suspicious when they didn't show up in a marked unit? Can't he give some type of description? Make? Markings? Color? Anything? License plate?" Reeves pressed, grasping for straws.

"Nada. No plate number. Not even a color. Phillips didn't suspect anything, so he didn't pay attention."

"I don't fucking believe this," Reeves wailed, cutting the call. "I'll have that kid's badge." He practically writhed in his seat.

"No you won't," Gates shook his head. "It was a rookie mistake. A bad one, I admit, but he shouldn't have been alone. We're stretched too thin. You know that as well as I do."

Reeves pounded the dash with his fist. "Can't you go any faster? Don't you have lights and sound on this thing?"

"Of course I have lights and sound." Gates rolled his eyes.

"Well, turn the damned things on and put the pedal to the metal!"

Gates reflected on his earlier opinion about lights and sound with the proverbial horse out of the barn, and ignored Reeves.

Reeves threw his phone into the backseat and stared out the front, dreading the arrival to their now-empty jail cell.

Chapter Seventeen

"Now what's he on about?" Hawk muttered, watching via the security monitors as one of the two detectives paced and apparently yelled into his cell phone, judging by the way the veins stuck out along his skinny neck. He turned to Joe Healing Water, who sat staring at the computer screen. Hawk waved, and the Indian glanced up.

"Can you get sound on any of these?"

Joe Healing Water shook his head, and Hawk turned his eyes to the grainy black-and-white screens. "I can't see their faces well enough to lip-read." He frowned. "We ought to find out what they're on about."

Joe stabbed at the computer keys.

Should I waltz up there and ask them?

Hawk sighed. Obviously, Healing Water was still pissed at him. "No, I'd rather not blow our location." He made swatting motions at Joe. "Move over. Let me at the computer for a bit."

Joe stood, and Hawk sat down. His fingers ran over the keys as he Googled local news stations.

"Where are we again?" he asked. Joe's gnarled hands reached around him. He hit the window he'd been using to type his communications with Hawk.

Pottawatomie County. Shawnee. Oklahoma. USA.

"Right." Hawk worked around the search engine some more, ignoring Healing Water's sarcasm. "Ah. This explains it." He slumped against the metal folding chair and stared at the screen in disbelief.

"Bloody fucking hell. They've gone and lost Jeremiah." He couldn't hear the report, but he could read the news feed crawling across the bottom of the screen. A grainy, black-and-white photo of two male figures replaced the reporter's face. His eyes narrowed and he leaned in for a closer look.

No mistake. Even with the poor quality, he recognized the Lee twins. Which meant the Charlie Network now had Jeremiah.

"Bloody fucking *hell*," he repeated. He stood and wove a crooked line to the bunks, slumped down on the bottom mattress to think.

This was a problem from numerous angles. It wouldn't take Chan Lee long to extract the information he needed from Tyler on the location of the bunker. He and Joe had at most a forty-eight-hour window to get to Jeremiah.

That would explain why the coppers on the monitor were so upset, but it didn't help Jeremiah's chances of being found. He looked up and saw Joe pointing to the computer screen. With trepidation, he rose and stumbled across the room.

Was this part of your plan, too?

Hawk released a sigh. "For the record, no. Nicking Jeremiah from a jail cell would not be my idea. He'd be safer behind bars." He leaned forward, confirmed he had not misidentified the photo. "You do realize these chaps are the ones I told you about?"

Joe's fingers stabbed the keyboard.

Asian twins good with rifles. In other words, bad news.

"Bloody fucking bad news." Hawk ran a hand through his grimy hair, then over the bristles covering his face. "The Lee twins have just checked us."

Joe glowered.

"Do you play Chess?" Hawk gingerly massaged the bandages on both ears, wished again for a miracle healing and a return of his aural senses.

Joe nodded, his lips drawn into a thin, irritated line as he typed again.

Right now you're looking a lot like the horse's ass.

"That would be the knight." Hawk retorted. He watched the news report again. "Damn him. Chan Lee's got us in a bad spot. How did they manage to nick Jeremiah from one of your county jails?"

Joe typed.

From the report, sounds like they swiped a couple of deputy uniforms and bluffed their way.

Hawk glanced at the security screens in time to watch the cops drive away, then re-read the news feed at the bottom of the computer window. He grimaced. "According to the news report, the police believe Jeremiah arranged the escape."

Hawk and Healing Water regarded each other for several moments before Joe began typing again. Sliding his hands into the pockets of his cargo pants, Hawk leaned over to read the screen.

Charlie will use Jeremiah to smoke us out.

Hawk nodded his expression grim. "That would be my guess."

Charlie is the best of the best. We're talking hours, not days, before she kills Jeremiah.

Hawk sighed. "Twenty-four hours tops before she breaks him. No more than forty-eight before she knows everything he knows, including the location of this bunker." Hawk regarded the now empty monitors. "It's a safe bet the police haven't a clue who's behind this. And by the time they figure it out, Jeremiah will be long dead."

Joe's fingers ran over the keyboard.

Because Jeremiah's their prime suspect, they're convinced he's behind it all, that he arranged for someone to spring him from jail.

"Precisely," Hawk nodded. "The circumstantial evidence against him is already damning. This will make things worse. They'll have him convicted and hanged in their minds for the murders and bombings, even if he survives the Charlie Network and makes it to trial." He swung his eyes around the room. His vision seemed clearer, his vertigo less intense. "The coppers are looking in all the wrong directions. They ought to be searching for Mattie."

He walked the length of the room and back again, the beamed ceiling so low as to create a mild claustrophobic feeling. His gait seemed more steady, his walking less erratic. Definitely signs of improvement. Now if the buzzing in his ears would just go away.

He stopped beside Joe. "Have you an idea where they'll take him?"

Joe gazed into space, then typed.

The Rez is too nosy. Mary Eagle Feather will want to keep Jeremiah's presence quiet. Last I heard she was in Victor.

Joe's expression blanked. Hawk was ready to poke him to see whether he had lapsed into some kind of catatonic state when he stirred and typed again.

I know where they'll take him.

Hawk's eyebrows quirked. "Do you now? Was that some kind of mental telepathy with our boy? Did you just send your spirit self out for a bit of a look?" He realized he must sound annoyed when Joe sent him a cold stare before turning back to type again.

You're the one who changed all the plans without bothering to tell any of us.

"I'm the bloody fool who volunteered to intercept the team Charlie sent," Hawk blew out a sigh. "And you and Jeremiah were too thick to realize I got myself into rather a spot of trouble because of it." He spun on his heel, lost his balance, braced a hand against the wall to prevent himself from falling.

Damn it all. A minute ago his vertigo seemed much improved. He guessed Joe was typing again, turned, then leaned forward to read.

You went rogue, you lousy Brit. Decided you were some double-oh agent instead of part of a team. There are always ways to contact team members when things get fucked up. Instead, you acted like a damned fool movie star wanna-be. And now Jeremiah and Mattie's live are both in danger.

Hawk met Healing Water's angry stare, wondered suddenly whether he would have reacted differently prior to the car bomb that almost took his life two years ago. He broke eye contact and carefully walked the length of the room. Running a hand through his hair again, Hawk released a heavy sigh and tilted his head to stare at the ceiling beams.

The answer shook him. Yes. He would have acted like a team member, would have put his faith in Joe and Jeremiah. Just like he had put his faith in Max, the CIA agent supposedly assigned to help locate the mole in their security network when in fact he was the mole and already knew Chan Lee to be a double agent.

Hawk shook his head in resignation. That whole experience shot holes in his ability to trust anyone else, which is what got him into so much trouble when Mattie took that infamous picture of him at the ball game. He no longer trusted what anyone told him, starting with her, and the distrust among himself, Healing Water, and Tyler had contributed to the cock-up of everything since.

And now, as if to prove his lack of faith, Hawk's instincts rejected trusting Healing Water despite the fact the old Indian had rescued him from surely ending up in a jail cell, hidden him away, even bandaged his wounds. He felt uncomfortably vulnerable, not being able to hear a bloody thing, and it would be too easy for the

Indian to sneak up behind him and put an end to it all. With his current deafness, Hawk wouldn't hear a train wreck if it occurred right in front of him.

Hawk turned and studied the old Indian, the wrinkles in his face carved like one of those bloody totem poles. The room shrank as time warped backward two years. He heard the explosion as the bomb annihilated the car he just stepped out of, felt the flames sear his back and legs as though he were on a barbecue. He winced as he recalled the agony during his long recovery, trying to build enough muscle to walk again, the months and months of constant rehabilitation to regain strength and mobility.

And now he felt the same loss of independence all over again. He hadn't suffered severe burns, but the vertigo and hearing loss made him an easy target, negated his ability to offer assistance of any sort. To compound the problem, not only was he physically useless, he possessed only surface knowledge of the region and the Reservations, while Joe knew the head of the Charlie Network, was intimately familiar with the surrounding territory.

The Indian smirked at him, waved him over. Hawk swallowed, straightened, and tried to walk a straight line to the desk. He hesitated before bending to read the computer screen.

Divide and conquer.

Hawk straightened and backed a couple of steps, unable to control the strong instinct of creating distance between himself and a potential threat. "They've been successful so far. They've got Jeremiah. And here we sit, pinned down in this underground grave." He didn't want to admit the distrust he felt.

Joe's grin broadened, exposing practically all of his teeth. Rather like a shark about to bite, Hawk thought. His gnarled fingers poked the keyboard. Hawk swallowed again and closed the distance.

How you ever made it into MI6 beats me. No poker face whatsoever. I could've had your scalp on a post any number of times since I picked you up out of those damned thorn bushes.

"Oh, my. How reassuring." Hawk breathed. "No bloody shotgun this time?"

Healing Water's eyes narrowed, the lines in his face deepened as he typed.

After losing Mattie, you deserve something slower.

Hawk released a sigh. "I would have to agree." He sat down in the metal folding chair. Healing Water nodded slowly as a sly expression slid across his features.

So, time to regroup, not kill each other. We need to divide and conquer.

Hawk reached over, stabbed a key and the news report re-appeared, poked his finger at the Asian twins' photograph.

Joe nodded.

"Right." Hawk propped his elbows on his knees and mas-saged his temples. Then he stood, slid his hands into his pockets, and retreated to the far side of the room. He sat down on one of the beds, rested his chin thoughtfully on top of his hands.

"I've a good notion how Chan Lee works. Problem is, he'll have acquired similar knowledge of me."

Joe watched him from across the room.

"Still, if we faced just Chan Lee, I could out-maneuver him." Hawk's eyes met Joe's. "It's his twin I'm unclear about. He's the fly in the soup."

Joe nodded and motioned Hawk over again. He sighed and stood.

"I'll be glad when I can hear again," he muttered as he once more crossed the room. Joe's fingers stabbed the keyboard.

You're not the only one. I'm tired of being stuck with a paranoid, deaf-as-a-post, would-be sniper. What do you think the Lee twins will do?

Hawk frowned. "I'm thinking they'll split. One of them will deliver Jeremiah; the other will set up an ambush to take us out."

Joe nodded as he typed.

My thoughts exactly. They'll head for the southwest corner of Colorado, which means they'll use Highway Eighty-Seven.

Hawk stared at what Joe had written. "Have you an idea where the ambush might occur?"

Joe typed.

Capulin National Monument.

Hawk frowned. "That sounds familiar."

Joe typed some more.

Probably from Mattie when you took her to New Mexico to get rid of her.

Hawk winced. "Right." He glanced at the Indian sitting be-side him. "Though, you must admit that for a foreigner, I was ra-ther spot on with the location."

Joe's mouth moved in what seemed light speed as he scolded. Hawk imagined well enough what he spouted off over the next several minutes, and felt rather relieved he could not hear anything.

Joe's lips snapped shut, ending his tirade. He turned and stabbed at the keyboard.

That's the only thing you were "spot on" about.

Hawk leaned against the hard metal back of the chair. "Tell me more about Capulin."

Joe typed.

An extinct ring of volcanoes in the northeast section of New Mexico. The Capulin cone is the tallest and most distinct. Ancient lava beds cover the entire area, which gives us ample terrain coverage for approach.

Hawk's lips curled into a grim smile. "Chan won't know the area. That'll be to our advantage. He'll focus on the availability of an elevated sniper roost. Which cone would you guess? Capulin?"

Joe shook his head, his fingers dancing over the keyboard.

Probably not the big cone because of tourist traffic. But there are smaller cones within a mile of the highway. Nice elevation for surveillance, excellent cover for a sniper.

Hawk stared at the computer screen, his black eyebrows furrowed in thought. "You're sure of the location? What about other routes?"

Joe shook his head, typed some more.

Highway Eighty-Seven is the most direct route to Wolf Creek Pass, where Charlie is hiding out. Other routes are too roundabout, will take too much time. They'll want to get Jeremiah to Mary Eagle Feather ASAP.

Hawk thought back to the empty, high desert prairie where he had taken Mattie. He remembered the flat terrain, the expansive horizon, the unimpaired visibility for miles. He had chosen that area because of the lack of roadways and townships on the map. It had been as open and sparsely populated as he could have hoped. A perfect location to get rid of a body.

A perfect location for an ambush.

His attention turned to the computer screen when he caught the movement of Joe's fingers from the corner of his eye.

You're not going to be worth much, since you're deaf as a post.

A hint of a smile curled the corners of Hawk's mouth. "Well, you're not young enough to be running any marathons." He motioned for Joe to move, took his seat at the computer.

"I want to check on Mattie." Hawk saw Joe shake his head, understood what he was thinking. "I realize we're not positive the patient in Norman Hospital ICU is Mattie, but it's as good a guess as any. She would not have been in shape to make it to Oklahoma City. I'm putting my money on the Jane Doe in the Norman ICU."

Joe shook his head again and leaned over until his fingers reached the keyboard.

If she was admitted to the hospital in Norman, they probably transferred her to one of the big hospitals in Oklahoma City.

Hawk pushed Joe's hands aside and went back to his search. "Then I'll run a search of Jane Does in those hospitals as well."

Time crept along as Hawk worked his way through security firewalls. Joe retrieved another bottled water, didn't eat any of the MRE's. He stood quietly beside the desk, his eyes flicking between the security monitors and Hawk's progress on the computer screen. The black-and-white security monitors showed strong winds and rain thrashing the trees and foliage surrounding the ruins of the Lamont Estate.

"There are several hospitals in the Oklahoma City area, and several Jane Does," Hawk murmured after a while. "No Jane Doe in any of the ICUs."

Joe leaned over, moved the cursor to the small window where he had been typing, then reached for the keyboard.

What about the morgue?

Hawk winced, worked through more security firewalls. A screen popped up, and Hawk's eyes scanned the list of names.

"Bloody hell." He sensed Joe grow still, knew the Indian had stopped breathing.

A Jane Doe appeared on the list in the morgue at St. Anthony's Hospital in Oklahoma City. Previously in ICU. Same age as Mattie.

Joe reached over, his fingers hovering, then typing slowly.

We don't know for sure it's Mattie.

Hawk shook his head. He didn't want to believe it, either, but his recent run of luck did not give Mattie good odds.

"Her leg didn't look good when I last saw her," he muttered under his breath.

Joe shook his head.

Don't believe that. I'm not sensing her spirit.

Hawk blew out a sigh. If the Indian wanted to be in denial, so be it. He closed the screen, went back to the one showing local news.

"Your law enforcement's got a bit of a sticky wicket." He watched news personnel crowding around an officer standing in front of the Pottawatomie County Courthouse.

"Is that the sheriff?" he asked Joe. The latter nodded, bent over, typed on the keyboard.

Just as we thought. They're trying to put the blame on Jeremiah. Saying he had cohorts who helped spring him from jail.

Hawk grunted. "Bloody idiots."

Joe nodded again, typed some more.

They'll never find Jeremiah in time. Won't even know where to look. Those twins pulled the perfect abduction. The police haven't a clue Jeremiah's been kidnapped.

Hawk stood and moved to the cabinets that held emergency supplies and gear.

"What have we in terms of clothes, weapons, and the like?" he asked as he started taking inventory. Joe joined him and shook his head.

"Emergency supplies. That's what you're saying?" Hawk guessed. "Any weapons?" He felt a sinking in the pit of his stomach. Deaf, ignorant, and weaponless. Could their situation get any worse?

Joe turned and strode to a tall cabinet that stood beside the tunnel entrance to the bunker. He opened both doors, reached inside, retrieved two hunting rifles and a pump-action shotgun. After Jeremiah had left, he had returned all the weapons from the table to the storage cabinets.

Hawk joined him, took one of the hunting rifles. The scopes were decent enough. The shotgun had a bead sight.

Joe made motions as though he were shooting a bow and arrow, then reached into the cabinet again and came out with an expensive compound bow. He held it out towards Hawk, who shook his head.

"Not my specialty."

Joe grinned at him, leaned the rifle and compound bow

against the wall, then motioned Hawk to the computer. Hawk put down the rifle and the shotgun and followed. Joe sat down, began typing.

I'm thinking you'd be the perfect diversion.

Hawk stared at the printed words for a long time. "As in bait. Chan's after me anyway. Why disappoint him?" Hawk's mouth curled into a devious smile. "You're the expert on terrain and such."

Joe typed.

Yeah, and with a little extra equipment, you'll stick out like a sore thumb.

"What about transportation?" Hawk asked, resuming his seat in the chair beside Joe.

We've got a beat up rusty, noisy, red truck I hot-wired when I came looking for Jeremiah after he quit answering his cell.

"Impossible to hide, easy to spot from a distance." Hawk paused. "No doubt the Charlie Network will have surveillance in place."

Joe's head bobbed up and down.

Hawk leaned back, his expression thoughtful. "But how will we spot them?"

Joe typed again.

Police don't know about you. And they've basically forgotten about me.

Hawk frowned. "You're off topic. That's not the issue."

When Joe continued to stare at him, Hawk tilted his head back and waited for enlightenment.

"I was unconscious when you plucked me from those thorn bushes," he declared slowly. "And I've been here since."

Joe's sly grin returned as he typed.

We're both off the map.

Hawk wasn't ready to accept they might have an advantage. "Not where Charlie and the Lee twins are concerned. They know we're involved."

Joe typed again.

They can't be sure you're still a threat. No mention of you in the news, no mention of total body count. For all they know, the blast might have killed you. And like you said, I'm just an old man.

"There's no mention of the coppers looking for me," Hawk mused, not wanting to believe he'd actually escaped detection.

"Despite the fact my prints were all over the van."

Joe grinned.

Hawk stood and managed to walk a straight line to the weapons resting against the wall. He picked up one of the rifles, checked the mechanism, peered through the chamber.

"Could use a spot of cleaning. Probably hasn't been zeroed in a while." He looked at Joe.

Joe turned and typed. Hawk knew the Indian's thoughts, knew it to be their only choice.

"Both twins are superb snipers." His statement elicited information rather than apprehension. "One of us will need to create a diversion. Too bad Jeremiah isn't available to help with that. I suspect we'll be facing off with one of them, as the other will be motoring Jeremiah to his death." He paused, stared at the Indian sitting at the desk. "We must assume both twins will know your background and involvement, and that you at least will attempt a rescue."

Joe's grin widened, revealing all of his impeccable teeth.

"And obviously that fact rather pleases you," Hawk frowned. "Because they'll know you're older than bloody sin itself, so they'll think they're invincible." He ran a hand down his face, felt the thick stubble of his growing beard. "And here I am, deaf as a post, stumbling about like a bloody toddler."

Joe nodded, motioned Hawk over to the computer.

"You needn't worry about getting rid of me when one of the Lee twins will do it for you. Either way, I'll end up with a bloody bullet through my skull," Hawk grinned as he sat down and squinted at the typed words.

I trust you know how to avoid a bullet long enough for me to put an arrow through the bastard.

Chapter Eighteen

Friday night FBI Special Agent Tony Mills parked his navy blue sedan in the small lot behind the Pottawatomie County Courthouse. The old three-story building looked down on him as he walked around to the front entrance, his dark summer suit hanging loosely on his tall, lanky frame. His white shirt and thin dark tie emphasized his Adam's Apple. Short gray hair looked like steel wool on his oval head. He glanced towards the southwest horizon. Born and raised in Enid, Oklahoma, Tony instinctively kept an eye on the weather during tornado season. The forecasters in this part of the country were some of the best in the world, but like any other prairie native, he kept his own weather eye out, just in case. The expansive horizon brought some of the most dangerous conditions, but it also gave good warning of approaching trouble.

Tony hurried into the building, climbed the stairs to the third floor. The desk officer greeted him.

"Can I help you?"

"Special Agent Tony Mills here to see Detective Gates." He held up his badge and ID.

The young officer's blue eyes widened with a classic deer-in-the-headlights expression when he saw Tony's credentials. He was young, overweight, his tan uniform shirt dark beneath the armpits. He might as well have "ROOKIE" stamped across his forehead.

"You the one who released Tyler to a couple of imposters?" Tony inquired, keeping his voice neutral. The young officer broke eye contact and looked away.

"Yes, Sir."

"I'd like to talk you through what happened, see if you can remember more about their description, mannerisms. Later, after I'm done with the detectives."

The rookie nodded. "Yes, Sir."

The kid picked up the desk phone and punched a button, then spoke into the receiver. He replaced the handset and buzzed Tony through the locked door that separated the reception area from the rest of the department.

Detective Harrison Gates waited for him in the hallway.

"Good to see you, Tony." He shook the agent's long, thin hand, felt the same surprise he always did when Tony's grip squeezed with unexpected strength.

"Seems like we always talk about getting together for that fishing trip, and then time gets away and we never follow up." Tony grinned at his long-time friend, his teeth yellow from too many cigarettes and not enough trips to the dentist. Gates led the way to his office and shut the door. Reeves sat at his desk and looked up when Mills entered.

"Detective Jason Reeves," he stood and offered his hand.

"Tony Mills." The agent shook hands with the young detective, then folded himself into a metal chair facing Gates' desk.

Harrison rounded the desk and collapsed into the chair. He pulled open a drawer, retrieved an ashtray in anticipation of his friend's next actions. He set the ashtray on the desk, wondered again whether he should take up smoking despite his wife's wishes, and lose some of the weight he had gained. "We've got a real mess on our hands."

Tony nodded. "So I've heard." He pulled a pack of cigarettes from an inside pocket of his suit jacket, then hesitated and glanced at Reeves, who looked at Gates.

Harrison grinned. "Go ahead. I know you think better with a cancer stick between your lips." He pushed the ashtray towards the Special Agent.

Tony grunted, lit a cigarette with a lighter he pulled from his pants pocket, returned cigarettes and lighter to their respective places, and inhaled a lungful of nicotine.

"So, six bodies, a kidnapping, and an escaped inmate who is your lead suspect?" He pursed his lips and sent smoke upwards in a thin, blue stream.

"And media screaming incompetence. They want our heads on a stick." Gates shook his head. "God I get sick and tired of their vigilante attitude sometimes."

Mills leaned forward in his chair. "So why are you thinking this is something bigger than local dirt bags?"

Gates opened a folder on his desk and pulled out some 8x10 photos.

"These are the ones found dead at the scene of the second

residential explosion. Three of them with execution style bullet holes. The fourth was found in a van we suspect held the kidnap victim. None of them are local boys, not even on state record. My gut's telling me this is big, especially after we found two more dead guys buried at the scene of the first explosion a day after we secured the area. We haven't released any of the photos to the media yet because, quite frankly, we don't know what the hell is going on."

Mills took the photos and studied each in turn. "What about gang related?"

Gates shook his head. "First, we really don't get much gang activity out here, since most of their interest is in the city. Second, none of these guys have any gang markings on them. And third, I just don't see two residential explosions as being gang related activity."

Mills paused on the last photo and stared at it for so long his fresh cigarette burned down to the filter before he glanced for the ashtray. He stubbed the butt out.

"This isn't just big, it's international. I'm having a hard time believing what I'm seeing." He glanced up, his light brown eyes scrutinizing first Gates, then Reeves. "We're talking Shawnee, Oklahoma, right? These bodies were found here? In your jurisdiction? Not somewhere in Oklahoma City?"

Reeves spoke up. "And the guy I'm thinking is behind it all is American Indian. Goes by the name of Jeremiah Black Bear Tyler. He's the one who managed to escape. The rookie at the front desk didn't know procedure and let a couple of Tyler's cronies bust him out."

Mills shook his head. "No, that's where you're wrong. I'm not sure what Tyler's involvement is, but it would be on this side of the law."

Gates leaned forward. "You know him?"

Mills nodded. "I know him by reputation. Hell of an operative. Successfully dropped off the map, although I think the big boss still uses him."

Reeves stared at him for a full two minutes. "You're kidding, right?" He finally managed to ask. "We're talking about a Southern Ute who married into the Lamont fortune?"

Tony Mills studied the young detective. "Same guy, wrong assessment."

Harrison Gates grunted. "Let me talk you through the angle we've been using." He propped his forearms on his desk and sent a quick glance towards Reeves, who leaned back in his chair and pressed his lips together.

"Circumstantial evidence indicates Tyler is involved, though at this point we're not quite sure how. At first we thought he was after the Lamont fortune. His wife's family have all died from apparent accidents over the last couple of years, the most recent being her parents, who died in a car crash this past January, and her only sister, who died from extended, self-inflicted starvation. That makes her the last of the Lamonts. That also makes her an extremely wealthy woman. We initially thought Tyler had her killed, but we haven't found a body. Tyler was found at the scene of the second explosion. It doesn't take a genius to figure his intent was to get rid of his brother in order to be the sole heir of the Lamont estate."

Tony looked down at the photos in his hands, tapped one with a long, thin finger, and thought over the detective's statement.

He admired Harrison Gates. The detective was a good cop, honest, not a bad bone in his body. His was a black-and-white personality, which helped him see clearly between right and wrong. He also had a loyal streak, which meant he would be the last to admit he and the young detective were at odds with each other. Tony sensed the tension between the two detectives. If one of them was being bull-headed about interpreting facts versus circumstantial evidence, he would put both of them in a very vulnerable position.

"Okay, let's put Tyler on a back burner for a moment," he suggested, laying the photos down on the desk and spreading them out. He pointed to the one on the far right. "This man is suspected to have been involved in several international assassinations. We've been working with the Brits trying to figure out who's behind them. We've managed to get a name. The Charlie Network. That's about all, though."

"International assassins?" Reeves interrupted, his face suddenly pale. "Are you serious?"

"Hang on a sec," Gates interrupted. "Did you just say you've been working with the British on this?"

Mills acknowledged with a small nod.

"My God, the stranger seen with Mattie," Gates swung his eyes to Reeves, then flipped through the pages in the folder. Reeves straightened.

"It's in with the report from the Lamont explosion," he offered.

Tony studied each detective in turn. "Mind telling me what you're talking about?"

Reeves explained. "A witness from the Lamont estate described a stranger who had an English accent with Mattie Tyler the night she disappeared. The night the house blew up."

"Let me see the description." Mills held out his hand. Gates found the page, passed it across the desk. Silence filled the tiny office. The Special Agent chose his next words carefully.

"Can't say as the description rings a bell, but I know MI6 has been trying to expose a mole in their network, someone who took out an important witness and almost killed one of their guys a couple of years ago."

"So why in hell would international assassins show up in Shawnee, Oklahoma of all places?" Reeves blurted, his eyes so wide that white showed around both irises.

"Good question." Tony laid the paper on the desk, then leaned against the straight-backed chair, pulled another cigarette out, dug around for his lighter. "It doesn't fit." He shook his head as he exhaled a cloud of blue smoke. Gates filed the report among the other sheets in the folder.

"It would if Tyler hired them to take out his wife and his brother," Gates offered, sliding his eyes in Reeves' direction. The young detective jerked.

"Are you actually agreeing with me?" he asked Gates.

Gates shook his head. "No, not really, but just because we disagree doesn't mean I'll ignore possible connections."

The men sat for several minutes in silence. Tony's eyes drifted to the small window behind Gates as he smoked. Thunder rumbled outside and rain spattered against the windowpane.

The phone on Gates' desk rang, breaking the silence. "Detective Harrison Gates," he answered, then frowned. "Okay, bring him back." He hung up.

"That was the front desk. Some lawyer friend of the Lamont family seems to think he's got something important we need to hear."

Tony stubbed out his cigarette, then made ineffective swatting motions at the lingering smoke. "Hope I don't get you into trouble," he grimaced.

A knock sounded on the office door, and the rookie popped his head in. "Mister Stephen Campbell wants to see you, sir."

Gates' frown faded and he nodded. "Send him in."

The men stood as an immensely tall, trim, elderly man ducked into the room. He was elegantly dressed in a tailored light tan suit with a light blue shirt and striped tie. His thick, wavy snow-white hair fell to collar length, his face clean-shaven, his brilliant blue eyes set wide apart, his cheekbones sharp and angular. His age could have been anywhere between sixty and ninety.

Harrison Gates smiled. "Stephen, good to see you." He made introductions. "This is Special Agent Tony Mills and my partner, Detective Jason Reeves. Stephen Campbell, a former attorney who manages the Lamont Estate for Mattie Tyler."

The four men shook hands, and Harrison pulled another chair to the front of his desk. "Have a seat."

Stephen folded his long frame awkwardly into the straight-backed chair.

"How long have you been managing the Lamont Estate?" Reeves asked.

"Since before the two girls were born. George and I go way back." Stephen pulled a yellow folder from a slender black leather briefcase.

"Quite a large sum of money and wealth, I believe," Reeves noted. Gates sighed. The young bull still wanted to hang onto his belief Tyler was behind all of this.

Campbell nodded. "Yes. The desk officer told me you were in a meeting," he said, turning his attention to Harrison, who resumed his seat. "Sorry to interrupt, but I feel its time I filled you in on a few things." He rested his forearms on his knees, the yellow folder dangling from his fingertips. His knees bent comically beneath him. "I have news about Mattie Tyler."

Three sets of eyes stared at him. Gates cleared his throat. "She's been found?"

Stephen held up a wide, long-fingered hand. Harrison recalled that the man had been a major basketball star in his youth. A long time ago. He wondered whether the man still played. He looked like he might still be able to run the length of the court.

"First, I need to explain what I know and how I found it all out." Stephen leaned back, shifted uncomfortably, and crossed one long leg over the other.

"This is Friday," he began. "Wednesday morning, just before sunrise, someone started ringing the front doorbell. I normally have domestic help who answers, but I was alone at the time. I debated whether to ignore the bell and wait for the person to leave." He paused and shook his head. "I am so thankful now I listened to my curiosity. When I opened the door, Mattie Tyler was standing on my doorstep."

"Why haven't you come to us sooner about this?" Reeves interrupted, leaning forward. "Her disappearance has been all over the news. Surely you would know the need to contact us about her location!"

Gates waved at Reeves to calm down. "I must agree with Reeves here. You know the deal, Stephen. For God's sakes, man, you're a lawyer."

Stephen held up a hand. "Detectives, please. Hear me out first before you start slinging accusations."

Gates shook his head. "You're coming to us at least forty-eight hours after Mattie Tyler was reported missing. Like Reeves just pointed out, her picture has been all over the news."

Stephen sighed. "Mattie was injured and in severe pain and not making a lot of sense. I took her in and wanted to call an ambulance right away. Her right leg looked terrible. She was feverish, showing symptoms of shock. But she wouldn't allow me to call anyone." He paused, his bright blue eyes drilled through Detective Gates. "Not even the police, Harrison. As I said, she was rattling a lot of gibberish, not making much sense."

"All the more reason to contact law enforcement," Tony Mills spoke up. "In her condition, her ability to make decisions would be unreliable, which underlines the fact you should have contacted these boys long before now."

Stephen ignored the FBI agent. "From what I could gather, she was kidnapped and managed to escape. She came to me because she didn't know whom to trust. I couldn't break that trust. Not with the shape she was in."

Harrison pulled out a notepad and pencil, and started scribbling notes. "You've been a close friend of the family for years."

"Yes," Stephen nodded. "I helped George establish trust funds for both Angela and Mattie, and also acted as their financial advisor."

"It sounds to me like she suspected her husband was involved with the kidnapping. Is that why she came to you?" Reeves prompted.

Stephen shook his head. "From what I could put together, her sister's husband was responsible for George and Ginnie's death, and also for Angela's death. I remember he swept into Shawnee at the beginning of the summer last year, then eloped with Angela shortly after George and Ginnie's funeral. Mattie was going on about something called the Charlie Network, but that wasn't making much sense to me. She kept saying this Charlie Network was targeting her and her husband because she killed Gary."

The room went silent.

"The Charlie Network?" Reeves finally spoke, his voice high. He cleared his throat and tried again. "You mentioned something about a Charlie Network?" His eyes slid to Tony Mills.

Harrison Gates paused, his pencil hovering over a pad full of notes. "Bill Parsons mentioned something about a brother-in-law." He turned to Reeves. "Remember? He said the guy married Mattie Tyler's sister recently. It was her funeral last Monday we've been hitting Tyler with because of the conflict between his statement and those we've gotten from witnesses at the service."

Stephen turned his clear blue eyes to the Special Agent. "The FBI has been on the case."

Tony stirred and reluctantly nodded. "Gary Tacque. Mattie's brother-in-law. According to police reports, she killed him in the southern part of the Colorado Rocky Mountains."

Stephen turned his attention back to the two detectives. "The brother-in-law was the one going after the Lamont fortune, not Jeremiah Tyler."

Gates stared at Mills. "Is he right that the FBI has been conducting an investigation all this time under our noses without bothering to tell us local yokels?"

The FBI agent nodded slowly. Gates jumped in before he could open his mouth. "And all along I've been accusing Reeves here of pushing theories that don't make any goddamned sense." He leaned back and snapped the pencil in his fingers, then threw the fragments onto his desk. "I don't fucking believe this."

Mills leaned forward. "We kept our investigation under wraps because we didn't want to tip the Charlie Network that we were onto them. We couldn't risk anything being leaked to the media."

Gates rubbed the stubble on his face. "So Mattie's brother-in-law was part of the Network, and the Network avenged his death by destroying her family home and the residence in Norman." Stephen continued. "I know this all sounds pretty strange, especially if you know Mattie and the Lamont family. George and Ginnie never boasted their immense fortune. Except for their estate, you would've thought they were just your regular folk."

"This whole mess is motivated by revenge, rather than by any of these guys going after the Lamont fortune?" Gates asked.

"We suspect Tacque was after the Lamont fortune," the Special Agent clarified.

"So, Tyler might still be after the family wealth. It would make sense he and Tacque were in it together," Reeves offered.

Stephen opened the folder he still held, pulled out several sheets of paper. "Here are copies of the financial arrangements George signed." He passed the sheets around. "You will notice Jeremiah Tyler has been excluded from any kind of inheritance."

Reeves frowned. "Tyler would have known about this. So why all the elaborate shit to try to get to the money? Maybe he hired this Charlie Network to help him get around the documents he signed?"

"I was afraid you'd be thinking along those lines, which is why I brought legal proof stating otherwise." Stephen shifted in his chair, obviously uncomfortable with being folded up like an accordion. He stood and stretched, then walked over to lean against the closed office door. "I'm not sure what role Jeremiah's played in all of this, but Mattie was insistent his life has been in as much danger as hers."

"Which would explain the healing bullet hole in his chest and his recent disappearance," Gates muttered, throwing an exasperated expression towards Reeves. "We've been chasing down the wrong leads." He turned to Mills. "You had to have seen the media circus around this whole case. You could've gotten us on the right track a lot sooner than now."

Stephen cleared his throat. "Mattie was kidnapped by mercenaries who belong to the Charlie Network. They blew up her house, then took her to Norman. It was their van parked in front of the Parsons' house."

"So if her husband wasn't part of all of this, why in the hell did we find him unconscious on the scene?" Reeves demanded.

Tony and Harrison exchanged looks.

"A rescue attempt gone bad?" The Special Agent murmured.

Gates nodded. "Makes sense."

"So…." Reeves paused, his expression troubled. "Tyler's disappearance from our jailhouse was not an escape."

Mill's shook his head. "I'm not so sure. Tyler's brilliant. He could've arranged a way to get out of jail and go under the radar."

Reeves shook his head. "No. His behavior prior to the jailbreak doesn't fit an escape scenario." He stared at Gates. "What was it he told you when you took the Parsons up to see him?"

Gates flipped through his notes. "He looked me straight in the eye and said he was involved." He grunted. "He also said we wouldn't believe him if he tried to explain things."

Reeves turned to the special agent. "Does this Charlie Network have the resources and information to impersonate law enforcement and snag their target from our jail?"

Special Agent Mills sighed. "Absolutely. They've been able to carry out successful assassinations all over the world without leaving a trace."

"Shit," Reeves spat out. "The jailbreak was this Charlie Network outsmarting local cops and making off with Tyler." His statement hung in the air. "Question is, what do they want with him?"

"Revenge, knowledge of the whereabouts of his wife, access to the Lamont fortune," Tony murmured into the silence.

One long stride carried Stephen back to the empty chair. "I agree, Special Agent. Which is one reason why I've kept Mattie's location secret. After hearing her story, I'm positive whoever Gary was in league with is still after the Lamont fortune. They don't know where Mattie is, so they've taken Jeremiah."

"What a screw-up." Reeves slumped against his desk chair. Stephen waited several beats before answering. "Yes." And now you're looking at a second kidnapping."

Gates frowned at the lawyer. "I appreciate your input, Stephen, but you haven't said yet where Mattie is, or what's happened to her."

Stephen's clear blue eyes settled on Harrison. "Mattie is currently in St. Anthony's Hospital in Oklahoma City. She collapsed shortly after she got to my house and hasn't regained consciousness since. I had no idea who might be after her, and I was afraid if I came to you, your staff might inadvertently reveal her location because you would've insisted on visiting her in the hospital, possibly to provide police protection. Her picture is already all over the news and I feared the media would get wind of her location and expose that, too. I wanted to hide her, especially after hearing all she has been through. So I had her admitted under my granddaughter's name, rather than using the typical 'Jane Doe' for unidentified patients."

Tony Mills stirred from deep thought. "Has she regained consciousness yet?"

Stephen shook his head. "She's in critical condition. They had to amputate her leg. And now she's septic, they've put her on a respirator. They're trying to get her stabilized, but things don't look good."

Tony reached into the pocket that held his cigarettes, realized what he was doing, dropped his hand to his lap.

Reeves spoke up, his voice sounding tired, defeated. "And her husband? If what you're thinking is true and he has been kidnapped, where would this Charlie Network take him?"

Stephen shrugged. "I have absolutely no idea. But I can tell you this. They will be convinced Jeremiah knows where Mattie is."

Gates shook his head. "Or, they will convince Tyler his wife is dead. In which case they only need to force him to sign over his inheritance rights to the Lamont fortune, unaware he has no access whatsoever to any of the family money."

"Well, that explains why members of the Charlie Network showed up in Shawnee, Oklahoma," Tony Mills commented, glancing at Gates, then over to Reeves.

"And in the meantime, we've now got six bodies, two destroyed homes, a wife in critical care, a husband who has been kidnapped, and absolutely no leads or suspects," Reeves sighed. "Where do we go from here?"

"Since our cases seem to be connected," Tony Mills spoke up. "I suggest we combine what we've learned, start treating this as one huge case."

"A little late on the cooperation move, aren't we?" Gates shot at Mills.

"Tyler was critically wounded in the confrontation with Mattie's brother-in-law," Reeves interjected. For now, we don't really need to know where the wife is. I'd suggest we run down the common connection between the six dead bodies, see if that gives us a lead on where the Network might be taking Tyler."

Gates nodded towards the stack of photos and then looked at the FBI agent. "Any more information you would like to share?" Tony picked up the photos again. "I'll give you any information that comes up when I run them through our system." "And in the meantime, do we assign police protection for Mattie?" Reeves asked.

The tall lawyer shook his head. "No. She's hidden. I want to keep her that way. I'll give you updates on her condition, but I want your word nobody from your office or anyone else to do with law enforcement," he shot a look at Special Agent Mills, "will show up at the hospital. We don't know whether any members of this network are still in the vicinity trying to find her. I've managed to successfully hide her." He stared at the three men. "I don't want her found."

Chapter Nineteen

Buckled in, his hands securely cuffed behind his back, Jeremiah slumped against the backseat door behind the passenger and watched the two men in the front seat of the sedan. Grudgingly, he acknowledged the twins' brilliance.

Dressed in Cleveland County Deputy Sheriff uniforms, the two assassins arrived late afternoon, during shift change, and in a perfect Oklahoma twang told the young and inexperienced desk officer they were transporting Tyler to the Cleveland County jail for further questions regarding the residential explosion in Norman. Their professional, abrupt manner intimidated the young desk officer into assuming they represented superior authority, and he failed to question the lack of paperwork or prior telephone notification. The two imposters confronted Tyler in the cell, cuffed him, escorted him to an unmarked black police cruiser and whisked away without the slightest suspicion that in fact they had just abducted the Pottawatomie County Sheriff's prime suspect.

Instead of heading south on Interstate thirty-five, which led to Norman and Cleveland County jail, they traveled west on Interstate forty, changed vehicles on the edge of the city, and then continued towards Texas. After almost four hours of non-stop driving, they neared Amarillo. By midnight under a night sky clear and dark, Jeremiah knew they had successfully dropped off law enforcement radar.

Any radar, for that matter. Pottawatomie Sheriff's department had surely put out APBs on the three of them by now. Instead of abandoning the police cruiser for state patrol to find, these two met a third man just off the Interstate, along a deserted two-lane side road, and changed vehicles. No doubt the unmarked police cruiser now sat in a chop shop, nowhere to be found. The person who assisted with the vehicles also provided clothes. The twins quickly swapped their Cleveland County uniforms for T-shirts, jeans, and baseball caps. They even changed the clothes he wore. Though neither of the twins looked familiar, Jeremiah guessed they were part of the Charlie Network. They executed their scheme with calm professionalism, detailed planning, and impressive support.

They both had kept their hats and sunglasses on inside the Pottawatomie County building, but Jeremiah suspected Hawk would recognize the photographs from surveillance footage. And recognition meant Hawk and Healing Water would leave the bunker to follow and attempt a rescue. Joe would know the source behind the kidnapping, would guess the connection to one of the Reservations, and would head west.

He watched the dark, flat terrain slide by as they cruised along the eastern portion of Texas. His assignments surrounding the Charlie Network had led him several times to the Ute Mountain Ute Reservation, so he suspected their destination lay in the Wolf Creek Pass area in Colorado.

He thought of Mattie, the only person in this world other than his little brother Mud Rain whom he held close to his heart.

Where was Mattie? Was she safe? Bill and Becky Parsons hadn't known her location. They promised they would take care of Mud Rain, hide him until things resolved. He fretted over where Bill and Becky could possibly take his little brother to keep him safe, then shook his head to clear his thoughts.

Trust them to care for him, he told himself.

They traveled through Amarillo, reached the exit that intersected Highway eighty-seven, and turned towards the badlands of northern Texas. The clear night sky sparkled with summer stars, streaks of white haze belied hot, humid conditions. They stopped at a station to fill the car, and the twins took turns watching him while the other made use of the facilities. Jeremiah watched stock trucks pass by, noted transporting livestock at this hour was typical to avoid the daytime heat.

The twin behind the wheel angled the car onto the highway. They unwrapped energy bars and bottles of water. The sight made Jeremiah's mouth water, but he swallowed and turned his head towards the window. The earthy stench of stockyards permeated the air-conditioned interior, and Jeremiah glanced at the driver's profile in time to see him wrinkle his nose and mutter an oath.

"Bloody sodding Yanks and their beef. Bloody foul odor, if you ask me."

Jeremiah barely controlled a startled reaction when he heard the man's British accent. Only one of them had spoken at the courthouse, and he had used an impeccable Oklahoma drawl.

It was drawing close to dawn Saturday when they reached northeastern New Mexico. Jeremiah's bladder had begun to cramp when the driver pulled over. The twin in the passenger seat got out, opened Jeremiah's door, and hauled him to his feet. Jeremiah wobbled slightly from being in one position too long, the pain of his chest wound sharp with the sudden movement, his head spinning from his recent concussion. The driver walked around to grasp his other arm, and the two men seemed to sense potential danger because they both checked his cuffed hands before leading him into a small grove of short, wind-blown trees, where he relieved himself with their assistance. He was led back to the car, firmly buckled again into the rear seat behind the passenger.

"How much further?" Wan asked as he angled into the passenger's seat.

Chan slid behind the wheel and cranked the engine over. "Another couple hours, I expect."

"What does GPS say?" Wan pressed as the car bumped onto the black, flat, straight highway pavement.

"Don't have it on. Too much risk." Chan's eyes squinted behind his sunglasses as the sun peeped over the eastern horizon behind them. Damn this American sun. Even at this hour, the brilliant reflection in his rearview mirror blinded him, promising yet another day of merciless heat. His clothes soaked with sweat against the imitation leather, he squirmed uncomfortably in the air-conditioned interior.

Wan felt equally uncomfortable. Not just from the humid conditions inside the car. Their prisoner had not uttered a word. No request for food or water, no complaints. Nothing. His stony silence unnerved Wan, and he didn't like the feeling.

With typical twin intuition, Chan glanced at his brother, younger by two minutes. "Relax. He won't give you trouble."

Wan shook his head. "You ought not change the schedule she outlined."

Chan's jaw muscles tensed. "We've a rare opportunity to take out both the Brit and the old Indian. I'm not passing up a gift."

Wan glared at his brother. "You're being a thickheaded git. That old Indian chap knows the terrain. You don't. Hawk might be dead from the explosion. We haven't heard any reports the coppers are looking for him. You've not sufficient reason to change plans just to go after the Indian."

"He may bloody well have gone underground," Chan retorted.

"All the more reason to stay on track, because if the Brit is with him, you'll be facing two wily adversaries with nothing to lose," Wan insisted.

Chan refused to back down. "We're on schedule. You will keep it that way, while I take care of those two." Wan gave in. "Then you'd best let me back-track and do the scouting," he barked, "Between us, we can determine who's after us, take them out faster than you would if alone."

Chan hesitated, mulling over Wan's argument. "You've a point," he admitted slowly. He didn't doubt for a minute Hawk was not only alive but aiding the old Indian in a rescue attempt. He didn't admit his suspicions to his twin, and Wan seemed too focused on their argument to pick up on his thoughts.

Chan glanced in the rearview mirror. Their prisoner sat motionless in the backseat, firmly secured by handcuffs and seatbelt. The man's eyes met Chan's despite his dark sunglasses, and Chan felt a shiver of premonition. He redirected his attention to the highway and mulled over his options.

Hawk and Tyler together had been formidable indeed. Add in the old Indian, and they'd achieved the impossible when they managed to kill Gary Tacque. His lips lifted in a tiny, self-satisfied smile.

Tyler, Hawk, and the old sod would soon be history. Not only would they never get the chance to reconnect, but soon, very soon, all three of them would be dead.

"Keep him belted in the backseat. Use your mobile to communicate," Chan instructed.

~ * ~

Capulin National Monument appeared on the horizon, first as small dark dots in the noon sun, then growing into various sized solitary cones framed against the expansive, cloudless sky.

Chan pulled onto the shoulder. Traffic was surprisingly heavy despite the deserted surroundings. He frowned. That might complicate things.

"Why so much bloody traffic?" Wan asked, exiting the passenger's side, voicing his brother's thoughts.

"It seems a main route. I'd have thought traffic to stick to the larger motorways." Chan strode to the trunk, opened the lid. Inside were a backpack, a bedroll, and two large nylon rifle cases.

"I'm still not keen on this idea of yours. I'd rather we leave Healing Water and Hawk to Eagle Feather and her lot," Wan commented as he watched Chan empty the trunk and drop the contents on the off-road side of the car.

He persisted. "You might attract attention neither of us wants. It's open terrain." Wan stared at the flat, high desert prairie. No cover of any kind grew between them and a nearby knobby little hill.

Chan unzipped the backpack and retrieved desert camouflage cargo pants, a long-sleeved matching shirt, and a small tin of face paint. Squatting against the off-road side of the car, he quickly changed his clothes, then covered his face and neck, wiped the excess paint from his hands onto his pants, while Wan stood nearby, blocking the view of passing cars.

Wan checked the camouflage backpack, bedroll, and the two rifle cases. When he glanced again at his brother, he could hardly see Chan's outline against the desert foliage. His doubts about Chan's ambush scattered, he grinned at his brother with a thumbs-up signal. "Proverbial snake in the grass," he complimented.

Chan returned his brother's change of heart with a tight smile. He still preferred to carry out his plans alone.

"I'll text when they pass," Wan stated, removing a pair of powerful binoculars from the backpack. He nodded at the spare rifle case. "I'll cripple their mobility. You can take them out at your leisure."

Chan adjusted the backpack and bedroll onto his shoulders, then lifted his rifle case. "They'll know Tyler's life is on a short timeline. I expect they're already en route. Keep a sharp eye." He nodded his head towards the direction behind them. "Find a location not more than a mile." His smile became a grin. "No worries. This will be the easiest hit we've made in our career."

Wan nodded. "Good luck."

But Chan was already gone.

~ * ~

Jeremiah watched the men's activity through his peripheral vision, catching snatches of their conversation whenever a lag in highway traffic occurred. He didn't pick up everything, but he heard enough to understand what the two were planning. Without attracting attention, he wriggled his shoulders around until he felt the seatbelt buckle with his fingertips, then relaxed his shoulders, leaned his head against the inside of the car, and closed his eyes.

Wan eased the spare rifle from the case and onto the front passenger's seat, then stored the case in the trunk before walking to the prisoner's side of the car. The man appeared to be sleeping, but he might also be cunning enough to fake it. Wan checked to make sure the seatbelt was securely fastened, then confirmed the man's hands remained cuffed. He shut the door, hurried around and slid behind the wheel. He checked the side mirror, waited for a long train of cars to pass, then eased onto the highway and searched for a place to turn around. Pre-occupied with finding a suitable spot to monitor oncoming traffic, Wan failed to notice Jeremiah's subtle change in position. He drove just under a mile before he found a satisfactory lookout along the oncoming side of the highway. He slowed and bumped onto a dirt roadway leading to a broad gate with a ranch brand on wrought iron sign. Settling into his seat, he didn't need to use the binoculars, as the straight highway gave him a clear view of oncoming traffic. With casual watchfulness he checked the occupants of each approaching vehicle. The sun crept across the sky, heating the inside of the car and forcing Wan to roll the windows down. He texted his brother at intervals.

Got yourself in position?

Chan's text popped up. *Perfect location. I've got a visual on you through my scope.*

Wan smiled. *I'll hit the tires as they pass. That should give you nice, easy stationary targets.*

Hours crawled by. Wan emptied one of the water bottles, considered giving one to the prisoner. He leaned over the seat and tilted a water bottle to Jeremiah's dry, chapped lips. The man downed the contents without taking a breath, then nodded a brief thanks.

The hot June sun dipped behind the western horizon, the extended desert plains twilight dimmed into darkness, and Wan began to feel anxious. He had not brought night-vision equipment, and his binoculars would reflect the headlights of oncoming vehicles. He unclipped the scope from the rifle. It had night-vision capability, which solved the problem. Identification would be more difficult, but he felt sure he would recognize his targets. He hesitated, then texted his brother.

We're behind schedule. We should abandon the plan and get Tyler to Colorado.

He didn't have a chance to read Chan's answer because at that moment the prisoner threw open the back car door and flung himself onto the dirt road.

~ * ~

Jeremiah suspected Healing Water and Hawk were in the vicinity, and he did not want either of them to walk into a head shot. A glimpse of movement right at sunset, far across the highway and among the ancient lava flows, gave Jeremiah a single, clear signal that Healing Water had spotted Wan's surveillance location. Jeremiah felt a wash of relief.

Now, he needed to provide a distraction. Waiting until full dark, he slipped his fingers over the buckle, quietly released the seatbelt, then twisted, opened the car door, and flung himself to the ground. With practiced ease, he folded himself double, got his bound hands in front of him, then rolled into the nearby prairie grass.

~ * ~

Wan dropped the rifle scope and leaped from the car. He glanced frantically around, alarm coursing through his body when he could not see the man anywhere. He whipped out his mobile, punched in his brother's number.

"What?" Chan hissed.

"It's Tyler," Wan panted. "He's gone."

"Well, find him, you idiot. And take him alive. She needs him to sign papers. Text me when you have him."

Wan reached for the rifle on the front seat then paused, cursing his lack of night goggles. The scope would be useless in terrain as wide as his surroundings. He crouched against the side of the car and considered his options. Carrying the rifle would slow him down, would be more cumbersome than helpful in a close fight. He emptied the rifle, placed it on the floor of the car, pocketed the ammunition, then checked the semi-automatic holstered at his back before peering into the darkness. A thought hit him, and he opened the passenger's door, leaned in and retrieved the car keys. Then he locked the car.

~ * ~

Several yards away, Jeremiah watched the twin's movements. He mulled over his options. Leading the twin on a wild goose chase opened a precious window for Healing Water and Hawk to locate and take out the twin brother without fear of a second gunman's crosshairs. He eased beneath the barbed wire fence that ran alongside the highway, pulled the wire taught and released it. The twang sounded loud against the silence of the dark, open prairie. Keeping his eyes on the twin, Jeremiah edged in a silent circle towards his quarry.

Wan cursed as he scanned the terrain. Damned bloody Indian. Chan and Eagle Feather both would have his head for this if he didn't find Tyler and fast.

His ears caught a sudden, strange sound. Staying low, Wan crept through the prairie grass, saw a barbed wire fence. With a grim smile he eased underneath the fence, continually scanning the terrain. Tyler must be panicking, he thought with satisfaction, not taking time to move silently, and thus giving away his location. Movement to his right caught his attention.

The faint blast of a diesel train drifted across the wide, dark high plains desert. The low, steady throbbing of powerful engines wafted through the cooling atmosphere, and the powerful headlight sliced a growing triangle of white light as the train approached.

Wan's heart thumped hard in his chest. The slow-moving train might allow Tyler the chance to jump on and make an escape. Cursing between his teeth, Wan squinted against the dark expanse, panic constricting his chest until he panted hard in the high altitude. As the train rumbled closer Wan's heart sank. There was just too much open space for him to monitor. Tyler knew the area; no doubt knew about the train tracks. He crept to within a few feet of the rails, hoping against hope Tyler was too weak, his mobility too restricted to make an effective escape on the train. The cars rolled past, clicking their way into the distance. Time slid by. Summer constellations, so bright Wan thought he might reach out and touch them, meandered their way across the night sky, and still he could not locate Tyler. He did not dare contact his brother to ask for assistance, vowed he would not text again until he found their prisoner. Anger scorched through him, and he decided it didn't really matter whether he presented Tyler dead or alive to the woman.

First, though, he needed to find the bastard.

~ * ~

Early morning wound inexorably towards sunrise and desperation filled him when a shadow leapt into his peripheral vision. Wan spun sideways just in time to avoid Tyler's vicious kick to his head. He tripped, fell, and twisted to his side as the Indian landed light-footed and leaped again. Lashing out with a foot, he caught the Indian in the chest. Tyler released a gasp of pain, fell hard, rolled, and stumbled to his feet. Springing up, Wan whipped out his semi-automatic, but the Indian leaped forward with lightning speed. His cuffed hands flew up and knocked the weapon from his grip. The uneven, rocky terrain caught Wan unaware, and he lost his footing and fell again. He rolled with his momentum, trying to put distance between himself and the Indian, jumped up, and twisted sideways. Tyler's feet swept his own, and he tumbled to the ground a third time, hit the jagged edge of a hidden lava crest. His hands covered his head as he fell hard over the short ledge. Twisting instinctively, Wan lashed out with a foot, catching Tyler on the side of his head as he sprang downwards.

The Indian crumpled.

Panting, his lungs searing from exertion and altitude, Wan peered at the motionless form for several minutes. His heart rate slowed, his breathing eased, and he hoisted the man into a fireman's carry, then stumbled his way across the field until he reached the barb wire fence. He dropped Tyler to the ground, rolled him beneath the fence, then himself, then waited as a line of headlights passed before dragging the man to the car.

Wan unlocked and opened the front passenger's door, fumbled with the glove compartment and retrieved the key to the cuffs. He re-cuffed Tyler's hands behind his back. Removing his own T-shirt, he ripped it into several strips, which he used to bind Tyler's upper arms. Wan secured the seatbelt, then slid behind the wheel. He sat immobile for a long time, panting, his bare back sticking against the uncomfortable fake leather seat. The dash clock told him the sun would rise soon, which meant he and Chan were hopelessly behind schedule. He texted his brother.

Got Tyler.

Chan replied almost immediately. *Get on the road. I've got one of them in my sights. I'll follow when I'm done here.*

Wan acknowledged. Neither of them could afford another complication, and now that Chan knew the location of Hawk and Healing Water, Wan felt better about things. Chan had the advantage, would take out both targets, which would be good news to bring to Mary Eagle Feather. He cranked the engine and headed west, reached Raton, pointed the car onto Interstate twenty-five towards Raton Pass. Walsenberg lay on the other side, and soon he would be rid of the Indian in the back seat. Wan followed the thin ribbon across La Veta Pass, wove through Wolf Creek Pass to a turn-off on the western slope. He followed a narrow dirt road through the thick pines and could not control a shudder when he glimpsed the sheer drop-off whenever he reached a break in the trees. He missed the turn-off, had to find a place on the forest maintenance road to turn around. He wasted time creeping forward and backwards in order to avoid slipping over the vertical drop, then retraced his path at a crawl until he spotted the track. He eased the sedan along the jagged terrain, thinking Eagle Feather should have thought ahead and offered some sort of four-wheeler for them to use. A Jeep would have been nice, a Hummer even nicer.

The car bounced around a narrow bend and a one-room, rough-hewn log cabin appeared. A soft square of light shone from a single small window in the shadows created by the surrounding trees. Wan coasted to a stop and cut the engine.

In the gray of pre-dawn, the door of the cabin opened, and pale yellow light outlined a slender, dark figure. Wan couldn't tell from this distance whether it was Eagle Feather or one of her cronies, but he did know whoever it was would be demanding shortly why he was so late. He texted his brother.

Are you on your way?

He looked up, studying the immobile figure in the doorway. Should he lie and say he got lost? After all, he and Chan had been instructed to leave all GPS gizmos turned off, including mobiles, which both of them violated when Chan decided to take out Hawk and Healing Water.

But he didn't have to admit that to Eagle Feather. He glanced at his phone. No answer yet from Chan. When he looked up again the figure in the doorway still had not moved. He opened the car door and stood, the scent of wood smoke mixed with pine reaching his nostrils, the chilly mountain breeze brushing his bare chest. Stepping quickly to the trunk, he rummaged around the contents and found a sweatshirt, which he shrugged on. Wan glanced down, realized his jeans were torn and stained. No way he would get away with some cockamamie story about getting lost. He slipped his mobile into a front pocket. He would know Chan had replied when he felt the device vibrate.

Mary Eagle Feather crossed the distance to the car. Even in the shadows, she could see the twin looked disheveled, disorganized.

And he was alone.

Something had gone wrong. Without a word she peered into the back seat.

Jeremiah Tyler slumped against the seat.

Mary Eagle Feather breathed a slow sigh of relief and straightened. "What happened? Where's your brother?" Her voice was quiet, barely audible in the silent mountain air.

Wan swallowed. "He has unfinished business with the Brit."

Mary Eagle Feather regarded the man in front of her for several silent moments. "That was not part of the plan."

"Nor was wiping out an entire team," Wan declared, trying unsuccessfully to keep anger out of his voice.

Mary Eagle Feather towered over the man. As much as she wanted to know exactly what had happened, did it really matter now? She had Jeremiah Tyler, and soon she would have the Lamont fortune. "Bring him into the cabin." She turned and walked sedately back to the small structure.

Mourning the loss of his semi-automatic, Wan opened the rear door and unbuckled Tyler. Retrieving and loading the rifle would take too much time, so he left it lying on the floorboard. He pulled Tyler from the car, spun him around.

"Walk to the cabin. Try anything, and I'll break every bone in your body."

Jeremiah made his way slowly across the rocky ground to the cabin. His head hurt, his chest wound hurt, and his shoulders had cramped from being so tightly bound.

Inside, the woman waited near a wood burning stove. He stopped a few feet in front of her.

"Do you know who I am?" Mary Eagle Feather asked.

Standing utterly still, Jeremiah met her gaze. Wan moved into view and watched the two Native Americans eyeing one another with blank, unreadable expressions.

"I do," he murmured after a long pause. "You are responsible for the deaths of my wife's family. And now you think I will sign over her estate."

Mary Eagle Feather smiled and stepped forward. "Gary Tacque was my son. You will sign over the Lamont fortune to me. Only by doing so will you save your wife from death."

Jeremiah regarded the black eyes mere inches from his own. His voice drifted between them with almost intimate softness. "The team you sent to kill my wife is now dead, as is the twin brother of this man. And soon you will join them."

The phone in Wan's pocket vibrated against his leg, and he allowed himself a small, self-satisfied smile.

Chapter Twenty

Chan Lee shivered in the late night high desert air, but his reaction wasn't due to the temperature. He had traveled all over the world, carried out hits in every conceivable climate. He had watched alligators creep within a yard of his location, snakes slither over him as he lay motionless waiting for his target. Nothing phased him, whether on two legs or multiples, in the sky or beneath the water, slithering, hissing, snapping, stinging, biting.

Out here in New Mexico there were no snakes, no alligators, no jungle cats, not even a moon. As full darkness fell, the clear sky became so full of celestial creatures he felt the entire cast of mythical gods was looking down upon him. He had lain all day in the summer desert heat without any sort of bad feeling or premonition.

But as darkness shrouded round him, he shivered. Instinctively. Uncontrollably. He didn't like it out here. He was not superstitious, did not believe in ghosts or other unworldly spirits. But they were out here tonight. They filled the vast emptiness, floating, hovering, invisible to the eye but obvious in so many other ways. Their whispers rustled through the desert grass, their formless essence crowded him, pressing, squeezing...

Chan shook his head violently; trying to dissipate the palpable feeling he was not alone. Never in all of his worldly travels had he ever felt anything like this, and it was thoroughly creeping him out.

The isolated cone he chose for his ambush was one of several extinct volcanoes that formed a rough circle. Unknown to him, the surrounding high desert prairie darkness hid frozen lava flows, so his approach to the cone proved much rougher than he anticipated as he had been forced to crawl over sharp, black volcanic rifts. His trek to the cone left him with torn clothes and numerous cuts and scrapes that burned and stung.

And gnats waited for him at the top of the small cone. Millions and millions of them, swarming around his face, collecting on his clothing in such thick numbers his sleeves shimmered and wavered on their own during the daylight, took on a silvery, ghost-like translucence in the darkness. They wiggled down the collar of his shirt, up his shirtsleeves, through the tears in his pants, flew into his eyes, ears, nose, crawled around the corners of his mouth until he thought he might be eaten alive one microscopic bite at a time.

The darkness created by the lava rock was like trying to see into a black hole. His thermal night vision goggles picked out wildlife, but did not give sight into the endless ridges surrounding the cone. From first appearance, the small elevation seemed the perfect place to establish a sniper's nest and wait for the Brit and his Indian companion. Mary Eagle Feather assured him Highway eighty-seven presented the most direct route to the southwest portion of Colorado, and Joe Healing Water and Hawk would no doubt choose this route when they realized who had taken Jeremiah from the county jail. On his recommendation, she phoned in an anonymous tip to the local Shawnee news station after Chan confirmed he and his brother had Tyler. Critical to their plans that the police get their photos into the news and onto websites quickly, so Hawk would know the Charlie Network had taken Jeremiah and Healing Water would realize their destination. Mary Eagle Feather expressed her certainty the old Indian would show up at the cabin, refused to elaborate on her plans to kill him. She waved off Chan's request to deal with the Brit.

So now he would take out both Healing Water and Hawk on his own terms and deal with Mary Eagle Feather's anger later. His plan was flawless, he reassured himself, and the ancient cones presented the perfect location. The weak link was his decision to allow Wan to remain in the area as a lookout, though at the time his idea to sabotage their targets' vehicle seemed an excellent suggestion. But now, Wan's texts were beginning to annoy Chan.

His mobile buzzed.

"What?" He hissed, then listened in disbelief. As good as Wan was, he tended to panic easily.

"Well, find him, you idiot. And take him alive. She needs him to sign papers. Text me when you have him." He cut the call and cursed his brother. His eyes narrowed through his night vision gear as a thought struck.

Was Tyler's escape an attempt to get away, or was that bloody old Indian and the British agent in the area and had managed to relay some sort of signal?

Either way, Tyler's actions complicated things. He needed this mission to proceed without problems. The location was perfect for taking out the two men. Out here in the middle of nowhere there were no witnesses, and at least several hours should pass before circling buzzards attracted someone's attention. If he took time to bury the bodies, it might be days or weeks before they were found. He focused his night goggles in Wan's direction. Headlights dotted the dark highway, and his goggles brought the surrounding terrain into clear, though dark, detail.

If indeed Hawk and Healing Water were nearby, Hawk, being familiar with Chan's sniper tactics, would attempt to outguess him. The Indian would no doubt know this area, know the existence of the cones and their ideal use as a sniper's roost.

Chan allowed himself a grim smile. He banked on the fact he and Hawk had worked closely together on several assignments. He was sure the Brit would recognize the security photos no matter how grainy they were, know Chan and his twin snatched Tyler. Even if Hawk and Healing Water were astute enough to spot Wan's car and realized they were heading into an ambush, he still held the advantage. His view from the top of the extinct cone covered miles, gave him the upper ground. All he needed to do was exert a little more patience.

Voiceless whispers brushed his ears and he shivered again. Gnats crawled and swarmed around him. Chan batted impatiently at the massive numbers of flying insects when another possibility slid through his mind and he swung his attention to Wan's stationary car.

If Hawk and Healing Water were indeed in the area, they might attempt to rescue Tyler. Had that been the purpose of Tyler's escape? To connect with Hawk and Healing Water? They would know a rescue now would save Tyler from torture and death. He lowered the goggles and peered through the night scope of his rifle. Traffic had thinned, and he would have an easy shot, should either of them pop up where his brother had parked the vehicle.

Chan glanced at his phone, willing Wan to text him saying he had Tyler. Yet another thought occurred, and he scanned other extinct, worn down cones dotting the landscape.

Would Healing Water or Hawk climb one of those knolls to ambush Wan? Two cones rose near enough to the stationary car for a sniper's rifle. He scanned the anomalies, then the flat terrain around him. He switched to the night goggles again and strained his eyes in an effort to detect movement in the vicinity of the parked car. He muttered oaths into the darkness surrounding him.

Grudgingly, Chan admitted the weakness of setting up an ambush without thinking things through. Now that he had time to reconsider, he should have insisted Wan continue on with Tyler and leave him to take out Hawk and Healing Water. He was already close enough to the highway to clearly see the occupants of passing vehicles with his rifle scope. That he allowed Wan to remain in the area with Tyler had been foolish. He should have anticipated Tyler would muck up things one way or another.

Minutes ticked into hours as stars crept across the night sky. Wisps floated across his straining eyes, only to vaporize when he jerked his eyes from the goggles. Gnats crowded on the lenses, impeding his ability to catch unnatural activity.

As the night slid into early morning, Chan reassessed his position and the strength of his plan, and he felt his confidence slip. No word from Wan, which meant Tyler had escaped. Very possibly Tyler had rejoined Healing Water and the Brit, and they would now know of his ambush. He should abandon his roost, rejoin his twin brother, face Mary Eagle Feather's wrath together.

His mobile buzzed, and he glanced at the screen.

Got Tyler.

Chan hesitated before typing a reply.

Get on the road. I've got one of them in my sights. I'll follow when I'm done here.

Not quite the entire truth, Chan acknowledged with a guilty twinge, but he wanted Wan out of the area. He read his brother's answer, watched the stationary car come to life and disappear along the highway, and breathed a sigh of relief. Wan was out of danger and would get Tyler to Mary Eagle Feather, which left him clear to finish what he started.

Chan's confidence surged. Tyler's escape had been a useless attempt to draw Wan away from the highway. The fact his ambush was impulsive lowered the odds of his targets realizing the danger they were in.

Wan was fine. He was fine. His plan was fine. Any attempt to climb one of the nearby volcanic mounds would expose Hawk and Healing Water completely. The feeling of complete control felt good, and he alternated scanning each of the extinct volcanoes dotting the landscape around him. He had not gone with the largest cone, the one that would afford the best position for a sniper. Instead, he had chosen the least obvious of the cones, but the one closest to the highway. If Hawk or Healing Water did suspect an ambush, neither would pay the smallest elevation any attention. They would concentrate on the larger cones, the ones with more obvious high-ground advantage.

He knew without a doubt Mary Eagle Feather would not agree to his change in her plans. She was focused solely on Jeremiah Tyler and the Lamont fortune. He also knew she would not honor any request he might make concerning the Brit.

And he wanted the Brit. Hawk had disappeared after the car bomb two years ago that almost killed him. He knew about Wan, he knew too much sensitive information about the Charlie Network. He was a superb operative and presented too great a danger to be left alive. And, after what Hawk had done to Gary Tacque's team, Chan wanted the pleasure of taking him out, and he knew Eagle Feather would never allow him the opportunity.

He swatted at the gnats crawling over his rifle obscuring his view through the scope, swarming around his eyes. The utter darkness of the open prairie hid a lot more than he realized. His sixth sense kept sending shivers through him. Concentrating on breathing, he felt his heart rate slow, and his breath floated on the misty wisps that drifted around him.

Had Hawk and Healing Water driven past the ambush while Wan searched for Tyler?

Both Hawk and Healing Water represented formidable operators in their own right. In his gut he knew the old Indian would suspect an ambush in an area with these raised cones. And Hawk, knowing how Chan operated, would anticipate he would set up a sniper's roost. He thought about that for a bit, and a smile tipped the corners of his mouth. He knew what the two operatives would do. While Healing Water headed for Colorado to rescue Tyler, Hawk would remain behind to investigate a possible ambush. In fact, Chan would need to deal with only the Brit. Mary Eagle

Feather would get her revenge when Healing Water made it to the cabin and tried to rescue Tyler. He divided the dark, expansive terrain into grids and kept his vision unfocused, relying on his instincts and his peripheral senses to pick up unnatural movement. Images of small animals, deer, antelope, and cows dotted the landscape. It would be easy to miss the prostrate form of a man approaching his lair, so he watched for sudden, startled movement of wildlife to give him indication something was present that didn't belong there.

The early morning hours grew unexpectedly cold until Chan's fingers felt numb. He shifted with small, imperceptible movements, unaccustomed to the radical temperature changes in the high desert altitude. With slow deliberation he once again surveyed his imaginary grid, wished he knew how many lava rifts each one held, reluctantly admitted he should have researched the area before deciding to use it as an ambush.

From his left, his peripheral vision caught the sudden leap of several dots. Antelope. He swung his goggles over and studied the darkness. For several minutes nothing appeared. He blinked incessantly, trying to clear the gnats that crowded around the corners of his eyes.

A small dot appeared. As Chan watched, the dot grew ever so slowly into a round oblong shape with slender arms and legs.

The Brit. It had to be. The Indian was too old for this kind of stunt. Hawk and Chan thought the same, trained the same, set up the same type of ambush. They would approach a sniper nest the same way, too. And that is where Chan had the advantage this time.

Chan's lips curled slightly. Hawk was good. He had guessed which of the cones Chan would use to establish his roost. He and the Brit were Grand Masters in a deadly game of Chess, each player trying to out-guess the other.

Only now he had the Brit in his sights.

Carefully, without any sudden movement, Chan lowered the night-vision goggles and shifted to the night scope on his rifle. The powerful magnification defined the blurred oblong object into the head and torso of a man lying prone on the ground. Chan watched as the Brit worked forward on his elbows, a rifle tucked beneath him, twigs and what could only be chunks of prairie grass poking up from his headgear. His head seemed high, making him an easy target. Chan watched the Brit's slow, inching progress and thought about that for a bit.

Why would he be carrying his head high, inviting a headshot? The Brit was too good for a rookie mistake like that. But he hadn't been in the field in over two years, and bad habits slipped in unless one constantly trained. And he was coming off a recent injury from his encounter with Gary Tacque, compounded by the severe burns he sustained in the car bomb two years ago, and no doubt his stalking abilities suffered.

Satisfied with his analysis, Chan settled the crosshairs onto the Brit's skull. Camouflage or not, it would take only one bullet at this distance to explode a human head. He calculated a scant half mile separated himself from the approaching figure.

Chan slowed his breathing, rested his cheek against the stock of the rifle. He felt his pulse slow. Gnats swarmed into his vision, and he fluttered his eyelids in an attempt to rid himself of them.

The gnats were a problem. He needed every part of his body still at this distance, couldn't risk allowing the Brit to sneak within range. The Brit no doubt would be wearing night vision gear as well, and even if he couldn't see Chan, he was good enough to make a dangerously close guess as to his location.

Chan's finger drifted to the trigger. He waited some more, felt his breathing and pulse slow further, relaxing his body until every motion became one. His finger gently squeezed.

The explosion rocked him, threw the weapon against the bipod that supported it, momentarily blinded and deafened him.

Immediately, he knew something was wrong. The three-oh-eight rifle had fired differently; the recoil was wrong. Something had impeded smooth launching of the bullet.

Gnats. They must've been inside the barrel.

Chan swore beneath his breath. Firing blew his position. Hawk would see the flash, would now be certain of his sniper nest. He strained to see through the scope, through the undulation of the gnats that crawled all over the optics. He chambered another round, then steadied the sites on the unmoving figure that had been crawling towards the cone a moment ago.

Chan frowned as he watched the motionless form through his scope. Years of training and experience prevented him from firing again. Another shot would expose his position further. But he felt sure his first bullet had missed the Brit, so why wasn't the bloody git seeking cover?

The dot lying prone on the ground did not move.

Chan made his decision fast. With quick, silent movements he removed the bipod, then crabbed his way to the edge of the cone, watched the motionless dot again for several minutes before crawling his way down the exposed side of black lava rock. He reached the base of the extinct volcano, drew a breath of relief when he realized the number of gnats significantly decreased. He still felt them crawling along his arms and legs inside his clothes, but he thought perhaps he imagined the sensation. He began a slow, cautious spiral inward towards the location of the Brit, the stock of the rifle planted firmly against his shoulder.

Chan cursed the lava rifts both for the time they took out of his approach and for their sudden appearance. He managed to avoid falling down any of them, but his progress slowed to a snail's pace. He approached the top of yet another lava shelf and peered across the edge. From this angle it was hard to tell, but it looked as though the Brit lay not too far away. He had not moved, and Chan began thinking that perhaps he hit his target after all. He glanced skyward; knowing the scent of death would soon attract winged scavengers.

Emboldened by the absolute stillness of the shadow, Chan stood and scrambled over the edge of the frozen lava rift. With his rifle leveled at the motionless figure, he thumbed the safety off and approached slowly, carefully, crouched and ready to fire a killing shot if the body on the ground moved.

Within thirty yards Chan's nostrils caught the metallic, stomach-churning stench of a large amount of spilled blood. He straightened and lowered his rifle, a satisfied smile curling his lips. He had killed the Brit after all, despite the deluge of gnats, despite his unfamiliarity with the location, even despite the misfire of his first shot. His instincts had seen him through, along with his expertise and patience.

Something sharp and piercing struck him hard between his shoulder blades, knocking him off his feet. He staggered, felt pain rip through his chest, then felt a second impact hit slightly below the first. He stumbled to his knees, threw his hands out to keep from planting face-first onto the ground.

No sound. He hadn't heard the report of a rifle. In the darkness he looked down and saw the brown earth beneath him turning black.

He was bleeding. If he'd been hit by a sniper bullet, he should be dead. For that matter, the killer should have put the round through his skull.

Breathing hurt like hell, but strangely he didn't feel faint. Blood wasn't gushing from him like it would if he had bullet holes. A sniper bullet would have torn up his insides enough he should be bleeding out. It didn't make any sense. Chan sank onto his right hip and strained to look at his chest.

Two barbed arrow heads jutted through his jacket. In complete disbelief he wriggled himself around. The silhouette of a shadowed figure stood several yards behind him against the gray of early morning, the outline of a compound bow held against his side. Comprehension dawned slowly.

He'd been shot with two *arrows*.

Well, he wasn't dead. Not yet. Pain scorched through his chest as though he'd been set afire but he could still breathe, and he could still think. It was only the Indian now, and he had his rifle. His problem was how to raise, aim, and fire his weapon before the damned Indian got off another shot.

The Indian wasn't moving in for the kill. He wasn't notching another arrow into his bow. Chan frowned. Was the shadow he saw actually there, or was he suffering a hallucination? Had the idea of ghosts gone to his head until his imagination started creating images?

He glanced down at his chest. The sharp, barbed points of two arrowheads looked real enough. He raised a hand and gingerly touched one of the bloody tips.

Yeah, they were real. The pain was real, too. Which meant the Indian had to be real. Chan glanced up and stared at the figure again. He began to think that perhaps time slowed down, that what he thought was taking minutes might in real time be taking only a fraction of a second.

He glanced down, saw his rifle on the ground. He reached over to pick it up, but slumped onto his side instead. God he felt weak. The shafts of the arrows might be plugging most of the bleeding, but he was still mortally wounded if he didn't get help soon.

From the corner of his eye, Chan saw movement from the direction of the dead Brit. He tilted his head and watched in horrified amazement as the prone, motionless form slowly rose like Hamlet's father from his grave. Blood covered the man, but when Chan squinted at him, he realized the Brit still had his head. He frowned, confused. His eyes must be playing tricks on him. He watched the Brit approach. The pale horizon seemed bright as full day. Blood soaked the Brit's clothes.

He has to be dead, Chan thought. *I'm hallucinating. I need to contact Wan, get someone here to help me.*

He thought about the mobile phone tucked in his vest. Mary Eagle Feather could wait. Wan needed to drive back, help Chan, bring emergency crews. He could stay alive so long as the shafts plugged the bleeding, so long as they had only pierced a lung. All he had to do was keep breathing until help arrived. He tried to move his hand towards the pocket that held his mobile but couldn't seem to generate enough strength.

"Hello, Chan."

The Brit's voice boomed in Chan's ears. He felt his chest constrict as pain seared through his body, forced his breathing down until he took small sips. The pain lessened, the constriction in his chest eased.

"H-how?" he mouthed. He did not have enough energy or air to sound the word.

Hawk knelt beside the wounded man. "You mean the blood?" His voice was low, gentle.

Chan managed a slight nod.

"Joe Healing Water's idea. A bag of antelope blood packed into an old army helmet crammed on top of my headgear. Rather clever idea, if you ask me."

Chan's eyes narrowed through the pain obvious in his face. He struggled to generate a tiny shake of his head.

The Brit leaned close, the stench of the blood making Chan's stomach churn in sickening, twisting knots. "Where did your brother take Jeremiah?"

Chan rested on his side and leaned his head back until he felt the cold, rocky ground beneath his skull. He didn't have the energy to mouth what he was thinking. Instead, he managed another slight shake of his head.

"To the cabin in the woods," another voice spoke above him. Chan snapped his eyes open and stared at the figure who now stood behind Hawk. He knew by the Brit's satisfied smile his own expression had given away the answer.

Hawk turned to Joe Healing Water. "I admit; I didn't think you knew what you were talking about."

Joe Healing Water's stony features emphasized the creases in his face. "Like I told you in the bunker, Mary Eagle Feather's cabin in the woods. Her home away from home, when she needs time away from the Rez and her work in Victor."

"And you know the directions to this cabin in the woods?" Hawk still sounded doubtful. He hadn't heard a word of Healing Water's answer, had to go by the satisfied though irritated expression on the old Indian's face.

"Have I been wrong yet?" Joe barked, annoyed.

Hawk turned his attention back to Chan. Deftly, he searched the wounded man's pockets until he found his mobile phone.

"You've got a text," Hawk told him. "Your brother. Wants to know if you're on your way yet." He turned to the Indian standing behind him. "And now we've a way to track the brother and Tyler."

"I don't need any damned technology to give me directions," Healing Water growled.

Hawk dropped his eyes to the phone and thumbed the keyboard, then looked at Chan. "There. I've sent him an answer for you."

Joe Healing Water stared at Chan, his black eyes cold as flint. "I want my arrows back."

Chan felt his body turn cold. He tried to shake his head, couldn't drum up the energy to create the movement. The only thing keeping him alive was the plugging effect the shafts created. He knew the arrows needed to stay in place until help reached him, took him to hospital. He tried to swallow, but his mouth was too dry. He moved his parched lips, hoping the two men would be able to intuit his thoughts.

Hawk glanced at the dying man in time to see the word form on his gray lips.

"Help?" He asked. He turned to Joe. "He waiting for help," he told him. "I assume he wants you to leave the arrows until help arrives."

Joe Healing Water stepped forward. "I want my arrows back," he repeated, leaning down. He planted a boot against Chan's shoulder, and grasped the bloody arrowhead with a gloved hand.

Chan's mouth opened in a silent scream as he felt his heart yanked against his sternum when the Indian pulled the shaft through. He had just enough life in him to feel the second shaft tear open his chest, then watched as his spirit joined the others now hovering above him in plain sight.

Chapter Twenty-One

"Chan is a fool, and you are incompetent."

Mary Eagle Feather stood at the window of her small cabin and heard thunder rumble overhead. The one-room structure had a fireplace, an old leather couch, a rough-hewn wooden table with two matching chairs, and a wood-burning stove that doubled as a cooking surface. A pole ladder led to a sleeping loft. She and her son, Wild Horse, spent a lot of time here over the years. It provided protection and isolation, a perfect location to work out details of targets and assassination plans without fear of discovery or interruption.

"Chan ignored my orders and pursued his need for revenge. If he had followed my plan, Hawk and Healing Water would have found this cabin, and he could have taken his time to kill them here."

Wan had difficulty swallowing. His throat felt tight. "I wasn't aware of his plans until he pulled over in New Mexico," he hedged. He sat on the couch and tried his best to appear relaxed, but he didn't like the woman's expression, didn't like that he was alone with her and Tyler. Thankfully Chan texted earlier, which meant he would be on his way as soon as he found transportation. He hadn't checked his brother's text yet, didn't want to take his eyes off the woman. But knowing Chan had finally answered gave Wan sufficient reassurance.

Most importantly, Chan's text meant he had tripped his ambush.

"Hawk and Healing Water are dead." Wan's words broke the uncomfortable silence in the cabin.

"How do you know?" Mary Eagle Feather challenged.

"He texted me. It'll take him a bit to find transportation, but he's en route." Wan smiled thinly at the woman. He just needed to keep her pacified until his brother arrived. He did not trust Mary Eagle Feather, did not want to mysteriously disappear like so many of her rich husbands.

Mary Eagle Feather regarded the man sitting on the couch, frowned, then turned her attention to Jeremiah Tyler, who sat bound in one of the wooden straight-back chairs at the table. He moaned softly, signaling a return to consciousness. She sat in the chair facing him, leaned back, and crossed one knee over the other. She wore floor-length soft leather tribal beaded skirt and moccasins. Her white woolen blouse hugged her throat, the long sleeves kept the chill inside the cabin at bay.

She picked up something from the table and watched Jeremiah closely as his eyes fluttered open. Pain glazed his pupils when he focused on the object she dangled in front of his face.

"Your wife's scalp, Black Bear." Mary Eagle Feather saw the alarm that flashed across his expression. Under normal conditions he might have maintained his poker face.

But not now. She timed her actions perfectly, when her victim reached the edges of awareness, in that interval before the brain is fully aware, when pain first registers with fresh viciousness. He would spend what strength he had trying to hide the pain. He would not be able to hide his reaction to yet another shock.

The wad of short, curly black hair and scalp covered in dried blood dangled from her hand.

"Look at the proof. I warned you. Sign the papers to keep her alive. And now, you cannot deny your wife is dead." Mary Eagle Feather shook the object. Jeremiah's eyes shifted to stare at her.

"One of my team slipped into the hospital and retrieved it for me. I knew you would not believe me if I had anything of lesser value." She studied him, waiting for her words to sink in. "And now, if you want to save your brother, you will sign the papers, naming me as sole heir to the Lamont estate."

Wan watched from his position on the couch. Mary Eagle Feather's expression showed no triumph, no satisfaction she had thoroughly beaten Tyler emotionally and physically. In fact, her face remained eerily blank. He shifted uncomfortably and cut his attention to the bound man. No doubt of the emotion there. Pain, disbelief, and horror crossed Tyler's face.

~ * ~

Jeremiah closed his eyes and withdrew his spirit into himself. Panic swirled through him, threatening to explode into shrieks and screams. Pain from his chest wound and his concussion compounded the pain inflicted by the woman sitting in front of him. But he had clung to mental strength because he knew Mattie, wherever she was, would be safe so long as Mary Eagle Feather concentrated on him.

Now, he could not breathe, he could not think. Mattie's death meant his own spiritual death. Physical death no longer mattered. He folded deeply into himself, to the mental hiding place of protection against the physical pain and torture threatening to rip him apart. His solace had always been Mattie, knowing she waited for him, her spirit wrapped protectively around his, shielding him from whatever physical danger threatened.

Her spirit wrapped around him now. He felt it as strongly as though she were in the room with him. Odd, he thought. Her spirit felt vibrant, alive. Was he feeling her essence through the physical part of her that dangled in front of him?

~ * ~

Thunder rumbled again, fainter, as a spring shower dampened the evergreens outside the cabin. Fat raindrops hit hard-packed earth as the high altitude storm passed over the ridge. Isolated storms like this were common during the summer months. Pines rustled outside the cabin, then grew still as the storm cloud moved on.

Mary Eagle Feather tossed the object onto the table, then picked up a long, thin tooling knife. Dried blood stained the sharp point. She leaned forward and traced a finger down the center of Jeremiah's bare chest, then held the tip of the dagger against one of his ribs near the exposed incision of the bullet wound.

"Are you ready to continue our little game?"

Wan listened to the soft sweetness of the woman's voice and felt a chill of horror crawl along his spine. Mary Eagle Feather was crazy. As stark raving mad as anyone he had ever encountered. And her son had exhibited the same kind of cold, heartless, soulless enmity for creating pain in another for his own amusement. He did not often feel sympathy for his victims, but he felt sympathy for Jeremiah Tyler now.

Holding the knife in place, Mary picked up a mallet from the table.

"Let's see. I've broken three ribs so far without damaging a lung. Would you like to know how I learned this particular art?" Mary tapped the mallet against the knife handle, driving the point through the skin of Jeremiah's bare chest. Three similar puncture wounds trailed down, knobby lumps showing where she had snapped three other ribs.

Mary Eagle Feather felt resistance as the point of the weapon embedded into the bone. Jeremiah couldn't control the gasp of pain as the knife probed deeper into his rib. His head tilted back, every cord in his neck bulging as he fought against the agonized screams that welled into his throat. He struggled against the rope that bound him to the chair, the steel cuffs that bound his hands behind him. He sought the safety of Mattie's spirit, silently begged for her protection to envelope him, but he couldn't feel her presence through the pain in his chest.

Mary Eagle Feather tapped the handle of the knife again, embedding the point further into the bone. She felt the rib begin to separate.

"It took me a long time to master just how much pressure to use to break a rib without puncturing a lung. The pain of a broken rib is one of the most delicious ideas I've come up with yet. Unfortunately, I couldn't use this on any of my husbands. Their deaths had to look natural." She tapped again and felt a rush of pleasure when Jeremiah released a hoarse, ragged cry of pain.

"So I've been saving this for a special occasion." She tapped the handle until the bone separated and the rib snapped. "The pain level never lets up, does it?" She asked, removing the knife and placing the mallet and knife on the table. "You must breathe, you must inhale and exhale. And with every breath, you can feel the edges of those broken ribs grating against each other."

She leaned forward and watched Jeremiah closely as he tried to breathe, as though she studied a lab experiment. Wan expected her to pull out a notebook and start writing down her observations. He squirmed on the couch, thought about retrieving his phone to text Chan about his estimated arrival time at the cabin.

"I haven't done this enough yet to know quite how to pace it so you don't faint," Mary cooed as Jeremiah's eyes fluttered. He was losing consciousness again. He was weak, his condition affected by the healing gunshot wound he sustained on the mountain and his recent concussion from the explosion. She leaned back in her chair and watched his head slump forward.

"Perhaps I should have put off this game until he was more fully recovered," she mused, casting a look at Wan. "After all, no one knows where we are. The police think he's an escaped suspect rather than a kidnap victim."

"Wait for Chan," Wan suggested. "The three of us will force him to sign the papers."

Mary Eagle Feather shook her head. "It's too late now to stop. He'll break soon, I think. Especially after seeing the scalp."

She wanted his signature on the legal documents, wanted control of the immense Lamont fortune. Closing her eyes, she imagined the projects the Lamont estate would fund, her own personal goals in addition to the desperately needed support for her People.

"How will you convince family solicitors you are the rightful heir?" Wan asked, his curiosity winning over caution.

Mary Eagle Feather turned, her black expressionless eyes regarding the man on the couch in silence for several minutes. "I'll arrive in Shawnee as his mother." She answered after a while. "With no other surviving relatives, the Lamont fortune will be mine. They'll have no choice. I'll find his younger brother and get rid of him, too, before I confront the estate lawyers."

She turned back to the unconscious man. "So, what do you think?" she asked Wan. "How many more bones in his body will I need to snap before he signs the document?" She pointed to a small stack of papers on the table.

Wan hesitated, unsure whether hers was a rhetorical question. The silence lengthened and he cleared his throat. "You didn't give him opportunity to sign before you started in on him."

Mary smiled, her expression misleadingly gentle. "He thinks he can withstand anything I do to him. He's proud and strong. I'll break him piece by piece. And then I will cut out his heart. He took my son from me. I will take his spirit from him."

"Even if he signs the documents?" Wan asked.

Mary Eagle Feather shifted her eyes to stare at the man on the couch. "Yes."

The absolute calm in her voice started alarm bells ringing in Wan's head. He suddenly felt he had made a grave mistake, but he wasn't sure what it was. He wished his brother was here. Chan understood the woman, had dealt with her over the years.

"Chan should arrive soon," he mentioned in an effort to change the subject. He reached into his pocket and retrieved his mobile. "I'll text him. Get an update."

Mary Eagle Feather stood and stretched, then looked down at Jeremiah. At least he was a warrior. The man on the couch was a coward and a liability. Never in all the years of managing the Charlie Network had anyone challenged her authority.

Until this assignment. The twins changed her directives, went rogue, and she didn't like it. If Wild Horse were here, would he kill the twins for disobeying orders?

She tried to imagine his reaction to Chan's decision. Thinking took more effort, decisions seemed more difficult, and she once again mourned the fact her son no longer physically stood by her side to help her at moments like this. She stared through the glass pane of the small window and tried to think through the problem. Outside, damp mountain air whispered among the pines. Stars sparkled through the tops of the evergreens as the storm clouds cleared.

She and the twin were alone. Getting rid of him would take care of half the problem. She could kill Chan the moment he arrived, before he had a chance to assess the situation, before he realized his brother lay dead. Darting a look at the twin on the couch, Mary Eagle Feather drifted to the table. With a smooth, invisible movement, she slid the thin knife into the sleeve of her shirt, the cold blade resting against the inside of her forearm. She would be a fool not to take advantage of the present opportunity.

She turned to Wan and paused, frowning. The color had drained from his face, and his expression held shock as he stared wide-eyed at the phone in his hand.

"Is something wrong?"

Wan locked eyes with the woman, his brain struggling to cope with the text from Chan's phone. *Impossible*, he thought desperately. *No way in bloody fucking hell those two blokes could take out his brother.* He held the high ground. He would have anticipated their movements. They should have been like a deer in his crosshairs.

"Wan?"

The woman's voice jerked him to her question. Wan swallowed, opened his mouth, realized too late he should be covering his shocked reaction, and snapped his lips shut.

"Nothing that cannot be dealt with," he declared his voice flat. To his immense relief, the woman turned towards the unconscious man. Apparently she was more occupied with breaking Tyler than pursuing an explanation for his shocked reaction.

"Help me move Black Bear closer to the wood stove." She motioned Wan over. He stood but did not close the distance between them. Instead, he watched the woman, his primal instincts suddenly at full alert. He did not have a weapon on him. His handgun was somewhere in the middle of New Mexico, the spare rifle lay on the floor of the sedan, the rounds still in his pockets.

"I'll be a moment." He turned towards the cabin door. He had been a fool to be caught unarmed, even with his hand-to-hand expertise. The shock of Chan's last text muddled his thinking, and he felt vulnerable.

Something shattered the window glass and whined past his ear. Automatically he hit the floor. He knew that sound. Mary Eagle Feather ducked behind Jeremiah's chair.

"Healing Water!" She shouted at Wan. "You told me Chan killed him!"

The words hardly left her mouth when a flaming arrow shot through the broken window and embedded itself into the opposite wall. Smoke trailed upwards as flames caught and spread along the lines of sap in the pine logs.

Wan saw Mary Eagle Feather's murderous expression, leaped to his feet, and turned for the door. Better to fight the woman outside the burning cabin.

Mary Eagle Feather sprang for Wan, knocking him face down to the floor. Straddling his back and seizing his hair, she banged his forehead brutally against the rough wood before he could twist from beneath her. Dazed, Wan tried to throw the woman off, but Mary Eagle Feather whipped the knife from her sleeve and thrust down with savage ferocity. The slender, lethal blade pierced his spine, traveled straight through his heart, jarring her hand as it deflected off his sternum. She leaped up, grabbed the mallet from the table, and used both hands to drive the knife point into the floor.

Wan's head rolled sideways, his face contorted with shocked disbelief. Bloody foam trickled from his open mouth as he tried to breathe.

Mary Eagle Feather's eyes jerked upwards as the whistle of another flaming arrow passed overhead. In moments, the entire back side of the cabin was ablaze. Her eyes narrowed on Jeremiah. They might be trying to burn her out, but they would not succeed. She would burn alive, and so would Black Bear.

The heat of the flames intensified and the rafters began to smoke. She started towards the unconscious man, intent on pushing him into the flames, when her eyes fell on the paperwork still on the table. The corners of the paper began to curl and smoke. She scooped up the documents and stuffed them inside the waistband of her skirt. Smoke swirled about her, stinging her eyes, clogging her throat and lungs, making it impossible to breathe. If she took the time to shove Black Bear into the flames, she would die, too. If she ran now, she would have the papers, would know Black Bear was dead, and might still find a way to access the Lamont fortune.

She turned towards the cabin door when it slammed open and two forms swept in.

~ * ~

Water drenched Joe Healing Water from head to toe. His eyes swept the room. A man lay on the floor, the hilt of a knife jutting from his back. Mary Eagle Feather stood in the middle of the room, blocking his way to Jeremiah. Beside him, Hawk moved forward, his soaked clothes steaming in the intense heat.

Hawk quickly assessed the situation. There was no time to untie Jeremiah before the fire consumed the room. Coughing and hacking in the thick smoke, he and Healing Water stepped around the woman, bent down and grabbed each side of the chair. Together they lifted Jeremiah; chair and all and turned towards the open door.

Despite her spasmodic coughing, Mary Eagle Feather blocked the doorway, her intent all too clear. Joe's clothes hissed and smoked. All four of them about to burst into flames, and still the crazy woman stood there, motionless. He stumbled when Hawk dropped Jeremiah, jerked his eyes in time to see a handgun appear in the Brit's left hand.

Hawk didn't hesitate, didn't take the time to order the woman to move aside. Deer blood still soaked his clothes and the stench, the heat of the fire, and the roar of the flames made his head spin. He squinted through the swirling smoke, aimed, and squeezed off two rounds.

Mary Eagle Feather saw the weapon and scrambled backwards through the door. The roaring flames covered the sound of the gunshots. Pain seized her right arm as she spun away and she staggered to the corner of the smoking building, the papers rustling against her clothes, blood flowing in a warm stream down her arm, soaking her shirtsleeve.

Hawk dropped the gun and heaved the chair that held Jeremiah. Flames roared and crackled around them, the heat so intense he felt his eyeballs frying in their sockets. His and Healing Water's clothes were smoking, and blisters welled on Jeremiah's back and chest. He looked at the distance to the doorway.

Too late. They weren't going to make it. His vision clouded, his legs wobbled, and he thought this time he wasn't going to escape with burns. This time he was going to die.

Hawk felt a sharp, painful jab in his chest, jerking him to full consciousness. Joe poked him hard again with the end of his compound bow. Hawk swore, pulled and lugged, and the three of them made the doorway as flames engulfed the inside of the cabin. Hawk smelled something burning, realized it was his clothes. He dropped the chair with Jeremiah just outside the cabin, then staggered onto the ground and rolled to extinguish the flames. Through hazy vision he saw Joe Healing Water doing the same thing. His hair gone, Jeremiah's chest and back looked as though he had been spitted and roasted to order. Mercifully he still seemed unconscious. Joe hauled the gallon jugs of water they'd used to soak their clothes and splashed water over himself, then over Hawk.

Dripping wet and shivering in the cool mountain air, feeling waves of heat from the burning building, Hawk dragged Jeremiah's chair further from the flames, then bent to untie him when something hit him hard between the shoulder blades. He fell forward onto his hands and knees, his head spinning from smoke inhalation and fatigue.

Someone whacked him again, hard, against the back of his head. He crumpled onto the ground, managed to roll as another blow glanced off his shoulder. Throwing an arm to ward off the next whack, he managed to get to his knees, then staggered to his feet. To his right the cabin burned, fully engulfed now, flames hissing, smoke billowing upwards. He swung around in time to see the woman coming at him with a thick tree branch. Blood soaked the right sleeve of her shirt, and she staggered slightly as she advanced on him. He thought fleetingly that her injury proba- bly saved his life. He fought to remain upright, trying to focus through the ringing in his ears and the dizziness in his head.

Something flew past him. As Hawk watched, an arrow em- bedded into Mary Eagle Feather's throat, knocking her onto her back. He staggered over until he stood beside her, then collapsed onto his knees and braced his hands on his thighs. Her expression frozen into one of shocked anger, the arrow had killed her instant- ly.

Hawk glanced up as Joe walked over.

"You're rather good with that." He panted, motioning to- wards the compound bow in the Indian's gnarled hand.

~ * ~

Jeremiah regained consciousness with reluctance. He didn't want to face Mary Eagle Feather again, nor did he want to see the scalp she claimed belonged to Mattie. It took him several minutes to realize he was on the ground outside the cabin. The smell of wood smoke and burnt human flesh assaulted his nostrils. He blinked his eyes open, then squinted against the pain engulfing him. He realized slowly he was no longer tied to a chair but on the ground. He turned his head sideways to look around.

"Well, you're finally back from the dead." Joe Healing Water walked over and knelt to assist Jeremiah to a sitting position. He figured the man hadn't understood a word he said. His expression looked more dead than alive. Jeremiah glanced up, met Joe's eyes, then looked around again with obvious confusion.

"Yeah, you're going to be slow for a while," Joe grumbled. He helped Jeremiah wriggle over until he could rest his blistered back against the bark of a pine tree. Joe removed his own shirt and used it to help pad the injured man's skin.

"What happened?" Jeremiah asked. Joe looked at him for a long moment.

"Can you understand a damned thing I'm saying?" he asked.

Jeremiah stared blankly at him.

"Then I'm not wasting my breath. You'll find out soon enough." Joe turned and retraced his steps to where Hawk knelt over a very dead Mary Eagle Feather.

"Was that the twin lying on the floor inside the cabin?" he asked. When Hawk didn't look up, Joe shook his head, looking at the bandages still covering the Brit's ears. "Why am I trying to carry on a conversation?" he grumbled. He turned and looked at the cabin. Flames roared towards the sky, sending a thick, heavy smoke plume upwards.

"Emergency responders should be flying over soon," he said aloud despite the fact no one could hear him. "We need to get out of here."

Joe caught whiffs of burnt human flesh. He wrinkled his nose.

"Do we have anything that could be used as a shovel?" Hawk asked, standing beside him.

Joe shook his head. "No time. We need to scram before we get buried in a heap of fire retardant."

Hawk squinted, trying to read Joe's lips. "Say again?"

Joe rolled his eyes skyward, started to make hand gestures, decided it would be a waste of time and energy, and shook his head again. "NO. SHOVEL." He mouthed.

~ * ~

Jeremiah's back and chest burned like crazy, and he felt immense heat all over his body despite the cool mountain air. His awareness waned, and he slipped into semi-consciousness. As he drifted, he sensed Mattie nearby, hovering over him, vibrant and alive. He opened his eyes, felt pain stab from the broken ribs as he inhaled, and stared at the flaming cabin and thought they needed to move before the surrounding trees caught fire.

Mattie's scalp lay in the cabin.

Had it been Mattie's hair? Her essence felt too vibrant, too alive for her to be dead. And his own spirit though struggling through physical aches and pains at the moment, remained whole. Not splintered, as it would feel if her life had been snuffed out.

~ * ~

Hawk and Joe strode to where Jeremiah sat on the ground. They both knelt.

"You look like shit," Joe told him.

Jeremiah gave up a thin smile. "Feel like shit."

Joe scowled at Hawk. "Since you've managed to lose Mattie and almost get Jeremiah here killed twice, this time I'm in charge of things." He didn't particularly care whether the man understood him or not, but Hawk nodded, and Joe figured his expression conveyed his message clearly enough. He and Hawk helped Jeremiah to his feet, then supported the injured man to the sedan and eased him into the front seat. The car keys dangled from the ignition.

Hawk straightened from the car and faced the old Indian, the compound bow slung across his bare chest.

"Clean up crews will find quite the delectable crime scene. My bloody semi-automatic, two bodies, and a cornucopia of other weapons and evidence," he declared. His ears still buzzed, distorting his words, but he knew from Healing Water's expression his statement was understandable. "Do we dally around and clean up the mess?"

Joe paused, listening. Approaching aircraft would be difficult to hear, although the fire did not seem to be spreading among the damp vegetation. He shook his head.

"Are you telling me no, or are you telling me I've the wrong body count?" Hawk challenged.

"I'm pissed, but we're still a team," Joe snapped. "And we've salvaged one life. It'll take all three of us to locate Mattie, if she's still alive."

Going by the old Indian's body language, Hawk shook his head, the slightest trace of humor touching the corners of his eyes. "So you're not going to shoot me with one of those bloody arrows?"

"Don't tempt me," Joe growled, stalking around the front of the car. He removed the quiver and bow, then slid behind the wheel. Hawk opened a rear door and angled into the car. Jeremiah's head drooped forward on his chest as he slipped once again into unconsciousness.

Chapter Twenty-Two

I looked down at the stump where my right leg should have been and couldn't control the repulsive shudder that wracked through me. I didn't understand why my leg was missing, didn't remember what day it was, or where I was.

I also had no clue who I was. I needed a mirror to tell me what I looked like.

I pulled open the drawer beneath the bedside table and rested my hand on the small mirror that would spring up if I moved my fingers. It took more courage than I thought to force myself to raise the stupid thing.

A tired, thin face peered back at me. A thin face with black collar length hair generously streaked with gray. Large green eyes with circles looking more like moon craters than facial features. My eyes were set deep into their sockets, although that might have been due to the thinness of my face. Not particularly attractive features, I thought. Especially if you added a missing leg into the description.

I tucked the mirror back into the bedside table drawer when the door to my room opened. A nurse in bright neon blue scrubs entered. Her short blonde hair curled around her well-proportioned face. Her blue eyes sparkled with humor, and her lips seemed curved into a permanent smile. Her small, petite frame practically bounced around the room.

"Well, hello, there, Mary Joe. How are we feeling this beautiful Sunday morning?"

I couldn't talk very well. My tracheotomy had been closed, but I could hardly breathe. A vapor mask spewed oxygen-rich mist into my face. My voice came out in a weak croak, and so I mostly didn't try. I gave the nurse a shrug and looked away.

I didn't like her perkiness, her annoyingly incessant good cheer. I wanted to be left alone. I wanted to remember who I was and what had happened, and why I was missing my leg.

I also wanted to find out why there was a thin tan line around my left ring finger.

I pulled a notebook and pencil and wrote my question down,

then held it for the nurse to see.

She smiled at me. "You don't remember what day it is? I just told you. Try to remember. And talk to me. It'll help your vocal cords get strong again."

I dropped the notebook onto the table and shoved it away. Miss Smiley Face raised the head of my bed as high as it would go. Obviously she was getting me ready to start the day.

I didn't want to start the day. I didn't want to suffer through another sponge bath, look at another breakfast when I wasn't the least bit hungry, or suffer through being forced to sit in a damned chair when I was missing a leg.

"Come on, Mary Joe. Give me a smile. The day is too beautiful to wear that frown." The nurse bustled around, tidying things up, filling the plastic basin with warm soapy water for my morning sponge bath. I didn't bother to look at her name tag. I didn't want to know what her name was. She was new, probably because the other nurses were tired of taking care of me. I didn't talk, didn't thank them for what they were doing for me, didn't interact with them at all.

Eight am rolled around and the kitchen staff delivered breakfast trays. I pushed around cheery looking scrambled eggs, stared at the cantaloupe, toast, and orange juice, then pushed the tray away. I closed my eyes, dreading what routine brought next.

Miss Smiley Face returned, bringing a second nurse with her. The unbearably cheery woman looked at my untouched tray and sent me what she must have thought was a comical frown.

"Mary Joe, you need to eat. Get your strength back, right, sweetie?"

Brother. A twenty-something kid calling me "sweetie". Someone needed to superglue her lips together.

"Okay, time for you to sit up in the chair." Miss Smiley Face stood beside the bed and pushed the bed controls. The head of the bed lowered, forcing me to sit up by myself. The other nurse, an older woman with thin, short graying dull brown hair and a thick, overweight figure, wrapped a supportive arm around my back. The bandages that covered recent chest tube sites hurt like hell when I had to use my trunk muscles to remain upright. I broke out in a cold sweat and began to feel sick to my stomach. I shook my head, trying to talk them out of forcing me to sit in that damned chair.

"Just for a little while, sweetie. It'll help you get stronger."

What Miss Smiley Face was really saying was that sitting up was doctor's orders, and she'd get yelled at if I wasn't in the chair for at least an hour. I knew from experience I'd be in the damned chair for closer to half the shift.

I was too weak to stand; my left leg looked like a skeletal stick, no muscle on it at all. The nurses stood on either side and basically lifted me from the bed to the chair. Miss Smiley Face hovered and fussed, straightening my gown, brushing my hair, putting on one blue no-slip sock.

One sock. Not two.

Miss Smiley Face tucked a light hospital blanket around my lap, covering up the abnormal stump where a leg should have been. Out of sight out of mind, I guess she was thinking. I sighed, closed my eyes, and leaned my head against the high-backed chair. Maybe I could sleep my way through the next four hours.

I must've fallen asleep because when I opened my eyes, a man sat in a chair near mine and stared out the tinted window. Flat prairie spread out under a clear blue sky. Trees swayed in the prairie wind, brilliant in fall colors of red, gold, and yellow.

"You've been asleep for a while. Do you feel better?" the man asked. He was older, with thick white hair that touched the collar of his pressed, light blue shirt. He wore dark double-pleated slacks and black leather shoes. Two shoes. The way he was folded up into the chair made him look like he might be very tall. His frank blue eyes set wide apart in his broad, kind face.

I reached for the notebook and pencil, scribbled a question. The man reached over and picked up the notebook, read what I had written.

"My apologies for not introducing myself. My name is Stephen Campbell. I'm the one who found you and brought you to the hospital."

My arm and hand cramped when I tried to write some more. Disgusted with my weakness, I pushed the notepad away.

"The doctors and staff nurses either don't know who I am or won't tell me." My voice came out in a cracked whisper.

The man nodded. "Yes, I talked with them."

I frowned at him, annoyed he wasn't more forthcoming. I

tried again.

"Who am I, and what happened to my leg?" I wondered whether he had heard a word I'd said over the noisy mist mask tucked close to my face.

The man's blue eyes regarded me in silence for several long, silent minutes. "Your name is Mary Joe Majors. You were in a severe car accident and have been in the hospital for over four months."

I frowned, shook my head, and croaked, "I can't remember anything. Not even my name."

The man nodded. "No, I don't suppose you do. Your primary surgeon, Dr. Lloyd Summers, warned me that you might suffer what's called traumatic amnesia. He's assured me not to worry, that your memory will come back in time." He fell silent and looked at me. His blue eyes dampened, and he reached into a front pocket of his dark slacks and retrieved a folded handkerchief, which he used to wipe his eyes.

"I'm sorry, Mary Joe. I thought we'd lost you. You were so sick for so long. It's a miracle, and I thank God every day for healing you." He wiped his eyes again, then tucked the handkerchief into his pocket. He uncrossed his leg, crossed the other one, and smoothed the crease along his trousers. I noticed his foot started wiggling and wondered whether he was nervous.

"I've been keeping tabs on your progress and when you could have visitors. I want to talk to you about helping you get back on your feet…." He stopped, and his pale-skinned face flushed beet red. "I'm so sorry. That was a very unkind, thoughtless slip. What I meant to say is I want to help you regain your independence and get things back to normal for you."

I didn't appreciate his slip, intentional or otherwise. And I didn't appreciate his assumption I would be willing to allow a total stranger to help me in any of my future endeavors.

"If I don't know who I am or who I was, it's going to be tough trying to get anything back to normal," I whispered. I broke eye contact and stared out the window.

Who was this guy anyway? How were we connected? How did I know he wasn't after something I didn't know I owned?

For that matter, was there anyone whom I could trust?

"Mattie," the man started, then stopped. "Ah…um, Mattie

was a good friend. You remind me of her." He uncrossed his legs and leaned his long arms on his knees. Folding his hands together, he stared at the floor for several minutes.

When he raised his head, his blue eyes searched my own. "Mary Joe, I realize that because you don't remember anything, you don't have a clue whom to trust. I'm asking that you trust me. I understand if you don't want to answer me right away. Think about it and I'll visit again. I don't want to come across as pushy, but I was a friend of your family, and I want to help you."

"What about my family? Why can't they help me?" I looked towards the door of the room. For that matter, why hadn't any family visited me?

"You're the first person to come visit me," I croaked.

Stephen Campbell studied me, and a look of anguish passed across his clear, blue eyes. "Your family is dead. All of them. I don't want to overwhelm you, and I don't want to set you back because you've made so much progress." He stood. He was very tall, very thin.

"I'll keep my visit short today. I really don't want to answer any more questions for now. I understand your confusion and hesitation about trusting a total stranger." He looked at me with a wistful expression. "I wish with all my heart things had turned out differently for you. I am willing to do whatever it takes to help you."

"Do I have any money to pay you?" I asked, craning my head back to look at him.

A sad smile touched his lips. "Mary Joe, you have millions. I am acting as your executor until you are healthy enough to take over. I promise if you will allow me to help you, I will ensure no one takes advantage of your situation. And, no, I do not want any pay."

He stepped over and planted a gentle kiss on the top of my head. He seemed more like a father figure. I wondered if he and my father might have been friends.

"Did you know my father?"

Stephen nodded. "Yes, I did. He was a very fine man. Your mother was a wonderful woman. And I am going to help you reclaim what you've lost."

I stared at him. "Even my memory?"

To my surprise, Stephen shrugged. "God will return your memory if and when He feels you're ready to face what that means."

I watched him stride across the room, his head almost brushing the doorframe when he walked through the door. Gently, he closed the door behind him.

~ * ~

Stephen Campbell closed the door to Mattie's room and turned to the three men standing in the hallway. He sighed inwardly and prepared for yet another argument concerning Mattie Tyler. He had been on the phone with Bill Parsons all morning. Bill and Becky were insisting on visiting Mattie, against Stephen's wishes. He wanted Mattie to improve, and he feared seeing anyone from her past might trigger memory and a resulting emotional crisis. In the end, Bill had reluctantly agreed to postpone their visit until Mattie was physically stronger. Stephen planned to have her safely moved to another location before the Parsons had a chance to see her. He broke from his internal thoughts and regarded the three men.

"She has no recollection of any events or who she is," Stephen told them.

"Still, we need to ask some questions. Maybe that will trigger something," Special Agent Tony Mills declared. Detectives Jason Reeves and Harrison Gates stood on either side.

"We've got four crime scenes and she's our only connection right now," Reeves offered tentatively.

"I don't care if you have a hundred crime scenes, you are not entering that room, and none of you will have any contact whatsoever with her. I'll post a guard at her door if necessary," Stephen told them sternly.

"Will you contact us if and when her memory returns?" The FBI agent asked.

Stephen nodded. "I will. I promise. For now, your questions must wait. Pursue evidence you've gathered from the body found in New Mexico and the two found near Wolf Creek Pass."

"Do you know where her husband is?" Detective Gates ventured.

Stephen shook his head. "I have no idea."

"He's completely dropped off the map." Reeves sighed. "We've managed to ID most of the bodies. It looks like this whole thing ties into the Charlie Network, like Mills here suspected."

"Yes," Special Agent Mills nodded. "It looks like most of the Network has been taken out. The two bodies found at the Lamont Estate, the four at the Parsons, the one in New Mexico, and two in the Colorado location. All but the woman showed up on Interpol's most wanted list."

"And we still don't know the details around Tyler's involvement," Reeves interjected.

"Cool it Reeves," Gates warned.

But the younger detective ignored him. "What about the papers found on the woman's body? They listed him as the sole heir."

"Reeves, shut up," Gates snapped. He turned to Stephen. "We need to find Tyler and get clarification on the chain of events. We also recovered arrowheads and weapons, some of which didn't come up as belonging to any of the deceased."

"Well, I can't help you," Stephen told him, then turned to Reeves. "Any papers stating Jeremiah inherits any of Mattie's wealth are forgeries." His blue eyes blazed at the three men. "Leave her alone. I mean it."

"And her surgeon? The one found dead in the doctor's lounge? Do you think there's a connection between his death and the others?" Reeves persisted, unwilling to follow Campbell's advice.

Mills shook his head. "Odd coincidence. We're still investigating that one. From the surface it appears to be unrelated. He died of a sudden, massive heart attack."

"Except for the odd text on his cell phone," Gates mused aloud to no one in particular.

"With as many bodies as we've collected on this case, it's easy to assume his death would be related. Frankly, I don't see a connection, but we'll be extra careful, cover every possibility before drawing any conclusions," Mills declared.

"None of which involves Mattie," Stephen reiterated. "Investigate all you want. Just leave her alone."

~ * ~

Cold high desert prairie air wafted across the porch on the south side of the adobe hut Joe Healing Water called home. Fall had come and gone, and now snow squalls seemed to be following one upon another. The afternoon was clear; the southeastern Colorado sky a brilliant blue. White puffs of clouds looked painted against the expansive, crystal clear horizon.

Hawk, Jeremiah, and Joe had all but finished the new gas station, and once the earth thawed trucks would install replacement fuel tanks. Hawk sat on the wooden plank porch and felt the warmth of the afternoon sun seeping through his heavy clothes. He had paid for all of it. The materials to erect the new building, the reserve tanks, the groceries and goods to restock the small store. He didn't like to think he had a conscience.

But he couldn't come up with another excuse for his generosity. He also could not explain why he continued to stick around. His ears healed, his health regained, he should have moved on well before now. But it was almost Christmas, and he kept finding reasons to delay his departure.

Maybe he was waiting for Joe Healing Water to throw him out.

Hawk's lips twitched. For all of his threats, the old Indian was more bark than bite. His thoughts turned to Jeremiah and he silently admitted the real reason he was sticking around.

He was keeping an eye on Tyler. Since Mattie's disappearance, Jeremiah had become even more withdrawn. He was gone a lot but would tell neither Joe nor himself where he was heading. When he showed up at Joe's adobe home he hardly slept, didn't talk, made little eye contact. Hawk suspected Jeremiah was tracking down what had happened to his wife.

Mattie's disappearance was a problem. If she turned up dead, Hawk had no doubt Jeremiah would come after him. So long as he had an eye on the man, Hawk didn't have to worry about always looking over his shoulder.

The sun touched the western horizon when Hawk's ears picked up the singular sound of Joe's rusty red truck, and shortly after it appeared along Highway one-sixty, the route that crossed the Comanche National Grasslands in the far southeastern corner of Colorado. Hawk stood and watched Jeremiah as he swung the truck into the graveled area that would eventually be home to the pumps. Tyler had been gone three weeks this time. Shadows stretched across the snow-covered terrain, the already cold temperatures plummeted as the weak winter light faded.

Hawk stamped his feet to get feeling going again, then went into Joe's adobe. Joe had boarded the windows to keep the heat in, which worked surprisingly well. Hawk thought he might go ahead and start dinner, which would consist of steaks, canned potatoes, canned corn. He had gone hunting a couple of days ago, brought in two antelope, which he and Joe skinned and divided into various cuts, mostly steaks. Joe didn't lean towards stews, Hawk noticed, which was fine by him. The wood burning stove that doubled as a cooking surface heated the one-room adobe nicely. The only drawback with Joe's accommodations was the outhouse.

He couldn't watch Jeremiah from inside, so he wandered through the front door.

The red truck parked in front of the gas station, where Joe spent his days watching a small flat-screen television. Customers were few, especially since he didn't have any petrol yet, but Joe manned the store anyway from eight in the morning until eight at night.

Hawk's eyes narrowed as he watched Tyler exit the truck. Anger showed plainly in his jerky movements, which did not bode well. Hawk mused over the possibility Jeremiah had information on Mattie, and if his behavior was any indication, the information was not good news. Hawk debated whether to retrieve his handgun, just in case. If Mattie was dead, Jeremiah would be out for blood. He would want things up and personal, and probably messy.

The messier the better. Hawk rubbed a hand over his scruffy beard. A good fistfight would relieve the tension much more thoroughly than a gunshot.

He heard raised male voices and took that as a warning, watched as Jeremiah stormed from the little store, his agitation obvious, his movements uncoordinated.

Hawk frowned. Jeremiah looked plastered. That was extraordinarily out of character for the Ute. He walked slowly from the adobe to the small field between the two buildings. He had on a heavy hunting jacket and overalls, but no gloves and nothing covering his head. The cold bit through his clothes as though he were naked.

Jeremiah had not used a razor nor seen a barber in well over six months. His hair was tied back into a black ponytail, a few scraggly whiskers made him look mean and unkempt.

Of course a lot of that came from the hard set of his jaw and the sullen, cold look around his eyes. He'd lost weight, his features were sharp and thin. He wore nothing on his head, nothing on his hands, and only a lightweight blue jean jacket over a black wool shirt and jeans. Hawk out-weighed him now by at least thirty pounds.

But Jeremiah was in a dangerous mood, and Hawk had no doubt he was in for a literal fight for his life. His eyes flicked quickly to the store as Healing Water appeared.

Bloody fucking hell, Hawk winced. The Indian had that damned shotgun in his hands.

"I take it from your expression you've news about Mattie," Hawk called out as Jeremiah closed the gap between them. Hawk kept his hands at his sides, watching Tyler's approach. The man was bunched up, his emotional control ready to explode. His gait wobbled, an alcoholic haze clouded his eyes. He glanced at Hawk, his black eyes cold, but he staggered past apparently heading for the adobe.

Hawk turned to keep his eye on Jeremiah, and a fist caught him in a solid uppercut just beneath his jaw. Hawk reeled, tried to roll out and regain his balance, threw a punch that missed. Jeremiah leaped on his back and drove him into the ground. Hawk bucked and twisted, managed to throw the lighter man off his back. He rolled away and sprang to his feet, arms away from his sides.

"Now wait just a sodding minute," he barked, his eyes fixed on Jeremiah, his peripheral vision catching sight of the K-Bar in the man's left hand.

"You fucking asshole," Jeremiah hissed, his words slurred, his eyes fixed on Hawk with murderous intent. "She lost her leg because of you. *She lost her leg.*"

Hawk knew with absolute truth he would never survive a knife fight against Jeremiah, even as drunk as he appeared to be. He started counting his life expectancy in measures of seconds.

The sharp explosion of a shotgun broke the stillness, and Hawk felt pellets fly through the air between himself and the Ute.

"Enough, Black Bear." Joe Healing Water's voice boomed. "The next round isn't bird seed."

Hawk watched Jeremiah waver on his feet, felt his fury in palpable waves, experienced a thud of apprehension and desperately hoped Healing Water could get through to the distraught man. He understood the bloodlust that wanted to maim him, then take his life. He balanced on the balls of his feet, unaware of the cold, unaware of the dying sunlight. He moved not a muscle.

"I'd rather like to avoid watching your guts spill out all over the snow, if Joe decides to use that thing," he ventured into the silence. "Though I wouldn't blame you for choosing death by a shotgun."

"Shut up, you lousy Brit, or I'll put a slug though you, too," Joe snapped.

Hawk acknowledged with a barely perceptible nod. Belatedly, he revised his assessment of Healing Water.

Joe's bark was indeed just as dangerous as his bite.

"He does not deserve to live," Jeremiah growled, his voice sounding more animal than human.

"Mattie went into the situation knowing the risks. Her decision was her own, not his." Joe moved into Hawk's peripheral vision, the pump action shotgun pressed against his shoulder and steady as a rock.

"He agreed to protect her." The knife Jeremiah held glinted against the white snow.

Not white for long, Hawk thought, and tried unsuccessfully to push the image away.

Joe leveled the barrel at Jeremiah. "You agreed to protect her, too. Where were you when she needed you?"

Deathly silence followed Joe's words. Jeremiah wavered on his feet, blinking as though trying to clear his vision. Hawk noticed two wet trails along the Ute's face.

Jeremiah steadied himself, then flipped the knife, caught the blade with his hand, drew his arm back with an exaggerated motion until the weapon poised just behind his shoulder.

Hawk stood motionless.

The knife flashed through the air, buried itself into a patch of snow between Hawk's feet. Joe lowered the shotgun, stepped forward, and whipped the knife from the ground.

"Don't want you reconsidering your aim." Healing Water's voice floated on the night breeze, gentle, forgiving. "I'm hungry. Let's eat."

The fight seemed to bleed out of Jeremiah. He slumped onto the cold ground, unmoving, his eyes closed, his mouth grim. Joe looked at Hawk and nodded his head towards a large, sagging barn that stood in a field behind the store.

"Right," Hawk agreed and gripped Jeremiah's upper arm. He felt bone and sinew and not much muscle.

"You really ought to start eating more than you drink," he grunted as he lifted Jeremiah to his feet. "I've something to show you."

He guided the Ute across the field and through the gaping hole where the barn doors had long ago blown away. Still gripping Jeremiah's arm, he felt along the wall and flipped the light switch. Pale yellow light illuminated the darkness, revealing an unmarked white moving van.

Jeremiah remained silent as Hawk led him to the back. "Help me open this, will you?"

Jeremiah's cold eyes stared at him, but after a moment he nodded. Together the men rolled the heavy door up. The pale light just barely revealed the contents.

Jeremiah froze, stunned. It took several minutes before he managed to collect enough thought to stare at Hawk.

"How?" His mouthed moved, but no other words came out.

"A peace offering," Hawk gestured. "I'll explain later. But I'd rather like to restore these to their owner. And I will do whatever it takes to bring her back. Tell me what you need."

Jeremiah's expression closed. "I want you dead."

Hawk grinned at him. "Precisely. Which is why I didn't ask what you *want.*"

Epilogue

Six months later and way too much time in a rehabilitation facility, I limped down the ramp and boarded a plane headed for the East Coast. It was nearing Christmas, and travelers packed the Will Rogers International Airport in Oklahoma City. I took a seat in the first class section, maneuvered the artificial device into a natural-looking position. Stephen Campbell followed and took the seat beside me.

"Ready for this?" he asked, giving me an encouraging smile.

I wore a calf-length skirt, as it was easier than pants when working with my device. I seemed to be perpetually cold, so I wore a long-sleeved turtleneck beneath a loose-fitting sweatshirt. I was still really thin, and the turtleneck hid the tracheotomy scar.

"I don't know," I admitted. I was nervous. I hadn't regained any of my memory, so I had no idea where I belonged, what I was supposed to do. Stephen had talked me through my rehabilitation, explaining his plans to help me make a new start on life. His solution hit a chord, sparked interest I thought I would never feel.

"The instructor is really anxious to meet you." He settled into his seat. A flight attendant stopped and asked what we would like to drink. I asked for a Coke, Stephen requested a bottle of water.

"How am I going to get around a barnyard on a plastic leg?" I asked. I wasn't very good walking with the artificial limb. I had a hard enough time on level sidewalk. Trying to get around a horse arena seemed daunting to say the least.

"The same way all the Special Needs kids do." Stephen paused as the flight attendant handed me a glass of Coke with a napkin and gave him a small bottle of water.

"Well...?" I persisted when he didn't seem to be forthcoming.

Stephen emptied his water bottle in one long swig, screwed the cap back on, and set the empty bottle on the foldout tray. When he looked at me, there was a twinkle in his eye.

I blew out a sigh. "Yeah, I know," I grumbled. "You've only been telling me for the last six months."

Stephen grinned. "And...?" He nudged.

I stared out the window of the plane, tried to keep the emotion out of my voice.

"One step at a time."

About the Author

F. Lynn Godfriaux (Lynn Godfriaux Maloy) has spent most of her adult life raising her two children and teaching piano. She received both a Bachelors and a Masters in piano from the University of Oklahoma and is an active performer, adjudicator, and presenter. Her writing career began through poetry and culminated in her first book, *The Well-Tempered Poet: 24 Pictures and Poems*, which was published in 2010. She has written articles about dyslexia in the music field in the CSMTA newsletter and *Clavier Companion*. Now that her family has grown, Lynn is focusing on writing, performing, and spending time with her husband and with her horse.

Mind's Eye

(prologue & 1st chapter)

(coming soon)

PROLOGUE

A frantic, high-pitched man's scream shattered the cooling desert October air in Southeast Colorado. Joe Healing Water's hand paused in the act of handing his customer change.

"Hang on a sec," the seventy-year-old Ute Indian muttered, stepping around the end of the gas station counter and through the front door. His adobe home stood a ways from the small station and was the only other building in sight, except for the remains of a barn that had blown down recently. Joe squinted against the setting sun and grinned when a long shadow darted across the high desert terrain behind the one-room adobe, from the location of the outhouse. He turned on his heel and re-entered the station, made his way around the counter and faced the customer, who eyed him with a surprised and confused expression.

"Nothing to worry about," Joe assured, retrieving a plastic grocery bag and filling it with snacks and drinks the man had just purchased.

"What was that, anyway?" The middle-aged truck driver pulled at his long, bristly brown beard. He wore a black plaid shirt and overalls. "It sure sounded like someone in trouble, if you ask me.

Joe Healing Water shook his head. "Naw. That was just our local Brit's first encounter with a tarantula."

CHAPTER ONE

"I don't care how much the two of you are crawling all over each other, tone it down next time! And shut the frickin' door! *Romeo!* Riley's voice rang from upstairs, where the bedrooms were located.

"You just want the door shut so you can glue your ear to the wood and pick up some hints." Aiden's rich baritone voice shot back. "Just because we were born together, *sister*, doesn't mean we have to do *everything* together."

I listened from downstairs, where I currently was fixing coffee for the three of us. I rolled my eyes, thought Riley had an excellent point. Aiden and his new girlfriend kept me awake most of the night, too.

"Half of the frickin' county heard the two of you!" Sounds of stomping accompanied Riley's retort. Yeah, she was pissed.

"Hopefully that means you know more about romance than you did before we started...." Sounds of scuffling feet followed by a loud *thud*, then, Aiden's voice panting, "Whoa ... okay, okay!! We'll keep it down next time!"

I grinned. No doubt, Riley had gotten her brother in another one of her famous arm bars.

Two sets of feet tramped down the hardwood staircase. Aiden appeared around the corner first, his dark brown hair in a crew cut that emphasized his high cheekbones and sharp jaw line. He stood six feet, with a thick chest and shoulders and trim waist, none of which gave him any advantage over his twin sister, younger by two minutes. Riley rounded the corner, her five-foot six stature muscular and lean, same facial features and high cheekbones as her brother, her dark hair almost as short. They wore jeans with loose, baggy gray sweatshirts that concealed their service weapons. They worked on the local town police force and would change into their uniforms once they got to the station.

An upstairs bedroom door opened and closed. Footsteps tapped down the wooden stairs, and a tall lanky woman with long arms and even longer legs glided into the kitchen. Designer jeans hugged her slender hips and a sequin long-sleeved T-shirt clung to her thin torso. Fancy cowboy boots with ridiculously pointed toes peeked out from beneath her jeans. Her long bottle-black teased hair sprang around her face like a banshee. Bangs fell just over her overly decorated wide blue eyes.

"Hi, Sweetie." The woman puckered perfectly painted pink lips and gave Aiden a dainty peck on the cheek.

Riley rolled her eyes. "Darla, the two of you were practically eating anatomical parts earlier, so you might as well knock off the respectable act."

A decidedly mischievous expression crossed Aiden's face as he reached for his girlfriend of two months.

I'd had enough of the twins' bickering. "Knock it off, Aiden," I told him. "You're baiting both Riley and me, and you know it." I watched the familiar sly look cross his expression, and he pulled Darla into an embrace. She moaned and leaned into him until I thought they might just get it on again right there in the middle of the kitchen.

"Darla, good to see you. Again." I interrupted, waving Riley away when she took a step forward. I really did not need another brawl. Aiden, you're going to be late."

Aiden straightened and broke the embrace. Darla stepped back and sent me a smile that did not reach her eyes. I didn't like her, didn't like the way she was monopolizing Aiden's time and focus. Of course it was none of my business, but that didn't stop me from feeling the way I did.

"Where are you off to this time?" I asked her, straining to remain polite.

"Got some business out in California, Mary Jo. I'll be gone for a month." She sent a comically fake pout towards Aiden. "I'm going to miss you."

"I'll bet you are." Aiden stretched and rubbed his chest. Riley rolled her eyes again.

"So will the rest of the county," she snapped. "Folks won't know what to do for evening entertainment, not having the two of you around to wow them with your *highly* descriptive audibles."

Darla brushed hair off her shoulder with a flip of her hand. "I'll see you when I get back." She sauntered across the kitchen and disappeared through the connecting door that led to the garages. Moments later the throaty roar of a Jaguar split the silence. Tires spun on loose gravel, and then the engine died away.

"God, Aiden, what do you see in that woman?" Riley ran a hand through her short spiked hair. "She's got floosey practically stamped on her forehead."

"She's got sexy tattooed…." Aiden started.

Riley threw up a hand. "Stop right there, Dork Brain. I don't want details. I want you to find someone who's interested in more than what's in your pants."

Aiden sauntered to the counter and picked up a black leather jacket. "She loves me for my brains and my brawn. I'm a cop. I'm her superhero." He flexed his biceps and posed.

Riley snorted. "Superhero my ass. You're a brainless dick head and you need to wake up and realize that you're just her gigolo until she finds someone else. You don't even know what she does or where she goes on these long jaunts of hers."

"Oh for the love of Pete," I butt in. "Would the both of you stop bickering! You sound like a couple of two-year-olds!"

The fraternal twins turned and gave me identical grins. Their movements and expressions couldn't have been more perfect if they'd been rehearsed.

"Driving you crazy again, eh, Aunt MJ?" Riley's brown eyes held the same mischievous gleam as her brother's.

"It's Mary-Jo, Riley. MARY. JO. Not MJ." I pressed my lips into a thin line. Riley was egging me and she knew it. I tried very hard not to fall into the trap.

Technically, I wasn't their aunt. In fact, I had no idea whether I was anybody's aunt, sister, daughter, or orphan, since my lifetime memory expanded only over the last couple of years. I had woken up in a hospital bed with no memory and apparently no friends or family, since no one had come to visit.

I had also woken up without a right leg. According to a very tall man claiming to be my attorney, I had lost my leg in a severe automobile crash that put me in a coma for almost two months. He told me my family had died in the crash, which explained why no family came to visit. He had not offered an explanation as to why no friends, work acquaintances, or even religious figures visited during my recovery and extensive rehab.

With the help of a wooden cane I limped on my prosthesis until I stood between the two siblings. At five feet ten inches, I split the difference between their heights. I had shoulder length black hair that had more gray than I thought I should have, especially since the tall thin man assured me I recently passed my thirtieth birthday. I also had green eyes that were too big for my face, and a Grand Canyon-sized nose, at least in my opinion.

I turned my head, locking eyes with each of them in turn. "Either the two of you get a handle on this constant bickering, or I will throw both of you out of MY house. I don't care what Stephen Campbell says about safety issues. You got that?"

"You wouldn't throw us out, Aunt MJ. You'd be bored in no time. We add spice to your life." Aiden's expression seemed always about to burst into laughter. He was one of the most spontaneously happy people I'd ever met.

Well, at least among the ones I remembered.

Aiden turned and poked his sister's left biceps with a finger. "Hear that? You need to stop picking on me and my girl."

Riley swatted at his hand, then stood on her tiptoes and thrust her face into his. "Listen, Dork Brain. I'm not the one broadcasting my romantic interludes across three counties."

"We need to get going." Aiden crossed his eyes at his sister. They mirrored each other as they checked their weapons and spare magazines. Mid-October had brought damp, foggy weather to the Blue Ridge Mountains of southwest Virginia. Aiden shrugged into his leather jacket, and Riley retrieved an identical one from the back of one of the kitchen stools. She turned to me as Aiden headed for the door leading to the triple car garage. "It's Friday, and Chief said he's gotten two sick calls for the swing shift, so we may end up pulling doubles."

"Is Randy coming over today? Or are you meeting him at the barn?" Aiden asked me, blocking the doorway. Riley gave him an irritated shove, but he didn't budge.

"I haven't heard from him. I'll probably spend the day at

the barn, as usual," I shrugged, looking through the open door-way and beyond the garage at the fog that hid the rural mountain landscape behind an eddying, sifting white blanket. Six o'clock on a Friday morning, and fog reduced visibility to a few yards.

"You'll use the indoor arena." Riley's comment didn't leave room for argument.

I bristled. "I'll ride where I want. Go on. Get out of here."

"C'mon, bossy. Let's go." Aiden nudged his sister. I limped to the door and watched them climb into a black Jeep Wrangler. Their police cruiser would be waiting at the station. A gray Ford Explorer custom-designed for my needs occupied the garage. The third bay stood empty at the moment, as I didn't feel like owning two vehicles.

The three-story stone house I currently occupied stood on a knoll in the middle of rolling lush green pasture hemmed in by the mountains deep in the southwest corner of Virginia. The upstairs held bedrooms, one on either end and two in the middle. Riley and Aiden each occupied the end rooms, which should have provided more than enough distance for privacy, seeing as how they were basically at opposite ends of the house. The main floor consisted of an expansive kitchen, an enormous cathedral ceiling great room with glass windows that framed a large stone fireplace, an office, and a master bedroom which I occupied. A broad, wood-planked, covered porch wrapped around three sides of the main floor, including a screened-in portion that opened off the master bedroom. The downstairs held two separate entertainment rooms and another bedroom. Broad oak staircases led to each floor, polished oak floors spread through the main floor and the upstairs hall and bedrooms. Warm, plush, forest-green carpeting kept the downstairs warm. The place had air conditioning during the summer when the cool mountain breeze wasn't enough to keep the heat and humidity at bay. A large wood-burning stove generated enough heat to comfortably warm the place during the winter. The décor echoed the wood floors with earthy brown tones and light tan accents.

I closed the door, limped to the kitchen, and wiggled onto

one of the six bar stools that stood around the large counter. Glancing at the clock on the wall, I debated whether to go back to bed. I was still in my pajamas. Things wouldn't get started over at the stables for another couple of hours. I could use the sleep.

If I could sleep. I'd had major issues with insomnia ever since I'd moved into this house eighteen months ago. Stephen Campbell, calling himself my benefactor and friend, helped me relocate to this remote place in the middle of nowhere. He'd grown up here, knew most of the people in the small nearby town, had arranged for two police officers to move in with me, to provide company and safety.

Safety from what? I'd asked. But Stephen would not explain, nor would he offer any information on where I originally was from, who I had been, or what I had done. It seemed odd at the time, and I'd asked him on several occasions why he was so unwilling to tell me anything about my past. Every time, he pressed his lips together and shook his head, telling me that he was looking after my best interests. Protecting me.

Which bothered the hell out of me. I mean, if my memory loss and injury had been because of an automobile accident, what in the world did I need protection from? He had not forbidden me to drive or to travel, both of which could be restricted if I had been the cause of the disaster.

But short of regaining lost memory, I had no way of finding out who I was or what had happened. I had tried searching on the Internet, but I had no name, date, or event to start with.

But I did have dreams. Lots of them. Vague images that I could not recall when I struggled awake. I would be streaming with sweat, and often would find Riley sitting beside me, leaning over me as she tried to get me awake. I would cry for no reason, shake with utter terror that gripped me with invisible, unexplainable talons, cling to Riley as though I were a toddler coming out of a nightmare. So while I couldn't figure out why Stephen felt I needed protection from an outside source, I was painfully aware that I desperately needed protection from something my subconscious was trying to tell me.

Figuring sleep wasn't an option I limped to the master bedroom and dressed in jeans, a long-sleeved green turtleneck and a black cotton sweatshirt, pulled on one thick sock and wiggled my left foot into a riding boot that zipped up the side. I had difficulty working the boot onto the prosthesis, but I really wanted to ride, and my stubbornness won over the awkward, man-made limb. I worked the prosthesis into the empty jeans leg, then stood and felt my stump sink into the padded socket.

The whole one-leg thing still bothered me. A lot. I wore wide-leg jeans that fit easily over the prosthesis, and I'd worked on my gait until I had only a minimal limp. I used a cane for security reasons and because at times I would forget about the prosthesis and try to walk like a normal person, lose my balance, and end up eating dirt, pavement, or whatever I'd been walking on at the time. I'd rather use a cane than end up embarrassed because of another face plant.

I went to the kitchen, drank another cup of coffee, then headed out.

The Explorer had been custom fit with hand controls, and it had taken me a while before I'd become proficient. The stables were ten miles north along the Interstate, and I had ten miles of twisting two-lane mountain road before I reached the Interstate.

Stephen introduced me to the owner of the stables when I first moved out. Kinsey Wells was about my age, had long, thick natural blonde hair that she kept in a ponytail, and had been riding horses since she could walk. She owned a thirty-horse boarding set-up that had a large indoor arena and three out-door arenas, including a grandstand for the numerous county horse shows and fairs. She also ran a therapeutic riding center and trained volunteers to work with children suffering with physical and emotional handicaps.

Eighteen months ago I had balked at what I considered a ludicrous idea of trying to put me on a horse. But Kinsey ignored my reluctance and bullied me onto a large bay gelding. With a volunteer on each side and one leading the animal, I had started my thirty-minute riding lessons twice a week, had felt incredibly tired and physically exhausted the first several months. Slowly, though, I'd recognized the improvement in my core strength and coordination, and in the process had fallen in love with Twister, the gentle twenty-year-old Tennessee Walker I now rode almost every day.

Fog reduced visibility to barely twenty yards along Interstate eighty-one. I made it without mishap, took the first exit into town, and turned onto the sloping dirt road that led to the stables. The outdoor arenas were invisible, hidden behind curtains of thick white moisture. The buildings appeared ghostly shadows through the fog, making me feel like I was the only person on earth. I pulled to a stop in the large parking area, retrieved my cane, and limped through the dense cloud cover to the side door leading to the indoor arena.

Kinsey was in the center of the arena, working with one of her regular private lessons. "Hey there! Wasn't sure whether you'd come out in this weather," she called. She turned her attention back to her lesson, a ten-year-old girl who beamed at me from the back of the black-and-white pinto pony she rode.

Little Amy Whitmore was the daughter of Randy Whitmore, the man I guess I could say I'd been dating for the last several months. Amy was largely responsible for my own riding progress. She had lost her mother in a freak equestrian accident that had instantly killed both rider and horse. Amy, eight years old at the time, had withdrawn into a world of her own, become non-verbal, even with her father, a renowned horse trainer. Soon after my arrival at the stables, Amy wandered over to sit beside me one day. To everyone's amazement Amy started talking to me, asking what had happened to my leg, if I liked horses, whether I wanted to ride. At the time I hadn't known how to answer her. Both of us eventually made it onto the back of a horse, Twister for me, Fuzzy for her.

Now, brown pigtails poked from beneath her pink furry hat, black jeans, little pink cowboy boots, and a matching pink zipped up winter coat and gloves. She had become a regular, and looked forward to my arrival each day. Which was a main reason why I made the effort to get to the stables.

"Miss Mary-Jo, watch this!" Amy turned her attention to her mount, her expression serious. Gathering the reins in her left hand, she leaned forward, clucked, and kicked her heels into her mount's furry sides. Fuzzy broke into a trot, then briefly into a bouncy canter before slowing back down into his normal lazy walk.

"Wow, Amy. That's terrific!" I called to her as she rounded the far side of the arena.

"Remember not to lean so far forward," Kinsey smiled. She glanced at her watch. "I think we're done for the day. Go ahead and walk Fuzzy around, make sure he's cooled off before you put him away."

"Okay." Amy reached a pink-gloved hand and patted Fuzzy on the neck as he walked along. "Has Daddy talked to you yet, Miss Mary Jo?" she called out.

I shook my head, puzzled. Aiden had asked the same thing. "No," I answered, "I haven't seen him this morning. Why?"

Amy's expression beamed. "He's got something for you. He made me promise not to tell you. It's really really pretty. I can't wait for him to give it to you."

Uh-oh, I thought with an inward cringe. It better not be something to do with commitment. I liked Randy. A lot. But I wasn't sure I wanted more than friendship, and I'd been the one who'd refused when he wanted to become intimate. He kept telling me things like how beautiful I was in spirit, nonsense like that.

Trouble with all of this was my reluctance to believe any of it.

"He's around here somewhere," Amy nodded, then turned her attention to Fuzzy. Kinsey walked to the railing where I stood. She was in her usual jeans, boots, wool jacket and wool hat. Her thick blonde ponytail streamed like a horse's tail down her back.

"She's going to be quite a rider before long," I commented.

"No kidding," she nodded, turning to watch Amy. "No one else can get Fuzzy to do anything he doesn't want to do. She gets on, and he's a different pony."

"She's really improved emotionally," I murmured.

Kinsey turned to me. "Because of you." She hesitated, then added, "So has Randy. You've been a Godsend to both of them."

I shook my head. "I don't know about that. I'm glad she's

better, though," I hedged.

We watched Fuzzy amble around the arena, then Amy pulled him to a stop in front of Kinsey.

"He feels good," Kinsey smiled, pressing her hand against the pony's chest to make sure he had cooled down. "Do you need help unsaddling him or putting him away?"

Amy shook her head. "No, ma'am."

"Okay. I'll open the door for you." Kinsey walked across the expansive dirt floor with the pair until they reached a large sliding double-door. She pulled it open and watched Amy guide Fuzzy through.

"Holler if you need help." She left the door ajar and walked back across the arena. She stopped, the arena railing separating us, and stared at me with incredibly clear blue eyes. "How's that contraption of yours working out?"

I shrugged. "Twister doesn't seem to mind it."

Shortly after we met, Randy carved a wooden prosthesis that buckled into the right stirrup of the Australian saddle I used. It was more for weight balance than leg signals, but I'd found my thigh strength had improved enough I could create a little bit of pressure, and Twister was sensitive enough to respond. "I still use mostly rein signals," I admitted.

"Whatever works," Kinsey nodded. I limped to one of the access gates, then walked with Kinsey towards the sliding door.

"Are you planning on riding?" she asked.

"I'd like to, if the indoor arena is open." We made it outside in time to see Amy leading Fuzzy back to his out-door run. The pony looked as though he'd just been to a spa. His coat shone, his mane and tail combed and silky.

Kinsey shook her head. "I'm afraid it's booked. Randy's conducting horsemanship classes, then I think he wants to work with that new Arab we got in a couple of weeks ago." She glanced over her shoulder. "Speaking of," she slowed and I turned around.

A man approached us. Tall, lanky, with a runner's build, his cowboy hat hid his features. "Howdy, girls," Randy smiled, his deep voice like velvet, his manner as easy-going with people as it was with horses. He wore jeans, boots, a padded jacket. His black hair tied back in a short ponytail. His broad face, strong nose, and black eyes reminded me of American Indian, though I'd never asked, and he never volunteered his background.

"Weather's supposed to get really crappy tomorrow and Sunday." He spoke to Kinsey, but winked at me. "Wind and rain. I don't like conducting classes when the weather's like that. Too much strain on the horses. So I've booked tomorrow's and Sunday's classes all day today." He turned to me. "You riding this morning?"

I nodded. "I'd like to, anyway."

"Twister's solid as a rock. The fog won't bother him," Kinsey said. "The wind's calm, it's not raining. You should be good. Keep an eye out for deer, that's all."

I grinned. "I imagine he'll pick up on them long before I see them."

Kinsey turned towards the indoor arena, leaving Randy and me alone.

"I'm going to work the new Arab in the back arena after my last class." He walked with me as I limped along the outdoor runs. I felt suddenly nervous when he slid a hand into his jacket pocket. He touched my arm, and I stopped. "I have something for you. I've been wanting to do this for a while."

I stumbled backwards, almost fell. Randy's strong hand caught and steadied me.

But I tumbled into an emotional free fall when he withdrew his hand from his jacket and showed me a small, square velvet ring box.

"I know this isn't the most romantic moment I could have picked." he started to kneel. I held up a hand and he stopped, then straightened.

"Wait, Randy. Wait, please. Don't open it." I began to shiver, and my face must have paled, because he slipped the box back into his jacket pocket and gripped my arm.

"I didn't mean to shock you," he apologized. "I just wanted you to know how much you mean to me. You have no idea how much you have helped Amy and me over the last two years."

To my utter horror, tears slipped down my cheeks. "I like you, Randy. I like you a lot." My voice started shaking. "I like

Amy a whole lot, too. I just ... I don't know ... I don't know...." I stopped and swiped a hand across my face. "Can we stay friends for now? Please?"

Randy's expression grew soft, supportive and gentle, the same manner that brought him so much success with horses. "I'm not in a hurry," he soothed. "I just wanted to let you know that it's yours, if and when the time comes." He glanced at his wristwatch. "My timing sort of sucks anyway. I've gotten you all upset, and now I have to leave to conduct the first horsemanship class."

I smiled, stepped close and gave him a hug. His warmth through his clothes felt safe, comfortable. "Don't give up on me," I whispered.

A soft chuckle rumbled through his chest. "You know I won't." His finger touched my chin, and I inhaled a steadying breath, then raised my face. He gave me a soft kiss on each cheek, understanding innately my emotional issues. I hugged him tighter, then backed away.

"See you later?" I asked.

"Definitely," he smiled. "Be careful in the back arena. Twister may be solid, but even the calmest horse can spook in these conditions."

I nodded, and we turned our respective ways. I limped to the run Twister occupied. He must have heard my voice through the fog because his brown shaggy head appeared at the gate, his ears pricked forward. He nickered when I got close.

"Hey there, fella." I rubbed his nose, and he dipped his head down for me to rub his ears. "You're spoiled; you know that?" I swiped at the wetness still on my face and turned to the tack room that held my riding equipment.

I had experimented with saddle types and settled on the Australian style saddle because of the side pommels, which I could grip with my thighs. The one I used also had a saddle horn, which helped when I was mounting. I wasn't good enough to hop and catch the stirrup with my left foot. Not yet, anyway. I was working on it, though, and planned to show off to Kinsey one day.

I left my cane in the tack room, retrieved Twister's halter

and got him from his run. I spent a lot of time brushing him down, picking his feet out, talking to him about Randy, my reaction, as though I were talking to a person. I secured the saddle and pad beneath my left arm, then used my cane for balance when I carried everything outside. It had taken a while and a lot of strength building, but I could now swing the pad and saddle up without help. I bridled him, propped my cane against the empty saddletree in the tack room, then led Twister towards the arena located at the back of the property. Woods currently invisible through the fog crowded around the enclosure, and I thought chances were good that wildlife of some sort would show up. Twister seemed calm and unconcerned, so I assumed that at least for the moment nothing was amiss. We passed through the gate, which I latched behind us, and then led Twister to the mounting block.

I'd tried several ways of working with the prosthesis, and the least awkward had proven to be removing the thing on the mounting block, then grabbing the saddle horn and swinging my stump onto the saddle before securing the stirrup with my left foot. Twister always turned his head to watch me. I think he sensed my handicap, because never in the time that I'd been riding had he ever moved a muscle when I was trying to get on. I settled myself into the saddle, folded the empty right jeans leg around my thigh, then worked my stump into the leg extension thing. Then I took up the reins and clucked to Twister. He raised his head and pricked his ears forward, and we set out in the vast empty whiteness that shrouded the arena.

The morning was cool and damp, and the warmth from Twister's half-ton body created vague washes of steam. I felt the same strength and warmth from him as I had when I hugged Randy. I pushed away the image of the ring box and focused on the utter silence surrounding us. It seemed that Twister and I were the only beings on earth. Nothing stirred the vegetation on the other side of the railing, no currents rustled through foliage. Conditions were wonderfully serene as we followed the railing. I urged him into his gait, felt the smoothness of his powerful muscles beneath me as he broke into the classic run-walk that made his breed so famous. It was like riding a magic carpet. My thighs gripped the side pommels, the extension gave me the extra feeling of balance, and for the time that I was in the saddle I could pretend that I was whole again.

I failed to notice when we were no longer alone. Twister warned me when his head came up and his ears perked forward, alert and tense. I slowed him to a walk, felt the tension through his body, and wondered what type of animal it was and whether it had joined us in the arena. Hopefully it was just a dog. Maybe a deer had leaped the railing. I gripped the saddle horn just in case Twister decided to shy.

As we neared the gated end of the arena, a shadow of a person appeared, hovering above the ground. Twister snorted, and I thought that he might take off. I wondered why Randy would appear suddenly when he of all people would know that he needed to say something that would calm Twister. "Easy, there," I murmured, rubbing his neck with the hand that held the reins and re-securing my grip on the saddle horn.

"I apologize. I did not mean to scare you," the shadow called out. "The woman in the office told me where you were." The man, a stranger, sat on one of the gateposts.

I felt Twister relax. Hearing a human voice helped him recognize and make sense of what he saw and smelled.

"Can't see a thing with this fog," I responded, guiding Twister closer. Something about the man's voice stirred deep-seated memories. We were within five yards before the fog parted and I got a good look at him. His shoulder-length black hair was tied in a ponytail. His cheekbones protruded sharply from beneath his black eyes, his skin color dark against the white mist that swirled around us. He dressed in jeans and a denim jacket that hung open to reveal a black button-down shirt. Recognition began whirling through my head and I felt the blood drain from my face. Vaguely I realized Twister sensed my shock, because he tensed and backed away.

I didn't stop him. I needed the distance. Memory flooded back, fast, furious. I felt as though I'd just been hit by a gigantic tsunami wave. I opened my mouth, struggled to choke out my next words.

"Hello, Jeremiah."

More mysteries await in these books from WolfSinger Publications

da sticks – Rich Kisielewski

Not long ago, Harry had moved back to the town where his ex-wife and kids reside and was trying to rebuild his life. The "work hard and play hard" attitude that carries Harry through life is balanced by the softness evidenced in his dealings with his children. Once again, he was going to have to be away from them and the new life he had been trying so hard to establish.

Going undercover at MechInsCo, Harry gets exposure to executives within the company including his lifer accounting boss, the psycho senior finance executive and a frantic company president. They all paint the same picture-a company losing money with no idea how, or why. His stint at MechInsCo supplies Harry with some raucous times: large amounts of information, booze and ladies provide him with much more than he signed on for.

da bug – Rich Kisielewski

Harry Mickey Shorts gets a call from M. Randle Trundle, a New York business tycoon, who is in need of Harry's help. Without a thought, Harry drops what he is doing and races off to help his benefactor, and his friend.

Trundle is a part owner in Board Room Farms—a horse racing stable—which is run by his brother, Danny Trundle. He informs Harry the stable's stud breeding stallion was found dead in his stall and Trundle feels something is wrong. Harry agrees to help Trundle with the case and does what he does best by going undercover and begins digging into the world of thoroughbred horse racing. Having bet on more than a few nags before in his lifetime, Harry is comfortable around the track and blends in very smoothly.

During his investigation, Harry forms an alliance with the ranch's female vet—in more ways than one. She agrees to provide needed intelligence on the current and prior goings-on at Board Room farms. Along the way, she becomes a serious love interest in Harry's life. Unfortunately, that conflicts with Harry's renewed part-time interest in his ex-wife that may prove to be a "pick one" dilemma, sooner, rather than later. His love for, and continued attempt to become part of his two children's lives, remains paramount in Harry's thinking.

da nuts – Rich Kisielewski

Harry Mickey Shorts, street wise private detective, gets a call from Max who just happens to be his favorite as well as his only son. Max doesn't ask his dad for much but he and his buddies are in need of Harry's help. Without a thought, Harry drops what he is doing and races off to help his son and his friends.

Max informs Harry he would like him to investigate the untimely events that prohibited Clint, their current cult hero, from participating in a first ever poker tournament. Clint had played over a quarter of a million hands of poker by the time he had reached his eighteenth birthday and, as evidenced by the size of his bank account, he had won a lot more of those hands than he had lost. All of that meant nothing when he turned up unconscious in his hotel room on the morning of the first day of the inaugural "Under 18 World Championship of Poker" tournament.

During his investigation, Harry uses his expertise that sets him apart from other private investigators and goes undercover to explore the world of internet poker. The twist with this version is only kids between the ages of sixteen and eighteen can participate and all winnings may only be paid to higher institutions of learning for the kid's college education. Once he uncovers the wrongdoings of the unscrupulous masterminds behind this scheme he partners with his benefactor M. Randle Trundle, a New York business tycoon, to set things right and preserve the previously dashed hopes of the winning poker teenagers. Harry's renewed part-time interest in his ex-wife and his love for and continued attempt to become part of his two children's lives complicates his own life but remains paramount in Harry's thinking.

da kid – *Rich Kisielewski*

Much to his surprise, Harry Mickey Shorts gets a call from Mel, his ex-brother-in-law, who needs his help. It is a rare occasion when Mel asks Harry for anything at all never mind his help. When it does happen Harry takes notice and drops what he is doing to see what it is that troubles "Big Mel."

Over a few cool ones Mel tells Harry a long-winded tale from his past involving a kid he had coached. Little Billy Burns had walked out of the gym before the end of a basketball game and soon vanished all together. Mel's belief that he had somehow failed Billy has lingered and he now sees an opportunity to rectify that wrong.

With the help of his friend, Tom, Harry's investigation takes him back to Central Pennsylvania to meet with Billy who currently resides in the Cumberland County jail. Their journey begins with an introduction to Billy's extended con-artist family and ultimately to some Las Vegas hustlers who are looking to continue their venture into golf course swindles. And at long last is Mel's reunion with Billy. At the same time Harry's part-time interest in his ex-wife, his love for his children and his continued attempt to become an integral part of their lives, continues to complicate his own life.

The Dolmen – *Matt Bille*

When attorney Julie Sperling's fiancée is murdered while researching a controversial museum exhibit, she calls on her ex-lover, science writer Greg nightmarish pursuit as very real predators from ancient folktales try to hunt down anyone with knowledge of their existence.

For Greg and Julie, the City of Angels has become the gateway to hell…

In Adam's Fall – *Phoebe Wray*

Old New England towns are infamous for their odd murder stories, but that had never happened before in Halton, Massachusetts.

When history teacher Nikki Sheridan trips over the dead body of a young Muslim girl in her backyard she finds herself at the center of a murder mystery. A mystery that will take her on a perilous journey with the police, the FBI, a nervous town ready to point fingers at neighbors who seem different, and a man calling himself 'the Patriot': a dangerous zealot whose hateful agenda could destroy the small town or bring them even closer together as they face a homegrown terrorist in their midst.

Murder Most Howl – *Margaret H. Bonham*

Dog Mushing Can Be Murder

For Stephanie Keyes, noted sled dog racer in Colorado, sled dog racing can be dangerous enough. But when a fellow musher and rival is found murdered and she's a prime suspect, Stephanie races to find the killer before he can strike again.

Missing sled dogs and deadly goals abound in this super sleuth tale—or is it tail?

www.ingramcontent.com/pod-product-compliance
Lightning Source LLC
Chambersburg PA
CBHW070851260626
47170CB00007B/2586